A CHOSEN PEO
BY FAITH AND
FIGHT FOR
PROPHECY

Saul—As a boy, he saw Israel's army shattered and its sacred Ark of the Covenant captured by the Philistines. But he would be saved from the slaughter to fulfill an even bloodier destiny—one the modest Benjamite hardly dared to accept . . . yet was powerless to refuse.

Samuel—Prophet and warrior, this fierce and uncompromising man of God gathered the scattered tribes together in their darkest hour and promised them the coming of a new king . . . a mighty man of power who would lead them to victory.

Eri—Once sold into slavery, this Child of the Lion would never forget the cruelty and depravity of the Philistines or the friendship of the young Israelite with whom he would one day join in a plan to destroy their common enemy.

Sarah—Many men sought her, both for her olive-skinned beauty and for her father's wealth, but an act of violence would force her into the arms of the one man who truly loved her . . . even as it robbed her of the ability to love him back.

Galar—Brutal, sadistic, merciless, the Philistine war chief put no limit on his lustful and barbaric appetites, and he has dedicated both to one goal: the destruction of the tribes of Israel.

Other Bantam Books by Peter Danielson
Ask your bookseller for the titles you have missed

Volume XVI

DEPARTED GLORY

PETER DANIELSON

Producers of **The First Americans,**
The Frontier Trilogy, and **The Holts.**

Book Creations Inc., Canaan, NY • Lyle Kenyon Engel, Founder

BANTAM BOOKS
NEW YORK • TORONTO • LONDON • SYDNEY • AUCKLAND

DEPARTED GLORY

A Bantam Domain Book / published by arrangement with Book Creations Inc.

Bantam edition / July 1993

*Produced by Book Creations Inc.
Lyle Kenyon Engel, Founder*

*DOMAIN and the portrayal of a boxed "d"
are trademarks of Bantam Books,
a division of Bantam Doubleday Dell Publishing Group, Inc.*

ISBN 0-553-56145-6

Published simultaneously in the United States and Canada

Bantam Books are published by Bantam Books, a division of Bantam Doubleday Dell Publishing Group, Inc. Its trademark, consisting of the words "Bantam Books" and the portrayal of a rooster, is Registered in U.S. Patent and Trademark Office and in other countries. Marca Registrada. Bantam Books, 1540 Broadway, New York, New York 10036.

PRINTED IN THE UNITED STATES OF AMERICA

RAD   0 9 8 7 6 5 4 3 2 1

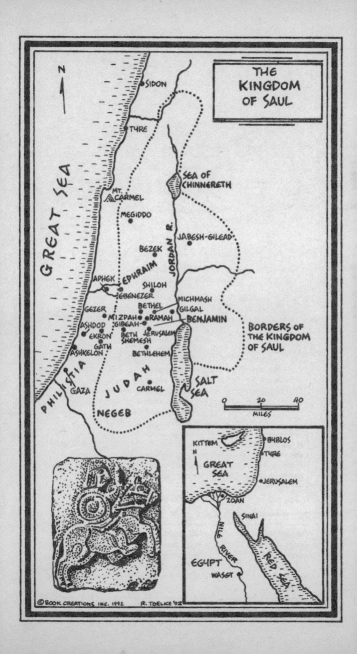

THE
KINGDOM
OF SAUL

GREAT SEA

SIDON

TYRE

SEA OF
CHINNERETH

MT. CARMEL

MEGIDDO

JABESH-GILEAD

BEZEK

JORDAN R.

EPHRAIM

APHEK

SHILOH

EBENEZER

MICHMASH

BETHEL

GILGAL

GEZER

RAMAH

MIZPAH

BENJAMIN

ASHDOD

GIBEAH

EKRON

BETH
SHEMESH

JERUSALEM

BORDERS OF
THE KINGDOM
OF SAUL

GATH

ASHKELON

BETHLEHEM

PHILISTIA

JUDAH

CARMEL

SALT
SEA

GAZA

NEGEB

0   20   40
MILES

KITTEM

BYBLOS

TYRE

N

GREAT
SEA

JERUSALEM

ZOAN

SINAI

NILE RIVER

EGYPT

RED SEA

WASET

© BOOK CREATIONS INC. 1992   R. TOELKE '92

Author's Note

~~~~~~

It is difficult to find agreement among Egyptologists on many things, not the least of which is the spelling of the names of the Egyptian kings and the proper place name for a city in one particular period of history. Our characters Kemose and Urnan arrive at the finest port in the Nile Delta—a city called at various times Zoan and Tanis—during the chaotic Third Intermediate Period, a time of vast political unrest. I have decided to go with Biblical place names for Egyptian cities and with John Henry Brested's version of Twenty-First Dynasty history, with his antique but interesting spellings of the titles of the rulers in the delta and at Waset. (The Greek name, Thebes, for this ancient Egyptian city didn't come into use until much later and was, in all probability, a corruption of the Egyptian pronunciation not of Waset but of nearby Ta-ipet.)

I do not think it would be true to the historical aspect of the book to use Greek versions of place names, i.e., Tanis for Zoan. And if you take that step, then you must not use the Greek name for Waset. Greeks were, after all, latecomers to history. To the best of my ability I have used place names that were concurrent with the era of Samuel and Saul.

I realize we get into some interesting differences in using Brested's out-of-date proper names, i.e., Pesibkhenno I instead of Pinudjem I; but Brested's names are colorful, and it would take an Egyptian scholar or someone willing to dig through as many books as I have to know whether or not, in this obscure period of Egyptian history, we are using fictional or historical names.

DEPARTED
GLORY

Prologue

On a snowy day much like that of old when Benaiah, son of Jehoiada, went down and slew a lion in a pit, the scholar drew his mantle more closely to his cadaverous chest. Cloak and tunic combined were scant protection against the cold wind that set the doves to fluttering around the tall ramparts of the great temple. The streets were less crowded than usual. Sensible people were snug in their homes. Outside the city of Solomon's glory, the poor and the hopeless, they who are always with us, they who pisseth against the wall, huddled around their inadequate fires in a communion of misery and covetous envy for those who dwelt within.

The scholar used his staff to tap his way to a point midway up the steps of the sanctuary. A disdainful priest glanced at him from inside before closing a huge brass door. Snowflakes agitated by the wind skittered across the cold stone. Only a very few saw and knew the scholar, and fewer paused in this weather to hear his words.

In contrast to his frailty, the old man's voice was virile. It soared to the cloud-touching towers of the temple and rang in the empty streets.

"Hear, then, the history of those who were before us," the scholar began.

"Speak of the deeds of the mighty Samson," a young man cried out, his voice muffled by a woolen scarf wound around his face against the cold.

"We would hear the acts of the first king," another voice called.

1

"To value more accurately the strong men of old, you must first know those who opposed them," the scholar said. "Is not the worth of a man measured by the strength of his enemies?"

The few who had gathered were shivering with the chill. They tugged on their garments in a fruitless effort to make them more protective.

"And so I speak of the warriors from Caphtor. I tell you of those who spoke a language unlike ours, a tongue written much like that of the sea islands."

"The Sea Peoples," said a young man knowingly.

"So they were called by the Egyptians," the scholar said. "The Peleset. They who were tall and slim in their betasseled kilts and hard-ribbed helmets. They came in heavily laden, solid-wheeled carts drawn by humpbacked bullocks. Their high-prowed ships sailed southward along the coast, through the green waters of the Great Sea. And behind them they left ruined cities, destroyed crops, and the dead. The mighty cities on the Halys River fell to their onslaught. The fleet and magnificent horses of Cilicia were their plunder, along with the treasures and the silver mines of Tarsus. They seized the secret of smelting iron as the weight of their inexorable advance borne under the proud Hittites. Cyprus, the Island of Copper, fell to them. Carchemish on the Euphrates was theirs. The Phoenicians tried to halt their incursion at Ugarit but failed. The fall of Ugarit was followed swiftly by the destruction of Byblos, Tyre, and Sidon."

"And what of our people?" someone asked.

"The seed of Abraham stood aloof," the old man said, "for ruin and death was being rained down not upon Israel but upon the hated enemy, the Canaanites. Israel was not at first directly affected by the wave of savagery that rolled on inevitably toward the Nile and old Egypt. So they watched. They observed from their hilltop redoubts. Israel raised not one hand as Ramses drew up his armies to face the alien hordes. It is said that the pharaoh's horses were like falcons amid a flock of tiny birds. The outcome of that great battle, and of Ramses's second triumph over the Peleset on the waves of the green sea, is written in the annals of Egypt. The pharaoh reckoned the totality of his *victory by hacking off the hands of the dead and wounded, so that great, reeking mounds of severed members rotted in the sun."*

A gust of wind sent snow swirling. Two members of the old man's audience turned their backs and hurried toward the warmth of home.

"Egypt was safe, but the battles took a lasting toll in blood. The renown of Egypt lived, but her will had been strained to breaking. The glory of Egypt departed with the death of the third Ramses, and the invaders remained close at hand, settled firmly into what had once been a part of the Egyptian Empire. The Peleset had failed to conquer the rich mud fields of Egypt, but they occupied the fertile plains of southern Canaan between the sea and the mountains."

"Now I know of whom you speak," said a young girl shyly.

"Say the name, then," the old man told her.

The girl blushed and hid her face.

"To the descendants of Abraham they were not the Sea Peoples, not merely those who built their cities along the shore. They were not the Peleset. They were then and will be throughout the millennia identified in the minds of all who hear or read the tales of the exploits of mighty Samson, of mystical Samuel, of the ill-fated Saul, and shining King David, as savagery incarnate. They were then and will be known always as cruel warriors interested only in material gain. They were then and will forever be thought of as godless blasphemers, mockers, amoral alien spoilers insensitive to the wisdom, the antiquity, and the beauty that they annihilated."

"Philistines," whispered the young girl.

"Philistines," confirmed the old man.

The wind rose and was more chill. The scholar, feeling the cold in his bones, hurried his words.

"From their cities on the plain of Canaan, from Ashkelon, Ashdod, Ekron, Gaza, and Gath, they pushed inland. The lords of those five cities acted as one in military matters, while Israel dithered internally, tribal pride rubbing against tribal rivalry. Their beer-drinking warriors wielded weapons of iron, and they closely guarded the se-

cret formula that they had stolen from the Hittites. Now the Philistines decreed there would be no smith in the land of Israel, lest the Hebrews make swords or spears and turn them against their oppressors. Every man among the Israelites went down to the Philistines to sharpen his share, and his coulter, and his ax, and his mattock. So the land that God had promised to Moses was in the hands of an enemy more cruel and more skilled in battle than any force ever faced by Israel."

The clouds were closing down, down, dimming the already weak light.

"They pitched at Aphek," the scholar said. "Their iron-armed warriors drank from the river Yarqon and threatened the road leading eastward into the mountains where Israel had settled. Israel pitched at Ebenezer to watch and to wait."

CHAPTER ONE

When Urnan awoke, his first thought was for his purse. He thrust his hand under the pack he was using for a pillow, palmed the weight of the gold, and felt reassured. He sat up and yawned mightily. To the west lay the luxuriant green fields of Philistine farmers on the Plain of Sharon. In the east the sun was rising over a low range of purple hills. Light reflected off the surface of the ponds around a spring that provided the liquid of life for the carefully tended fields of grain and the olive groves that climbed partway up the brown, barren slope below Urnan's camp. The sky was white with moisture, which would dissipate with the heat of the day.

When he cast aside his woolen coverings and stood, the movement startled a lurking jackal, who had been attracted to the campsite by the lingering scent of Urnan's evening meal of cold mutton and coarse bread. The animal's quick flight caused the ears of Ramses the donkey to jerk forward in momentary fright.

"Easy," Urnan soothed. As he walked past in search of a place to empty his bladder, he patted Ramses on the rump.

The man wasted no time in getting started on his journey. His route lay to the southeast, deeper into the wooded mountains. For several days he had skirted the cultivated areas populated by the tall, slim Philistines. More than once he had seen patrols of soldiers dressed in tasseled kilts and ribbed helmets. By sticking to the more difficult trails in the hills, Urnan had managed to avoid contact, but he was prepared for that eventuality. He was dressed as a poor man. Ramses, although stout of heart, was aged and spavined, a beast not worthy of seizure by the descendants of the people who had looted the fabled horses of Cilicia.

Only two things belied Urnan's disguise: the pouch of gold, proceeds of his trade in Megiddo, and a well-balanced, beautifully crafted short sword of his own design and manufacture. The gold was bound tightly to his waist under layers of odoriferous, ragged garments. The sword rested in the bedroll that lay across the shoulders of the donkey in front of the pads that made Urnan's seat astride the little animal bearable. He knew that should he be accosted, the well-made weapon would be worse than useless against the iron swords of a Philistine patrol. He was a worker in gold, silver, and the baser metals—an armorer, a craftsman, not a warrior. The sword was for use against bandits, who killed without question; Philistines were dangerous only when they had something to gain.

The narrow trail wound its way upward, toward the western massif of the mountains. As he rode, Urnan ate cheese and bread, then washed them down with swigs of warming water from a goatskin flask. The sun climbed to the zenith. Urnan was thinking of resting his rear and Ramses's old bones when he noticed the soaring carrion birds.

They were in the hundreds—black dots in the azure sky. The stench of death assaulted his senses and caused his lip to curl in revulsion. There was constant agitation among the circling birds as dozens more of their cousins came from hazy distances to drop down, down, then out of sight behind a rocky ridge.

The odor of decay grew stronger as he topped the rise and looked down upon a scene of carnage that caused the hair to rise on the back of his neck. The gaunt old donkey snorted and pranced.

"Dead Israelites," Urnan whispered as he struggled to bring Ramses under control. Bloated and rotting, the dead had been denuded by looters. Now they lay sprawled on the rocky earth, their swollen flesh shredded and torn by winged and four-footed scavengers.

A great battle had been fought in the dry, rocky valley. Only here and there was even a hint of green. Above and surrounding the valley the wooded hills brooded in silence. With a combination of kicks and reassuring words Urnan forced the donkey down the slope. With his stomach rebelling against the stench, his mind numbed by the slaughter, Urnan began to count but lost track at around three hundred as Ramses picked his way through the human debris. Stunned, the traveler was not yet grieving the loss of warriors whom he considered to be his adopted countrymen.

When there was movement in that valley of death, Urnan tensed. His hand plunged into the open end of his bedroll to close over the haft of his sword. The donkey jerked his head nervously.

"It is only jackals," Urnan said, then heaved a shuddering breath. A stone's throw from where he sat his mount, two beasts snarled in dispute over the same tidbit of carrion.

"In the name of God," Urnan despaired, "is there not enough for all?"

Movement came again on the far slope just below the tree line. He squinted. Something was alive there, something that was not an animal, something that moved erectly but jerkily on two feet. Urnan urged Ramses forward, ready for flight or fight. Neither was necessary. Staggering toward him was a boy dressed in a drab woolen tunic. The hem of the coarse garment had been gathered and tucked into a cloth girdle to allow for more freedom of movement. The exposed flesh of the boy's legs was lacerated, torn by thorns, bruised, soiled.

"Water," the boy rasped. "Do you have water?"

Urnan dismounted and quickly extended his goatskin flask. The boy reached for it but missed and stumbled, to fall heavily. Urnan knelt and felt the boy's brow. It was burning with fever.

He stood, looked over the field of ruin, and sighed. "Well, Ramses," he said, "a lad who has survived this deserves our best efforts."

In spite of the strength in his arms, the smith grunted as he lifted the boy to lie prone across the donkey's bony back. The Israelite was a sturdy lad. Urnan judged him to be around sixteen years old. Ramses turned his head and brayed as if to protest the burden.

The man noted the direction of the wind—from the sea. He led Ramses southward to escape the reek of the field of battle and finally saw vegetation ahead. Ramses smelled water and, with his ears pointed forward, increased his pace. In a little glen the clear, cool elixir of life flowed from a cleft in the rock and pooled enticingly before running through a miniature oasis to disappear back into the earth, which had given it birth.

While Urnan positioned the unconscious boy on woolen robes, Ramses drank his fill. The man rinsed a cloth in the pool and cleaned the Israelite's face. The coolness caused the boy's eyelids to flutter, then open with a start.

"Rest, friend," Urnan said, putting gentle pressure on the Israelite's shoulders.

"Who are you?" the boy asked in a strained, hoarse voice.

"I am Urnan, the smith." He unloaded his pack from the donkey.

"I know you," the boy said, once more trying to sit up. "Your forge is near Shiloh."

"Yes. How long has it been since you ate?"

Tears welled into the boy's large, brown eyes. "I cannot think of food."

"Then eat without thinking," Urnan advised as he broke off a hunk of bread. He cut a chunk of cheese. In spite of his protests the boy stuffed his mouth full and chewed hungrily.

"Did you take part in this fight?" Urnan asked.

"It was not God's will that I be here to smite the Philistine," came the bitter answer.

"Be thankful that it is his will that you still live."

"Israel is dead," the boy said around a mouthful of food. "Would that I were as well."

"If death is all you seek, be patient. It will come to you," Urnan said. "What is your name?"

"I am Saul, son of Kish."

"Ah, Kish the Benjaminite," Urnan said, nodding.

"I was sick when the men of my tribe left to join the main body of the army."

"So you were not in the battle."

"I came as soon as I was well enough to travel," Saul defended. "When I arrived I saw what you have seen."

"You are still feverish. Lie back and rest."

"Messengers came to my father's village to tell us that the Philistines were pitched at Aphek," Saul continued. "Our warriors gathered at Ebenezer."

"And met the enemy there," Urnan said, pointing toward the scene of the battle. "An ill-chosen place, indeed."

"I came as quickly as I could."

"Yes, I'm sure you did."

"The enemy had looted the dead. I walked among them"—his voice fell to a whisper—"looking for my father and my brothers."

"And?" Urnan asked gently.

"I found them not. A few survivors had hidden in the hills. Thanks to God, my father and my brothers had been seen, alive and well, heading homeward, to Gibeah." Tears flowed freely from the boy's eyes. "But Israel is dead. The godless Philistines have taken the sacred Ark of the Covenant."

"Is this true?" Although Urnan had lived among the sons of Abraham all of his adult life, he had never fully understood the fanatic, all-encompassing attachment that the Israelites had for their god. He was aware of the importance put upon the Ark by old Samuel, the holy man of Shiloh, and, indeed, by all of the seed of the wanderer Abraham; but to Urnan the Ark was just a rather nicely constructed box. He had seen it in its place of honor at the holy of holies in Shiloh. He thought that the winged cherubim atop the chest were well executed but not really works of art to rank with his own creations in gold and silver or, for that matter, to match the skill of both the ancient and modern artists of Egypt.

"Why in the name of heaven was the Ark here?" Urnan asked.

"When the first clash went badly, the Ark was sent for," Saul said. "It was thought that its presence would bring victory."

"The cherubim do not wield swords," Urnan pointed out.

"The glory has departed from Israel."

"Yes. Well." Urnan hid a smile engendered by the boy's pomposity, so incongruous with his tender age. He lifted the water flask. "Drink, and then rest."

The man was beginning to feel threads of apprehension. Before the battle Aphek had marked the northern and eastern boundary of Philistine domination. Now, with the Israelite army ruined, the hill country lay open to enemy penetration. To him the Ark of the Covenant was an object of superstition, but the fact that it had been captured and carried off by the Philistines defined the seriousness of the situation.

"Do you think you are strong enough to ride?" Urnan asked.

Saul nodded. "Yes, but we will have to travel far to the south. The hills are full of enemy patrols and foragers. Three times I tried to travel eastward. Three times I was forced to turn back."

Urnan's brows came together. If the boy was right, if there were Philistine soldiers in the mountains, then all of Israel was vulnerable—including his own home at Shiloh.

"We will rest here until the sun begins to set," Urnan said. Again he dipped the cloth in cool water, squeezed it out, then set it on the boy's head.

"If you will be so kind," Saul said, "I am hungry again."

Urnan handed over bread and cheese. The boy lifted his eyes and prayed aloud to the one God, to Yahweh of the Hebrews. Urnan bowed his head, even though he had no need for gods. He was a Child of the Lion, marked by the red-wine-colored brand of Cain, by the imprint of the lion's paw just above his left buttock. His was a noble heritage that matched that of the descendants of Abraham, although the details of his family's past were but hazy memories of tales told to him by his father and his mother before he was left to survive on his own in a strange land with only the skills learned at his father's forge to sustain him.

It cost nothing, however, to be respectful of the god of the Hebrews. His wife, Shelah—she of the dark, flashing eyes, honeyed lips, and perfumed, ebon tresses —worshiped the god of Abraham, and their son, Eri, had been brought up as a Hebrew.

With the sun touching the top of the hills to the west, painting the horizon with red, he helped the boy mount Ramses and led the animal toward the heights. There was a moon, and by its light they negotiated the mountain track. Once, they had to skirt a Philistine camp. They heard the drunken voices of the soldiers raised in song, and, as a breeze wafted up toward them, Urnan caught the scents of roasting meat and rich, strong beer.

With the morning they approached a village with great care, only to find that it had been destroyed. A woman lay half in and half out of a burned house. Above the waist she was blackened by fire. Her legs were long and slim. Her female core was exposed, the soft flesh there bruised and torn.

Urnan felt a burning in his stomach. He had known fear before, but never such an all-consuming panic. It seared his guts and left him weak. For seven years he had lived in the mountains at Israel's heart, near the sanctuary at Shiloh, where the Ark had rested. To remain so long in one place was unusual for a Child of the Lion. But as a boy of fifteen, he had fallen in love with the sultry Shelah, daughter of a priest of the tribe of Levi. Urnan was skilled in the making of sharp-edged tools of death, and the men of Shiloh and Israel needed his skills to help them meet the Philistine threat. He sublimated the urge to roam by periodic trips to Megiddo and other rich cities to the north to peddle the gold and silver trinkets he fashioned in his workshop.

Now, as he looked numbly at the half-burned body of the woman, as he smelled once again the stink of death, he was concerned not only for his wife but for their twelve-year-old boy.

"I must hurry home," Urnan told Saul.

The Benjaminite sat old Ramses. His head rested on his chest. "My way lies there," he said, pointing.

"You're still weak," Urnan said.

"Thanks to you, I am much recovered."

Saul dismounted slowly to stand without swaying. He offered his arm and hand in a clasp that Urnan accepted.

"If you ever have need, smith, you have only to ask of me or of any member of the tribe of Benjamin. It is true that we are the smallest of the tribes of Israel, but we have a long memory for those who befriend us."

Urnan smiled. There were times when the boy's voice lost its manly quality and reverted to the pitch of childhood. Looking into Saul's face he had to lower his first estimate of the boy's age.

"May your god go with you," Urnan said.

"As he goes with you, my friend," Saul replied.

Urnan watched until the boy reached a rocky outcrop and turned to wave before disappearing behind the shoulder of a ridge. Saul walked slowly but strongly.

"Yahweh," Urnan said in a normal voice, not that of prayer, "if, indeed, he is one of your Chosen People, he needs your help."

He mounted the donkey and urged the animal into motion. The sun was just past the center of the sky dome. He covered his head and, with trepidation, settled in to cover the remaining distance to home.

* * *

Before he emerged from the trees and rocks to see smoldering devastation of what had once been the peaceful village of Shiloh, he smelled that which he had most feared. There was no sign of life, only the reeking evidence of the decaying flesh that remains after life has fled. He kicked Ramses hard and shouted at him to hurry. Home was a short ride to the south of the sanctuary at Shiloh. His stone house and his forge were tucked snugly into a sheltered glen beside a clear spring.

Impatient with the donkey's slow pace, he leaped to the ground and ran toward the stream that flowed out of his private little paradise. He let out a hoarse cry when he saw that the once-clear water was tinted red with blood. A leather sandal lay beside the stream. He had to leap over the body of his manservant, his helper at the forge. The corpse was badly butchered by many blows. The man's head lay in the shallow water. His glazed, open eyes stared unseeingly toward the sky. Blood oozed into the clear water from a great gash at his throat.

Ahead, Urnan heard raucous male laughter. He recognized shouted words as being of the Philistine language. He ran around the stone wall that backed his shop and jerked to a halt. In the open area in front of the stone house, four soldiers were holding his wife, Shelah, on the hard, clean-swept earth. A fifth man, his kilt lifted to his waist, worked energetically between her outstretched legs.

Red rage dazed Urnan and dimmed his vision. He heard, as from a great distance, a small voice calling.

"Father! Father!"

Eri, his son, was lashed to the door of the shop. His face, so like his mother's, was stained with tears. A noose around his neck was tied to tighten if he struggled.

"Father . . ." The voice was a wail of despair, a clarion call to vengeance and action.

Urnan's short sword was in his hand. It was of perfect balance. The bronze blade was as sharp as the skill of a master craftsman could make it. As Urnan tightened his grip on the haft, the Philistine soldier using

Shelah's soft body stiffened and grunted at the moment of his ejaculation.

Urnan bellowed his outrage and was on the soldiers before their attentions could be distracted from the woman they had been sharing. A mighty blow slashed through the neckbones of the rapist. A gout of his blood splashed into Shelah's open mouth. Her dark eyes caught Urnan's for one terrible moment, and in that instant he saw anguish so intense that he screamed again in rage and lifted his sword for another strike. But he was not a warrior. He knew weapons, of course, from the making of them, but their use was left to the warriors for whom they were fashioned.

A sixth Philistine emerged from the doorway of the snug, stone house, his arms laden with loot. Urnan's sword made contact with a soldier scrambling to reach his own weapon. When the man released Shelah's hand, she clawed at his eyes, and distracted, the Philistine took Urnan's blow to the neck and joined his comrade in death.

Now Urnan faced three soldiers, each with a sword in hand. The outcome was inevitable, but he was saved from death by the intervention of the man who had been robbing the house. A heavy earthen ewer smashed itself to bits over Urnan's head. He felt the earth move under his feet, saw a flash of light, and then nothing.

CHAPTER
TWO

Urnan felt himself being dragged across the hard earth and began to perceive dim light as his arms were jerked behind him and secured roughly to a post. From a great distance he heard a woman screaming. When at last he could lift his head, he saw that the Philistine soldiers had returned to their pleasure. Shelah's screams grew weaker. Eri, still tied to the door of the workshop, was reviling the Philistines at the top of his boyish voice.

A Philistine officer, tall, looking as if he had been long in the field, stalked to slap Eri ringingly and say in the language of the Hebrews, "If you value your tongue, boy, you will hold it."

"Captain, hear me," Urnan called, the effort making his head throb.

The officer turned toward Urnan. His face was that of a man of no more than thirty years. He had eyes that

15

were the blue of a winter sky, a prominent, strong nose, a jutting chin. His purple kilt was soiled and frayed at the hem.

"Sir," Urnan cried out, his voice shaking with horror and desperation, "my family and I are not of the Twelve Tribes. I am Urnan the smith, a craftsman, an armorer. Those are my wife and my son. We are not your enemy."

"And for whom do you fashion your arms?" the officer asked.

"An armorer has no country. Stop them, please," Urnan begged.

The officer turned his head and mused for a moment as two soldiers switched positions around the woman.

"Tell them to stop," Urnan wailed. "In the name of all the gods tell them to stop!"

The officer laughed.

"I have sold my crafts in the Philistine cities," Urnan said, his voice distorted by his weeping. Shelah was throwing her head from side to side as if in negation of what was happening to her. Eri was sobbing from pain and fear. "I am known in Ashdod, and in Ashkelon—"

"This man of Ashdod knows you not," said the officer. He turned, shouted in his own language to his men. Urnan knew enough of the Philistine tongue to understand that the officer had told them to hurry.

Urnan's scream of rage and helplessness was so powerful that it hurt his throat.

"By the way," the officer asked benignly, "can you see well enough from your position?" He chuckled. "I would think that you would treasure these last few minutes of seeing your wife alive." He turned, barked an order. Two soldiers came to lift Urnan to his feet and secure him to the post to which he had been tied.

"After all," the officer continued, "the Hebrew slut is being honored to have the attentions of so many of our brave soldiers."

Eri was sobbing. His eyes were closed tightly.

"You, boy," the officer said, turning to him, "open your eyes."

The officer moved to Eri's side and with the edge of his sword lashed at his bare legs below his short tunic.

"Open your eyes and see what happens to those who oppose us," the officer ordered.

For Urnan, it seemed to go on forever. Madness threatened him. His vision blurred as man after man tormented Shelah. She no longer moved.

"Enough!" the officer shouted. "Leave the Hebrew slut."

For a moment Urnan dared hope that Shelah would live. Her legs moved feebly as those who had been pinning her to the ground released her. The last man to use her brushed down his kilt, took his weapon from a companion who had been holding it, drew the iron sword from its sheath, and plunged it into Shelah's stomach. She screamed, clasped the iron blade with both hands, and tried to sit up. For a moment, before Shelah slumped over in death, Urnan looked into dark eyes made wide by agony.

"Mama! Don't die! Please don't die!" Eri shrieked.

With an effort that would have done credit to the mighty Samson, Urnan broke the bonds that had secured him to the post and rushed toward the man withdrawing his sword from Shelah's body. With an animalistic scream Urnan threw himself at the soldiers, taking them by surprise, bearing two, including the man who had killed Shelah, to the ground. He managed to strike a few wild blows before he was pummeled into dazed submission.

"We have here," said the murderer, "a fellow of some spirit. I think he will be worth a good price."

A cold, numbed calm had replaced Urnan's madness. "Tell me your name," he said.

But the murderer said nothing.

"Will it console you to know the name of he who killed your whore?" the senior officer asked.

"And yours," Urnan said. "I would know your name as well."

"I am Galar of Ashdod," the captain said. "And
this, the one who is so skillful with his sword, is Jobal,
my lieutenant."

One of Urnan's eyes was slowly being closed by
swelling. He tilted his head to get a good look at Jobal.
The visage was hard, the face of a common soldier
rather than an officer. The pale eyes were slits of evil;
the lips and mouth were set in cruel lines. Jobal came
over and searched Urnan's filthy robes. He came upon
the pouch of gold and, smirking, tossed it to Galar. The
captain tucked it into his belt. Then Jobal took Urnan's
short sword. This the lieutenant was allowed to keep.

Urnan did not speak. He knew that his position was
hopeless. He was dazed, bruised, bleeding. The shock of
having seen Shelah despoiled and murdered had taken
his reason and left only an apathetic shell. When his
hands were lashed in front of him and he was led away
from his home, from the body of his beloved wife lying
in the dust, from the cries of his son, it was as if the
events were happening to someone else.

"Father! Father . . ."

He was not sure whether he dreamed it or whether
Eri, too, had been lashed behind a horse and was running at his side.

The well-mounted Philistines were eager to get
back to their city. Time and again Urnan lost his balance, fell, and was dragged across the rocky earth until
he could manage to get his feet under him again. The
physical pain became more powerful than his mental
anguish. The searing abrasions on his legs and arms, the
ache in his head, and the protestations of the muscles in
his back where he had been beaten told him that he was
alive. His son, too, was alive. He could do nothing at the
moment but struggle for survival. His fate and Eri's was
to wear the brand of a slave; but as long as there was
breath in him, the hope also lived that one day he would
kill the Philistine officer who had ordered his home
plundered, his wife killed, his son led away into slavery
with a noose around his neck. He would never forget
the face of Galar of Ashdod. He would go to his grave

with the hard, cruel visage of the killer, Jobal, vivid in his memory. He would not rest or allow himself to succumb to the degradation and the rigors of slavery until he saw those faces smashed, saw those two pairs of blue eyes filmed over with the dryness of death.

CHAPTER THREE

Urnan had been wrong in guessing that Saul the Benjaminite was around sixteen years old. The youngest son of Kish, a mighty man of power, had just observed his fourteenth birthday when he was bundled across the back of Urnan's donkey and carried unceremoniously away from the site of the disaster at Ebenezer. Saul looked to be older than his years because he was a tall, strong lad. At fourteen, even when his voice broke and he sounded like the boy he was, he showed the promise of the man he would become.

As he traveled southeastward, away from the vicinity of ruined Shiloh and into the lands of Benjamin, the sickness that had been upon him gradually released its hold. He began to encounter other travelers, some of whom had fled the slaughter at Ebenezer. He camped one night with followers of Samuel, the holy man of Shiloh, a man to whom God spoke. The travelers were trekking south to join the seer in the hills north of Jerusalem, there to continue the fight against the encroaching Philistines. This news made Saul glad, for Samuel, a judge and acknowledged leader of Israel, had created some sense of organization, at least, among the vanquished.

To his joy Saul learned that the enemy had not penetrated the rugged hill country surrounding his native village, Gibeah. He was greeted there by Kish, his father, and by his brothers.

At first Kish was full of reprimand, but as he examined the ravaged face of his youngest son he relented.

"I looked for you, Father," Saul said. "I looked for you at the field of death."

"You were there? At Ebenezer?" the old man asked.

"I came too late."

"What did you see there?"

"I saw Israel dead and being eaten by carrion birds and the beasts of the field."

"And the Philistines?" Kish asked.

"They are in the mountains," Saul said. "I have been told that Shiloh is destroyed. Soon, I suspect, they will come here."

"There is still this," Kish said, lifting his bronze sword. "Not all of Israel is dead."

Saul's weakness returned. His head was swimming. "I looked for you," he repeated, and sat down.

"Your brothers and I were ordered by the captains to spy into the Philistine plain. We were far away when the battle was fought. Of course, we heard of the defeat. But was it so cataclysmic that we did not even tend our dead?"

"Their bones will whiten in the sun," Saul said. "And Israel is lost, because the Ark of the Covenant is taken."

Raphu, an influential man in the village, emitted a wail at this calamitous news. Grief-stricken, he tore his striped tunic.

As the word was spread, others echoed his sorrow.

"With the sacred Ark in the hands of the Philistines, what hope can there be for Israel?" wailed Raphu.

But in Saul's opinion, Raphu was always the naysayer and predictor of doom and gloom. Villagers of similar pessimism always rallied around the man.

"There are still those who will fight," Saul said, dismayed by the lamentations. "There are those who follow Samuel."

That was powerful news. Samuel, as the last of the judges, wielded great influence over the tribes. Aside from his direct access to God, he was a man of great moral stature and strong personality. But Raphu seemed not to hear as he continued to rend his garments in despair.

"It can be nothing more than a last stand," said one of Saul's brothers.

"Last stand or not," the boy said, "where men of Israel stand to fight, there we should be."

"Saul is right," Kish said, his voice ringing out, quieting the moans and sobs of the women. "Men of Benjamin, gird yourselves, for we will march!"

"This time I will go with you," Saul said, leaping to his feet. But he experienced such a wave of dizziness that his brothers had to catch him to prevent him from falling.

"You have not yet recovered fully from your illness," Kish said.

"Saul," said the eldest son, "someone must protect the women and the old ones. After you have regained your strength, you will be their guardian."

So it was that once again Saul was left behind while his brothers, his father, and the men of Gibeah and the lands of Benjamin marched off to face the enemy. For two days he was too ill to be much concerned, but good food, the love of his mother and his sisters, and the solicitude and concern of all brought quick recovery. Within a few days he was as strong as ever. He honed his weapon, a battered sword that had been discarded by one of his brothers. He scouted out from the village, but fortunately, the Philistines had chosen not to penetrate the mountains as deeply as Gibeah.

To that date only Saul's size had set him apart from other lads of his age. He seemed to his mother and to his sisters to be an ordinary enough boy, just another junior member of Israel's smallest and poorest tribe. In ordinary times his duty was the care and watching of his father's asses, to see to it that they had graze during the day and were safely in the pen at night. Now he was one of the few able-bodied men—or in his case, a near man —left in the village. He took his responsibility seriously, for he knew that his older brother had not been speaking idly when he said that Saul would have to be a guardian for the women, children, and old men. He combined taking the donkeys to pasture with scouting forays into the surrounding hills, thus fulfilling both his assigned duties.

When he was alone in the hills, while tending the animals, he prayed to God, for his faith was strong and not yet diluted by events. The weight of the terrible defeat at Ebenezer was heavy on him. He asked God why he had allowed the Philistines to seize the Ark, the most sacred artifact of the long and terrible flight from Egypt.

"I ask you, God of my fathers," he prayed aloud, "why have you allowed your Ark to be so desecrated, to be taken by the uncircumcised Philistines?"

In Saul's young mind it was an intolerable situation. He wondered when the world would end, for no priests of Yahweh were guarding that which lay between the cherubim. Sacrilege was being performed against the Ark and against God, and the weight of it bore him down and crushed him. So, when God came to him in a dream, he did not question why the presence was made known to a lad of fourteen years.

God came in the form of a blinding and gloriously golden light to the young lad of Gibeah. No words were spoken, but there was communication from the Most High to the mind of Saul.

"You know what you must do," he was told by the shining presence.

The young Israelite was awed. He knew that he had been blessed, that he, like Moses on the Mount, had been in the presence of God. He, like Moses, had not been shown the face of Yahweh, but he recognized the majesty of the Supreme Being when it came to him, even in a dream.

To avoid remonstration from his mother and to spare himself the need to make an explanation, he left the village in the dead of night. He carried his battered old sword, enough food to last him through his journey to the Philistine plain, a cloak to ward off the chill of night, and a goatskin container of water.

He slept a few hours in the early morning in a cleft in the rocks, then was traveling again with the sun. Late in the day he topped a ridge and looked down upon the field of battle near Ebenezer. The bones of Israel's dead, whitened by the sun, had been scattered by sharp-toothed scavengers. He knelt and prayed that the God of Abraham would bring retribution and revenge to those who were in the process of subjugating the Chosen People.

Saul slept that day on the side of a hill looking down upon the plain. With darkness he began his penetration of the enemy's country. At first he moved among the poor huts and tiny fields of Canaanite farmers and herdsmen. He felt no pity for those who were the mere remnants of a race that had once lived prosperously in large areas between the Jordan and the sea, for the Canaanites were worshipers of heathen idols. They denied God. That they had been beset first by Joshua and the Israelite warriors of old and then pushed aside by the Philistines seemed to him to be no more than God's punishment for the wicked. He felt no hesitation in stealing food from the gardens and, from a drying line, coarsely woven garments left outside by a Canaanite housewife. Now he could travel by day as a Canaanite beggar.

Saul used his disguise more to seek information than to acquire petty coin. He learned quickly that the prisoners taken at Ebenezer had been marched as slaves to various Philistine cities. Of more immediate interest, however, was the discovery that the sacred Ark of the Hebrews had been taken to the city of Ashdod.

To the best of Saul's knowledge, no member of the tribe of Benjamin had ever traveled so far from the hills northwest of the great Salt Sea. To a more experienced, older man, the prospect of traversing the heart of Philistia would have seemed daunting. Saul merely bared his dark, shaggy head, let his tight curls blow in the breeze as if he were a Canaanite beggar boy, and started southward. Below Azor he was in the land that had once been given to the tribe of Dan, but the descendants of Abraham had, for the most part, fled into the interior hills.

He soon learned that the proud Philistines were more likely than the subjected Canaanites to toss a minor coin toward the outstretched hand of a handsome boy. The Canaanites had been reduced to little more than servants for the conquerors.

Actually he fared much better than he would have guessed. Becoming a skilled thief was relatively simple. He took sustenance from the fruit trees and gardens along his route; the few coins that he begged purchased bread and meat. He rationalized that because his cause was godly, he would be forgiven for eating flesh not butchered in accordance with the dietary laws of his people or blessed by a priest.

He was unprepared for the chaos, the noise, the crowding, and the bustle of a major Philistine city. He leaped to one side as a pair of mounted officers rode recklessly down the street. Then he found himself directly in front of a heavily laden oxcart with huge, solid wheels.

"Get out of the way, beggar!" shouted the driver.

Saul, acting like a beggar, made a rude gesture to the driver and skipped aside to collide with a bearded man in rich garments.

"Scum!" the man shouted, shouldering Saul back into the street.

"Eater of swine," Saul retorted. He dodged a quick blow from the Philistine's staff and decided that retreat would be wise. He ran, weaving in and out, occasionally jostling others, until the street opened into a market square teeming with people. The cornucopian produce of the fertile plains was displayed in luscious mounds of yellow, red, and green. Merchants hawked their wares in more than one tongue. Women, both free and slave, haggled loudly over prices.

Saul, wide-eyed and amazed by the surplus of plenty that surrounded him, slowed to a walk. Nowhere in Israel had he ever seen such abundance.

A voice called out near his ear, "Here, boy."

He turned to see a buxom woman seated on a stool behind a small display of clay objects.

"You look as if you need some luck," the woman said, smiling. She was missing two front teeth.

"Perhaps you are right," Saul said politely.

The woman picked up an oddly shaped clay image and extended it. "This brings luck to beggars."

"It looks like a chair," Saul said, taking the object and examining it closely.

"No, look," the woman told him, pointing to two conical breasts protruding from the back of the chair below a long, extended neck and an egg-shaped head with huge, staring eyes. "It is the goddess Ashtoreth, seated upon her throne."

Saul almost dropped the object in his eagerness to give it back to the peddler. He knew full well what happened to those of the Chosen People who adopted the heathen images of the Canaanites.

"The lady Ashtoreth is the consort of Baal," the woman said. "She is yours." She named a small sum of money and held the crudely fashioned idol out toward Saul. "She will improve your life."

"I have no money," Saul said, knowing that the small lie would end the woman's persistence.

Indeed, the smile left her lips, and she looked away. "Begone, beggar. Leave room before my stall for those of worth."

It occurred to Saul that he knew nothing about the city and might have inadvertently made a tactical error. Already he had almost been ridden down by Philistine officers, nearly run over by an oxcart, and attacked by a man of the city. "Perhaps," he said, "I might have one or two small coins."

The eyes of the seller of charms, amulets, and small

household idols gleamed again. Saul took the idol from her hand as he prayed silently for forgiveness. He took two bronze coins from his purse, and the exchange was consummated.

"Old woman," he said, "I am a stranger in Ashdod. I have come to see the wondrous objects that our brave soldiers seized from the Hebrews in their great victory."

"Do you speak of the box in which the Hebrews carry their god?" the woman asked.

Saul's impulse was to correct the woman's mistake, to tell her that it was not God but the commandments of God that resided inside the Ark; fortunately he managed to think faster than his tongue could speak. "I think that I have heard it called the Ark of the Covenant," he said.

"It rests in the house of Dagon."

Saul nodded. "And where may I find the house of the honorable Dagon?"

"Honorable indeed. What backwater slut spawned you," the woman asked contemptuously, "that you know not of the god Dagon?"

"I am but a poor orphan of Canaan," Saul said, lowering his gaze.

The woman was looking at him closely. "And yet the Philistines brought their god to Canaan."

"Do I look like one who has communion with gods?" Saul asked. "In truth I have had, in my unfortunate life, little contact with them." So saying he began to edge away.

"Come back!" the woman called.

He turned and ran, dodging among the stalls and the milling crowds of Ashdodians. He fled into a narrow alley and was alone for a moment. In disgust, he flung the clay idol from his hand, and it smashed against the cobblestone of the street. For some time he wandered through a reeking, poor residential district, where thin, naked children played in the streets and waded in the human waste that ran in the gutters. When he found his way out of that quarter and into wider avenues, he walked carefully, for these streets were patrolled by armed soldiers who peered at him with suspicion.

Hunger drove him back to the market. He stayed away from the idol-seller's booth and bought honey cakes with one of his coins from an old hag.

"This, boy, is your change," she said kindly, handing him a small coin that had been shaved down to make it more oblong than circular. On one side of the coin was a lion. On the other was an image of a being with the torso, arms, and head of a man and the lower body of a snake or a sea creature.

"What does this image indicate, old mother?" Saul asked.

"You see on that coin the glory of Dagon," the old woman said.

Saul's mouth was watering with hunger. He bit into a honey cake and mumbled around his mouthful, "Good, very good."

"I have long experience," the old woman said offhandedly, but she smiled at his praise.

He swallowed and wiped his mouth on the sleeve of his tunic. "I am told that Dagon lives here in Ashdod."

"He does," the old woman confirmed.

"Would a beggar like me be allowed to see him?"

"He is the god of all," she said.

"I would see this great god, old mother, if you would be so kind as to point my way."

The old woman used her hands to describe the turns that Saul would make to arrive at Dagon's temple. He thanked her, then used his last coin to buy more of her honey cakes and left the market square in the direction opposite his last egress.

Her instructions proved accurate. The temple of Dagon was constructed of cyclopean blocks of limestone. It rose to a great height. Wide stone steps led up to entrance doors, which were great slabs of wood sheathed in bronze. Saul stood across the street for some time and observed. Only a few came and went from the temple. Each time someone entered or left, one of the massive doors was opened by a shaven-headed priest in a flowing purple tunic with gold trim at the neck and hem. Below the tunic showed a length of some delicate white undergarment.

It was growing late by the time Saul decided that it was now or never. He walked across the street, then up the stairs. As he neared the door it was opened, and the priest, who was not only barren of hair on his head but also clean-shaven, looked down at him.

"Pardon me, holy one," Saul said, bowing slightly, "is it permitted for an unworthy beggar to see the god?"

"Dagon is the god of all," the priest said with a smile that creased his fat cheeks and showed the red of his gums. "Enter and be blessed."

The priest closed the door with a creak of hinges and led Saul through a narrow, high-ceilinged entrance and into a huge, ringingly empty chamber. There were no windows, but the vast room was lit by torches in holders along the stone walls. The god Dagon stood on a pedestal at the far side of the room, but after one glance at the tall stone image Saul had eyes only for one object.

Saul held his breath. He had never seen the Ark of the Covenant, but there was no doubt in his mind as to the nature of the great box that sat on a wheeled cart that was its permanent means of transportation near the evil, towering statue of Dagon.

The box was elegantly carved, gleaming in the richness of its wood. On the end and side that were visible to Saul were columns carved in bas-relief. The chest was closed, and the two cherubim facing each other atop the lid glowed with the red reflected light from the torches.

"You may approach," the priest told him in a kind voice.

Saul walked slowly toward the raised dais on which sat both the idol and the sacred Ark. He threw himself to his knees, fell forward, put his forehead on the cool, rough stone, and prayed not to the heathen idol but to Yahweh.

He arose to look closely at the idol. Dagon clutched a trident spear in his right hand, a tambourine in his left. His lower body tapered off into a sinuous, serpentine coil. Saul, feeling revulsion and hatred, turned his eyes to the cherubim atop the Ark and continued to pray silently to the one God.

"You are a devout lad," the priest said as Saul turned away from the dais.

"You are most kind, sir, to allow me to enter this sanctuary."

"Dagon loves young lads." The priest showed his red gums in a wide smile. "Tell me, have you a place to stay, a home?"

Saul hung his head. "I am an orphan, holy one."

"If you should prove to be worthy, there might be a place for you here."

"Here?" Saul looked up. The unexpected kindness filled him with suspicion.

"Have you thought of devoting your life to Dagon?" the priest asked.

Saul's heart lurched at the blasphemy, but he managed to keep a calm face. "I had not dared to aspire so high."

The soft, pudgy, hairless priest put his hand on Saul. Fingers kneaded the boy's shoulder, then slid toward his buttock. A feeling of discomfort and uncleanness caused the boy to step away.

The priest continued to smile. "It is time to give the god his rest. At sunset we secure the doors. If you will come back tomorrow, perhaps we can explore your future more fully."

"You overwhelm me with your generosity," Saul said. He turned and marched toward the exit. The priest strode ahead of him, opened the portal, and smiled at him redly as he walked out into the evening light.

With dusk, a feeling of terrible loneliness came over Saul. He was, after all, young and farther from home than he'd ever been before. He looked toward the heavens in an effort to gain solace from God, but there came to him only a reinforced awareness of his helplessness.

He made his way to the market. Most of the merchants were gone, their stalls closed for the night. The old woman from whom he had bought honey cakes was packing up her few remaining morsels.

"So, young one," she said when he walked up. "Did you find the temple?"

"I did, old mother."

The hag laughed and shook her head. "I am surprised that the good priests did not make you a guest for the night."

Saul was puzzled. "How so?"

Again the old woman cackled. "If there is anything that the priests love more than kissing the stone hands of their god, it is kissing goodly young boys."

Saul's face flared red.

"Ah," the old woman said, "so you *were* invited to stay."

"No, only to return with the day," he said.

The old woman clucked at him. "And will you accept the invitation?"

"Should I, old mother?"

She seemed genuinely flattered to be consulted for an opinion. She licked her dry lips with a long, pointed tongue. "A Canaanite boy without a protector and without means could do worse, I imagine."

"And what would the priests want of me, old mother? Are they so needful of recruits that they would accept a Canaanite orphan into their membership?"

The old woman laughed with genuine amusement. "If you don't know, child, I suggest that you go back to the countryside." She sobered. "It is strange, indeed, that the priests let one who is so innocent escape them."

"I don't understand," Saul pressed. "If the priests want to help me—"

"Well, then, I will spell it out for you, child," the old woman said. "Some would use you as a woman. Others would be content to have you do the same to them."

The idea of it caused Saul's face to flush again, but in the fading light the old woman didn't notice.

"Go back to your own people," she urged.

"You are wise."

"And take these," she said, handing him the pieces and crumbs of several broken honey cakes. "For I am sure that you have no more money."

Saul chewed on the cakes and watched the old woman hobble away. The marketplace was deserted. He

looked around in the growing darkness for a place to
take shelter against the coming chill. From the other
end of the square a patrol of three soldiers entered the
area and began a sweep. Saul retreated into an alley
that ended against a stone wall. He sat on the cold
stones to drink from his goatskin and ponder his situation. Weariness enveloped him, and he fell asleep. . . .

He was dozing when another entered the dead-end
alley and staggered toward his resting place. Saul took
his sword in hand, hiding the blade in a fold of his tunic.

"What have we here?" the newcomer asked, swaying in drunkenness as he tried to make out Saul's face in
the shadows.

"No one who concerns you," Saul said.

The man, short, stout, smelling of beer and highly
seasoned food, threw himself down beside Saul. "Have
mercy, sir, for I have no bed."

"There are other alleys," Saul said.

The man put his hand on Saul's knee. "But they are
empty and lonely."

"I have not asked for company," Saul said and
moved away.

"Well, you're quite young, aren't you?" the man
asked, following, pushing his hand up Saul's leg.

"Are you a priest of Dagon?" Saul asked, remembering what the old woman had told him.

The man laughed merrily. "So you know the
priests, eh? That's good, for you will find me much more
gentle, my young beauty."

Saul gasped as the man's hand slid over his geni-
tals. He jerked himself away and leaped to his feet.

"Here, don't go," the man pleaded, rising to his
knees to reach for Saul.

Baring his sword, Saul stepped backward. The man
came to his feet and, moving with surprising swiftness,
threw his arms around Saul and pulled the boy to him
strongly. Saul met the force of the man's insistence with
a thrust of his arm. His bronze blade penetrated just
below the v of the Philistine's rib cage and thrust upward to paralyze him instantly. There was no outcry.

Saul jerked his blade free and let the body slump to the ground.

He had never killed a man. He stood dumbly for a long moment and looked down at the crumpled, dark form on the stones before he fled the alley as if pursued by demons.

CHAPTER FOUR

The world of Eri, son of Urnan, ceased all movement after the Philistine officer Jobal thrust his sword into the stomach of Eri's mother. For twelve years the boy had been loved, cherished, and pampered. His maternal grandparents lived nearby in the sanctuary at Shiloh, and in addition to being the darling of his grandfather and grandmother he was the favorite of dozens of uncles, aunts, and cousins.

As he neared the end of his childhood and approached that age where a young lad of Israel ceremoniously entered manhood, Eri knew that he was one of the fortunate ones. As the son of an honored craftsman and a grandson of a priest, he had status in the community. His father was not actually rich—Israel was a poor nation—but the family of Urnan wanted for nothing. He dressed in white tunics of fine weave. His mother always insisted that he wear an undershirt of linen that reached to his thighs, just short of the length of his outer garment. His leather sandals were of the finest manufacture. He bathed regularly and smelled of a sweet balm that Shelah applied every morning to his dark, thick, wavy hair.

Until the Philistine foragers smashed their way into his family compound beside the clear, sweet spring, Eri's most painful experiences had involved a stubbed toe, a cut finger, and a burn caused by his own carelessness as he apprenticed at his father's forge.

He was shocked into nonresistance when a Philistine soldier punched him in the face with a closed fist and knocked him to the ground. He bawled and cried out for the family's manservant as he was lashed to the door of his father's forge. His split lips hurt, and his nose was bleeding from the blow. Blood ran into his mouth and down his throat.

At first he was in shock, unable to assimilate what was happening to him and his mother. That their servant was dead had not even occurred to him. To a twelve-year-old who had known nothing but love and security, the events seemed to be a nightmare, something that might happen to others, but not to him. When the soldiers, laughing, making obviously lewd remarks in their own tongue, began to use his mother, reality intruded. Eri screamed out his protests until his throat was raw. Exhausted, he slumped against the bonds that secured his wrists to the hooks on the door. But when he put his weight on the ropes, his arms pained him severely, and a noose tightened around his neck.

Gradually a blessed numbness blurred the scene before his eyes. There was a sameness to it as man after man took position atop his mother. Then he saw his father. Hope burst in the boy as brightly as the rising sun on a cloudless day. But then there was new despair after Urnan ran into the compound to attack the Philistines and was swiftly overcome. He hated his father in that moment for his weakness.

Eri cursed the Philistines and prayed his grandfather and the strong warriors of Israel would appear. He kept looking toward the entrance to the family compound, hopeful that his prayers would bring salvation.

After he witnessed the brutal and casual murder of his mother, God gave to him the same gift he gives the frog taken unawares by the predator serpent—the gift of oblivion. Eri had observed that phenomenon once, to his shuddering disgust. A snake had seized a frog by the rear legs. The frog was alive, breathing, eyes blinking; but there was no struggle, no gasps of pain as the serpent's teeth slowly and inexorably worked the frog deeper and deeper into the abhorrent maw. The frog felt nothing as it accepted its fate.

So it was with Eri as he saw his father beaten into the ground to lie as if dead, saw his mother's lifeblood gush out onto the earth. He was oblivious to the pain in his wrists as he was half dragged behind a Philistine horse. A protective blankness enveloped his mind.

After the soldiers halted their march and made camp for the night, he was vaguely aware that his father was still alive. Urnan was tied to a tree on the opposite side of the campfire. Once, Urnan called out, "Eri! Eri!"

The boy turned his head and stared with blank eyes across the fire. He did not react when a Philistine soldier slashed Urnan across the face with a crop and told him to be silent.

He remembered little of the trip from Shiloh to the Philistine city of Ashdod. He arrived there spent, bruised, his fine clothing soiled and in tatters. The only recollection he had was that of hearing his father call out to him. That he would always remember, for men were leading Urnan away.

"Eri, remember me! Remember your mother!" Urnan cried out.

And then he was gone, and Eri was alone. Life, as he had known it, was over.

He was pushed roughly into a bare, small room. The door slammed, closing him in dimness. Before darkness, two male slaves came into the room and gave him a bowl of moistened, ground grain and a jug of water. He slept the sleep of exhaustion on the earthen floor, curled into a fetal position as protection against the chill of the night. The two slaves came back at daylight. One of them carried a bowl of water and a cloth.

"Clean yourself, boy," he was told.

When he didn't obey, the slave did the job roughly but not cruelly, swabbing dirt from Eri's neck and face, arms and legs. He was given a rough, dun-colored tunic to replace his ruined finery. Thus dressed, he was taken into an open square, where a small group of men was gathered around a raised platform. A young woman with the dark tresses and honey skin of a Hebrew stood on the platform, her head lowered to her chest, her arms hanging loosely at her side. A slim and sinister-looking Philistine stood beside the woman, pointing out her obvious good qualities to the bidders. The woman reminded Eri of his mother, and acid tears formed in his eyes. For a few moments he was the victim of reality, and the tears slid down his cheeks. But then the kind haze of oblivion washed over him again.

"You'll be next," said the slave who had washed Eri.

He stood on the platform next to the evil-faced Philistine and looked out over the crowd. His eyes lingered on the bloated face of a man with large, bushy eyebrows, a bulbous nose, and a mouth that pouted in the manner of a displeased child. One of the man's large, dark eyes winked at him.

It was the man with the pouty mouth and a soft belly who came to take Eri's arm when, after a brief flurry, the bidding for the young Hebrew slave boy ended with an offer that pleased the auctioneer.

"Come, pretty one," the pouting mouth said.

"Where are we going?" Eri asked indifferently, for surely the events of the day were happening to someone else, not to him.

"You will have your own room. You will have good things to eat."

It didn't matter. Nothing mattered. Eri made no objection as he was led away. A slave in a short work tunic took his arm and guided him down the street, after the man with the pouting mouth.

"Well, boy," the slave said, "you could have been purchased by a worse master. You will find that Liath is a fair man, and one of the richest in Ashdod. If you'll just do as you're told and stay out of trouble, your life won't be bad."

Eri did not answer.

"I am Moah," Eri's escort continued. "When I came to this house as a slave of our master's father, I was no older than you. I learned to keep my mouth shut and to obey orders, and now I am house steward. So you see, you are not entering into a completely hopeless situation. A slave who applies himself and serves the needs of his master can advance."

The house of Liath sat behind a great, mud-brick wall amid a grove of almond and apple trees. The air was deliciously scented with fruit and blossoms. Lilies and small purple flowers sprinkled the gardens with color. As the master walked through the main door, Moah took Eri into the sprawling edifice by way of the slave quarters.

From the kitchens wafted aromas that did more than anything else had to penetrate the trauma that shielded Eri. Moah gestured the boy to stop outside an open door from which came the most enticing of the smells, that of bread fresh from the oven.

"Mernan?" the steward called out.

A plump and motherly Hebrew woman came into view around the ovens. Her face was flushed from the heat of the kitchens, and her black hair was damp with perspiration. Strands of it clung to her forehead and her neck. She reminded Eri so much of his grandmother that the protective shield of shock was stripped away from him, and he realized all that he had lost. Tears flowed down his cheeks.

"Give this lad some food," Moah said, "and put him in the small room next to yours."

The Hebrew woman looked compassionately at Eri, and her brow was knitted in concern as she held out her hands to him. "Come, little one."

Moah gave Eri a small shove to send him Mernan's way.

The woman put her arm around his shoulders. "Some hot bread with honey will make you feel better," she said soothingly.

"Please, honorable mother," Eri said politely, "I am not hungry."

"Moah," the woman said, "has this boy been mistreated?"

The steward shrugged eloquently. "How can you ask such a thing? Mistreated? Just because he has been seized as a slave in a raid? Just because his entire family has probably been slain or sold on the block? Does that make him any less fortunate than you or I?"

"Hush," Mernan said, looking around fearfully.

"One of the first things you must learn, boy," Moah advised, "is to recognize your friends. Go with this good woman and heed her advice."

"Perhaps you would like to rest," Mernan suggested.

"Yes, please."

She led him through the steamy, aromatic kitchens and into a dark, narrow hall. "This is my room," she said, indicating a door. "And here is yours, at least for the time being."

The tiny cubicle had only one window, small and high and barred.

"I'll bring you some food and water," she offered, "just in case you change your mind."

"Thank you." Eri sank down gratefully onto a hard couch. It held a smell of old sweat and mustiness. He was asleep within minutes, the nirvana of unconsciousness replacing the fading oblivion that had been God's temporary gift. . . .

He awoke to darkness and to hunger. Mernan had left a plate of bread and cheese on the floor beside his couch. He ate slowly, for his appetite fled him when his memory began to function. He relived the terrible moments in the family compound, saw in his mind's eye the tortured face of his father as he was led away, calling out, *Eri, remember me! Remember your mother!*

Hate flared up in him and gave him strength. He hated his father for being unable to protect him and his

mother. He hated Moah and Mernan and Liath. He
tried the door. To his surprise, he found it unlocked. He
stuffed the remainder of the bread and cheese into a
fold of his slave tunic and crept into the hall. Mernan's
door stood open, and he could hear her heavy, regular
breathing. He tiptoed into the kitchens, where he found
several loaves of newly baked bread covered by a cloth.
He took one heavy, round loaf.

The door leading to the grounds was locked. But
Eri remembered seeing a window behind the ovens. He
was halfway out, hesitating only because he could not
see what was immediately below, when strong hands
clasped his legs and hauled him back into the room. His
ribs banged hard against the sill, and he tried to jerk
away but was set firmly on the floor, then slapped on the
side of his head.

"Why must you all be so predictable?" asked the
steward. "I cannot remember when a new one had
enough common sense to resist the temptation to try to
leave us on his first night."

"Let me go, Moah. Let me go back to my village."

"You wouldn't make it out of the city, little fool,"
Moah said. "You're far too pretty to be wandering
around the streets after dark."

"This afternoon you spoke as if you felt sorry for
me," Eri said.

"And so I do," Moah replied. "Enough to be sure
that I make an impression on you." He held Eri's arm in
a strong grip and steered him back to his room.

"Who's there?" Mernan called from the darkness.

"Moah. I am returning our small guest to his chamber." He chuckled. "I fear, Mernan, that there will be
some slight noise to disturb your sleep further."

"Be easy with him," Mernan said. "He is only a
boy."

"And I want to be sure he survives to become a
man," Moah told her.

In the room, by the light of a small oil lamp, Moah
removed his leather girdle. It was the width of his hand
and quite thick. He pushed Eri facedown on the couch.
The child stiffened with the first impact of the

leather strap, and he cried out in pain and outrage at the second. Then the injustice of it stiffened his resolve, and he was coldly silent as the leather smacked across his buttocks ten, fifteen, twenty times.

"Sit up," Moah ordered. "Look at me."

Eri's dark eyes were squinted with hatred. His backside ached, but he knew that Moah had been careful not to cut his flesh. There would be welts, but they would soon heal. It was not the first time he had been punished, for his father and mother had lived by the belief that to withhold discipline and guidance from a child was a serious sin and an indication that the child was not loved. Of course, his father's hand had never been as heavy as Moah's strap.

"There are no guards in the slave quarters in the house of Liath," Moah said. "The locks on the doors and bars on the windows are to keep robbers out, not to keep slaves in."

"I will run away as soon as I have the chance," Eri said.

"Little fool." Moah shook his head sadly. "Did you not hear me say that the streets of Ashdod are unsafe for a boy alone and unprotected? The fate that awaits you here is a kind one compared to what would happen should the animals of the streets get their hands on you. Listen to me: Mernan is of your people. She is a good woman. For the time being you will be her helper. Make the best of it."

Eri wiped his eyes with the back of one hand, then glared at the steward. "And when I am no longer Mernan's helper?"

"You will know the answer to that when Liath calls for you," Moah said. "I'm going to leave you now. I am going to my bed, and I sleep soundly. I tell you this in all honesty: I have saved you from your own foolishness once. I will not do it again. I will say, however, that our master paid for you in gold, a commodity he values highly. His punishment for trying to leave his house is far worse than mine."

The door had scarcely closed behind Moah when Mernan entered the room. She smelled of the compound of glasswort, which some people used to clean their skin. She wore a long night tunic with a robe thrown over her shoulders. Her glossy black hair was down, hanging to her matronly breasts. She sat on the edge of Eri's couch and put her hand on his shoulder.

"Moah's advice is worth following," she said gently.

"Did you ever try to escape?" Eri asked.

"I thought about it, of course. I was a mere girl when I was bought by Liath's father."

"You have been here so long?"

She nodded.

"Mernan, what will happen to me?"

She sighed. "Let me explain it this way. When the soldiers raided my village and killed my parents, I was a soft, full-bodied girl. When Liath's father saw me on the slave block, he bought me as a gift for his son, who was then of an age to me. The first night I was in this house, I was bathed and anointed, clothed in finery, and delivered to Liath's room. I was, of course, a maiden. I knew not what to expect, and I quaked with fear. I need not have concerned myself. Liath was civil to me, but he did not touch me. I was still a maiden when I left his room and went to the chamber assigned to me."

"I don't understand," Eri said.

"He will call for you, little one, and you will be bathed and anointed with oil. But you will not escape untouched from Liath's chamber, as I did."

Eri flushed with shock and sat up. "I will die first! I will swallow poison before I will have him use me as a woman."

"It will be just the opposite," Mernan said, obviously embarrassed by the subject. "And, I believe, it will be much less harmful to you than the taking of poison."

"What's he waiting for?" Eri asked, shivering with the thought of it.

"He will keep you in the household long enough to be sure that you do not have some loathsome disease." She stood. "Try not to think of it now. Try to sleep."

He slept, but his rest was interrupted by many wakings from the nightmares that came to him. He saw his mother die over and over . . . and saw the look of helpless desperation on his father's face as he was led away.

Urnan had discovered that the will to die was not the father of the act. When his son and he were separated on the outskirts of Ashdod, all desire to live left him. His back, shoulders, and arms were heavily bruised, swollen, and crusted with scabbed abrasions from his severe beating by the Philistines. But he welcomed the pain that came with each step as punishment for his inadequacy. It was an elemental justice that either he or the men who had raped and killed his wife should be dead.

As the slave coffle moved toward the north, Urnan's wounds healed, including the slave brand burned into his neck. His bruises lost their angry coloration and faded to shades of brown and yellow. The number of slaves grew constantly, most of the newcomers being Hebrews brought down from the hills as the Philistines continued their subjugation of the countryside.

Urnan heard, without realizing that he was listening, that the Philistines now controlled all of Israel with the exception of small enclaves in the mountains north of Jerusalem, where the followers of the prophet Samuel held out. None of it mattered to him, for the part of Israel that had been his life was gone. The God of Abraham, he felt, had not done well in protecting his Chosen People.

The coastline of the Philistine plain was difficult, devoid of good harbor. The growing group of slaves were marched to the north, toward the excellent harbor at Tyre. On the way they passed the fertile fields in the Plain of Sharon, then traveled to the west of Megiddo where, only weeks before, Urnan had sold his cunningly crafted items of gold and silver. The caravan moved along a narrow coastal strip into the land of the Sidonians. To the east rose tree-covered highlands, source of the cedar that had, through the centuries, brought traders from great distances, from the sea islands and from old Egypt.

At last they came to the great harbor at Tyre. The

tangy smell of the sea, which had always inspired Urnan to dream of travel to faraway places, did nothing to bring him out of his apathy. His body lived, but his mind existed in a haze. His whole world was dead. Everyone he loved was gone. The benevolent, sensible order to life was turned upside down.

He turned to snarl an insult at a Philistine guard who had lashed him across his bruised shoulders. The whip fell again, but Urnan felt the pain only dully. He lowered his head and followed the man ahead of him out onto a pier.

The harbor was crowded with vessels of various types. Huge, arklike commercial vessels squatted heavily at their moorings. A small boat rowed by two slaves moved toward the pier. Seabirds soared, called out harshly, and landed on pilings to peer with bright, small eyes at the activity of the humans.

Tied broadside to the pier was a bronze-armored warship. Just above her waterline were horizontal slits for oars, which were retracted with the ship at rest. Around the gunwale were circular bronze shields. The rectangular sail, left unfurled to dry, flapped loosely in a slight sea breeze. The stern of the vessel curved upward to project a decorative extension into the air, and the bow was heavily armored for ramming.

Urnan assumed that his fate was to join the slaves on the oar benches below the warship's wooden deck. Soon, then, his wish would be granted, for the life expectancy of a galley slave was a brief period of unendurable misery. *So be it,* he thought grimly.

He and the other slaves, their hands still chained in front of them and attached to a longer chain that connected them to a long, single-file line, were herded onto the deck of the warship. Lashes curled around scantily clad shoulders and cracked cruelly until the human cargo was huddled in a group on the forward deck before the mast.

With great shouts and purposeful actions the ship's crew loosed her from her moorings. Oars bit into the calm water of the harbor. She moved slowly toward the sea, and Urnan could hear the rhythmic poundings of the beater's wooden hammers from below as he marked time for the oarsmen. Sailors tightened the sail's riggings, and the great mass of cloth filled. The ship seemed to leap forward. Soon she was tossing and rolling in a quartering sea as she sailed northwestward away from the Phoenician coast.

Urnan soon realized why the slaves had been given only a swallow of water that morning instead of the usual breakfast of gruel. The motion of the ship sickened large numbers of slaves, and their retchings and spewings, scant as they were, filled the air with stench and brought the sickness to others. Philistine sailors drew buckets of salt water and drenched the slaves, deck, and all to wash away the vile accumulations.

"May God help us," a young man said in the language of the Hebrews. "For they are taking us to the Island of Copper, to the mines."

CHAPTER
FIVE

Urnan lost count of the days, for he was taken by a sickness that burned him with fever. When thin gruel was distributed to the slaves on the forward deck, he could not eat. Many men died during the voyage. He watched them tossed unceremoniously over the rail and desired that end for himself; but his fever abated, and he lived to see the rocky coastline of Kittem, the Isle of Copper. He was so weak, his fellows supported him as they were taken away from the port and into the hills. Still he did not die.

Urnan's strength began to come back as he was warmed by the sun and as he breathed clean, fresh air. But then their journey came to an end. After he and the others had been herded into an area of small, stone-walled cells carved into solid rock, they were released from the long chain. Urnan was shoved into a cell, and the door clanged shut behind him. His hands were free, and it was an excruciating luxury to stretch and move his arms. Now he wore shackles around his ankles, with those chains locked into a heavy iron ring in the stone floor. He could walk but a few steps, with a slow, shuffling pace governed by the length of the chain that connected his shackles. He sank onto a stone bench covered with straw and slept. . . .

The complaint of unoiled hinges awoke him as the door was opened. He looked up to see a giant entering the cell. Startled, Urnan sat up. Reaching out one huge paw to seize Urnan's arm and jerk him off the bench, the giant spoke harshly in an incomprehensible language. He spoke again, this time in Aramaic, a language Urnan knew. "You have my place."

Urnan chose not to contest the issue. He moved as quickly as he could to an identical stone alcove on the other side of the stone ring in the floor and sat down. The big man threw himself onto the bench and turned his back. He said nothing more, not even when slaves brought clay bowls of gruel and ewers of water. Urnan and the giant ate in silence. The larger man was soon asleep. His snores seemed to shake the cell's stone walls, but Urnan's exhaustion allowed him to sleep soundly until the ring of a guard's club on iron bars announced the dawn. The guard came in to release the shackles from the floor, then ordered Urnan to queue up outside the cell.

He fell into line behind the big man. Bread was distributed to the slaves, who ate as they walked into a ruined landscape of scattered rock and heaped soil. A well-worn pathway climbed a mountain of spoil. No vegetation broke the sameness of that devastated countryside. At the top, Urnan looked down into the open pit of a copper mine. Below, overseers bellowed and whips whistled through the air.

The giant took an iron-headed mattock from a rack, then glanced at Urnan, who stood uncertainly.

"Take this," the big man rumbled, handing Urnan another mattock.

An overseer glared at them for speaking and twitched a lash threateningly. Urnan took the tool and followed his cellmate down a winding ledge to the bottom of the cut. The man's broad shoulders were sun browned, but under the color were the marks of many lashes. It seemed that he had not been an easy one to tame.

By midmorning the sun had turned the open pit mine into a caldron where laborers stewed in their own sweat. Young boys circulated with water bags among the workers. Urnan took each opportunity to drink, but still his throat was dry, his tongue thick. He watched his cellmate and took his lead from him, for the big man moved with snaillike slowness, lifting his tool and letting its weight drive it a fraction of an inch into the rock.

Slaves with woven baskets scooped up the loosed ore and, staggering, carried it up the winding ledge toward the top of the excavation.

"They're the ones who die first," the big man said.

"Then I shall join them tomorrow," Urnan responded.

"If death is all you want," the giant said, "be patient, and it will come to you as a nice surprise."

Urnan let his pick fall. As the point struck the rock, the impact sent a jolt through his hands and arms.

"You have an accent that I don't recognize," Urnan said.

"So I have." The big man cast a look at Urnan and winked.

That moment of levity seemed so out of place in the forbidding surroundings that Urnan, to his surprise, chuckled. "I am Urnan."

"Of the Hebrews," the big man said.

"No. Of the Lion."

"Who?"

Urnan held his answer as a guard sauntered past.

"He, too, sweats," the big man philosophized when the guard was at a distance.

"But not so much as we," Urnan said.

"You said that you are of the Lion. I knew an armorer, a smith—"

"Who had the paw mark of a lion on his back?"

"Exactly."

"A cousin," Urnan said. "We are scattered widely."

The giant glanced with new interest at Urnan. "I am Kemose."

"Kemose is an Egyptian name."

"It is."

By midafternoon Urnan was too tired for talk. Kemose seemed to feel the same. The big Egyptian lifted his pick slowly, then let it fall. He had put aside his tunic and was working in nothing more than a loincloth.

The slaves were herded back to their stone cells as the sun set over the distant sea. Urnan sank onto his bench immediately and fell asleep. Kemose shook him awake when the food slaves came.

"I can't eat," Urnan said weakly.

"You will eat."

"Leave me alone," Urnan begged as the big man pulled him into a sitting position and forced his bowl into his hands.

"Eat," Kemose ordered.

Urnan drank the thin, starchy gruel, guzzled his ewer of water, then fell back onto his hard bench.

"You will not die, smith," Kemose grumbled in a low, deep voice, "for I have use for you."

Bitter tears came to Urnan's eyes. He certainly had been of no use to his wife or to his boy.

"Sleep," Kemose said.

That was an order easy to obey.

The days were a grinding sameness. Once, before Kemose could stop him, Urnan moved away from the tool racks and picked up a woven basket. He joined the carriers of ore, and before the day was half spent he understood why the bearers died first. The sun heated the rocky ledge and burned the soles of Urnan's bare feet. The basket, which had seemed small, magically gained weight with each trip up the winding ledge. At the top of the open pit, other slaves toiled to extract copper from the crushed ore.

By the end of the day, Urnan was numb with fatigue. He was grateful to be back in the cell. But Kemose seized him by the shoulders and with two big hands jerked him around to look up into a pair of angry eyes.

"I told you, fool, that you are not to die," Kemose said.

"Leave me alone," Urnan moaned. He had no strength to resist.

"Look at me!" the Egyptian ordered.

The Child of the Lion lifted his gaze. Kemose's eyes were brown and large; but as Urnan's gaze was captured and held, the Egyptian's eyes became pitch black and as hard as iron. They seemed to glow with a life of their own. They bored into Urnan's very soul, and he heard words without seeing Kemose move his lips.

You will not die, smith. You will not go with the bearers again. You are with me and will be with me when I escape this place.

Urnan shook his head to dispel dizziness. The giant released his grip on Urnan, who stumbled to his bed and fell asleep quickly. He dreamed that a pair of large, midnight-black eyes were penetrating his skull, seeking the very core of him.

He worked side by side with the big Egyptian under the blazing sun. As luck would have it, they had chosen a relatively soft area that day, so the bearers were often with them, filling baskets with the ore broken free by their tools. In a moment when they were alone Urnan asked, "Did I dream that you said you were going to escape this place?"

Kemose jerked his head to glare at Urnan. "Shut up. Never speak of that."

It was Kemose who brought up the subject in the cell that night, after they had eaten their meager evening meal.

"Can you remove these?" Kemose asked, lifting his feet to rattle his leg chains.

"With the proper tools," Urnan answered.

"I will never accept slavery," the Egyptian said.

"To rebel or to attempt to escape brings the lash or worse," Urnan said.

"I endure," Kemose said. "As will you."

Urnan did not want to admit to himself that the

Egyptian's words gave him something akin to hope. He felt guilty for not desiring death. A man who could not protect his family did not deserve to live.

And yet the faint possibility of deliverance was there, and with it a desperate hope that once freed, he might be able to find Eri and release him from his bondage.

"The time will come," Kemose said. "One of the guards will become careless and will die."

Urnan was silent. He had no doubt that Kemose could kill a man with his bare hands. To kill an overseer would solve all problems, for death by torture was the punishment for that offense.

"First we have to find a way to get out of this cell," Kemose said. "Then we will find the tools you'll need."

Urnan closed his eyes. He told himself that his friend was indulging a foolish dream, but as sleep came to him, he felt a surge of elation, a moment so pure that he felt like shouting out his joy. It was, he told himself, completely irrational. There were chains at his ankles, and those chains were attached at night to a ring of iron anchored in the stone floor of the cell. Even if Kemose and he found some way to loose themselves from the restraining ring, there was the matter of the iron-barred door.

At the slave steward's direction, Eri joined Mernan in the kitchen of Liath's great house. The boy's appetite returned under the woman's kind care. The day seemed endless in spite of the many chores she gave him, but it did end—as did another and another until the moon, which had been a small, faint crescent when he had arrived in Ashdod, was a swollen, golden globe in the night sky. He had been branded on the neck as a slave of Liath's, and that excruciating wound was healing, too.

Now he was gaining the rhythm of a moderately pleasant routine. His work for Mernan was not demanding. He lifted heavy pots and jugs for her, kept the fires of the oven stoked when she was baking, carried away the scraps of the fine meals served to Liath and the nonslave members of the household to feed a pack of

dogs kept by the master at the backside of the garden.
Dogs were, according to his mother's people, unclean
animals. Indeed, Liath's pack seemed vicious, noisy, and
contentious with one another and overtly hostile to the
slave boy who shoved the food at them through a hole
in the enclosure wall.

But a constant bleak undercurrent during these
passing days was Eri's apprehension. Both Moah and
Mernan assured him that the role he would play with
the pudgy master would not be painful or harmful; but
as the grandson of a priest of the tribe of Levi, Eri had
been raised with the morality of the Hebrews. The vice
of the Philistines was virtually unknown among the worshipers of Yahweh, although he had heard the older
boys in Shiloh sniggering about it among themselves
and thus knew what it was.

He was enough his mother's son to say in his
prayers, "Lord, I want to believe. Help thou mine unbe-
lief." Yahweh, the one God, was mystery and majesty
and guidance toward a way of life. Eri would readily
have admitted that he did not understand all there was
to know about the faceless God of Abraham. In fact, at
times he had doubts about his faith. He never actually
realized how deeply the teachings of his mother and his
grandfather were ingrained in him until Moah entered
his room one evening, a fine linen tunic folded carefully
across his arm.

Mernan was behind the steward. "Come, little
one," she said gently.

Eri didn't have to ask. He knew that his time had
come. He followed without comment. He protested only
slightly when Mernan stripped away his slave tunic and
helped him to step into a tub of warm water. Not too
long in the past his own mother had casually disregarded his nakedness to scrub him thoroughly, as Mernan did now, rubbing his hide vigorously with the
scratchy cleaning compound. Then he was dried,
dressed, led upstairs, and abandoned at the master's
door.

Liath waited in his bedchamber. Plump, soft,

sweetly perfumed, he greeted Eri with a pouty smile and a beckoning wave of his hand.

"I see that they have cleaned you up nicely," Liath said.

"Sir," Eri quavered.

"You are quite a comely lad."

"Sir," he said, letting his head sink. His heart was pounding, his stomach was churning, and in his memory was the thunderous voice of the holy man of Shiloh, Samuel, preaching against the abominations of the flesh.

"Come to me, little sparrow," Liath said, putting his soft, warm arm around Eri's shoulders and pulling him to a mass of softness into which Eri felt he was sinking. He felt the wet lips on his cheek, then on his neck. He squirmed and tried to pull away.

"I can understand your fear, little sparrow," Liath whispered. "Believe me when I say I wish you no harm. Stay with me, and there will be sweets to eat and soft linen to wear."

Panic set in when Eri felt the master's soft, pudgy hands caressing the small of his back and the hard little mounds of his buttocks. The boy wrenched away, breathing hard, his eyes wide and dilated.

Liath was not pleased. He reached for a silver bell and rang it furiously. Within moments Moah was bowing in the doorway.

"I told you to prepare this Hebrew imp!" Liath screamed. "You know I hate to be resisted! Take him away and teach him his place! You have done nothing, *nothing,* to make him ready for me."

Moah ran across the large chamber and seized Eri roughly by the ear. "Come, you ungrateful cur," he snarled, jerking the ear angrily.

The pain was almost welcome, for it was the means by which Eri escaped the sick sweetness of Liath's perfume and the cushiony softness of his body.

In the corridor of the slave quarters, Moah released his grip on Eri. The boy rubbed the side of his head tenderly.

"I told you and I told you, little fool," Moah

seethed. "Do you have any idea what the master meant
when he told me to prepare you?"

"No . . ."

"I was to train you, to use you as he would."

Eri's jaw dropped. He looked up in shock at the
steward.

"Once, I was Liath's favorite, and I jeopardized my
soul to secure my position here. Do not force me to
commit an abomination with you in order for you to be
able to please the master."

"Moah," Eri said, going into his room, "as much as
I respect you and am grateful to you, if you touch me in
that way, I will kill you or myself."

Moah followed Eri and looked closely at the boy.
"Do you mean what you're saying?"

"I do."

"Just be sure that you do."

"I know what death means. I saw a soldier drive his
sword into my mother's stomach."

"If you insist on defying Liath, then be certain that
you choose death. If he sells you, it will not be with your
well-being in mind." With that, he turned and stalked
out.

Mernan passed Moah in the doorway. "I beg you,
little one, to reconsider."

"I cannot, honorable mother."

She took the fine white tunic and handed him his
gray slave's garment, then looked into his eyes. "I, too,
once thought that death would be preferable to the fate
planned for me. But I still live. I beg you to choose life
as well, little one. It offers simple pleasures for one who
looks for them."

"I cannot," he repeated.

"So be it," Mernan said grimly. "But perhaps you
might be willing to give yourself one small chance?"

"I would be willing."

"Rest, then. When the moon is high, be ready. I
will come to you with food and a warm cloak. I will also
bring you an iron knife from the kitchen."

* * *

Eri tried, but he couldn't sleep. When he heard a small sound in the corridor he sat up and watched as Mernan entered the room. True to her word she had a satchel filled with food, a thickly woven cloak, and a Philistine knife used for butchering meat. She placed the weapon in his hand and closed his fingers over the hilt.

"If you are about to be taken by the street people, be sure you choose death. The surest way is to position the point of the knife thus."

She put the sharp point of the knife at the v at the bottom of Eri's rib cage. "Don't push the knife straight in. Tilt it so." She demonstrated. "One push, I am told, penetrates to the heart for a quick and painless death. Above all, do not let yourself fall into the hands of those who own the streets at night."

"I hear," Eri said.

"It is time." She led him to the back entrance to the house. The garden outside was lit by the moon, which hung low in the western sky. Mernan pointed at the orb. "Put the moon at your back. Stay in the shadows, and if you see anyone on the streets, hide. When you reach the outskirts of the city, continue to keep the moon behind you until you travel into the rising sun. Conceal yourself by day, and travel by night. When you reach the mountains, you will be south of Jerusalem."

"Mernan, you have my eternal thanks," Eri said.

"Give Mernan a hug," she said, holding out her arms. He embraced her and for a moment reveled in the warm comfort. And then he was in the garden, running lightly toward the wall that surrounded Liath's compound.

Eri had gone only a few feet when he heard a hiss of warning from behind him. He looked over his shoulder to see a sight that chilled him. Two of Liath's dogs were closing on him, their paws scrabbling on the loose gravel pathway between banks of flowering shrubs.

He put on a burst of speed, but one look told him that he had no chance of reaching the wall before the animals overtook him. He skidded to a stop, dropped the pack of food, threw off the cloak, then drew the knife from his girdle and waited. With a low snarl and the rattle of claws against loose gravel, the lead dog launched himself, his open slobbering jaws aiming for Eri's throat.

The quick instincts of youth and the strength of resentment that had built within him since the Philistine raid saved him. He slashed out as the dog's bared teeth came within an arm's length of his throat. He felt the sharp point of the knife engage flesh. He followed through with all of his might, at the same time stepping aside to avoid the momentum of the dog. The animal fell heavily and began to thrash around. Eri had just enough time to kick out strongly with his sandaled foot at the second animal. He put all his weight behind the kick and felt the top of his foot contact the dog's jaw, lifting the animal and sending it to land hard on its back.

At his feet the first dog's legs kicked feebly. In the glow of moonlight he saw a dark stain spreading from the animal's throat across the gravel. Eri stood poised on the balls of his feet, knife at the ready, but the dog he had kicked under the jaw was crawling away, dragging its hind legs and whimpering softly.

The boy turned and snatched up the satchel, then ran to the wall. He used the overhanging branches of an apple tree to climb to the top, vaulted over, then dropped onto the stones of the city street. He crouched in shadows until he was certain that he was alone. His heart was pounding from his encounter with the dogs. He knew that Mernan believed she was sending him to his death, that she thought, as he did, that for him to die would be preferable to being coaxed into bed by Liath. But he knew he would survive. Defeating the vicious dogs was a good omen. Heartened by that train of thought, Eri set out.

Staying in the shadows under Liath's wall, he moved down the street slowly and turned east at the first juncture. The city was quiet save for the barking of a dog and, once, the bray of a donkey. He guided himself by the moon and had traveled some distance when he turned a corner and almost ran head-on into two drunken men of the streets. His heart leaped as he ducked back and ran into the dark maw of a narrow alley. He kept one hand against the blank stone wall of the houses to his left as he penetrated the blackness. Looking back, he saw that the two men had halted at the mouth of the alley and were staring intently toward him. He froze.

"It'sh nothing," he heard one of them slur. "A dog, or a jackal."

He held his breath as the pair moved on. He waited for several minutes. Reluctant to go back the way he had come lest they be waiting at the alley's mouth, he walked on into the blackness. At last he saw a lighter area indicating that the alley opened into another street. He began to move more swiftly and ran directly into someone larger and taller than he, someone who wrapped him in arms of steel, pinning his knife hand to his side. Eri struggled but lost his footing and caused his larger opponent to fall atop him. He caught a glint of metal and knew that a knife was aimed at his heart.

"Yahweh," he prayed aloud, "help me."

CHAPTER SIX

When Eri called upon the God of Abraham for help, that help was instantly granted, and in the nick of time. The sharp and deadly knife that had been aimed at Eri's throat was swung to the side and plunged harmlessly into the earth.

"You're Hebrew?" Eri's assailant asked.

"Yes."

"Then peace be with you."

"And with you," Eri croaked. "You're breaking my arm."

There was a release of pressure. The weight of the body atop his was removed. A hand fumbled, found his, and helped him to his feet.

"You're just a boy."

"I am Eri, son of Urnan the smith."

"In God's name, that's odd."

"How so?"

"I know your father! I owe him a debt."

"How?"

"I'll explain later, when there's time. What are you doing in this alley?"

"First," Eri said, "I need to know to whom I speak."

"Saul, son of Kish the Benjaminite."

"Have you run away from slavery, too?" Eri asked.

Saul puffed out his chest. "No one would dare try to enslave me."

"Ho," Eri said. "Because you are such a mighty warrior?"

"Because I would die first, taking many with me."

"Then," Eri said with sarcasm, "I have indeed encountered a worthy ally."

"You are an escaped slave?" Saul asked.

"I fled from my place of servitude only an hour ago." This time Eri's boyish chest inflated.

"They'll be looking for you with the morning," Saul said. "What am I to do with you?"

"If you know this city, I would be grateful if you could direct me toward the eastern wall."

"The wall is well guarded at night," Saul said. "Your best chance of reaching the open countryside will be during the day, when many come and go through the gates."

"That leaves the night before me," Eri said.

"Come along," Saul said, putting his hand on Eri's shoulder.

The boys walked to the end of the alley, where Saul had left warm woolens that he had stolen from the rear courtyard of a prosperous home.

"I left my cloak behind," Eri apologized.

"Don't worry. I've got two." Saul pulled Eri down to lie close beside him atop one cloak and covered with another.

Eri awoke with the dawn. His back was pressed against the back of his new companion. He was chilled, so he pulled the woolen cloak up and under his chin.

"Are you awake?" Saul whispered.

"Yes."

"Come then, it is time to go."

"You're just a boy, too," Eri said when he saw Saul in the gray light of morning.

"I am past fourteen," Saul said indignantly.

"Oh, then I beg your pardon," Eri said. "You are indeed a man."

"You have a sharp tongue," Saul said. "Be careful lest its thrust be reversed to bring you pain one day."

"I did not mean to prick your feelings," Eri apologized. "Such observations are my nature."

Saul bundled the woolens and stuffed them into a large crack in a rock wall, then led the way to the mouth of the alley. A vendor was leading two donkeys laden with bolts of fine fabric down the street toward the market. A three-man patrol of soldiers appeared from a side street.

"We'd better go this way," Saul said, turning toward the temple of Dagon.

"That is not east," Eri said.

"Perhaps you'd like to ask those soldiers which way is east?"

"I see your point," Eri said.

The priest who had taken a fancy to Saul was just opening the main doors to the temple when the two boys came bounding up the stairs.

"Good morning, young sirs," the priest said, taking a close look at Eri.

"Good day to you, honorable priest," Saul said. "I have brought a friend to see the god."

"Your friend looks hungry," the priest said. "As do you."

"You have excellent eyesight, holy one," Saul said.

The priest, who introduced himself as Habi, led Saul and Eri to his private quarters and gave them bread to be soaked to a delicious softness in goat's milk. He watched them as they ate, his eyes hungry.

Eri glanced at his new friend, but Saul seemed oblivious to the priest's growing agitation. Eri realized that there were certain dangers inherent in being inside Dagon's temple with one of his priests. He recognized in Habi's slack-mouthed stare the same passion that had pervaded the home of Liath. His desire was, to Eri, a steamy aura that was almost visible.

"Thank you for the food," Eri said, making a half bow to the priest. "You are very kind."

"Give your thanks to Dagon, not to his humble servant," the priest said.

Beside him, Saul stiffened. Eri understood Saul's reaction but was himself not so rigidly controlled by his beliefs. Obviously, Saul would die before acknowledging a heathen idol like Dagon.

"If indeed this kindness is due to Dagon," Eri said, "then I do thank him."

"He is a gentle master, and there are many rewards for being in his service," Habi said. "It is odd that we live in a time when blasphemy and disregard of the old gods are becoming endemic."

Eri thought that it was in his and Saul's best interests to keep the man talking. "How does one enter the service of Dagon?"

"Through dedication and piety," Habi answered. "I myself have been a true believer since I was a boy."

"And in return does the god grant food and a home to his priests?"

"Yes, of course," the priest said. "Although the priesthood is not always an easy life. There is work to be done, and certain mysteries to be studied and understood. Unfortunately, in recent years the number of servants dedicated to the temple has been declining steadily."

"Would the god accept two homeless boys as his servants?" Eri asked. Saul glared at him.

"I can only hope that you are serious," Habi said. "Actually, most of our recruits to the ranks of the priesthood are not unlike yourselves."

Eri could not resist being flippant. He rubbed his back and then his belly. "After sleeping on the stones of an alley and going without supper, both my back and my stomach are quite serious."

"And you?" The priest looked at Saul. Eri jabbed Saul in the side with his elbow.

"Yes, I am serious," Saul said in a tone that was not, to Eri's ear, designed to convince. Somehow, it seemed to please the priest, who rose and left the room.

Saul was seething with anger. "Do not include me in your blasphemy!" he hissed. "I am here for one reason and one reason only, to take the Ark of the Covenant back to the Chosen People."

Eri widened his eyes to show that he was impressed with Saul's ambition. "I admit that I have no such divine purpose. I was thinking only of food and a bed and a place where I can hide until I can escape this city."

"Don't tease this priest, or you'll find yourself in the position of a woman under his advances," Saul warned.

"I know. And I shall try to avoid that at all costs." Eri fell silent, musing, his eyes going blank and staring into distances. When he spoke, his voice was soft. "The Ark used to be in the sanctuary of my village. Do you know where it is now?"

"Of course," Saul blustered. "It's right here, in this temple."

Eri was going to ask how the Ark came to be here but decided against it. If it had been stolen from Shiloh, then there was a good possibility that his grandfather the priest and others of his family were dead, killed by the Philistines in the same raid that took his mother's life. Some things were better left unknown.

"Have you seen the holy man Samuel in communication with God?" Eri asked.

"Yes. Why?"

"You have seen him, then, giving out oracles from a trance, at times roaring reproof and damnation, while at other times promising sweet and abundant life?"

"I just said I had," Saul said.

"And you are truly serious about returning the Ark to its rightful place?"

Saul nodded.

"Then I suggest that you, like Samuel, have been touched by God," Eri said thoughtfully.

"And I think you have been touched by the sun."

"No, listen," Eri said, bending forward in earnestness. "Be like Samuel. Roll your eyes back in your head. Drool. Whimper. Rant meaninglessly in a great voice for a time before you let these priests of Dagon know that the wrath of the God of Israel is upon them because they have dishonored the Ark of the Covenant."

Saul's eyes twinkled, and he confessed that, in fact, he and his brothers had, as a joke, imitated old Samuel by pretending to fall into a God-induced trance and bellowing out prophecies. It had been a favorite game, although there had been times when Saul was not totally certain that he was playing.

"I would do it," Eri offered, "but you, being older than I, will be more convincing."

The friendly priest came back with a colleague. The men hid their hands in the sleeves of their robes and looked down with pious expressions at the two seated boys. The newcomer was the high priest, and he explained that he was studying the two potential recruits to decide which one would become his personal disciple. He decided to choose the smaller of the two.

Food was brought in. Saul and Eri gorged on the meat of a lamb hot and juicy from the fires of sacrifice, topped off with sweet, ripe figs. The two priests competed with each other in indoctrinating the apprentices and created many opportunities to practice the laying on of hands—not in the manner of healing but of exploration. Eri was hard put to keep Saul from using the deadly little sword that was hidden in the folds of his tunic.

When the two priests took the recruits into the large chamber that was the home of the god, Eri saw his chance. While the priests prayed, prostrating themselves before the graven image of Dagon, Eri winked at Saul and whispered, "Now."

Saul was kneeling, but he had turned himself slightly away from the idol to make it clear to Yahweh that he was paying homage to the holy Ark and not to Dagon. He swallowed and nodded. Grinning, Eri urged, "Now. Now!"

Saul turned his face toward the high ceiling and let his eyeballs roll back. He began babbling in nonsense syllables. His voice rose to a shrill peak, causing the praying priests to turn as one. Eri pretended to be awed by Saul's divine seizure. He clasped his hands together in front of him in a gesture of submission while murmuring a real prayer under his breath to Yahweh.

Saul cried out in a deep voice. Saliva dribbled from the corners of his mouth. He fell onto his back, arms outflung, and quivered, all the while speaking expressively in a nonlanguage composed of random sounds and syllables.

"What language does he speak?" the high priest asked Eri.

"The language of God," Eri answered portentously.

The priest's eyes went wide. He and his companion bowed low to the one who was being used by the gods.

Saul became still, sat up slowly, climbed to his feet, and pointed dramatically at the kneeling priests. "Hear me, priests of Dagon."

"Speak to us, holy one," the high priest said.

"The wrath of the God of Israel is upon you!" Saul bellowed, his voice breaking boyishly.

"How can this be so, holy one?" whined Habi in real terror.

"The Ark of the Covenant has been dishonored," Saul said, keeping his voice as low as possible. "Grief and pestilence will come to those who defy the Lord God of Israel. His punishment will be swift and harsh. The wrath of the God of Israel will bring low those who dishonor his holy Ark."

Suddenly Saul went limp and collapsed to the floor. There was a long moment of silence. Eri began to mutter a prayer. The high priest made a sign to the stone idol and begged, "Dagon, hear me. Dagon, protect those who honor you."

Saul sat up and shook his head as if to clear it. In a normal, youthful voice he said, "I'm sorry, honorable priest. I must have fainted."

The two priests peered at him with squinted eyes.

"Forgive me?" Saul implored.

"Come," the high priest said. "There is work to be done. You boys must go."

Dusk was falling. Eri and Saul were told that they would not be allowed to spend the night within the temple until they had completed the necessary studies of the temple mysteries and taken their vow of service to Dagon.

"If this is the gratitude of Dagon . . ." Saul grumbled as they made their way toward the alley where the woolens had been concealed.

"It's for the best," Eri said. He explained his next plan, and Saul grinned widely.

In the small hours of the morning the boys climbed to the temple roof, using the uneven, projecting blocks of stone as hand- and toeholds. They entered the priests' quarters through a trapdoor and crept past the individual cells, then through the long, dark hallways to the main chamber of the temple.

Dagon had been carved from native stone. The statue was heavy. It took both of them working together to topple him from his pedestal. He fell onto his face directly in front of the Ark of the Covenant, and his nose broke off and skidded across the marble floor. Eri was sure the crash would awaken every priest in the complex. Saul and he dashed to the front door, ready to flee. If the boys had to unbolt the door, the priests would know that someone had been inside the sanctuary and attribute the statue's fall to robbers; that would defeat their whole purpose. But after having cast down the idol, it wouldn't be healthy for them to stay to try to make explanations, either.

They waited, poised for flight, for at least five minutes. There was only silence. They shrugged at each other and made their way cautiously back to the priests' quarters to hear snoring and, from one cubicle, moans of either ecstasy or pain. The crash of the falling idol had awakened at least one priest, but obviously his thoughts had turned to other things.

* * *

When Eri and Saul came to the temple the next morning, they strolled unnoticed through the front door to find half a dozen stunned priests standing around the fallen Dagon.

Eri walked to stand beside the high priest, who looked at him quickly and nodded acknowledgment.

"Do you see?" Eri asked in an awed voice.

"I see," the high priest said testily.

"It is as if Dagon pays homage to the Ark of the Hebrews," Eri said.

The high priest flushed. It was evident that he had not taken that meaning from the idol's prostrate position near the Ark.

"The wrath of the God of Israel," Eri whispered, and Saul took that prearranged cue to fall to the floor. His eyeballs rolled back so only the whites showed, and he went into a trance that, in Eri's opinion, was a bit too noisy and dramatic. Once again, after an interval of babbling and drooling, flailing and moaning, Saul pronounced the wrath of the God of Israel on the priests of Dagon and, indeed, the entire city of Ashdod and all of Philistia unless the Ark of the Covenant was returned to its rightful place. Angry, the high priest banished the two boys from the chamber.

"Don't you think you overdid it?" Eri asked Saul when they were alone in the kitchens.

Saul, having helped himself to bread and cheese, spoke with his mouth full. "I find these priests to be less than logical."

Habi came into the room. "There will be no time to train you boys today."

"We can study the mysteries by ourselves and stay out of the way," Eri said.

"See that you do," Habi said, "for we will be very busy, all of us."

"What will you be doing?" Saul asked.

"Performing mystic rites to restore Dagon to his rightful place," Habi answered.

"I am strong," Saul said. He flexed a biceps. "I can help you lift the idol back onto his pedestal."

"Little fool," Habi said. "That has been done already. Now it is the work of the priesthood to erase the shame of the god's fall and repair the damage."

Eri and Saul went into the temple's library and stayed there, whispering and giggling like much younger boys as they exchanged their impressions of the reactions of the priests to Dagon's fall. After a while, Eri decided to pay another visit to the kitchens. He found the kitchens to be empty.

Saul joined him. "No one's in the temple, either," he said, looking around.

"Where do you suppose they have gone?" Eri asked.

"To perform mystic rites," Saul said with a wink.

"But where?"

The answer was discovered when they crept quietly along the hall from which opened the doors to the sleeping cells of the priests. Grunts and moans came from several of the rooms, and through one open door the two boys were, to their shock, exposed to the hairy, bare-rumped mystic rite of the Dagon priests.

In the evening, as the sun set, all of the priests gathered in the main hall of the temple to bow and pray to Dagon. Some of them walked gingerly. As they knelt, more than one moan of pain was heard. Saul chose the time when the high priest had just finished his hymn to Dagon to perform another of his trances, and when he specified the physical ramifications of the vengeance of the God of Israel, Eri almost laughed aloud.

The priests did not laugh. There were, in fact, a few moans of real or remembered pain.

Again, in the dead of night, Eri and Saul crept down the crude ladder leading from the roof of the temple to the priests' quarters. When they pushed the idol from its pedestal, this time it landed on its face. The noseless head broke off, bounced, and rolled to a stop. The crash did not awaken the priests. Saul picked up the idol's head and used it as a mallet to break off the hands. Then he placed head and hands before the Ark of the Covenant.

There was great consternation in the temple the

next morning. Once again Saul pronounced the wrath of
the God of Israel on the priests of Dagon and the entire
city of Ashdod. The frenzied "worship" of the priests
spread to others in the city who claimed Dagon as their
god.

"It was pure inspiration," Eri told Saul with a
chuckle as they watched the pained walk of two Dagon
priests.

"It was clear to me," Saul said, lifting his nose con-
descendingly, "that the religious practices and mystic
rites of the cult of Dagon make his followers exception-
ally vulnerable to the plague that God promised
through me."

"Hooo," Eri said. "Now God speaks through you?"

Saul, frightened at his effrontery, whispered, "Forgive me, God of Abraham."

The lords of the city came to observe the fallen
idol. They noted the position of Dagon's hands and
head in relationship to the Ark of the Hebrews. The
high priest made an impassioned speech in which he
advised the rulers to rid Ashdod of the cursed artifact.

The high lord of Ashdod nodded in agreement. "It
will be done."

Eri and Saul looked at each other with satisfied
smirks. At the first opportunity Eri approached Habi.

"What will happen to the Ark?" he asked.

"It is to be taken to another city."

"To another temple of Dagon?" Eri asked.

"Yes."

"Then pray for the priests who will be exposed to
the curse of it and to the anger of the God of the
Hebrews."

It was clear from Habi's look that he was thinking,
Better them than us.

"Perhaps it would be pleasing to Dagon if the
priests in the new city were given warning," Eri suggested.

"Perhaps," Habi agreed.

"Dagon has given my friend the gift of prophecy,"
Eri said. "With your blessing, wise priest, Saul and I will
accompany the Ark and tell others of its curse."

There was relief on the priest's face. He would, they knew, be glad to see them go, for when he looked at them he could not help but be reminded of the shame that had been brought to his god and, by association, to him. It required no further coaxing from Eri to convince Habi to write a letter introducing the boys as aspirants to the Dagon priesthood who had been touched by the god with the gift of prophecy.

When the Ark of the Covenant left Ashdod, being carried southeastward to Gath, City of Giants, Eri and Saul trailed along, making themselves useful to the soldiers who guarded the cart carrying the artifact. In Gath the Ark was taken to the temple of Dagon, and the letter from Habi gained them swift introduction to the high priest. As soon as he had an audience, Saul went into a prophetic trance and repeated the dire warnings that had brought such excellent results in Ashdod. Once again Dagon was thrown down in the middle of the night. Once again there was frenzied "worshipful" activity among the priests and the more ardent followers of Dagon.

Later, Saul was to admit that it was quite possible that God himself had lent a hand, for in the coastal cities of the Philistines, pestilence struck a severe blow. To the discomfort of the priests and devoted worshipers of Dagon, real death was added in the form of an epidemic of fever. The word of Dagon's fall spread rapidly in Gath, and the people raised an outcry so great that once again Eri and Saul were traveling.

This time they were heading north, ahead of the slowly moving Ark to the city of Ekron, not far to the east of Jerusalem and even nearer to Beth-shemesh, a village of the Hebrews.

CHAPTER SEVEN

The overseer Naboth was a small man with knotty leg and arm muscles and a leonine head made to appear larger by masses of hair on both his pate and his face. He was a lowborn man in a lowly job, that of guarding slaves in a Kittem copper mine. At the end of each day, when all of the slaves were in their cells and the ravaged countryside lay in silence under the sky's blanket of uncaring stars, Naboth retired to his hut—a domicile not much more luxurious than the cells—and paid homage to the only god he recognized, the god of wine. Only with wine could he forget his misfortunes. The internal caress of intoxication soothed away the omnipresent knowledge that he would never, never rise above his current miserable station.

In the heat of the day when Naboth poured sweat as copiously as any slave and gasped for a cooling draft of fresh air amid the baking heat and stifling dust of the mine, he cursed the gods that had decreed he be born a bastard, that the passage through which he entered the world had been familiar to uncounted but impressive numbers of Philistine soldiers, that his mother, a simple Hebrew girl who ended her life as a scullery maid in a Philistine kitchen, could not even guess the identity of the soldier who had planted the seed that became Naboth. He cursed the gods for having given him inferior Hebrew blood and for his stringy, undersized body.

Any man brave enough or foolish enough to defy the gods could be a potent force in his own day-to-day life, even if his function concerned slaves who labored briefly in the mines before dying of exhaustion, starvation, disease, accident, or sheer hopelessness. Moreover, the lowliest man had his purpose. Naboth's goal in life was to prove his own manhood and to thumb his nose at the gods for having made him small and half-Hebrew by breaking men larger than he.

When he was transferred to the mine where Urnan the smith and Kemose shared a cell, he immediately singled out the big Egyptian. Kemose stood half a head taller than the next tallest as the work line snaked its way to the pit and down the winding ledge and a full head taller than almost everyone else. It was inevitable, in view of Naboth's nature, that a relationship develop between overseer and slave, a one-sided imbalance that weighed malicious, unrelenting cruelty against helpless but stubborn suffering.

"You are too strong and healthy to be of so little use," the overseer said in the language of his unknown father. He had come to stand near the spot where Kemose and Urnan worked side by side, picking slowly at the hard, rocky earth.

Kemose made a motion of subservience but raised his eyebrows in puzzlement, pretending not to understand the Philistine tongue.

Urnan worked on. He had to force himself not to give in to the impulse to work harder, to put more force behind his blows, to work faster. He had learned that it was a terrible mistake to increase one's productivity in the presence of one of the lash-bearing overseers. Slaves who did so were forced to maintain that pace and were soon dead.

"Do you hear me, animal?" Naboth asked, this time in Hebrew.

Urnan knew that Kemose spoke not only Hebrew but the tongues of a dozen other peoples who lived around or near the Great Sea. In the weeks that Urnan had been cellmate to the big man, he himself had picked up a few words of Egyptian.

Kemose bowed low and spoke in the odd, rapid-fire language of the Nile. "Command me, master," he said, "and I obey."

Naboth's lash whistled through the air and wrapped itself painfully over Kemose's shoulder, the leaded tip curling upward to leave a mark of blood on the Egyptian's side under his muscular arm.

Kemose fell to his knees and began to bow rapidly, talking in a high voice intended to make the overseer think that he was frightened. Urnan understood only one word in several, but he gathered that his friend was begging for mercy, while his downcast eyes burned with hatred.

Naboth let the lash fall again. A fresh welt sprang up on the Egyptian's scarred back. Kemose prostrated himself on the rocks and grunted when the overseer kicked him in the side.

Urnan said in Hebrew, "Lord, he does not understand. Tell me what you want of him, and I will relay your orders."

For a moment Urnan thought that he was going to get a taste of the lash. Instead the little man laughed. "So you are a pig of the hills?"

Urnan nodded, accepting the insult, knowing that it would be pointless and dangerous to try to explain that he was not a Hebrew.

"Have mercy on the big one, master," Urnan said. He tapped his temple. "He is somewhat like a child."

"Tell him that I will not abide sloth." Naboth coiled his lash and turned away.

Kemose rose, lifted his pick, and glared at Urnan. "So I am like a child?"

"That one is to be watched," Urnan said. He had seen the unreasoning hatred in the overseer's eyes when they were directed toward Kemose. "You play a deadly game, my friend."

"I have managed to survive," Kemose said. "There may yet be some advantage in their not knowing that I understand their barbaric languages."

Urnan swung his pick. The iron tip clanged off rock. He rested as he looked around carefully. "To you, anyone who was not washed in the Nile at birth is a barbarian."

"You have said it, not I," Kemose said with a wry grin.

Urnan had discovered that banter helped make the days bearable, but the talk between them was not always frivolous.

"When your ancestors were nothing more than scattered farmers along the Nile," Urnan said, "long before your scribes learned to use the picture words, my ancestors had built towers to the gods and recorded their laws, their legends, and their far-reaching business activities on clay tablets."

"So you claim, my friend," Kemose said. "But in all of my travels I have not seen these wondrous towers that reach to the heavens."

Urnan spoke in the old tongue, the language of his forebears, the tongue that Belsunu the Babylonian had learned, along with his craft at the forge, before the fall of the great city of Ur. "Nor have I seen the tombs of your Egyptian kings rising from the desert. But that does not mean they do not exist."

"What tongue is that?" Kemose asked.

"The language of my fathers, of those you call barbarians, those who built their great cities in the land between the two rivers."

"I have heard of that land," Kemose said. "How do you come to speak the language?"

Urnan shook his head. "I have to confess, my friend, that my knowledge of the tongue is limited. It was a family tradition to pass the native language along, but I fear it has been diluted and weakened by neglect through the centuries."

"I have heard tales of a great conqueror, of the king called Sargon," Kemose said. "I would not be surprised if you tell me that you are of his seed."

Urnan shook his head in amusement, although he was too tired, too hot to smile. "I am of much more humble origin." He lifted his short slave tunic and pulled aside his breechcloth to bare his left buttock. There, in maroon, like a splash of raw red wine, was the paw mark of an animal. "The mark of the lion. The brand. It is said that it was first applied to Cain, the first worker in metals."

All talk stopped abruptly, for Naboth the overseer stalked toward them, his small, dark eyes squinting at the big Egyptian. Past them, he whirled, thinking to catch them leaning on the handles of their picks, but both of them were working.

"Tomorrow, big one," Naboth said, "you will join the bearers." He nodded to Urnan. "Tell him."

"The lord overseer says that tomorrow you will be a bearer," Urnan said in very bad Egyptian.

Kemose bowed to Naboth, who turned and paced toward the ledge leading up and out of the pit. "Before we reach my country," Kemose told Urnan, "I will have to give you lessons, lest you disgrace me with your mutilation of my language."

"There seem to be several obstacles between us and that worthy goal." Urnan nodded toward Naboth, who had paused and was again looking back at them. "For one thing, you seem to have caught that one's attention."

"That one," Kemose said, "will be the instrument of our delivery."

Urnan said nothing. He feared for his friend's sanity. If Kemose was losing his mind, he would not be the first driven mad by the burning sun and the hopelessness of his situation.

* * *

The next day, when Naboth used the handle of his lash to push Kemose into the line of bearers, Urnan went with his friend.

"Are you mad?" Kemose asked when they were at the bottom of the pit, filling their baskets with the copper ore. "You are too frail to be a bearer."

Urnan was already regretting his impulse to remain with his friend, but he twitched his lips and said, "I did not want to be far off when Naboth becomes the instrument of our delivery."

"Look at me," Kemose ordered.

They were on their knees, scooping ore with their hands into their baskets. Urnan looked into the large, brown eyes of the Egyptian and saw them become hard and black, with small points of light dancing deep inside. It seemed that the burning orbs held his eyes for only a moment.

"Do not cry out," Kemose said. "Do not move suddenly."

"I hear," Urnan said.

"Look at the ground beside your left knee."

The Egyptian horned viper, like other deadly reptiles, was fashioned by the Creator to make its nature known at a glance. Urnan had never seen the snake that some called the asp, but there was no doubt in his mind that the sandy-brown horror coiled near his unprotected flesh was poisonous. His breath caught in his throat. He froze, afraid to move lest the reptile strike.

Kemose reached out one hand, and to Urnan's amazement, the hand seemed to merge with the snake. Then Kemose snapped his fingers, and the viper disappeared. "Thus will we use Naboth," he said. "But first we must be alone with him."

"He seems to me to be a very careful man."

"But desperate," Kemose said. "It is his love of gold that will help us."

Urnan made scratches on the wall where he kept track of the days spent in the backbreaking job of carrying ore. He had made eight scratches when Naboth decided that the cruel labor was not accomplishing his desired purpose quickly enough. In fact, the overseer seemed a bit disappointed. The big man apparently had no spirit to break. It required only a touch of the lash to set Kemose to blubbering with abject fear and to cringe and cower on the ground at Naboth's feet. The only pleasure available to Naboth was the ruination of the big man's body. But as the days passed, it became evident that Kemose thrived on being a bearer.

Such was not the case with Urnan. In spite of warnings and coaxings from Kemose, he insisted upon loading his basket to the top, just as Kemose did—but Urnan did not have the massive body and powerful muscles of his friend. The labor was beginning to tell on him. Toward the end of the workday all of his will was required to carry the last basketful of ore to the separators, and each day the labor became more difficult.

Then, on an evening with a growling thunderstorm moving in from the sea, Urnan stumbled and almost spilled his load. Such an accident always resulted in immediate lashings, and Kemose feared that his friend could not survive any punishment. He seized Urnan's basket, shifted it to his own left shoulder without losing the balance of the basket on his right, and carried it the remaining distance.

Naboth was standing beside the ore piles. His eyes narrowed, and his thin lips curled into an obscene smile when he saw Kemose with two baskets. He leaped toward the two slaves eagerly, his lash singing, cutting first across the big, broad back of the Egyptian, and then over the shoulders of Urnan.

Kemose cried out with pain, quickly dumped the two baskets, fell to his knees, hands clasped before him in supplication, and blubbered in Egyptian. Naboth turned his attentions to Urnan, and the whip struck twice, three times, with Urnan standing defiantly.

"Fall to your knees, fool," Kemose said in his high-pitched, panicky voice. "On your knees, curse you!"

Urnan heard his friend's voice as if it came from a great distance. He went down to his knees.

"Howl with it," Kemose said. "Beg him to stop."

Urnan moaned as the lash cut new welts on his back. The overseer switched his attentions back to Kemose. The Egyptian wept and wailed. Urnan felt a surge of fierce elation, for even though Kemose was pretending to cry out for mercy, he was cursing the overseer and all of his ancestors back several generations in the language that Naboth did not understand.

The overseer held the lash at the ready. "So," he said, "you are strong enough to carry two baskets. Fine. Tomorrow you will do the work of two men."

For four days Kemose carried not one but two ore baskets from the bottom of the pit up the slanting ledge to the separators. By the afternoon of the fifth day, it was obvious to Urnan that the strain was beginning to tell. The flesh seemed to be melting off the giant's body. His dark eyes were sunken, and his sun-browned face looked sickly.

As the cellmates knelt at the bottom of the pit and began to fill their baskets Kemose said, "It must be soon."

"Yes," Urnan agreed. He, too, was growing weaker every day with just the single basket.

"When next Naboth comes near," Kemose said, "here is what I want you to do." He told Urnan what was required of him.

"Dangerous," Urnan said. The plan depended entirely upon Kemose's being able to hold the overseer's eyes for a count of at least ten. To look directly into the eyes of an overseer was considered to be a challenge to authority.

"So," Kemose said, "we die slowly of exhaustion, or we die quickly here and now. Does the difference really matter?"

Urnan shook his head. "I'll be ready when you are."

Naboth walked slowly toward them, smacking the handle of his lash into his open palm.

"Now," Kemose said.

"Master," Urnan called. "Master . . ."

"Why do you call, pig of the hills?" Naboth came to stand over them.

"My friend asks a boon," Urnan said.

The overseer laughed. "The only boon that the big one can expect is a merciful death."

Kemose spoke rapidly in Egyptian.

"My friend says, master," Urnan said, "that it would be a kindness befitting a god if you would put us back into the pit, if only for a few days."

Naboth laughed and raised his lash. Kemose cringed and sputtered in fear.

"He says, master," Urnan went on, "that he can reward you for this boon."

Naboth held his blow and narrowed his eyes at Urnan. "Is that so? And how does a slave reward his master?"

"He has four gold coins," Urnan said.

"He lies," the overseer said, but he was looking with interest at Kemose.

"No, master, it is true. He swallowed them before he was captured and—"

The overseer made a face. "I hope he has washed them."

"Yes, master."

Naboth looked at Kemose thoughtfully. At that moment Kemose lifted his face to stare into the deep-set eyes of the overseer.

"He has kept them hidden," Urnan said. He was counting on his fingers, one, two, three, four. The overseer continued to meet the eyes of the Egyptian. Urnan saw the blackness come, saw the brown orbs deepen and flash the reflected light of the sun.

Five . . . six . . .

"Just a few days, master, until we are rested," Urnan begged.

Eight . . . nine . . .

"Enough," Kemose said quietly.

Urnan looked at the overseer. He stood motionless, lash poised, eyes wide and unblinking.

"You will come to me tonight, Naboth," Kemose commanded. "You will come after the meal, when the night is dark. You will come alone. And once you are with me, you will do as I tell you."

The black, burning eyes bored into the eyes of the overseer for a few more moments, then shifted away and down.

Naboth lowered his lash. "I will come tonight, big one, after you have eaten, when the night is dark. I will do as you tell me."

"I will have the gold for you then, master," Kemose said.

Naboth did not seem to notice that Kemose had spoken the Philistine language. "Put down one of your baskets," he said, blinking and recovering. "I want you alive, at least until tonight."

"Thank you, master," Kemose said, and inclined his head.

Urnan was almost too exhausted to eat. He did so only on Kemose's orders.

"You will need your strength this night," Kemose said.

Naboth came in silence and was standing in front of the bars before either slave noticed he was there. "Give me the gold," he said.

Kemose rose. He moved slowly to prevent his chains from rattling. He stood facing the overseer through the bars. "Look at me, master," he said.

At first Urnan was afraid that the Egyptian's magic had failed. Naboth shifted on his feet and looked away before turning his head to stare into Kemose's face.

"First you will open the door," the Egyptian said.

Naboth opened the door. Kemose took the overseer's arm and pulled him into the cell.

"Now you will remove the rod that secures our leg chains," Kemose whispered.

The overseer bent and unlocked the iron rod that went through rings on the shackles and prevented free movement to the two men in the cell.

"Quickly, where is the guard?" Kemose asked.

Urnan peered out of the cell. "He must be in his hut. I don't see him."

"Be ready."

"I am ready."

There was a snap, as of a dry twig. Urnan turned to see Kemose lowering the overseer to one of the hard, stone benches. Naboth's head lolled at an odd angle.

Crouching, they moved away from the cell. They held the leg chains in their hands to keep them from rattling against the rocky ground. The forges that served the mine were located near the refining area. There, on great iron anvils, the tools of the slave miners were fashioned, sharpened, repaired. Familiar smells filled the open sheds covering the forges, the residue of burning charcoal and white-hot metal.

"I must be able to see," Urnan whispered once they were under the shed. He used a broken pickax to stir the banked coals in a fire box. Wood shavings from a tinderbox burned quickly, illuminating the anvil surface with leaping, wavering flames. After locating a sharp chisel and a sledge, he positioned Kemose on his back on the blackened earth beside the anvil and lifted his legs to place one foot alongside the iron.

"This cannot be done quietly," he warned.

"As long as it is done quickly," Kemose said.

Urnan positioned the chisel and with one heavy blow cut the iron link that secured the cuff around the Egyptian's ankle. He positioned the other foot, and with one loud clang of iron on iron Kemose was freed of his shackles. The Egyptian leaped to his feet and, holding a pickax as a weapon, waited, his head tilted to catch the slightest sound.

Now Urnan lay on his back and lifted his legs. "Place the chisel across the iron link," he instructed. "Strike one hard blow."

Kemose cursed in his own language when the sledge slipped off the head of the chisel. He hit it again, and the iron link parted. There was no indication that anyone had heard. He managed to part the other iron link with one blow, and for the first time in months Urnan had complete freedom of movement.

They used their unencumbered legs to walk swiftly out of the slave compound surrounding the mine. Because of the tight security at the mine, escape had never been a problem. The guard at the gate was sleeping comfortably, leaning back against the wall of his watch-tower.

The Kittemian village near the mine was mainly a fishing town. Hardworking seafarers went to bed early. Urnan and Kemose skirted to the north of the fringe habitations, made their way to the shore, and approached the village by way of the narrow, pebble-covered strand. They found what they were looking for without having to venture into the village center and its docks. A small boat was pulled up onto the shingle shore. It had one frail-looking mast, a furled sail, oars and oarlocks, and most importantly, two goatskin water bags lashed inside the gunwales. One bag was full, the other half-full.

Together the men pushed the boat into the water and rowed away from the shore and into the wide harbor.

"We'll need food," Urnan said.

"We had food when we were chained to the floor of the cell," Kemose said.

Urnan nodded in the darkness. Truly, it would be better to starve as a free man than to die as a slave.

CHAPTER EIGHT

Ekron, the northernmost of the five Philistine cities, was not as cosmopolitan as mighty Gath or as sophisticated as Ashdod. In its markets Canaanites mixed with their conquerors to give the city a rustic flavor. The old gods of the country's original inhabitants competed with the gods of the Philistines for the favor of the population.

Eri and Saul left Gath well ahead of the procession that moved the cart-borne Ark toward Ekron. They arrived at their destination several days ahead of the caravan. From a distance the city looked much like the other Philistine strongholds. Impressive walls constructed of huge stone blocks rose toward the sky. All gates stood open; because the Philistines controlled all of the countryside, there was no threat to the city's security.

The two boys entered Ekron just behind a farmer driving two donkeys laden with the produce of the rich farmlands surrounding the city.

During his months in Philistia, Eri had shown himself to be a quick study with regard to language. His command of vocabulary was still limited, but his accent was acceptable. He was usually assumed to be a Canaanite boy who had lived his brief life under Philistine rule. He fell in step with the farmer and asked directions to the temple of Dagon. The farmer was, by his dress, a member of the indigenous race.

"Why would a good Canaanite lad want to know about the god of the Philistines?" he asked, disapproving. "If you seek the help of the gods, call on Baal. He is the god of Canaan."

"It seems to me that he's been off duty lately," Eri said, unable to resist making the observation.

"I'll have nothing to do with blasphemy," the farmer said, turning away.

Close beside the city wall were stables and shops. Eri sniffed the air, flashed a quick grin at Saul, then turned into a small alley and followed his nose.

"Why this way?" Saul asked.

"To find a man who speaks my language," Eri said.

"I would have little regard for the Hebrew who lives by choice in a Philistine city," Saul said, but he followed Eri until they heard the clang of iron on iron. The smells of burning charcoal and hot metal were strong.

The smith's shop was opened to the street by simply folding back a grillwork of wooden strips and iron bars to rest upon the low roof. The glow from the fires of the forge shone from the interior. Eri stood inside and waited until the smith ceased his clanging attack on a glowing piece of metal that was taking the shape of a spearhead. The smith, naked save for a leather apron, thrust the unfinished weapon back into the shimmering coals in the forge. A similarly dressed, strong-backed lad began to pump the bellows.

"Honorable craftsman, sir," Eri said in the language of the Philistines, "may I have a word with you?"

The big Philistine glared down at Eri.

"We are strangers," Eri said, "and—"

He did not finish. The boy who had been pumping

the bellows was distracted by Eri's voice and had accidentally pressed his bare hip against the hot bricks of the firebox. He leaped back, screaming in pain. The flesh was inflamed.

"Fool!" the smith roared, snatching the bellows from the helper. "Let me see what you have done."

"I am in great pain, master," the helper moaned.

"Go inside," the smith said in disgust, "and put oil on it." He held the bellows in one hand and lifted the unfinished spearhead with his tongs in the other. He cursed loudly. "Now it will be ruined."

"If I may, sir?" Eri said, taking the bellows from the smith's hand and applying the nozzle to exactly the right position. He blew hot air to the glowing coals.

The smith's eyebrows shot up as he watched the boy work the bellows expertly. He turned the spearhead and positioned it to gather the heat. "You've done this before?"

"At my father's forge."

"You are Canaanite?"

"Sir," Eri said, neither confirming nor denying the smith's assumption.

When the iron was glowing with white heat, the smith removed the spearhead from the firebox, and the din of his hammer filled the shop. Eri competently banked the fire in the box and then handed the smith a smaller hammer without having to be told.

"You do know your way around a shop," the smith said.

The spearhead had taken shape. The smith thrust it into a barrel filled with dirty water, and steam sizzled up to disappear quickly in the dry air.

"Do you grind and polish in your father's shop?" the smith asked.

"I have, yes," Eri said.

"And where is this shop?"

Saul was looking at Eri worriedly. Eri smiled as much for Saul's benefit as for the smith's. "My father is dead, sir. The shop now belongs to the lords of Ashdod."

"Too bad," the smith said.

"Now, sir, if you please, can you tell us how to get to the temple of Dagon?"

"It is dangerous for such as you to wander the streets," the smith said. "There are those who favor young lads, and there are others who sell orphans into slavery."

"We have the protection of the priests of Dagon," Eri said.

The smith frowned with distaste. "Are you considering joining that collection of Sodomites?"

Eri widened his eyes in innocence. "They feed their acolytes well, sir."

"If it's a position you want, I can use an apprentice here."

Eri, truly honored, bowed his head. "Thank you, sir. But I have my friend to consider."

"I can always use a good strong back at the furnaces," the smith added.

Eri was intrigued. "You know the magic of separating the metal from the rocks of the earth?"

"Not magic, boy," the smith said, grinning. "But, yes, I bring forth the metal in a liquid, glowing stream. Would you like to learn how?"

"Yes, sir," Eri said. He frowned. "But I have made a commitment to the priests, sir, and my father taught me to honor my word."

"I can respect that," the smith said. "But if you change your mind, I'll be here. Just ask for Melech. I'm well known in the city." He walked to the street with them and pointed them toward the temple.

Armed with the letter of introduction from the priests at Ashdod, they were welcomed into Dagon's temple in Ekron. It had none of the grandeur of the sanctuary at Ashdod, where the two lads from the hills of Israel had first implanted the belief that the God of the Hebrews had the power to smite those who dishonored his Ark.

Saul was becoming adept at pretending to be seized in prophetic trance. His performance for the Dagon priests in the mud-brick temple confirmed rumors that had traveled ahead of the self-appointed oracle of the Ark.

Eri had witnessed Saul's performance several times, but he still had difficulty containing his laughter when his handsome young friend reached the climactic moment of his dire warning and specified the plague that God had decreed especially for the followers of Dagon. It was evident that the priests in Ekron shared vulnerability to the malady that Saul threatened. Like their peers in the first two Philistine cities to house the Ark of the Covenant, they were influenced by their personal predilections and the sexual expression specified by Dagon during times of stress. Thus Saul's work in Ekron was quickly accomplished. The physical discomfort suffered by all the priests and devout worshipers at the temple was translated into dire warnings that spread throughout the city.

When the little caravan of which the Ark was a part finally arrived at the gates of Ekron, it was met by a horde of screaming, protesting citizens. As the day progressed, a crowd grew outside the temple and became unruly. The lords of the city, surrounded by elite units of troops, forced a path through the mob and up the broad stairs to the sanctuary doors. Just outside the temple's entrance, the high priest of Dagon stood waving his baton and his hands at the Hebrew artifact while chanting prayers designed to diminish the Ark's power.

Eri and Saul stood within a few paces of the high priest, near the front wheels of the cart carrying the Ark, but being very, very cautious not to call attention to themselves.

The high priest of Dagon in Ekron was an old man. The top of his wrinkled scalp was naturally bald, so he had to shave only the fringes of his hair. His body was soft from decades of good living. Long had he been secure in his position as chief spokesman for Dagon. The mob quieted, interested to hear his words.

He bowed low in respect to the lords of the city, but he showed no hesitancy in speaking out.

"My lords," he said in an amplified voice that reached many in the crowd, "are we to accept what

Ashdod and Gath have rejected? Already we in this goodly city suffer the same plagues that have accompanied this hateful box from the moment our brave soldiers seized it from the pigs of the hills at Ebenezer. Are we to accept this situation without a protest?"

"No! No! No!" screamed hundreds of throats.

Saul nudged Eri with his elbow and grinned. The shared risks and pleasing rewards of their joint efforts in Philistia had bonded them as close as brothers.

"I say, my lords," the old priest bellowed, "that this object of Hebrew worship be destroyed where it stands."

"Burn it! Burn it!" the mob chanted.

"We must destroy it and the vehicle that carries it," the high priest said, holding his arms overhead. "Only thus can our lord Dagon be honored. Dagon must not share his temple with this—this abomination as he was forced to do, to his eternal dishonor, in Ashdod and Gath."

The rulers of the city, while trying to retain their composure, were looking with open speculation at the Ark, the object that had brought so much misery and death to Ashdod and Gath.

"This isn't going too well," Eri told Saul.

"It's time God spoke to the Philistines again," Saul decided.

He pushed his way to stand directly in front of the high priest. The old man ignored him and lifted his arms in preparation for another exhortation. Saul fell to his knees, lifted his own arms, let his eyes roll back in his head, and chanted the nonlanguage in which he was becoming so fluent.

"Be gone with you," the high priest ordered.

"Hear the word of the Lord God of Israel!" Saul shouted. "Hear his dire warning!"

"Who is this beggar?" asked one of the lords of the city.

"He is a prophet, my lord," said one of the priests, his hand gingerly rubbing his buttocks. Eri presumed the man had been hard smitten by God's curse on the followers of Dagon.

"Touch not the holy Ark," Saul said, lowering his voice so that the lords had to lean forward to hear him. "You have seen and felt God's punishment. Tempt him no more. Return his Ark to his Chosen People."

"This boy has prophesied well," said one of the priests. "He warned in Ashdod and in Gath of the consequences, and death stalks both cities. Hear his words."

"God says that his Ark must be returned to his people," Saul said.

"What say you, High Priest?" asked the leader among Ekron's lords.

"Send it back!" yelled someone from the mob, and the call was taken up in the form of a chant.

Due to his advanced age, the high priest was suffering horribly from the curse. It was his duty, however, to participate in the cleansing rituals of Dagon. "It is not a particularly valuable artifact," the high priest pointed out. "It will be no great loss. The Hebrews are defeated, so they will gain no advantage from the return of this object." He nodded importantly. "Dagon says yes, return the Ark to the Hebrews."

A cheer of relief erupted from the crowd.

"So be it," agreed the supreme lord of the city.

"Hear the words of the God of the Hebrews!" Saul bellowed.

The high priest frowned, clearly displeased with the presumptuous boy. The lords of the city, who had begun to turn away, looked back.

"The holy Ark must not be returned empty to the Chosen People," Saul proclaimed.

Eri was making frantic motions to his friend to desist, but Saul's eyeballs were rolled back, and the look of trance was on his face.

"God says," Saul bellowed, "that his wrath will be cooled only by the tribute of twenty-five golden mice—one for each of the five lords of the five Philistine cities."

A frown distorted the face of the supreme lord.

"Moreover," Saul continued, "gold models of the symptom of God's curse must be fashioned."

"Nonsense!" the high priest protested. "We do not pay tribute to a defeated rabble."

One small gray cloud had formed directly over the city, but few had noticed. It did not blot out the sun; it did not even touch the sun. Suddenly the brilliant day was speared by bolts of lightning from the cloud. One tower on a corner of the city wall was blasted. The heavy stone blew apart, shattered. A sentinel was hurled high into the air by the force of the bolt. The man was dead before he hit the ground with a thud that was heard by the stunned gathering around the Ark.

Saul, as startled as the rest, managed to remain calm. He lifted his arms and chanted nonsense syllables.

The supreme lord of Ekron paled. The high priest had lost control of that portion of his musculatory system affected by the curse, and his robes were stained. He chanted loud praise to Dagon when the supreme lord of the city announced, "So be it. Do as the oracle says."

For two days, while the golden mice and the other objects specified by Saul were being fashioned, the Ark of the Covenant remained outside the city walls. The two boys slept nearby. On the third day the priests of Dagon came out through the city gate. Two of them carried a chest that, for its size, seemed disproportionately heavy.

"Put your burden inside the Ark," the high priest ordered.

The priests carrying the small coffer of gold peace offerings stepped up to the cart holding the Ark. One of the holy men brushed against the side of the Ark. Suddenly he stiffened and cried out in agony. Saul, standing beside the Ark, caught the box as it fell from the stricken priest's hands.

It was evident by the slackness of the holy man's body that he was dead. A murmur of dread rippled through the small crowd that had gathered to have one last look at the curious object of the Hebrews before it was taken away.

"Your offering will be carried here," Saul said as he

placed the coffer by the side of the Ark. He was extremely careful not to touch the sacred object.

Drawn by a matched pair of milch kine, the cart holding the Ark rumbled slowly to the east. A procession of Dagon's priests followed the Ark to the outskirts of the Hebrew village of Beth-shemesh, where they were met by several Levite priests. Those men took glad possession of the Ark and used the wood of its cart to start a fire. When the flames were high and powerful, the oxen that had pulled the Ark were sacrificed as a burnt offering to Yahweh.

The Philistines who had followed the Ark turned on their heels to return to their own city. Eri was surprised to learn that the Levites knew of the two boys who had followed the Ark all the way from Ashdod.

"You have done well," a bearded elder told them, clasping them in his arms.

Eri asked the high priest if he knew anything about the Levites from the sanctuary at Shiloh, and what he had feared was verified: his grandfather had been murdered by the Philistine raiders on the day he himself had been enslaved. Saul and the high priest were comforting Eri when another holy man interrupted them.

"High Priest," someone called out, "you must see this."

The coffer containing the Philistine peace offering had been opened.

"Mice?" asked a puzzled priest, holding up one of the small golden sculptures.

"Twenty-five of them," Eri said, "one for each lord of each of the Philistine cities—Ashdod, Gaza, Ashkelon, Gath, and Ekron."

"And these?" asked another priest, holding an oddly shaped nugget of gold.

Saul hesitated, suppressing a grin.

"Tell them," Eri urged.

"Sire," Saul said respectfully, "the, uh, object you hold is an image of the curse that God put upon the priests of Dagon who trespassed against the Ark."

"I don't understand," the high priest said, taking

one of the gold lumps between thumb and forefinger, then examining it by holding it close to his face.

"God smote them in their secret parts," Saul delicately explained. "What you see is a golden image of the symptom of their pain—an emerod."

"The ways of God are, indeed, mysterious," the high priest said distastefully.

CHAPTER
NINE

The Hebrews, confined to the rugged mountains of the interior west of the great Salt Sea, had developed an insular view of the world. The great wanderings of the past were a part of their lore. The story of the Exodus lived in the heart of every Hebrew, but those who had trekked the emptiness of the desert with Moses had long since been called by God. Those who lived in the time of the great judge Samuel did not often venture beyond their own immediate area. Every small glade, every hill, and every meadow in that relatively small area peopled by the seed of Abraham was identified, but the sea that washed the shores of Philistia had no name to most Hebrews. When it was referred to, which was not often, it was called alternately the Philistine Sea or the Western Sea or—and this was the label in Ur-nan's mind—the Great Sea.

The Great Sea gave Urnan and Kemose its ugly

face just two suns after they rowed quietly away from the harbor at Kittem and into the blue vastness. A storm stripped away the small sail, breaking the mast in the process. Kemose felt that it was imperative to put as much distance as possible between the small craft and the Island of Copper, but his great strength had been severely tested by the excesses of the overseer, Naboth. He rowed for as long as his body allowed, then he rested, drank sparingly of the water, and rowed again. Urnan, more weakened than Kemose had been by the ordeal of being an ore bearer, could manage only short stints at the oars.

Using thread pulled from the remnants of the sail, Urnan rigged fishing lines and used scraps of wire for hooks and flesh from a small flying fish that had soared into the boat for bait. But his efforts were totally without success.

"My friend," Kemose said after they had been without food for three days, "I think we would have been wiser to eat that small flying fish."

On the fifth day another flying fish landed in the boat. It struck Urnan directly in the face, dealing him a blow that disoriented him for a moment. The flopping of the fish in the bottom of the boat galvanized him into action. While Kemose, at the oars, looked on dully with sunken eyes, Urnan threw himself onto the creature and with both hands subdued its struggles. Hunger told him to devour the fish—its scales, skin, fins, and all. His stomach told him that the fish was his, his, his. Urnan used a knife taken from the forge at the mine to scrape off the scales and gut the fish. He cut it carefully in half, then sawed the halves into smaller pieces.

"Be careful of the bones," he warned Kemose as he handed over a portion.

The big Egyptian began to tear into the raw flesh with an intensity that matched Urnan's own efforts. All too soon the food was gone.

Urnan saved one tidbit, the hard flesh near the fish's tail, to bait his makeshift hook and was rewarded as darkness fell by pulling in a small shark just over a cubit in length. There were an interesting few moments as both starving men battled to smother the powerful creature. The shark's rough skin left red abrasions on Urnan's thigh; but he finally managed to hold the struggling fish while Kemose drove the knife into its head between the cold, unblinking eyes.

Skinning the animal in the dark was an adventure that Urnan longed not to repeat, but there were rewards in the form of more raw flesh than either man could eat.

In the middle of the night Urnan's stomach rebelled, and to his regret, he vomited his meal overboard.

"The gods are with us," Kemose said at midmorning.

"So it seems," Urnan agreed.

Since dawn a northwest wind had been pushing them farther and farther from the mines on Kittem, and by the middle of the day soft, low clouds had refreshed them with rain. They let the precipitation pool in the sail remnants, then poured it carefully into the goatskin water bags.

Urnan kept down his second meal of shark's meat. Soon there was nothing left but bones and pockets of flesh in tight places along the skeleton. Urnan used these as bait. Now the sun beat down with unremitting vigor on the open boat. When the heat was at its peak and the sun turned to fire on his back, Urnan covered himself with sailcloth and tried to sleep. Kemose had, for the most part, given up on rowing. The constant wind was doing the work for them.

They sighted the sails of a ship on the eighth day. They were hungry again. Their water supply was low. Urnan saw the tip of the ship's sail first. He cleared his throat and croaked, "There."

Kemose muttered a prayer in his own language, using the names of at least half a dozen gods.

"Philistines?" Urnan asked. His heart was pounding. Surely fate could not be so unkind as to deliver them back into the hands of their captors.

"I don't know," Kemose said. "Perhaps they won't notice us."

That possibility presented Urnan with a dilemma.

The ship could provide food and water and shelter from the relentless sun. But there might well be a lash and shackles and a swift return to the mines. If he were taken back to Kittem, he knew he would never leave the island alive. Urnan decided that he would prefer death by starvation or drowning on the Great Sea to enslavement in the mines. He prayed for deliverance. He was still praying to the God of the Hebrews and to an assortment of Philistine and Egyptian gods for good measure when it became obvious that the ship had seen them and was changing its course to bear down on them.

"The gods are truly with us," Kemose said when the ship was close enough for him to make out the emblems on the flag flying from one of the masts. "It is Egyptian."

Sun-browned, scantily clad sailors helped them climb up and over the ship's rail. An impressively handsome man stood on a raised platform beside the ship's tiller. He wore a short white kilt, ornately decorated sandals, and a headdress that shaded the back of his neck from the sun.

"Captain," said one of the sailors who had assisted Urnan, "this one bears the brand and the ankle and wrist scars of the slave."

"As does this one," said another sailor.

The ship's captain strode toward them. He was half a head taller than Urnan, but he had to look up into the face of Kemose.

"Your flag tells me," Kemose said, "that you are in the service of Amon."

The captain cocked his head and looked at the giant through squinted eyes. "You are observant."

"Then you know this sign," Kemose said, making a quick motion with his left hand.

The captain's face went pale. He fell to his knees. "Great One," he breathed, "can it truly be you?"

"Rise," Kemose commanded. "You will be rewarded, my friend." He looked at Urnan and showed his teeth in a wide smile.

"To serve you, Prince, is reward enough." The captain turned and called out orders. "Prince Kemose will have my cabin."

"Such kindness is not necessary," Kemose said.

"Great One," the officer said with a bow, "I wish only to serve you."

"I would be eternally grateful for some decent food, some water, and a great ewer of the sweet wine of Egypt," Kemose said.

"At once, Great One," the captain said, turning. "And food for Prince Kemose's slave."

"Like me," Kemose said, "my friend is no longer a slave."

"I will find him a place," the captain said.

"He is with me."

"As you will, Great One."

The large reed boat was just days out of its home port near the mouth of the Nile. There were fresh meats, vegetables, and fruit aboard.

For a time Urnan directed his attention totally to the food, the fresh water, and finally, a wine so dry and pleasant that it made his throat glad. When at last he had almost eaten his fill, he looked at his friend and asked, " 'Great One'?"

Kemose smiled and shrugged.

" 'Prince Kemose'?"

"I fear so," Kemose said with a wry grin. "And high priest of Amon."

"Perhaps, Great One, I should bow down before you," Urnan said, only half in jest.

"Only occasionally," Kemose said. "No more than a dozen times a day."

Urnan raised an eyebrow.

"Or perhaps once a month, at the time of the full moon?"

"In all seriousness," Urnan said, "I will bend my knees to you any number of times per day. I owe my life to you."

Kemose reached to clasp Urnan's arm. "You freed me of my chains, and you were my friend when, but for your good wishes and your optimism, I would have despaired. No, my companion, never bow to me, but stand with me as my equal. As soon as we reach my country, my home will be your home, and whatever you desire, you shall have."

Urnan looked to the east. Somewhere out there was land, the Philistine coast. "One day, Kemose, I will leave you to search for my son."

"When that time comes, I will understand," the Egyptian said.

The ship's captain approached, making little bows.

"Come, sir," Kemose said. "Tell me what has occurred in the land of my fathers during my enforced absence."

"Gladly, Great One," the captain said. "And perhaps, if it pleases you, you will tell us of your adventures across the sea."

"I, too," Urnan said, "would be interested in hearing how a prince of Egypt came to be a slave in a mine on the Isle of Copper."

"Well, my friends," Kemose said, smiling broadly, "it was not easy. And I will tell you about it someday, I suppose. But I'd rather not even think about that now. Let's turn our conversations to happier topics for a while and busy my tongue with food."

CHAPTER
TEN

It was easy for Eri and Saul to blend with the population in the village of Beth-shemesh. Their ragged clothing was no worse than that of most of the inhabitants of the town. They were not in the minority, as they had been in Philistine cities, with their dark skin and glowing black hair. They were among their own, and the Ark of Yahweh was back in Israel. Although it was still the property of the Philistines, it was in the care of Levite priests who knew the sacred and ancient code of reverence for the holy object. For this accomplishment, both boys had reason to feel proud. But fever and sickness had followed the Ark from Ashdod to Gath and Ekron. Now they came to Beth-shemesh, too.

As people took sick and died, the outcry from frightened Hebrews was loud. Their protests, Eri thought, were not unlike the demonstrations in the Philistine cities.

"Why would God strike out at his Chosen People in the same way that he smote the Philistines?" Eri asked Saul. The boys stood on the fringes of a growing crowd and listened to the frenzied demands that the Ark be taken from the village immediately.

"God's ways are not to be questioned," Saul admonished. "Perhaps he is angry because the men of Israel allowed his Ark to be dishonored in the first place. Or maybe he wants the Ark returned to its original place at Shiloh."

Whatever the answers, the Ark had to be moved. Because the two boys had followed it all the way from Ashdod, they tramped the roads of the countryside once more. The holy relic was taken to a place called Baale-Judah. There, at last, the Ark found a resting place, and the boys knew it was time for them to say good-bye to each other. Their job was done.

"It's time to go home," Saul said.

"I have no home," Eri told him matter-of-factly. He was not fishing for sympathy. He was going on thirteen years old, and scars heal more rapidly among the young than the old. Yet there were times when he seemed to be an empty vessel containing only aches of regret and loneliness. He still grieved his mother, and the wounds regarding his grandfather's death were fresh.

"My home is yours," Saul told him. "We will go to Gibeah, where, I am sure, my father will beat me severely for leaving without his permission."

Eri laughed. "It won't be difficult, my friend, for you to convince everyone that you are a homecoming hero, solely responsible for the return of the Ark to Israel."

"Not solely," Saul said, putting his arm around the younger boy's shoulder. "And I have gained more than the return of the Ark. I have found a brother."

"I am honored," Eri said.

"Then let's go. I'm lonesome for the sight of the hills around my home village."

But Eri was not convinced. "Saul," he said, "the

Philistines will be there, too. If they're not there now, they will come soon."

Saul sobered. "What are you saying?"

"The Philistines have iron weapons. You told me that your father and brothers left Gibeah to join Samuel near Jerusalem to fight the Philistines. They will do battle with swords of bronze against the hard, keen weapons of the enemy."

Saul frowned. "I think I know where you're leading me, and I don't like it."

"The smith at Ekron knows the secret of bleeding liquid iron from the very rocks of the earth," Eri said. "He would teach me. One day, if all goes well, I could bring that secret to you in the hills."

"Your idea is a good one, little brother," Saul said, "but I hate the thought of leaving you behind in this godless land."

Eri laughed. "My mother believed that God is everywhere. That would mean that he is in the land of the Philistines, too."

"Yes," Saul agreed, "he is there if you call on him in all sincerity." He looked at Eri in concern. "You are determined to do this thing?"

"I watched the Philistines rape my mother, then kill her. I saw my father cry when they led him away into slavery." Eri's voice took on a hard edge. "Oh, yes, I owe the Philistines a debt. I am too young and too small now to wield weapons against my enemies. There is little I can do except use what my father taught me about the craft of my ancestors. Yes, I am very determined. Keep me in your prayers, and after I have mastered the Philistine secret, I will come to you in your home village . . . if it still exists. Otherwise, I will find you wherever the men of Israel gather to fight the enemy."

Filled with emotion, Saul seized Eri by the shoulders. "I will pray for you every day," he promised, then kissed Eri on each cheek in the manner of his people.

Moving back, Eri grinned. "Have you adopted the habits of the Dagon priests so quickly?"

Saul snorted and punched his friend lightly in the belly. "Go with God, little brother," he said.

He shaded his eyes and watched as Eri turned his steps westward, toward Ekron. As Eri's form became smaller in the distance, Saul thought about the commitment his young friend had made to the cause of victory over the Philistines and how he would spend the next several years in the shop of Melech, the big Philistine smith, near the city wall. Saul's chest swelled with pride as he realized how Eri had turned the adversity of his life into fuel for the future.

Saul knew he himself was lucky; his own village had escaped the Philistines' savagery. More than that, he had been sent on a holy mission and done what had been asked of him. How, he wondered, could he return to Gibeah and tending sheep? There could be no "normal" life for him now. Surely his work for God must continue.

And so, instead of pointing his toes toward his father's home, Saul took another path. His way led him back toward the south and the east. He decided to seek out the stronghold of the men of Israel who had gathered north of Jerusalem with Samuel. He had decided to fight the Philistines.

CHAPTER ELEVEN

The reed vessel carrying Urnan and Kemose toward the Nile Delta dipped gracefully and leisurely through small waves as she ran before a favoring wind. For several days Urnan had done little but eat, drink, and sleep. He had eaten so much that his stomach protruded. Already his face was more full, and the flesh was beginning to cover the protruding bones on his torso, arms, and legs. Kemose appeared to have been restored to full health.

As the ship neared the delta, Kemose spent much time in conference with the captain. Urnan, feeling optimistic and content, and lazy because of his full stomach, asked no questions about the prince's conferences with his ship's officer. He noted, however, that the nearer the ship came to its port in the old city of Zoan, the grimmer seemed Kemose's demeanor.

When land was a dark smudge on the horizon, Kemose came to the place on the deck that Urnan had chosen as his own. The prince sat on the edge of his friend's pallet.

"We will land shortly after sunrise tomorrow," Kemose said.

"It will feel good to have the solid earth under my feet again," Urnan said.

"My identity must not be revealed in the city," Kemose continued.

Urnan looked up, indicating his interest with raised eyebrows.

"Much has changed since I left Egypt," Kemose explained. "I have heard of it from the captain, who is loyal to Waset."

"Loyal to Waset? Is that good? I mean as opposed to being loyal to someone or something else?"

Kemose did not answer directly. He rubbed his newly shaven chin and looked out over the rolling waves toward the dark hint of land low to the south. The captain approached, then stood within earshot, but Kemose did not appear to mind. His voice had a musing tone.

"When the third Ramses ruled the two lands, Egypt was a safe place to live. A twelve-year-old virgin girl could walk the streets of Zoan at midnight and fear no harm; but now my country suffers from a long line of weak rulers, men who—even though they adopted the proud name of the great ones and called themselves Ramses—allowed lawlessness to grow in our cities." He spat in disgust over the rail. "*Ramses,* they called themselves. *Great king,* they called themselves." He spat again.

"I gather that things are about as bad in Egypt as they are in my adopted homeland," Urnan said. He remembered his donkey, Ramses, and wondered briefly what had become of the animal. "The glory of Israel was said to have departed when the great Ark was taken by the Philistines. What has been stolen from Egypt and by whom?"

Kemose shook his head. "Nothing has been stolen, but the glory has departed from Egypt. It is no longer one land."

"That is true, Great One," the ship's captain said. "Egypt as one nation is no more. The empire? Ha! People in Zoan and in Waset will tell you that Egypt still rules the far lands and that the two lands on the Nile are united, but that is not true. What has happened is that the self-styled kings in Zoan and the high priest in Waset claim to rule the two lands."

"You tell me the empire is gone," Urnan said. "But it has not existed for a long time—not since the great Ramses vanquished the men of Caphtor. But what of my country, Captain? What do you hear of Canaan? Of Israel?"

Urnan's questions were ignored as the captain continued to address himself to the Egyptian dilemma. "Both Waset and Zoan will claim lordship over all of Syria. That, I assure you, is a lie to which lip service is paid in the courts of the two cities."

"Captain," Urnan said, exasperated, "you are a well-traveled man. What is your suggestion as to the best route for me to return to Canaan?"

But before the officer could respond, Kemose cut in firmly. "We will have no talk of your leaving. First of all, you are not in any condition to attempt such a long journey. Secondly, my friend, I am going to need you." He put his hand on Urnan's wrist. "I am going to need that strong right arm."

"I am not a warrior," Urnan said.

"Any fool can be trained to wield a sword or a spear," Kemose said. "I need the skills that are contained here and here." He patted Urnan's arm and then touched his temple.

"But I must go," Urnan protested. "I must find my son. I'm afraid to think what might have happened to—"

"Urnan, look at me," Kemose said.

"No! I do not want to see your eyes turn black."

"Nor will they." Kemose turned Urnan so that he could look into his friend's face. "Can you, single-handed, conquer Philistia? Can you go among them with the brand on your neck and the scars of shackles on your wrists and ankles and take back what they have seized by force of arms? Even if by some stroke of fate you should find your Eri, you would be helpless to wrest him away from his owner. Those who steal slaves are harshly treated in the Philistine cities."

"But—"

"I know. And I share your sorrow," Kemose said. "I have two things more to say. One will sadden you. May I speak?"

"I will listen."

"In all probability, your son is dead."

Urnan felt as if he had taken a booted kick in the gut. He had feared that possibility, of course, but hearing the words seemed to give weight to the thought. "My reason tells me that," he admitted. "My heart disputes it."

"If the boy lives, you will stand a better chance of finding and freeing him if you accompany me at the head of an Egyptian army."

Urnan looked up, startled. "You have that much power?"

Kemose shrugged. "There seems to be a dearth of leadership in Egypt, from what our friend the captain tells me. In the delta the Libyans have won by immigration and by breeding like the mice of the field what they failed to gain by armed invasion. Lower Egypt is, for all practical purposes, a Libyan kingdom. The national army is commanded by Libyan officers. My people, the high priests of Waset, maintain a small militia made up of loyal Egyptians, and it is this force I will rely upon as my cadre when the time comes to rise up, as Upper Egypt has done in the past, to throw off foreign domination."

"How does this concern me?" Urnan asked.

"An army needs weapons. My men will need iron-tipped spears and swords, also lances and daggers of the gray metal—and all must be of the finest workmanship. My army will need chariot wheels that run true. We need the skills that only the Children of the Lion possess. That, my friend, is why I need you."

Urnan opened his mouth to speak but was silenced by Kemose's upheld hand. "You yourself have said that you owe me a debt. I am calling on you to repay me now, even if it risks our deep friendship. I need you. You must come to Waset with me."

Urnan thought of Eri and how the boy's face had looked when last he saw his son. His eyes filled with tears, and emotion constricted his throat. His heart exhorted him to go to Canaan. His reason counseled him to agree with Kemose—Eri was probably dead or, at best, lost hopelessly among the hundreds of thousands of slaves in Philistia. And it was true that Urnan was still weak from his ordeal. He was just a man, not a hero. When he thought of traveling alone over the boundless sea and through hostile lands to reach Canaan and Philistia, fear shook him. Fate had not treated him well. Already he had lost his wife, his son, his home, his profession. Why should he think that his quest for his son would be a success? More than likely he, too, would end up a corpse from the fool's errand.

Even in an Egypt polarized by competing dynasties, even in an Egypt weakened by the infusion of alien blood over a period of centuries and torn by warring factions, there would be safety with Kemose and, in all probability, comfort and perhaps even luxury.

"I do owe you a debt," he said seriously. "Without your strength and your magic, I would be dead in the copper pits of Kittem."

"Then you will help me?" Kemose asked.

"I will teach your armorers how to build the proper facilities," Urnan said tiredly. "I will teach them all I know of working the dark metal, although you must remember, my friend, that the working of iron is still a Philistine secret."

"A secret not unknown to the metalworkers of Waset," the captain said.

"But if your smiths can work iron, then you do not need me," Urnan said.

"But you will learn from our smiths the secrets of the Philistines and the Hittites before them," Kemose said. "You will therefore gain something. And you have your own particular secrets and knowledge. I would bet my life that within weeks of starting to work with our armorers in Waset, you will have improved and quickened their processes and that you will have found a dozen ways to make our weapons stronger, keener, and more deadly."

Urnan smiled and spread his hands. "You have found the key, my friend—shameless flattery."

"Do not worry that you are doing the wrong thing," Kemose said gently. "You never had a choice. The gods put us together in that cell, then just as easily allowed us to escape. They have provided me with a Child of the Lion. That, my friend, is your destiny!"

CHAPTER TWELVE

Under Pesibkhenno, the Libyan-affiliated king who ruled the delta and Lower Egypt, the city of Zoan was showing her age. The flood of trade goods that had flowed through the city at various times in her history was slowed to a trickle. The finest harbor in Egypt was going to ruin. Once-busy quays were rotting away. A seagoing vessel had been abandoned in the shallows and showed only her mast and the decorative tip of her prow above the water.

The captain of the ship that had rescued Urnan and Kemose was loyal to the older regime, with its capital upriver at Waset. But he was a practical man, and his livelihood depended upon the sea. The Libyan who called himself king in Zoan controlled access to the sea. Therefore, the captain pledged his loyalty aloud to those in power in Lower Egypt while praying to all of the old gods to bring a true king to the Two Lands, godkings of the caliber of Ahmose the First, who had driven foreign invaders from Zoan in an age of greatness, and of Seti, also the first of his name, who rebuilt the city to erase all trace of the Hyksos aliens.

"I will be sending dhows upriver," the captain told Kemose. "You and your friend can pose as boatmen."

"Your loyalty will be remembered," Kemose said. Although there was no open warfare and trade continued between the Libyan pretenders in Lower Egypt and the high priests of Amon at Waset, relations were strained. Pesibkhenno would have liked nothing better than to embarrass the priests of Upper Egypt by holding hostage a prince of Waset and one of the priesthood's loyal followers.

Dressed as common fellahin, Urnan and Kemose worked side by side with the laborers who transferred cargo to the small lateen-sailed dhows that would travel the long, watery distances up the Nile, past the eastward curve of the river, and to many-gated Waset.

After the cargo was loaded, the initial portion of the journey took the flotilla of dhows through areas of waving, windblown papyrus reeds and past fields made verdant by the annual enrichment brought down by Father Nile. Soon after the desert squeezed the green areas into a narrow strip on either side of the river, Kemose called to Urnan, who was resting, to come to his side. Ahead of them on the western bank rose the gleaming, white-towering, man-made mountains of the tombs of the old kings. The polished stone of the steep sides of the tallest structure threw back the sunlight in a harsh glare. Even at the distance from which Urnan was viewing the pyramids, he could not believe the immensity of them. He whistled softly in amazement.

"There is evidence in stone of the greatness of our people," Kemose told him.

"I wonder if the slaves who built them felt the same," Urnan said.

Kemose spoke sharply. "Not slaves! Pious men who served the gods! To this day the descendants of those laborers can look upon the monuments to the old gods and feel comforted. Even the poorest of men needs the solace of knowing that there is something greater than self, something more important than this fleeting life."

Urnan did not dispute his friend's statement. It was Kemose's country, and the smith was a guest there. The world had become a hostile place, and Urnan was reluctant to face it alone. He valued Kemose first as a friend, but he was realistic enough to understand that any hope he had of making his way back to the Philistine plain to search for his son depended upon aid from the giant Egyptian.

Sometimes sailing conditions were unfavorable. The journey was long and slow. Well before the winds pushed the fleet eastward as the Nile took an abrupt turn toward the distant sea, Urnan had regained his health and strength. The disc of the sun god smiled day after day. Following the example of Kemose, Urnan stripped to a kilt for coolness, and his skin was darkened by the sun to be as tawny as Kemose's and the boatmen's who worked in loincloths tucked around and between their muscular brown legs.

Kemose was standing in the prow of the boat when the great pylons of Amon's temple came into view. The prince was silent and moody. At his side Urnan respected his friend's preoccupation. Kemose had not seen his home city of Waset for seven years, and during most of that time he had been either hostage or slave at the hands of the Philistines.

"Once, this city was the navel of the world," Kemose said. "Once, this was the center of an empire that stretched from the mountains of Punt to Canaan and beyond. Babylonia and Assyria bowed to the standards of the god Amenhotep. The rulers of mighty Mitanni sought the friendship of Egypt." He spread his hands wide and sighed. "I fared forth as a prince of Egypt, Urnan. But unlike the great kings, I had no army at my back—only a letter of introduction and a small purse of gold and silver. The purse was stolen from me, and I was sold as a slave. To such depths has the pride of Egypt fallen."

"The glory lives here," Urnan said, glad that Kemose was, at last, beginning to talk about his travails.

"In memory, at least," Kemose agreed.

There was grandeur on both banks of the river. To the east stood the city that had once been the capital of the Two Lands. Its great temple, Ipet-Resyt, soared toward the cloudless sky on the city's southern end. Beyond Waset proper and connected by arrow-straight, sphinx-lined avenues was the impressive spread of the northern temple complex, Ipet-Isut.

When Kemose spoke again, pride and regret were mixed in his voice. "Look past the green of the fields," he said, pointing to the west bank, "to the structures rising at the edge of the desert. Can you see?"

"I see wonderful things," Urnan said.

"There, standing as the greatest of them, is the temple of the second Ramses," Kemose said. "Next to it and to the south is the monument to Thutmose, then Merneptah's remembrance, and the evidence of Amenhotep's greatness."

Urnan was very impressed. "How can a nation capable of building wonders such as these and the ones we saw downriver ever become fragmented and weak?"

"Complacency and smugness," Kemose answered. "Even though our scribes had recorded the lessons of history, we disregarded them. We believed that we were so strong, so secure, that disasters such as the invasion by the Hyksos could never happen again. This misconception seemed to be confirmed when the third Ramses scored his great victories over the Peleset. We lost Canaan, but it was not an armed invasion that was to be our problem. A much more subtle sort of invasion was going on under our very eyes, a conquest made possible by misplaced compassion and greed. Some among us said that we should, out of basic human kindness, allow the hordes of poor people of the Libyan desert to enter Lower Egypt. Others promoted open entry for the Libyans out of greed; they provided cheap labor."

His eyes were sweeping the vista, right to left, then back again, as if he could not gather in all of the sights and beauty of his city quickly enough to satisfy his hunger for home. "In times of political or military crisis my people rise up and fight like lions in a pit. In times of peace, however, they are content to work their fields, to have children, to take whatever ease the gods send their way while their betters pursue the goal of worldly riches. The conquest of Lower Egypt was peaceful, slow, and silent. Almost without notice the immigrants changed the ancient customs, established their own language, diluted the Egyptian race, and abandoned the old values. We had allowed the northern army to disintegrate into ill-prepared units with nothing more to do than guard the mighty and their wealth. The army in the south, meanwhile, gradually came under the command of Libyans."

Kemose sighed. "There was the glory," he said, pointing upriver to the gleaming, color-accented temple complex. "The second Ramses, sometimes called the Builder, gave his testimony to the gods by restoring the old temples, adding to those that are the most holy, and constructing new ones. He built in stone to outlast the ages, but he neglected the defenses of the Two Lands. By the time the Peleset came to threaten our empire and the very borders of the Two Lands, being a soldier was out of fashion. The third Ramses had to call on heroic efforts in mobilizing the manpower and wealth to defeat the enemy. The sudden transition from peace to war depleted the Two Lands of young men of fighting age, material wealth, natural resources, and will." He shook his head. "The empire is no more. The Peleset occupy the plains where they had been vanquished by the great kings. The blood of Egypt flows not in the veins of those who claim rule from the mouth of the Nile."

Urnan could feel his friend's sadness.

"So there is glory in stone," Kemose said. "But in the hearts of my people?" He shook his head. "None."

The dhow reached dockside, and Kemose wasted no time in going ashore. The streets of great Waset were alive with activity. Dark Nubians wearing long, sweeping white robes strode the streets. Officers in gleaming, gold-encrusted armor drove their shining chariots recklessly through the streets, forcing the mass of humanity to scuttle aside to keep from being crushed beneath the iron wheels. Hawkers of goods of every description called out the praise of their merchandise.

Kemose's destination was the sprawling southern temple of Amon. The way intercepted the avenue of human-headed sphinxes that led to the northern Ipet, outside the city proper. Kemose acted as Urnan's tour guide, pointing out the chapels of Sarapis and Hathor just within the walls. As the men walked across a grand concourse, Urnan tilted his head back to see the top of the grand pylon built by Ramses the Second and entered the colonnade surrounding the shrine of the triad and the great court of Ramses.

At the entrance to the enormous forest of columns in the hypostyle hall, their progress was stopped by stern-faced priests with shaven heads.

Urnan's eyes could not take in the vastness, the grandeur, the sea of brightly painted images, the walls of picture writing in the complex.

"You can go no farther, commoner," a priest said rudely.

"I'm sure you do your job well," Kemose said, "but you must remember, brother, to be polite. It is the commoner, in his masses, who feeds you."

"Who are you, low one, to teach me my job?" the priest demanded.

Kemose smiled gently. He spoke his name in a low voice. The harsh Egyptian syllables piled atop one another so quickly that Urnan did not understand. And as Kemose spoke, he used his hands to give a sign so secret that only the priesthood knew it.

"Are you indeed he?" the priest asked, bowing his head and bending his knee. "Are you the prince Kemose, who was sent abroad so long ago?"

"I am he. Tell my brother that I am here."

"At once, Great One!" The priest turned and shouted, "Here, you! Bring beer for the Great One! You, bring seats."

"That will not be necessary," Kemose said.

Four priests, dressed in the high regalia of office, came running through the columns to fall to their knees before Kemose.

A priest of advanced years and shriveled visage spoke. His very words shook with age. "In the name of the great king Paynozem, He Who Will Live Forever, we welcome your return, Prince. The great king awaits."

One of the priests seized Urnan's arm as he started to follow Kemose. Kemose made a motion, and the priest loosed Urnan and leaped back.

They walked down a grand corridor, their bare feet cooled by the smooth marble floor. Huge doors were opened at the walkway's far end, to reveal an audience chamber. And at the far end were a dais and a golden throne with a man standing before it.

Kemose's brother was in the prime of manhood. Although there was the softness of the good life about him, he still appeared to be strong and vigorous. Paynozem wore the combined crowns of Upper and Lower Egypt, but, Urnan remembered, so did the Libyan king Pesibkhenno in Zoan. He stood with his arms crossed, the emblems of his office in each hand, until Kemose, with Urnan trailing along, approached the dais.

"Son of my father," Paynozem said, laying aside the wands of office to run down the broad steps. "It is really you!" He threw his arms around his taller brother and embraced him before stepping back. "Thank the gods, you seem to be in health."

"A few scars," Kemose said. "Nothing of lasting consequence."

"The gods are kind," the king said. "And your return is most timely, for your country needs you, Kemose. *I* need you. I need the strength and courage that are in your great heart."

"I have always been ready to serve my country," Kemose said.

"Come, let us celebrate your return." Paynozem took Kemose's elbow and steered him toward a door.

Urnan followed until the king stopped abruptly and turned to glare at him. "Does your slave go everywhere with you?" he asked, indicating Urnan.

"He is my friend," Kemose said. "You don't know it yet, Brother, but you need *him*, too."

"Ah?" Paynozem raised his eyebrows in question.

"He bears the mark of the lion. When we fight the Libyan pretenders, we will wield iron weapons made at his forges."

"Then," the king said, nodding to Urnan, "you are indeed welcome. The best we have to offer will not be good enough for you." He waved one hand, and two servants sprang from their position along the wall. "Take this man to the guest quarters in my palace. See to it that he has fresh clothing. Choose women to assist him."

Urnan looked at Kemose, who nodded as his brother led him away. "Go with them," the prince called. "I will find you later."

Urnan followed the two servants of the king through a maze of hallways to exit the temple by way of a hidden doorway. It was a short walk to the palace, where he was shown into a suite furnished in such luxury that he was overwhelmed.

"We will send women to tend you," said one of the king's men, before bowing out of the room.

Urnan explored the suite to find a bedchamber, an area furnished with comfortable chairs and couches, a small room containing certain conveniences, and a patio with steps leading down into a huge bath. He was contemplating taking off his soiled clothing and partaking of the bath when he heard movement behind him and turned to see two young women, neither of them yet fully mature in body or face. One carried folded clothing, white and pristine. The other had a tray that, he was to discover, held perfumed oil, scrub brushes, anointing gel for his hair, and towels.

"Will you bathe now, my lord?" asked the smaller girl.

"Yes, thank you."

The girl carrying the clothing set it aside, came to him, and began to remove his tunic.

"Thank you, I can do that myself," Urnan said, pushing her hands away.

"My lord?"

The other girl, having deposited her tray within reach of the bath, loosed his kilt and let it fall away.

"Here now," Urnan protested.

The girls giggled at his modesty and, urging him to cease his resistance, pulled him into the bath. They scrubbed his back and belly. After the bath, they rubbed scented oil onto his limbs and massaged them. They were very thorough in their work, neglecting no part of his anatomy.

Urnan had not known a woman since he had left his home on what turned out to be his last trading trip to Megiddo. He was young and healthy, and the girls sent to him by the king were knowledgeable and willing. At first he tried to send one of them away; he considered union between man and woman to be a private matter. After a few minutes of trying to make himself understood, he realized that both girls intended to stay. He gave up and accepted his fate. His twin tormenters knew just when to tease and just when to consummate. He decided that what he was doing could not be shameful because the girls were so freely eager to give their all and he enjoyed it so much.

CHAPTER
THIRTEEN

After having dined sumptuously, Urnan met the young priest appointed by Kemose to be his guide. The holy man took Urnan to the royal armory, where the smith examined collections of bronze blades and bronze-tipped spears, leather shields and body armor. Although the armies of the third Ramses had brought the secret of the gray metal back to Egypt from the Hittites and the Peleset, not much had been done to modernize the forges and shops that produced weapons for the army of Upper Egypt.

A tour of several forges confirmed this oversight. Urnan and the priest had to travel to the southern outskirts of the city to find furnaces for bleeding iron from the rocks of the earth. Production was almost at a standstill, and to Urnan's dismay, the iron weapons that had been forged at the shops were inferior in design and craftsmanship.

He had a huge task ahead of him, and the hope of repaying his debt to Kemose quickly, then finding Eri in the near future, seemed a distant wish.

"And what is the state of our weapons industry?" Kemose asked that night after they retired to the royal quarters assigned to the prince. They had partaken of a grand, formal feast in the pharaoh's palace.

Urnan, pleasantly sated and comfortably drowsy, burped, then yawned. "Let me say only that I will be a very busy man for a long time."

"Good, good," Kemose said. "I have spoken to the king, my brother, and he has granted you the authority to make any needed changes. Feel free to ask for any manpower or materials you need."

Urnan nodded. He had other things on his mind at the moment. He was remembering a pair of almond-shaped eyes, as dark as the depths of the night, eyes ringed with startling black kohl. Her name was Tania. She was the granddaughter of the brother of Kemose's father, a part of the extended royal family. A comely girl with golden skin, slim waist, and long legs, she had sat next to Urnan at the meal.

"Where do you begin?" Kemose asked Urnan.

Urnan laughed. "At a place familiar to both of us. The mines."

"Deliver me," Kemose said, rolling his eyes.

"The ore on hand is unsatisfactory," Urnan said, becoming serious. "My guess is that the men managing the mines don't know what qualities to seek in the rocks of the earth."

"The way to the mines is long and tedious," Kemose said. "Before you go, perhaps you would like to see more of the handiwork of our artists and craftsmen."

Urnan looked up expectantly.

"I have been given a commission that is not totally to my liking," Kemose admitted. "It is in itself not especially onerous, but it illustrates the chaos that rules in Egypt."

"Go on. . . ."

"I have pointed out to you the breakdown of law and order, have I not?"

"More than once," Urnan said.

"The extent of the rot at the heart of our society is measured by growing crime," Kemose said. "There is no honor. There is no personal responsibility. Too many of our people are no longer content to earn their bread and beer with honest work. It became apparent some time ago that we were no longer able to protect the tombs of even the greatest of our god-kings. Robbers have desecrated the royal sanctuaries. To better guard the kings, some of them were transferred from their own tombs to a central location, but now even that cannot be properly guarded."

"It sounds as if you're going across the Nile," Urnan said.

"*We* are going to cross the river," Kemose said. "You and I."

Urnan had heard of the place of the dead, that desolate region known as the Valley of the Kings on the river's western bank. He had mixed feelings about going there. He had not learned all there was to know about Egyptian beliefs regarding death, the dead, or Anubis, god of the dead. But he knew enough to feel uneasy about the vast desert necropolis, where corpses of the great and not so great were preserved forever. At the same time, he wanted to know more. His curiosity to see the funerary temples of the great kings stilled his half-hearted protests.

Urnan crossed the Nile with Kemose and found himself riding a tiny donkey through a cultivated green strip. Kemose was similarly mounted, but his legs were so long that he had to ride with his knees bent to prevent his feet from dragging on the ground. The prince said that there would be time later to visit the temples on the west bank. The landscape changed instantly into an area of desolation. The line of demarcation between land irrigated by the life-giving Nile and the desert was knife-edge sharp. Ahead lay the boundless desert. By turning his head Urnan could look back into contrasting greenness. An ancient track wound between arid hills.

Gradually the barren, brown heights closed in on either side. The pathway skirted along the edge of a cliff, through a narrow gap, then into a tightly enclosed area that was more wadi than valley. On either side were steep, irregular cliffs, which looked as if the weather had gnawed at them. The disc of the sun god poured heat down to reflect off the rock-strewn earth, turning the resting place of the kings into a caldron.

Kemose, once again the guide, pointed toward dark openings in a perpendicular wall of stone. "Those have long since been pillaged," he said. Then he indicated entrances to the tombs of Amenhotep the Second; of Horemheb, the general who became a king; of the great third Ramses.

The work force and priests selected by Kemose waited beside the entrance to yet another tomb. "Here lies the great Seti," Kemose said. "This is our destination."

Steps carved in stone led downward. Some workers carried torches, others carried cedar coffins. Kemose, holding his own torch, led the way into a long, sloping corridor that disappeared downward into the depths of the living rock. Hieroglyphs stood out in raised relief, covering the surfaces of the wall. Another steep flight of steps led to a chamber whose walls were covered with beautifully colored figures. Kemose gave names to the goddesses, but Urnan, totally enthralled by the magnificence and profusion of the artworks, was inattentive to his words. Jackals and vultures stood in pairs. The colors revealed by the flickering light of the torches were bold and breathtaking.

Kemose halted Urnan with an outspread arm. The smith peered ahead and down into a black pit. The distance to the bottom of the tomb's well equaled the height of five men the size of Kemose. Wooden beams had been laid across the well to a small entrance on the opposite wall. The group walked carefully across. Urnan was very glad to be on the far side.

The deeper into the interior they went, the more

brilliant became the colors of the wall decorations. At last Urnan followed Kemose into a huge, vaulted chamber. The dome of the room was blue. The walls were wonderfully decorated with glyphs and figures. A procession of gods and goddesses paraded along both of the outer slopes of the vault, which was a representation of the night sky. Urnan could make out familiar stars. Entranced, he stood with his head thrown back until he heard an anguished groan from Kemose.

The big Egyptian was standing near the wall of the chamber. At his feet was a pile of decaying rags. Urnan walked over to join his friend and saw the desiccated face of death. Vandals had ripped away the wrappings of several mummies to expose the calm, sleeping faces. Brittle, preserved flesh and bone had been smashed, holed at the chest as the tomb robbers searched for the jeweled heart scarabs of the dead.

"Behold the great kings," Kemose said with crushing sadness. He knelt and held his torch close. The priest who had moved the mummies into the tomb of the first Seti had scrawled identification onto the wrappings.

"Forgive us, great Ramses," Kemose whispered.

"Is it truly he?" Urnan asked, feeling a shiver of dread run up his back.

"Ramses the Builder, the second of the name," Kemose said. "And here is the first Seti, who ruled so long and so well; and this one is the first Ramses."

Behind them the workmen were muttering prayers. The torches flickered; the air of the great tomb was stale in their nostrils. The priests appointed to handle the remains of the great kings moved forward and with appropriate gestures and prayers began to gather the ravaged mummies and place them in the coffins.

The kings of Egypt made one more journey during the next week. Some were carried by reverent workers to a hidden spot in the wadi, to the tomb of an obscure queen who was identified by her royal cartouche as Inhapi. The tomb was entered by way of a rough passage at the base of a cliff. Other kings were removed from tombs that had been ravaged by the robbers to a place high in a cliff, another tomb of a secondary queen. At both sites the scribes recorded the names of the kings, along with a record of their last movements. Workers sealed the entry to the new hiding places. Last prayers were said. Vows of secrecy were exchanged. The greatest kings of the Two Lands slept again, this time without benefit of priests or guards but, for a time at least, in solitude.

To Urnan's great pleasure, the beautiful, lithe Tania had prepared a reception for her kinsman and his friend when they returned to the city. She herself supervised the handmaidens who attended Kemose and Urnan at their shared bath in Tania's royal apartment. When Tania shed her linen gown and joined the men in the bath, Urnan's lips went dry, and he had difficulty swallowing. He had never known such temptation and wondered how he would ever get out of the water without humiliating himself. His Shelah had been lush and womanly and beautiful, and she would live in his heart and memories as long as there was breath in him. But it was impossible to compare Shelah's memory with the living wonder of the almond-eyed Egyptian. Shelah had possessed her own type of loveliness—wholesome, motherly, earthy. Tania was a creature of the clouds.

"I think, my friend," Kemose whispered to Urnan as Tania splashed him playfully and smiled at him teasingly, "that my cousin has eyes for you."

"Can it be?" Urnan asked. "Would it be allowed?"

"Knowing my cousin as I do," Kemose said, smiling fondly at both of them, "I don't think anyone would dare not allow it. Besides, my brother needs you. Encouraging you to marry Tania is one way to keep you in Waset."

Urnan did not have to ask for permission to marry the beautiful Tania; he was told by the king himself that the marriage would take place. The following week Urnan the armorer, Child of the Lion, and Tania, princess of Waset and the Two Lands, were joined in an elaborate ceremony with the king's blessings.

To Urnan's surprise, Tania was a skillful lover of obvious experience. He asked no questions. She was his —wondrously his, unbelievably his—and he was willing to accept the customs of the country that had bred and perfected the most beautiful woman he had ever known.

Urnan lived the life of a prince, happy in the arms of his beautiful wife. He discovered quickly that being married to a princess of Egypt was different from taking to wife the daughter of a Levite priest of Israel. For one thing, Tania had no desire to spawn children, and she had ways of controlling the functions of nature. This saddened him, and thoughts of Eri came often and unbidden. Another difference was that Tania believed in taking an active part in Urnan's work. So it was that as the armorer began the reorganization of the weapons makers of Upper Egypt, Tania was at his side. He did not object. He took advantage of her willing influence and power to get things accomplished quickly. Kemose wondered if Urnan had become a magician, so rapidly was the quality of weapons improving.

Tania was at Urnan's side during the trek to the mines that supplied the forges of Upper Egypt with the gray metal. She took it on herself to force an improvement in the living conditions of the mine's slaves, and by so doing she impressed Urnan with her compassion and her practicality.

"There are times," Tania said sternly to the overseers, "when the slave is more valuable than the ore he digs. Both are property of the great king and are to be treated with regard to their relative worth."

Soon the baked clay furnaces below Waset poured out the red heat of the bleeding earth, to be shaped and cooled and hammered into blades and arrow tips and spearheads.

Kemose had taken a position in the army and could be found daily on the training fields, teaching recruits how to handle the ever-increasing supply of iron weapons that came from Urnan's shops.

Day by day the will and strength of Upper Egypt grew. Week by week the army became better trained. Month by month life was rich and good and pleasurable, so that Urnan rarely let his thoughts dwell on the end result for his product. War would come, he knew, for the traditions of the Two Lands demanded the union of Upper Egypt and Lower; but as the months passed and the inundation of the Nile came and went and came once more, war seemed to be something for the remote future.

Then the word came that Pesibkhenno, the Libyan king of Lower Egypt, had agreed to give Kemose's brother, Paynozem, his eldest daughter as wife. Urnan began to hope that war would not be necessary. Pesibkhenno was old and infirm.

True to Urnan's hopes, Paynozem gained by diplomacy what could not, as yet, be achieved by force of arms. Pesibkhenno went to the netherworld. The crown of Lower Egypt passed to Paynozem through his wife, and Egypt was united once again. Paynozem would move his court to Zoan, and Kemose would remain in Waset, as high priest.

"My friend," Urnan said one evening as he, Tania, and Kemose were enjoying grapes, cheese, and flatbread in an open court beside Tania's private lake, "although I hate to mention it, I wonder if it isn't time for me to think of going home."

"You are at home," Tania said crossly. Quickly, however, she lifted her hand. "Forgive me, Husband. I know you still long for your son."

"Perhaps it will not be long before I fulfill my promise and send you into Canaan at the head of an Egyptian army," Kemose said.

Urnan laughed. "I believe I could move faster and less obtrusively alone."

"You will not go alone," Tania reminded him.

"Let's not be hasty," Kemose said. "If there is one thing an Egyptian knows, it is that time is endless. There is seldom need for quick decisions. Here, my friend, let me pour you more wine."

Urnan held out his glass and, shrugging, allowed Tania and Kemose to convince him to postpone his departure. He felt only a little guilty for postponing his trip to Canaan.

When he did leave Waset with Tania at his side to sail down the Nile, it was to travel at the command of Paynozem, king of Upper and Lower Egypt. He had orders to enter the city of Zoan incognito and to make contact at a specific place and in a certain manner with the king's agents.

Urnan, posing as a merchant traveling with his wife, arrived in Zoan and rendezvoused with Paynozem's agent at an inn near the waterfront. Urnan identified himself with a letter signed by Kemose. The king's man proved his identity by giving Urnan a golden ring engraved with the king's cartouche.

"Great king who will live forever has work for you," the agent said in a low voice. "I am to take you to a safe house, where you will be welcomed and well treated."

"What is the nature of this work?" Urnan asked, wondering if he had gotten in over his head.

"The king said that you would be impatient to know all," the agent said. "I am empowered to tell you this much: The Libyan interests are still much in evidence in Lower Egypt, and Paynozem suspects that there is an active plot to seize the throne. He wants to arm those who are of pure Egyptian blood and who are loyal to him. Your job will be to accomplish here, in secret, what you did in Upper Egypt."

"There is no end to it," Urnan muttered, thinking of how long it had taken him to accomplish the impossible in Waset, then multiplying it by two in Zoan.

"My husband will do his duty," Tania said with a fond smile and a pat to the back of Urnan's hand.

CHAPTER FOURTEEN

Melech, the smith of Ekron, had no sons. In his efforts to implant male seed into the fertile wombs of his wives he filled his spacious, functional home with lively, dark-haired, sloe-eyed daughters. Because he had no son to work at the forge with him, and since good help was hard to find, Melech was most happy to see young Eri walk through the door of his shop.

Melech was a big man, taller than most and thick of chest. His work at the anvil had developed the muscles of his right arm to massive size. His thighs were as sturdy as tree trunks. And he had a heart to match his bulk.

As Eri's apprenticeship moved from weeks into months, a closeness developed between the big Philistine and his helper. Melech was a good craftsman. He had the artisan's appreciation for talent, and he saw in Eri an ability not only to match his own but to surpass it once the boy had mastered the various techniques. Even with the head start Eri enjoyed from having worked with his father and by having the mark of the lion on his flank, he still had much to learn.

Eri's body grew with his knowledge of metalworking. The muscles across his chest, shoulders, and back and in his right arm were expanded by wielding the hammer. It was evident and a wonderment to him that once he attained his full height, he would be taller than his father. He was not yet a man, however, and to accomplish his goals—to make the arms borne by the Hebrews equal to those of the Philistines and to wield his own iron weapons in battle against those who had destroyed his home and his family—he needed the bulk of a man's body and the strength of a bull.

With that in mind, Eri worked to prevent the uneven physical development that marked other smiths. With the permission of Melech, he engaged in activities that included all of his muscles. Every night and on the one day that Melech did not order him to stoke the fires, Eri took weapons training with other lads on the verge of manhood. Bearing the weight of a Philistine shield, he developed the strength of his left arm under the tutelage of the personal guards of the lord of Ekron.

He had more than one motive for learning the art of arms. By tradition, an armorer, a smith, confined his interests to the making of weapons, not to their use, but Eri would never forget how his father had fought unsuccessfully to save his mother. The boy vowed to himself and God that he would never be as helpless and as ineffectual as Urnan had been during the Philistine attack on the Shiloh settlement.

Eri became known among the aspiring young warriors as a fierce one who took his exercises in the use of sword, spear, ax, and bow very, very seriously. More than one young Philistine learned that the muscular arms of the smith had fearsome power. One did not spar with Eri without sustaining bruises or, at worst, a broken bone.

Eri's life revolved around his work and the weapons training. He ate enough food, or so claimed Melech's wives, for two boys; and when he found his bed in a small room behind the forge, he slept soundly.

For the moment he was content, for he was becoming a master of working the dark metal of the Hittites under Melech's supervision; and he was becoming ever more skilled in honing a blade to a lasting, deadly edge. Nonetheless, Eri kept sight of his primary goal in life: One day he would leave Ekron, reunite with Saul, and perform his near miracles of skill with metals for Israel's people.

He would wait. He was still growing, although he was a match for many men in size and strength. To his confusion, it was not only his body that was maturing. The desires that come most strongly to the young were building in him.

Melech's daughters came and went as they chose, although they were careful not to interfere with the work in the shop. The younger ones were fascinated by the clang and crash, by the fiery sparks that flew when the hammer smashed down on white-hot metal, and by the hiss and bubble and the acrid smell when a blade or a tool was tempered by being plunged into a tub of blackened, stale water. The girls watched wide-eyed until a butterfly flew past the open side of the shop to lead them on a wild, whooping chase. At midday, the older daughters brought bread and meat and cool water in beautifully decorated earthen ewers or goat's milk chilled in the cistern underneath the house.

To the younger daughters, Eri was a smiling, teasing friend. When the older girls, who were nearing the age of marriage, were in the shop, he was helplessly mute, afraid to look into merry, dark eyes, reluctant to let his gaze fall on the frontal bulges or the sleek curves of rump pushing against thin, cool robes of summer. There was mystery there, in addition to a beauty that made his throat tighten.

And then there was Meda.

Of all of Melech's daughters, Meda of the laughing eyes was by far the most beautiful. She was of an age to Eri, so that in the time he had been Melech's apprentice, he had watched the girl develop from having a slim, angular body to a youthful plushness that made her stand out from all of her sisters, even the older ones. Even before her body began to develop the sweetness of coming maturity, she did not walk; she danced. Her sandaled feet seemed scarcely to touch the hard earth of the shop floor when she brought a water vessel delicately balanced on her shoulder.

From the earliest days of Eri's apprenticeship she had a smile for him, a pleasant word. He could look at her, could exchange comments about the weather, or answer questions about the particular project he had under way. But Meda was especially interested when Eri worked in gold. He had impressed Melech early on with his knowledge of the yellow metal. He remembered designs that had been developed by his father, and as time passed, Melech allowed him to spend time making jewelry for the ladies of the city. Quite often when Eri removed the delicately cast items from their ceramic molds, Meda was at his side, exclaiming in awe at the beauty that Eri had wrought.

For his part, Eri had eyes not for the feathery designs of a brooch but for the beauty of dark, slanted eyes, of olive skin that smelled like flowers even in the acrid smoke of the shop, of the softness that he felt when, in her eagerness to see some new piece of gold work, Meda touched him momentarily.

He dreamed of her at night and in the morning felt guilty for lusting after the daughter of the man who had taken him in and treated him so well. In the day he wondered how it would be to hold her in his arms, not daring to allow his imagination to go any further.

Eri could not have defined a particular time when Meda's attitude toward him underwent a change, but in his fifteenth year he became aware that things were different. The touches became more frequent and of longer duration. As he bent over the workbench and carefully removed the mold from a casting, she would bend with him, and the softness of her breast would be on his shoulder, a sweet but burning weight. Now and again she would reach out with one soft, small, delicate hand to brush back his mass of dark, wavy hair from his wide forehead. She smiled at him with her eyes as well as with her lips.

On a day of lowering cloud and changing weather, with a coolness moving in over the city to hint at the coming winter, Melech lay ill with a fever. The work was fairly well caught up at the forge, although the demand for weapons by the army of the lord of the city never flagged. Eri was free to spend the day cutting away the mold marks and polishing a commission of jewelry. It was Meda who brought his midday meal.

"How is your father?" he asked as she placed bread and cheese on his workbench and poured a mug of cool milk.

"He is sleeping," she said. She leaned over his shoulder and pressed against him.

He felt a burn, a fattening of his manhood, and a guilt that forced him to move away from her touch.

"One day, Eri, will you make beautiful things for me?" she asked in a throaty, soft voice.

"I would, gladly," he managed to say.

"Would you? Why?" She was smiling teasingly.

He lost himself in her dark, tilted eyes and could not answer.

"Because you think I'm beautiful?" she asked.

He could only nod.

"Can't you say it?"

He swallowed, forced his voice. "You're beautiful."

"You'd like to touch me, wouldn't you?" she asked, and there was something in her voice that caused Eri to shiver. He glanced at his hands. Usually they were grimy, soiled by charcoal, metal fragments, rust, just plain dirt. He had washed them thoroughly before beginning the work of polishing the gold items, so except for the black crescents under his fingernails, they were clean.

"Wouldn't you?" Meda asked.

"Yes," he said. "Oh, yes."

She took his hands and put them on her breasts, then reached to cup his buttocks.

"Meda—" he began, but lost his train of thought as she moved her hips against him.

"One day you will make beautiful things for me?"

"Yes, yes."

As her hips continued to move, she bit his earlobe teasingly. "Beautiful things of gold?"

"Yes," he promised hoarsely.

Now there was another element in his life. Metal-working skills and the art of warfare no longer were his burning considerations. His every waking thought seemed to involve Meda. Twice more they were alone in the shop, and the second time he was allowed to insert his hand under her tunic to feel the warm, flowery flesh of her breasts and to shiver in mysterious want as his fingertips were dampened by the dew of her femininity.

When she pulled away he stood helplessly, hands outstretched.

"I am at the age of betrothal," she said.

His heart leaped. He had seen more than one daughter leave Melech's house. First there was betrothal and then marriage. To think of Meda's being touched by another man was torment.

"Have you nothing to say?" she asked, lifting one eyebrow.

"What can I say?"

"Speak for me."

He did not understand. He lifted his hands and shrugged.

"Speak for me to my father," she said. "Ask him to betroth me to you."

"But I am only an apprentice."

"You will not always be an apprentice. Your gold work brings new clients to my father's shop. One day he will make you a colleague, not just a helper."

Wild dreams sprang up in Eri's mind. In the glow of his infatuation, in the burn of his first venture into the preliminaries of man-woman togetherness, his determination to return to Israel was forgotten. Before that most powerful of all human passions his friendship for Saul was relegated to temporary oblivion. There existed

for him only Meda, she of the heated, moist softness. At
that moment and, indeed, for a week as he mustered his
courage to obey Meda's injunction to speak to Melech,
he was willing to spend the rest of his life in Ekron. He
knew his own mind, that love was all that mattered.

CHAPTER
FIFTEEN

As a member of the Egyptian royal family, Tania's life experiences had been somewhat limited. Her father's residence, although not as regal as that of her kinsman Paynozem, was spacious and luxurious. The girl had never been without the services of a number of slaves trained to obey her every whim.

Urnan began his work immediately after meeting secretly with the agent of the king. He directed the building or alteration of small forges and smelting furnaces hidden among the fields and marshes of the delta. Ore was transported from the desert mines on the little riverboats. The money to finance the operation was delivered to Urnan by the king's agent in a seemingly endless supply.

At first, while Urnan did his duty to the king, Tania's life in Zoan was novel enough to keep her amused. In the manner of the newly wed, she accompa-

133

nied her husband on his first ventures into the rural
areas of the vast delta; but she found that the accommo-
dations among the fellahin were even less desirable than
their modest house on the outskirts of Zoan—there, at
least, she had two servants. Although that was appropriate for her role as the wife of a merchant, it was a
depressingly small number of slaves for a princess. She
was often alone, and it took only a few short months to
convince her that there was, after all, little glamour in
being the wife of a secret agent for the king. She was far
from the temples and palaces of the mighty, who were
also her friends and relatives.

When her own personal Nile refused to flood red
for the second time in as many months, she reached the
end of her patience. It did not occur to her to blame
herself, although she had become careless in the practice of methods of preventing the inconvenience that
had befallen her. She placed the fault squarely where it
belonged. She blamed Urnan.

"But my dear," he protested, "I have always depended upon you to take the necessary precautions."

"That is the trouble with you men," she stormed.
"You are mindless and uncaring as long as your desires
are satisfied."

"In truth," Urnan ventured cautiously, "I would
welcome a child."

She threw back her head and screamed.

"Am I to understand that you don't agree?" Urnan
asked, amused by her reaction.

"Go," Tania said. "Go back to your little men with
their leather aprons and their huge hammers. Go make
iron weapons for my kinsman, and hurry, so that we can
leave this place of misery and return to Waset, where we
belong."

Urnan was willing to leave her to her mood. Knowing her as well as he did, he held no hope that she would
present him with a child. Trying to discuss the matter
would prove futile. He returned to his forges, where he
had more say than he enjoyed at home.

Urnan had been moderately successful in training a
half-dozen country craftsmen in the making of weapons,

and the king's secret caches of blades, arrowheads, and spearheads were growing. His most recent project was to teach two of his most gifted pupils how to make iron rims for the king's chariots.

Left alone with her problem, Tania came to a quick conclusion. She was, after all, a woman of standing. The blood of the mothers and wives of kings flowed in her veins. She took finery from a chest that had not been opened since she had made the trip downriver with Urnan and ordered one of the house servants to go into the city and summon chair bearers. She sent a deposit in silver, knowing that without it the servant would not be able to convince those who served the rich at the center of the city to venture into the outskirts.

By the time the servant returned with two husky men carrying a litter, Tania was dressed in fine white linen. Her dark skin was accented at her neck and on her arms with jewelry that caused the chair bearers to blink in wonderment at seeing such riches on the mistress of so modest a home. She gave orders with the confidence of a woman used to commanding servants.

When the bearers were stopped at the gates of the king's palace, she spoke imperiously and was admitted to the presence of a dubious steward. She had to put on a full measure of condescension and bluster to convince the steward to ask his superiors if the king did, indeed, have a kinswoman named Tania.

Things began to happen quickly. Four armed members of the king's bodyguard ran into the courtyard where Tania waited with the curtains surrounding the chair pulled aside to admit a cooling breeze. Orders were barked. The chair bearers moved swiftly, and she was carried into the women's wing of the palace, where an angry king awaited.

"You little fool," Paynozem stormed, "what have you done?"

"For one thing," Tania said arrogantly, "I have tired of living like a slave."

"You have endangered our entire plan!" the king shouted. He paced in front of Tania. Finally he threw up his hands in defeat. "Well, whatever the damage, it is done. May I ask why we are honored with your presence?"

"I have need," Tania said.

"Of what, in the name of the gods?" Paynozem asked. He had decided that it was not gainful to be angry at her. Perhaps her visit to the palace had gone unnoticed by his enemies, of which he had many. The Libyan faction in the delta had proved to be stronger and more deeply entrenched than he had guessed.

"My needs can best be met by allowing me time here in the women's quarters," Tania said.

The king rolled his eyes in silent acceptance, thinking that the silly little wench had merely run out of kohl or some other feminine luxury item. "Fine," he said curtly. "And you will be escorted from the palace when day is gone. I pray to the gods that you have not endangered your husband's work by coming here."

"I was careful not to be seen," she said, pouting.

"Here even the walls have eyes," Paynozem told her. "I do not want to see you here again."

Tania was welcomed by one of the king's lesser wives, a lady whom she knew well. After much embracing and excited questioning, Tania stated her problem.

"I could not trust the crones of the fellahin to undertake so delicate a task," she said. "If you could have one of the court healers attend to it, I will be most grateful."

"I have strict orders from the king to remove you from the palace in secrecy with the night, so there is no time to have the healer uproot the swelling seed and for you to recover from his pruning."

"Then you must send the healer to me at my wretched home," Tania said.

"Perhaps that is the best solution."

"Promise me," Tania implored.

"I do."

Tania left the palace just before dawn. It had been a wonderful night of levity, dancing, music, drink, and good food in the women's quarters. She dozed in the chair and cursed the bearers with mild impatience when she was jostled. She was too pleasantly intoxicated to notice that the litter was followed all the way to the modest house that she shared with her husband.

Although Zoan itself was a hotbed of sedition against the king, his most powerful opponent lived upriver in an area of growing power that had come to call itself Middle Egypt. There the Nile sent a portion of its life-giving water westward into the desert to create a huge oasis of cultivated fields. This region had become, through the years, a Libyan stronghold. In that nome of Egypt the word of Buyuwawa was law. His power was absolute.

Buyuwawa had made his son, Musen, high priest of the temple of Amon and commander of a potent mercenary army. Father and son shared the same ambition: to overthrow Paynozem, whom they considered a leftover from the old and dying portion of Egypt, and put a king of Libyan blood, preferably of the blood of Buyuwawa, on the throne of the Two Lands.

With this goal in mind, Musen was generous with his father's gold for the purpose of obtaining information about the affairs at the court in Zoan.

This was a time when even the tombs of the godkings were not safe, when the word *sacrilege* was not known by many, when greed was the rule, and it was an accepted adage that one had to look after oneself. Thus it was a simple matter for Musen to build a network of spies that penetrated to the women's quarters and to the very throne room in Paynozem's palace.

Musen and his father had known for months that an unusually high number of shipments of iron ore had been made from the mines of Upper Egypt. Their spies in the delta had, in fact, located more than one forge that was turning out acceptable weapons made of the gray metal. Musen knew that the state of the armorer's craft in Lower Egypt had been at a low for some time. But the new weapons seemed to be the work of a master armorer—a man who knew the secrets of both the Hittites and the Philistines . . . perhaps the same man who had instructed the fellahin in the delta.

Musen informed his father of this new development, and both men agreed that the effort to revive Egyptian weapons-making skills had to have been ordered and financed by Paynozem. Only the pharaoh had the power and the wealth to amass such a hoard of iron weapons.

"Weapons made are weapons used," Buyuwawa said moodily.

"And since Paynozem does nothing more than pay lip service to restoring the empire," Musen said, "he is not buying weapons to mount an expedition into Canaan or Nubia."

"No," the old man said. "We are his target."

"Is he ready for civil war?" Musen asked.

"The problem is, my son," Buyuwawa said, "that we are not yet ready for war."

"My army could isolate Paynozem in his city," Musen said. "We could starve him out."

"And you think that Prince Kemose, who directs the army of the priests of Amon at Waset, will let you get away with that?"

Musen bowed to his father's wisdom. "The time will come," he said.

"Yes," Buyuwawa said. "I had hoped to see you, my son, with the double crown on your head. Perhaps that will not be. Perhaps I will not live to see you, or your son, or even your grandson rule the Two Lands, even though the oracles have told me that such will come to pass. Perhaps I will have to look down from the pathway followed by the god of the sun to see it, but you must promise me that you will not forget my vision."

"I promise," Musen said. "In the meantime, Father, we must seek out this armorer who is working magic among the unskilled smiths of Lower Egypt."

The old man nodded agreement.

Musen's spy in the women's quarters of the palace had already passed along the information that a member of the royal family visited unexpectedly. Musen knew every member of Paynozem's blood. Suddenly he connected that report with the present conversation.

"The princess Tania," he told his father, "was given in marriage to a foreigner who returned from the sea with Prince Kemose. It was after the return of the foreigner and Kemose that iron-smelting activity increased in Upper Egypt."

"This foreigner, then, could be the armorer who is mobilizing weapons makers for Paynozem?"

"I find it odd," Musen said, "to think that a princess of Egypt is living in a modest house once occupied by a small merchant on the outskirts of the city."

"Ah?"

"She was followed there," Musen said. "She has been alone. There has been no sign of her husband. My sources tell me that the husband, one Urnan, travels into the countryside quite often."

"I think, my son, that a conversation with this Urnan might be of interest."

"You are wise," Musen said. "I go to Zoan this day with an armed escort disguised as priests."

CHAPTER SIXTEEN

It was difficult for Eri to approach Melech on the delicate matter of asking for Meda in marriage. It took two days beyond a week before, over the midday meal, he blurted out, "Master Melech, I have something to ask."

Melech chewed slowly and contentedly. He nodded and mumbled around a mouthful, "What is on your mind?"

"Your daughter," Eri said, almost choking on the words.

Melech wasn't sure he understood. He swallowed, looked at Eri musingly. "Which daughter?"

"M-Meda."

"Has she been bothering you? I have been patient with her interest in your gold work. You know how women are about gold. But if she is interfering with your concentration, I will, of course, speak to her."

"No," Eri said quickly. "It's not—she's not—" He braced himself, and the words tumbled out of his mouth seemingly without his cooperation. "She asked me—she wants me—"

"She wants you to make her golden trinkets." Melech laughed. "I have told her that I am not a rich man. I have told her repeatedly that the daughter of a smith, especially a smith who has so many female offspring, does not wear golden baubles."

"Oh, Lord," Eri said in befuddlement. "Master, it is that I want to ask for Meda in marriage."

It took a moment or two for the words to soak into Melech's understanding. After they had, he swung his right arm and the back of his hand connected with Eri's face. The boy was swept off the stool on which he was seated to land on his back on the packed earthen floor. Melech stood over him and for a moment Eri feared that the smith was going to kick him.

"If I hurt you, I am sorry," Melech said.

Eri shook his head to dispel blurred vision. There was a numbness in his left cheek, and a taste of blood in his mouth. He had received discipline from Melech before, but never had the big smith struck him in the face. In spite of his regard for the man, Eri felt an underlayer of cold anger in him.

"Perhaps I misunderstood you," Melech said, holding out both hands.

Eri, ignoring the smith's offer of help, came to his feet. His eyes were on a level with Melech's. His height had increased by half a cubit since he had first entered Melech's shop.

"You must understand," Melech said in a tone that was almost a plea. "What you ask is impossible."

"Then you didn't misunderstand me," Eri said.

"You asked to marry my Meda," Melech said.

"Yes."

Melech's voice was calm, but there was something deep in his eyes that made Eri wary. "Tell me what gave you the idea that my daughter would have you as a husband—you, a Hebrew."

A revelation of uncommon clarity came to Eri. It

was an understanding of multiple dimensions. It told him that he was right in thinking that there was danger in Melech's eyes, even as it made him wonder what sort of spell Meda had cast over him to cause him to forget his origins. In that blinding moment of awareness he saw himself for what he was, a boy not yet ripe for manhood, a boy who had been dazzled by his first infatuation with a girl. Given time to consider, he would not have contemplated marriage with a woman of the Philistines. He had forgotten his purpose. He had come to Melech's shop with only one intention, to learn the secrets of the gray metal. Now he had those secrets, but the flowery scent of a Philistine girl had wiped all traces of responsibility from his mind. He had forgotten that Philistines had destroyed his home and his family and that he was bound by oath to his dead mother, his father, the God of Abraham, and to himself to avenge those wrongs.

He fully understood the look in Melech's eyes. Melech, too, was the product of his own circumstances. To a Philistine, a Hebrew was not only the enemy but a less-than-human enemy, a pig of the hills. Hebrew women were for momentary satisfaction to be followed by death or slavery, lest they breed more pigs of the hills. For a Hebrew man to take a Philistine woman to wife was an unbearable thought, to be prevented at all costs. The army fought bravely to keep the Hebrews confined to their hills, away from the homes of Philistine women. For a Hebrew to ask for the hand of a prominent citizen of Ekron in marriage was unthinkable.

Eri could only guess how near he had come to death, for he would have been unprepared for a sudden assault, and attack was being urged by every fiber of Melech's being. He was restrained only by his need to know.

"Tell me why you thought you could ask for my daughter in marriage," the big smith repeated.

"Master," Eri said, "it was no more than a momentary madness." He edged closer to his workbench. On the wall behind the bench his sword hung in its sheath.

He would not use it except in self-defense, but he was warned into alertness by Melech's cold eyes.

"On your part alone?" Melech asked. "Or have you spoken to Meda about this madness?"

Eri weighed his answers, and defiance gave him tongue. He was close enough to the sword to reach it before Melech could get his huge, powerful hands on him. "It was she who suggested that I speak."

Melech's face darkened. He leaned forward, and Eri tensed himself to leap for his weapon.

"He lies, Father!" Meda's voice came from behind Eri. He kept his eyes on Melech's face, ready to move swiftly.

"I don't know what gave this Hebrew the idea that I would be receptive to such a revolting idea," Meda said.

Eri accepted Meda's betrayal with a calmness that surprised him. He felt no pain, only relief.

"As I told you, master," he said softly, "it was nothing more than madness on my part. I can see now that I was dreaming of the impossible. I ask that you forgive me."

His mind was racing ahead. He saw in his memory the wooded hills, the dry washes, the hidden meadows and glens of Israel, and he longed to be there.

"Let me be sure," Melech said. "Meda, has this boy spoken to you? Has he—" He seemed to have trouble forming the words. "Has he touched you?"

Meda laughed and cast a contemptuous look at Eri. "No, of course not. He mentioned no such nonsense to me. If he had, I would have spit in his face. Touch me?" She laughed. "Would a daughter of Melech stand for such insult?"

"Leave us," Melech said.

Meda ran from the shop.

"I had hoped that you would work at my side," Melech said.

"Is my offense so great that that is no longer possible?" Eri asked.

"My daughter—"

Eri lowered his head as if in contrition. Actually he

was wondering how quickly he could shake the dust of Melech's forge from his feet and clear his nostrils of the stench.

The smith straightened. "You must promise me, Eri, that you will never again look at my daughter. At any of my daughters."

There was still danger. To Melech, he was just a Hebrew, a handy unpaid helper in the forge.

"You cannot, of course, ever be your own master in Philistia," Melech said. "The law strictly forbids that a Hebrew be a smith lest he become a traitor and make arms for the enemy."

"Yes," Eri said, angered more by that statement than he had been by Melech's insulting refusal to consider his suit for Meda.

"But you may stay," Melech said. "You may continue to be my helper."

Eri nodded. He knew that now was not the time to mention leaving. Clearly a Hebrew would not be allowed to leave Philistia with the secret of iron to be given to the enemy. Melech's hand had closed over the handle of the great hammer, which lay atop the anvil.

"I am grateful, master," Eri said. "I will not step out of my place again."

Melech's hand relaxed. "We will speak of this no more."

Eri nodded. "I will finish my work," he said, turning to the bench.

He spent the rest of the day polishing the gold trinkets that would ornament the wife of a rich merchant. He ate his evening meal alone, then retired to his room behind the shop. When the rest of the household was asleep he gathered his belongings by the light of a half-moon. He considered taking the gold items he'd just finished, but did not. He had worked hard for Melech, but his payment was in his memory, the knowledge of how to turn rocks of the earth into gleaming, keen-bladed weapons of death.

While apprenticing at the forge in Ekron, he had heard tell of the fury of a big Hebrew warrior, had heard the name of Saul spoken along with that of Samson. He had heard the Philistine soldiers speak of the Lion of the Mountains, of Saul the Benjamite. Some said that among the living, only Goliath of Gath, the young giant who had the strength of half a dozen men, could ever hope to be Saul's match in a man-to-man encounter.

Saul would be much changed—a man now—just as Eri himself was changed, on the verge of manhood. Had their friendship endured the intervention of time? he wondered. *Well, I'll find out soon enough,* he thought.

He crept away from Melech's establishment in the small hours of the morning, made his way to an isolated section of the city's wall, scaled it, lowered himself by a rope to the earth outside Ekron. He awakened two vagrants, for the Philistine cities, too, had their share of hapless ones. The two loafers saw what they thought to be easy pickings, with two against one, but were quickly dissuaded by Eri's flashing blade, which he applied flat side against a cheek, an outstretched arm, and finally the retreating rumps of the idle ones.

By morning he was climbing the low hills above the Philistine plain. He was going home. He allowed himself to think of Meda, of her soft, wet mouth, and the warm, moist secret under her tunic. He put the memory behind him and instead thought of Saul . . . and the iron weapon he would make for his old friend.

Tania had given up hope that a healer from the palace would be coming to her aid. Nearly two weeks had passed since her visit to the women's quarters, but she was afraid to go back—the king would be infuriated if she showed her face again. When the princess was told by her one serving girl that a priest of Amon waited outside, she assumed that the healer had been sent at last from the palace to rid her of her inconvenience.

"Send him to me," she said, then waited with mixed emotions, for she had been told that the procedure she would soon undergo was at best painful and at worst dangerous. When two men dressed as priests entered the room, she became confused. Why two? she wondered. Then her black-ringed eyes widened in surprise

when she saw that one of the priests was wiping blood
from a short sword with a cloth of the same material
that her serving maid had been wearing.

"What are you doing?" she demanded.

"We want to see your husband," said the larger
priest, a Libyan by his face and voice.

"If you have not been sent to me from the palace,"
she said, "I am not expecting you. You may leave."

"In time," the Libyan said. "When do you expect
your husband to return?"

"I have no way of knowing," she said. "My husband's business is unpredictable."

"Let us hope, lady, that the wait is not too long, for
my servant can become impatient. Allow me to intro-
duce myself. I am Musen."

Tania did not recall ever having heard that name.

The other man finished cleaning his blade, tested
its sharpness with his thumb, then tossed the bloodied
cloth to the floor.

"This is not some alley where you can discard your
trash," Tania said sharply. "Pick it up."

"Pick it up," Musen said mildly. He smiled at Tania.
"I fear, my lady, that he has left trash of another sort
lying on your floor. Your maidservant became frightened and tried to flee. We will pick up the remains and
dispose of them later."

Tania had begun to realize that something was
wrong, but her haughty expression did not change. "I
had gathered that your jackal had used the weapon of
which he seems to be so fond."

"Pray that he is not forced to use it on you," Musen
warned.

"Do you know the penalty for threatening harm to
a member of the king's family?" Tania asked.

"Oh, yes," Musen said evenly. "Now let me ask *you*
a question: Have you ever known pain, Princess Tania?
Have you ever experienced *real* pain?"

She did not answer.

Musen nodded to his man. The mercenary leaped
forward to seize Tania's arm. With one swift movement
he jerked it behind her back with one hand. Tania tried

to whirl out of his grasp, reaching for his eyes with the fingernails of her free hand, but he was too quick, too strong. Excruciating pain shot through her like a hot knife as he twisted her arm high. She heard something crack and feared that a bone had given way. She screamed.

Musen nodded. The mercenary relieved the pressure, stepped away.

"This one will die quickly," Tania said to Musen. Tears of pain and rage wet her cheeks. "He merely takes orders. You will be kept alive until you beg for death."

"Again," Musen said, nodding to the mercenary.

She stood the pain as long as she could, and then she begged, "Please . . . please . . ."

She sank onto the floor, tucking her legs under her, cradling her injured arm.

"Where is your husband?" Musen asked.

"He is in the delta on business," she said.

"What business?"

"I don't concern myself with his business."

"Again," Musen said, and his servant stepped toward Tania.

She scuttled backward until her shoulders were pressed against the wall. The kohl with which she lined her eyes was running with her tears. "No, please," she whispered.

"What is your husband's business?"

"He is a smith."

"An armorer?"

"Yes."

"Where are his furnaces?"

"I've seen only one. I know only that we traveled west from Zoan into the fields."

"Again?" the servant asked eagerly.

Musen shook his head. "When do you expect your husband to return?"

"I don't know. Soon, perhaps. He doesn't like to stay away more than a few days at a time."

The mercenary laughed. "If I had something like this at home, I wouldn't leave in the first place."

"Do not insult a princess, low one," Musen said.

"Sir," the man said sullenly.

"How many more servants are there in the house?" Musen asked Tania.

"Only one," she said. "He is an old man and harmless."

"Go see how harmless this old man is," Musen ordered.

"Who are you?" Tania asked. "Why are you here?"

"I just want to have a chat with your husband," he said.

"I don't believe you." The pain in her arm was diminishing. She could not believe that she, a princess, had been so harshly treated.

Another man dressed as a priest entered the room and gave Musen a military salute. "We have found papyrus documents in another room, sir, but they are written in a code." He extended a roll.

Musen unfurled it, knitted his brow in puzzlement. "What code is this?" he asked Tania.

"My husband told me that it is the old language of Ur and Babylon."

"Can you read it?"

"No."

"Not even if I have one of my men remind you that pain can be unpleasant?"

"Not even if you kill me," she said defiantly. "To me it is nothing but wedge-shaped scratchings."

"I believe you," Musen said. "No civilized person could make sense of such bird tracks." He turned to the soldier. "Nothing to indicate where the armorer might travel?"

"Nothing, lord."

"Post your men," Musen said. "Prepare to stay here as long as it is necessary."

"Sir," snapped the soldier.

The man who had killed the maidservant came back into the room. "Lord Musen," he said, "the old man, the other slave, has fled."

"Put someone at the front gate. If anyone inquires, tell them that there is illness in this house, that we priests are here to care for the sick and to prevent the disease from spreading."

Musen stayed only long enough to be sure that Tania was securely confined in a room and guarded by one of his most trustworthy men. He was not pleased with the situation. It could get very touchy unless the armorer returned quickly.

CHAPTER
SEVENTEEN

Urnan's work was the meat of his life, and coming home to Tania the honey cakes that made the meal complete. He traveled downriver in a dhow manned by loyal Egyptians who, after dropping him off, would make their way southward to fetch another cargo of iron ore.

The winds could not fill the sails powerfully enough, and the current of the Nile was not swift enough to match the man's eagerness. He wasted no time after landing at a rickety pier away from the city's main riverfront, but darkness had fallen before he reached the area just beyond his home on Zoan's outskirts.

The light of oil lamps flickered from the windows of his far neighbors. The aroma of roasting meat lingered in the air. From the fields to the east a jackal howled, setting off a chorus of barking from dogs in the town.

Now he could see his house. A light glowed from the window of the bedchamber he shared with Tania. He walked rapidly, staying in the center of the narrow street. When a figure stepped from the shadows of a house and called his name, his hand went to the hilt of his sword. He waited warily, but as the figure approached, Urnan recognized the gait of the old man who was the servant in his house.

"There is trouble, master. Soldiers have come dressed as priests."

Urnan's throat tightened. "What are you saying?"

"They lie in wait for you, master."

"And your mistress?"

The old man bowed his head.

"Speak to me," Urnan ordered. Fear roiled in his stomach, the same queasiness he had felt so long before, trying to get back to his family in Shiloh.

"I know not, master. But they killed the girl who was maidservant to my mistress."

Urnan drew his sword and began to run down the street. He was reliving another homecoming, and in his agitation he could smell the blood, could hear the protests of his son as the Philistine soldiers took their pitiless pleasure with Shelah.

Sanity returned as he neared the wall enclosing his gardens. He slowed to a walk, then stood and listened outside the gate. He heard two men talking softly from the shadows under the tree nearest the entrance to the house. Urnan crept among the trees and shrubs of the garden to the kitchen and entered the back way. In the darkness his foot touched something soft. He bent, put his hand into blood. His heart skipped. He explored the body, felt cold skin, felt the coarse cloth of the maidservant's tunic, but only when he felt the ring in her ear was he certain of her identity.

Once before he had come home to find a servant dead. The similarity to that time made his knees weak, but there was one difference. He had made a vow during the time when he was enslaved that if the gods would give him another chance, he would never again be defenseless against the ravagers and murderers of the world. From the time of his arrival in Egypt he had lived with a sword in his hand or near at hand. During the time he had spent in Waset with Kemose he had trained with the weapons masters of the palace guard. His blade was of iron and, because of its superior craftsmanship, more than a match for anything that a soldier of the Libyan-dominated army might carry.

Urnan stepped out from the shadows into the pleasant, airy room where he had enjoyed leisurely meals with his wife. A man dressed as a priest was standing guard at the foot of the stairs leading to Tania's chamber, cleaning his fingernails with the point of a blade. He did not look up as Urnan slipped behind him.

"How goes it?" Urnan asked.

"Quiet," said the guard.

"The woman?" Urnan asked, moving closer.

"She fancies herself to be a princess," the guard said with a laugh. "A few minutes with me would make her humble."

"That you will never do," Urnan said, swinging his keen-bladed sword with so much power that the sharp point slashed flesh, tendons, and blood vessels, leaving the man's head attached by nothing more than the bones of his neck.

Urnan caught him, eased him to the floor, listened. There were only the sounds of his own beating heart and the distant barking of the dogs.

He crept up the stairs and slowly and carefully opened the door to the bedchamber. Tania was sitting in front of her dressing table. Her eyes widened, and she opened her mouth to speak when she saw him. He held his finger to his lips. She ran to him, threw her arms around him, then cringed away as she encountered warm, sticky blood.

"You're hurt!" she whispered.

"Not I," he said. "How many are there?"

"I don't know. I saw four, but perhaps there are others."

"There were at least three," he said.

"They asked questions about you. They are Libyan."

"We will leave that way," Urnan said, pointing toward the window that overlooked the back garden. He took Tania's arm and pulled her toward the opening.

"My jewels," she protested.

"Quickly," he said.

She ran to pick up a small, gold-inlaid cedar box. Urnan waited near the window. He motioned Tania to be silent. The two men who had been at the front entrance were walking through the garden toward the open window. The window was one and a half times Urnan's height from the ground. A large fig tree shaded the wall. Limbs brushed the mud-brick side of the house.

"Wait for my signal," Urnan said, "then drop the box to me."

"Look," she said, thinking he was not aware that the two men were now standing below the window.

He shushed her. She clung to his arm so tightly that he had to lift her fingers to free himself. He climbed into the aperture, then perched momentarily, sword in hand, on the window ledge. At the right second he launched himself out and down, to land with his knees in the back of one of the men. When they hit the ground, Urnan heard the air rush from the other man's lungs. The armorer leaped to his feet and swung a killing blow at the second man. His lessons had paid off; the sword dug deeply into soft flesh, and the Libyan bent double, clutching his belly. Urnan turned and finished the stunned man on the ground with one swift slash.

The fellow with the stomach wound was on his knees and looking up with surprise at Urnan. The moon showed his eyes. His mouth was open in supplication when Urnan silenced him by severing his throat.

Tania tossed down the little chest containing her jewels. She eased herself onto the window ledge, reached for a spreading limb of the fig tree, hung there for a moment, then dropped. Urnan caught her but lost his balance. They tumbled to the ground and lay there for a few moments as he listened for movement. The garden was still, save for the tiny sounds of leaf movement in a night breeze.

He helped Tania to her feet, then led her to the back gate and into the fields directly behind the house, making a wide circle before coming back to the streets of the town.

"We must go directly to the king," Tania said.

"I think it best that we find a boat and make our way upriver to Kemose," Urnan said.

"But Paynozem will protect us," she said. "It is he you serve with your armories, isn't it?"

Urnan decided to stay with his own plans. As Tania and he approached the riverfront, however, they saw members of the Libyan-dominated national army patrolling and standing guard.

Urnan pulled his wife to a stop. "I cannot be that important," he told her. "Surely they are not looking for me."

"I choose not to ask them," Tania said. "Please, let's go to the king."

They made their way to Paynozem's palace through dark, deserted streets. Twice they had to hide in the shadows to avoid small groups of soldiers. Urnan was relieved to see that the king's own bodyguard had sentries posted around the temple and palace complex. He had begun to fear that the army was in revolt.

They ran across an open square. Urnan expected to hear the sounds of pursuit at any time, but it was a member of the royal guard who challenged them. Urnan let Tania do the talking. The guard, although dubious, called his watch supervisor. Soon the couple were in the pharaoh's presence.

Paynozem was irritable, for he had been awakened from sleep only a short time after falling into his bed. Urnan suspected that the ruler's exhaustion was due to a round of experimentation and satiation with no fewer than three deliciously youthful dancing girls. The king listened impatiently as Urnan explained that the Libyan elements had discovered the nature of his work in the delta.

"If you will supply us with transportation, Great

One," Urnan said, "I think that we will be safer with Prince Kemose in Waset."

"We will speak of this when the sun is high," Paynozem said, dismissing them with a wave of his hand as he stumbled toward his quarters.

The sun was high—indeed well past high—before they were summoned to the throne room the next day. The king looked as if the double crown of the Two Lands rested heavy on his head. His face was drawn, his lips pursed. Tania and Urnan knelt before him, rose with his impatient gesture.

"My loyal subject Musen, son of Buyuwawa the Libyan, has made petition before me," Paynozem said. "He claims that a common criminal killed three priests of the temple last night."

"We are not familiar with common criminals, Great One," Tania said.

"My loyal subject Musen thinks that the criminal will try to escape by traveling upriver to the rebellious and independent nomes of Upper Egypt. He has a full regiment of the national army guarding the riverfront."

"Great One, if you will keep Tania safe here in the court, I can lose myself among the fields of the delta," Urnan said.

"No, that will not do," Paynozem said.

Urnan waited. There was something in the king's manner that roused tendrils of uneasiness in him.

"You have served me faithfully, Urnan," the king said. "I do not know what mistake you have made to allow my enemies to discover your mission, but they do know. Units of the army are searching the delta for your forges and furnaces. You may well ask why I don't take the situation in hand. I can tell you only that you are not in a position to know the entanglements of politics."

Urnan nodded, but not in agreement. He knew enough about politics to know that the king lived in constant fear of a Libyan uprising.

"Because of your relationships to my kinsmen, Tania and Kemose, I will not abandon you," Paynozem said. "But the political situation precludes your going upriver. Nor can I risk your being captured in the delta. The bravest man talks when he is persuaded by an expert, and my loyal Libyan subjects have skilled practitioners of the torturer's art." He shook his head. "No."

"There is a solution, Great One," Urnan ventured.

"I listen."

"I have longed to return to my homeland, to search for my son. Perhaps, since the army guards the way to the south, I can go north, across the sea to Canaan."

Paynozem mused, nodding. "So let it be. You will remain here in the palace until you are called."

When Tania and Urnan were alone in the room assigned to them she put her arms around him and kissed him. "I was not consulted about this wild scheme of yours."

"No," he said. "Perhaps, my love, it would be best if you stayed here with your kinsmen."

She kissed him again. "You have introduced me to living the life of a tradesman. I did not like it, but I survived. Perhaps a princess of Egypt can endure traveling to your barbaric homeland as well."

"No. There will be danger," he said. "I would rest easier if I knew you were safe here in Zoan."

Her dark eyes flashed. "Where is there safety? What safety will there be after the Libyans seize power?"

"That, surely, will not happen," he said.

She shrugged. "Nothing is certain save that Anubis awaits all in the netherworld." She clung to him. "You are mine. You are my Child of the Lion, and where you go, I go."

"As the king says, so let it be," Urnan said, embracing her, covering her mouth with his. In the comfort of a royal bed she had never been more willing, had never been so soft, so warm. They seemed to melt together in a closeness that made them, truly, one.

Urnan was awakened harshly by four men who had crept into the room, covered his mouth with cloth, seized him, and with sheer force muffled his struggles.

He was half dragged, half carried out of the room and out of the palace, then tossed—with his hands and legs trussed—into a cart. He could not see where he was being taken, but he soon caught the familiar smell of the river. He was carried onto the deck of a dhow. The boat put out into the slow current and drifted until it was well away from the city.

A man came, squatted in front of Urnan. "Are the ropes too tight, master?"

Urnan noted the respectful form of address, the polite voice. "Where are you taking me?"

"A ship awaits," the boatman said.

"My wife—"

"If the ropes are too tight I can loosen them," the boatman said, "but I have orders, master."

"What, exactly, are your orders?"

"To treat you with respect, but to see to it that you are taken on board the ship that awaits."

"Untie me," Urnan said.

"And there is one other thing," the boatman said. "I am to tell you that what you had planned is impossible, that . . ." His voice trailed off.

"Speak, man," Urnan said impatiently.

"Let me be sure I remember how I am to say it." The boatman rubbed his head. "I am to tell you that a princess of Egypt would never be allowed to venture alone into the lands of the barbarians. I am to tell you that your wife will be safe and will occupy the position to which she was born. And I am to tell you that you are not to try to return to Egypt."

"Tania," Urnan whispered. Pain stabbed him and probed his heart. There was small comfort in knowing that Tania lived and would continue to live in ease and luxury; but the feelings of loss and emptiness in him were not unlike how he had felt when his wife and son were taken from him. As far as he knew, Tania was still with child. The boatman left him alone with his misery.

When the dhow pulled alongside an oceangoing ship, Urnan's bonds were cut away. Two sailors helped him onto the deck. The sun was just rising, and in the gray light he saw a familiar face, the face of the ship's captain who had rescued Kemose and him from the sea.

"So, my friend!" the captain said.

"We are well met!" Urnan said, feeling hopeful. "Please, if you are my friend, you will help me."

The captain shook his head. "Because I am your friend, I will make you stay right where you are. If you go back to the city, you will be killed or sent back into slavery." He shook his head sadly. "You've made someone in high places unhappy with you. After we are safely at sea you must tell me all about it. I'm curious to know what sin you have committed against our great king who will live forever."

"The sin of loyalty," Urnan murmured.

"I'm going to have to lock you in your cabin, old friend," the captain told him. "I would hate to see you lose your hands, tongue, and head, and I would most certainly be averse to joining you in that state of deprivation."

Urnan nodded. His heart was empty, but his reason told him that the events of the night were for the best. The king of Egypt was not secure enough on his throne to protect his loyal supporters and those who served him. Even if the Libyans had not discovered Urnan's work, his continued presence in Egypt would have endangered Tania. She was safe. If the Libyans eventually overthrew Paynozem, she would still be safe in Egypt, because the legitimacy of the kings passed through the bloodlines of the royal women. With the double crown on the head of a Libyan, Tania would probably become the wife of a nobleman of the court. But what would happen to the child she carried in her belly, he wondered. Had the Fates conspired against his progeny?

His heart ached as he followed the captain to a cabin. He agreed that food would be welcome, but when it was brought to him, it was like dust in his mouth.

The ship reached the open sea. The door to his cabin opened, and the captain smiled at him. "You may join me on deck, if it pleases you."

He stood at the stern of the ship and watched Egypt disappear down the horizon.

"I never feel that a voyage has properly begun until we are out of sight of land," the captain said.

"Where are we bound?" Urnan asked.

"Unfortunately for you, we are not going directly to Canaan," the captain answered. "We have a few island ports to visit before we swing back down the Philistine coast. In compensation, we will eat well for the first few days. There is an ample supply of good Egyptian beer; and the wine of the islands is a caress on one's tongue."

The captain slung his arm across Urnan's shoulders. "Now, old friend, I want to hear what you did to tweak the tail of the lion of Egypt."

CHAPTER EIGHTEEN

The orders to move out had been issued to Dera, the young officer in charge of the column, by the Commander of the Army of the East, General Galar. The supply column consisting of three solid-wheeled oxcarts left the Philistine plain at daybreak to wind its way into the hills. Recent rains had brought forth a profusion of greenery and flowers to brighten the landscape, and the early morning air was sweet.

Intended for the garrison at Michmash, in the area the Hebrews called the land of Benjamin, the food supplies in the wagons were guarded by a score of heavily armed, well-mounted soldiers. Four horsemen led the carts. When the terrain allowed, others acted as outriders, but the main body of troops rode at the rear. Each man wore a full complement of body armor made of bronze and iron plates mounted on leather.

As the column climbed the steepening track into

the convoluted hills, the sun reached for the zenith. Some of the soldiers began to doubt the wisdom of their superiors in ordering so much protection. After all, the only threat came from poorly equipped die-hards among the defeated Hebrews. Not one man in the group doubted that the elite force of mounted soldiers could handle anything that a few renegades could manage. In the years since the battle at Ebenezer, the Hebrews' meager attempts at resistance had been under Samuel, and he was an old man and a seer, not a warrior. Besides, Philistine weapons could make short work of whatever the Hebrews might scrounge up—at least until recently. Sketchy military reports held that something different was going on, but the commander said that further information was needed before it was viewed as a serious, organized threat.

The temperature rose. Sweat formed under the soldiers' ribbed helmets and ran down to sting their eyes. Beads of moisture formed on heated skin under breastplates and girdles and felt like crawling insects as it soaked undergarments. In order to get some air, several of the men loosened fasteners to broaden the spaces where armor joined with armor. When no officers objected, other troops did the same.

The interstices gave easy access to well-aimed, bronze-tipped arrows that flew in a storm of death as the Philistine column entered a steep-walled wadi. The flight of arrows came from the shelter of boulders on the slopes. Men and horses screamed in agony. The young officer shouted orders but was cut off in midcry when an arrow found its target, piercing his helmet.

Suddenly a big-shouldered, shaggy young Hebrew warrior bounded down the western slope of the wadi, leading a rabble of ragtag men of various ages. He threw his heavy spear on the run, putting the strength of his arms and shoulders behind it.

The surviving Philistines threw themselves off their mounts and formed a protective square. Iron-tipped spears protruded from the wall formed by their shields. Gleaming swords were at the ready.

Saul, son of Kish, was no longer a boy. He was at

least a full head taller than any other man, Hebrew or
Philistine, on the field. He wore a helmet of leather
reinforced with bronze plate. His massive chest was protected by Philistine iron, taken in a previous encounter.
The Philistine sword that had tasted blood more than
once was in his hand. For ease of movement he dis-
dained greaves to protect his legs. The iron tip of his
hurled spear sliced between two shields, and a cry of
pain escaped a Philistine soldier.

The Philistines held against the abandoned hand-
to-hand assault for one shouting, moaning, screaming
instant. To his left Saul saw one of his own go down
under an all-out blow from an enemy sword. To his right
another of his men cried out in frustration as his bronze
blade was broken by contact with Philistine iron.
Weaponless, the young man died with a Philistine spear
thrust into his stomach. Saul roared out his own anger.
Hebrew bronze against Philistine iron was an unequal
match. Only surprise and pitiless determination could
overcome the disadvantage, even when the enemy was
outnumbered, as they were now in the shadowed wadi.

A wounded horse screamed and screamed and
screamed until a ragged man of the hills took pity on the
animal and finished it with a hefty swing of a captured
iron sword.

Saul looked around wildly for another target for his
blade, but the enemy was no more. The stolid oxen,
undisturbed by the brief and deadly encounter, chewed
their cuds, content to be at rest.

"Gather the weapons," Saul ordered. "Get the
carts moving."

Twenty more Hebrews would be armed with Philistine iron. The supplies in the carts would feed the people of Gibeah for a time.

As the laden carts got under way, one of the patient
oxen lifted its tail and dropped steaming excrement
onto the ground, where blood mixed with the drying
earth in dark splotches. Flowers brought forth by the
rains had been trampled.

* * *

Saul stood atop a boulder and gazed down the track toward the plain, on watch lest there be another force of Philistine soldiers. He was tall. His dark, curled hair, damp with his exertions, hung to his shoulders. His leather and bronze shield was a light weight on his left arm. An iron-tipped lance was in his right hand, butt resting on the ground.

The impressive, big-boned, well-muscled figure was seen by a pair of eyes made hazy by pain. He could see the big Hebrew standing on the rock, legs like pillars, arms that would have made fabled Samson envious. For among the fallen men and horses, Dera, the young Philistine officer, lived, partly covered by the body of one of his men. He had been unconscious when Saul's men stripped him of his armor and weapons. Blood, his own and that of others, had wet his hair, covered his face, and soaked the tunic under his breastplate.

When Dera opened his eyes and moved his head, an ocean of pain ebbed and flowed inside his skull, and his vision blurred. He had held his breath as the Hebrews gathered the bodies of their fallen comrades. When the carts were urged into motion, the wheels of one came within inches of his outflung arm. He waited, heart pounding.

Now, as the young officer looked up at Saul, he felt a surge of hatred and humiliation, but the enmity was colored by respect. With inferior weapons and nothing more than an untrained mob, the big Hebrew had wiped out a specially prepared penetration unit. Worse, the Hebrews had come through it with alarmingly small losses.

A voice came from somewhere on the heights, calling, "Saul . . . Saul?"

The big Hebrew looked toward the sound. To Dera, it seemed that the intense brown eyes lingered on his face for a moment.

"Saul!" the voice called.

The big man waved his spear, leaped down from his stance atop the boulder, and took long strides to overtake the rear guard of the force that was moving deeper into the hills. As he passed, Dera had a good look at the commander's face. It was worth remembering: high of brow, strong of nose, eyes like those of a desert lion.

The sun burned down, and dizziness overcame Dera. When he was aware again, he heard the flapping of many wings and opened his eyes to see that the carrion birds were arriving. He moaned in horror as a hooked beak tore an eyeball from a dead face.

He pushed himself to his feet and in a staggering run removed himself from the place of carnage. He fell into the dust, but death was behind him. He could hear it in the rustling wings and greedy squawks as the birds squabbled.

Movement sent a surge of alarm through him. He raised his head to see his horse, Menos. He thanked the gods that the Hebrews had not found the stallion and taken him away.

"Come, my friend," Dera whispered hoarsely, holding out his hand. He had trained the stallion from a colt. Menos snorted at the acrid smell of drying blood and nodded his head in agitation, but he came toward the fallen man. Dera whispered soothingly, reached up, and seized a trailing rein.

It took all of his strength to mount the nervous animal, and as Menos found his own way down the track to the plain, there were times when awareness left Dera entirely. He clung to the back of his stallion through instinct alone. He was drifting in and out of consciousness when Menos reached a field camp of the Army of the East.

When next Dera was conscious he tried to sit up, for the first thing he saw was the face of his commander, General Galar of Ashdod.

"Rest," Galar said. "Be at ease."

"Sir," Dera croaked. "I have failed."

"Tell me," Galar said.

"I should have been more alert," Dera said weakly.

Galar curled his lower lip impatiently. "Where?" he demanded.

"We were moving into the hills, sir."

"How many?"

"At least a hundred."

"How armed?"

Dera closed his eyes, thinking. "One of them, the big one called Saul—"

"Saul," Galar said, and from his lips the name was a curse. "How do you know it was he?"

"He was called by name."

"Tall? A head taller than you? Muscular?"

"His eyes," Dera said. "His eyes—"

"What about them?"

"Burning. Burning."

Galar rose from the stool on which he sat. The young man had fainted. Well, he was in the hands of the gods, for a head wound was a serious thing. Sometimes it appeared that a man was well on the road to recovery, and then, suddenly, he was moaning in pain and clutching at his head as death claimed him.

The general's field armor was functional, not at all as glorious as the uniform he wore at formal functions in Ashdod. He was a plain and simple man, a man who had reached his position as commander of the Army of the East as much through deeds, he believed, as through having won the heart and hand of the youngest daughter of the high lord of the city. It was his responsibility to keep the conquered Hebrews in submission, to keep the tribute flowing from the settlements and towns in the interior. For years it had been a relatively easy job, which he had directed from his fine residence in the city; but starting with the last season of cold, a campaign of hit-and-run terror had begun against isolated Philistine outposts and small units.

Whenever Galar sent large fighting groups into the hills, the soldiers found only hardworking, submissive noncombatants. Punishments had been meted out. Able-bodied men suspected of fighting with the renegades had been summarily executed in public. One entire village that had conspired to hide a smithy with a forge working not in iron but in bronze had been destroyed, for the Hebrews were forbidden the use of the forge, lest they turn it to the making of weapons.

When certain tortures were applied, captured Hebrews talked freely and readily. It was from a moaning, screaming man who had just been deprived of his right hand that Galar had first heard the name Saul.

"Saul. It is he, Saul," the man had said. "It is he who continues the fight. Saul and the holy man Samuel."

Now, again, the name was in his ears.

Saul.

"Saul," Galar said aloud. "Your head will decorate my spear before the coming of winter."

In the season of in-gathering the Feast of Tabernacles was enriched by the contents of the three oxcarts brought to Gibeah by Saul. The last harvest of the year was near completion. At dawn the women and the children went into the olive orchards. Young boys climbed the trees to shake down the last, reluctant fruit. Women beat the lower limbs with sticks. The crescent moon announced the coming of Bul, the eighth month, which fell between the early and the later rains.

With the new moon a traveler came to the small village hidden in the hills. He came warily, for his clothing marked him as one who dwelt on the plains of Canaan. He came armed with a short sword of iron hanging from his belt.

Sarah, daughter of the widow Sapha, was the first to see him as he skirted around the olive orchard on a slope below the town. He was well built and taller than some. Over his tunic he wore an open vest of ox hide. His arms were bare from the shoulders down, and Sarah noted with interest that his arms were strong, impressively developed. His wavy dark hair glistened blue-black in the sun.

It was the traveler's face that caught and held Sarah's attention. It was a visage of such masculine beauty that she felt soft and melty inside. It was a face to inspire confidence in a girl, a face so pleasant and open that she forgot that its owner was a stranger. She made no attempt to conceal herself as the newcomer approached.

His eyes were merry, his smile engaging. When he

spoke, his voice was warm. "I greet you, lady of Gibeah."

Sarah let her eyes fall. She felt her cheeks getting warm as she flushed in confusion. She answered his smile, for he had called her lady. There was no amusement in his eyes, so he had been sincere in addressing her as an adult. She had observed her fifteenth birthday on the day of the Feast of Trumpets. During the year leading up to her birthday, she had ripened with the olives, her body filling out, her breasts becoming more rounded. A cascade of ebony hair covered her shoulders. Her lips were full, soft, and womanly. The sparkle in her brown eyes matched the congeniality in the eyes of the stranger.

"I seek Saul, son of Kish," the stranger said.

"I know no man of that name," Sarah said, for it was well-known that the Philistines had a price on Saul's head.

"I have come far."

He was *comely.* And, she realized as she examined him shamelessly, he was quite young, not much older than she. His smile breached all of her defenses.

"How is it you speak our tongue so well and yet you wear the clothing of a Canaanite?" she asked.

"Ah," he said, "because, as it happens, what you call your tongue is the language of my mother. As for the clothes, they are the only ones I own." He smiled and added, "My lady."

Trusting her instincts, she told the stranger how to find Saul. Her eyes followed him as he walked past. His back was straight, his stride proud and powerful. She felt weak, but her breast was filled with wonder. She drew in four long, shuddering breaths, then ran through the orchard, taking the short way to the village.

"A stranger comes," she told Saul's sentry on guard at the place where the pathway to the village narrowed.

"Go to your mother, my little one," the sentry said.

"I am not your little one," Sarah said.

She ran up the path and concealed herself behind a bush to wait until the stranger came striding up the hill, to be halted by the sentry. She could not hear what the two men were saying, but neither could she tear herself away. Only after the stranger had handed over his sword and walked ahead of the soldier up the pathway did she run into the village. Behind her she heard the sentry sound a warning on his ram's horn.

Armed men with suspicious faces had awaited his arrival and now surrounded him. These were fighting men, Eri realized, not cowed shepherds or farmers.

"I am Eri, son of Urnan, the smith of Shiloh," he said in a strong, confident voice.

"Shiloh has been ruins since shortly after the battle at Ebenezer," a man said, a blade pointed at Eri's heart.

"This I know," Eri said. "I was there when Galar of Ashdod made it so."

"He is a spy, sent by the Philistines," someone said.

Eri looked around. There were too many able-bodied men for the size of this village. The girl had not lied; Saul must be there. In fact, Eri had a feeling that Saul was quite near. He lifted his face, cupped his hands to his mouth, and bellowed, "Saul! Saul of Gibeah!"

A soldier lifted his hand to strike, but Eri seized his wrist in a grip of iron.

"I have come in friendship," Eri said, a cold note of warning in his voice.

"Who calls Saul?" a deep voice boomed.

"One who helped him bring home to Israel the Ark of the Covenant and golden emerods," Eri bellowed.

Moments later Saul came bounding down from a hut farther up the hill. "Eri, is it you?"

"It is I," Eri said, opening his arms as Saul pushed his way through the encircling men.

"God be praised," Saul whispered as he engulfed his friend in his powerful arms and lifted Eri from his feet. His great chest vibrated with pleased laughter.

Eri threw his head back and howled. Saul set him down, then held him at arm's length and examined Eri's face closely.

"How do I look?" Eri asked.

"I see a youth hardened by experience. I see a man in body and attitude if not in years."

Eri flushed with pleasure at his friend's words.

"You are a man now."

"Yes," Eri said.

Saul felt his friend's massive, hard biceps. "These are the arms of a man who knows the smell and heat of the forge."

Eri nodded.

Saul expressed his happiness in soaring laughter.

"They fed you well in Ekron."

"It doesn't look as if you have suffered deprivation," Eri said with a fond grin.

"Saul, he carried this," a man said, handing over Eri's sword.

Saul held the sword, hefted it, checked its balance. "A fine weapon," he said to Eri. "A Philistine weapon."

"Uh, no . . ." Eri said, enjoying himself hugely.

Saul raised an eyebrow. "Not Philistine?"

"Mine," Eri said. "I learned my lessons well at the side of the smith of Ekron."

"By the name of Yahweh," Saul whispered, running his thumb along the razor-sharp edge of the sword. "If we had two hundred blades like this, three hundred—"

Eri laughed. "I can't promise you that many today, but that's why I have come."

Saul's eyes hardened, glinted like those of a hunting raptor. "I thank you." His voice was low and serious. "We must talk, my friend."

He slung his arm affectionately around Eri's shoulders and led him toward his hut. "You can make swords like this?" Saul asked, making the iron blade whistle through the air.

"It will take time," Eri said. "I will need men to build the furnaces. We will have to find new sources for the ore of the gray metal, and we will have to hide our works well from the Philistines."

"The Philistines are blind pigs," Saul said.

"But even a blind pig finds a tuber now and then," Eri said.

A maidservant bowed before them at the entrance to Saul's shelter. "Wine and meat," Saul said, "for my friend who was lost but is now found." He pounded Eri on the back as he followed his guest inside.

Eri said, "Gently, gently. There are breakable bones there."

"We will build the things you need in the fastness of the mountains," Saul said. "And after you have equipped my army with these—"

"It may take a day or two," Eri said.

Saul joined him in laughter. The servant returned with a jug of new wine and a plate of cold meat. There was much to be told, first by Eri and then, under questioning, by the less glib Saul. It was worse in the mountains than Eri had suspected. No place was safe from Philistine incursion. Saul's village was one of the few that had escaped being looted.

"They are uneasy in their victory," Saul said. "The Philistines still force us to come to them merely to sharpen our field tools."

"I wonder if a certain Hebrew giant whom they call the Lion of the Mountains has anything to do with that?" Eri asked wryly.

Saul lifted his head and clasped his hands in a prayerful attitude. "Pray God that it is so." His eyes were burning when he looked back at Eri. "God spoke to me when I was a boy but not since then, no matter how I have prayed for it." He shrugged. "I can only hope that he is on my side and directs my actions and my words."

When Saul fell into morose silence, Eri filled the void. "Let me tell you what I'll need. First, a secure place. And while we're seeking this place it might be advisable to start men gathering ore. Three or four good stonemasons. Two men who know how to work with clay. A supply of wood for making charcoal. Limestone for the furnace."

"It will be done," Saul said. He picked up the serving tray. "More meat?"

Eri raised a hand, shook his head.

"You're tired," Saul said with sudden concern. "You've traveled far today."

"That I admit," Eri said.

"My home is yours," Saul said, spreading his hands and grinning. "It's not as grand as the home you rejected in Ashdod, but you won't have to put up with a Philistine sodomite here."

Eri made a face. "I hadn't thought of my onetime master in a long time," he said. "Which bed is yours, Lion of the Mountains?"

"Take whichever pleases you," Saul said.

Eri sat down on a hard couch and pushed aside woolen coverings, for it was quite warm in the hut.

"Sleep well," Saul said, moving toward the door.

"By the way," Eri said.

Saul turned.

"I was first greeted by a girl. Fourteen or fifteen, I'd guess. Slim, but—" He made rounded motions in front of his chest. "Long hair, lively eyes, a bit sassy."

"Ah," Saul said with a smile.

"I was just curious," Eri said as he lowered his head to the couch. "It was just that she was so—so—"

"I think you have encountered Sarah, daughter of Sapha. You are not the first to notice that she has blossomed."

"Just curious," Eri said, turning his face away guiltily.

"Yes, of course," Saul said. "And to answer the question you have not asked, she is not betrothed. Her mother, a widow, recently married a fellow named Raphu, who never has a good word to say about any suitors." He snorted. "Come to think of it, I've never heard him say anything good about anything. You know the kind. But if Sarah were in my eyes as she is in yours, I would not let that deter me."

"I said I was just curious," Eri said with some irritation. He felt a little silly, after his infatuation with Meda, to be attracted so immediately and strongly toward another pretty face and shapely body. Well, as the weeks passed, he would know if his interest was genuine or merely a way to get Meda out of his thoughts. In the meantime, he had more than enough to keep him busy.

CHAPTER NINETEEN

The ore came from the south in woven baskets balanced on each side of patient donkeys. The workings of the mine were well hidden. The ore carriers moved at night until they were deep into the desolation of the Wilderness of Judah near the Salt Sea. There they made their way slowly through the sunbaked rocks and sands of the desert to a hidden wadi from which rose the smoke of Eri's furnaces and forges.

The construction had begun in the eighth month, only days after Eri's return to Israel. Now, in the season of highest temperatures, the smell of glowing charcoal filled the deep canyon. Men stripped to loincloths gasped with the heat, wiped sweat from their dripping foreheads. Eri, too, wore only a loincloth. His black, wavy hair had grown long, and he had gathered it with a leather thong at the nape of his neck.

There were two furnaces. They sat in the open, ex-

posed to the burning midday sun. Flat roofs of brush
had been built over the six forges to provide shade, but
little relief was felt from that effort. The shelters for the
workmen—and for Eri—were also nothing more than
brush arbors.

Saul had overtaken a small donkey train carrying
ore not far from the wadi and had accompanied it. He
yelled out a greeting to Eri as he rounded a curve in the
canyon. His friend seemed to shimmer in the waves of
heat. Eri waved but could not take time from his work
to greet his friend. Saul came near.

"You have arrived at a good time," Eri said.

The heat was a presence, a thickness, a physical
thing that seemed to Saul to burn the sweetness out of
the air that he sucked into his lungs in deep, laboring
breaths. Heat from the sun . . . heat from the stone
and clay furnaces . . . heat from the forges . . . but
there was something else in the air—an air of expectation, an excitement. Now, at last, the Hebrews were nar-
rowing the odds and had a serious possibility of
throwing off the hated Philistine oppression. And the
need was dire; how much longer would he be able to
hide from Galar? How long before one of his own
would betray him under pain of torture?

A workman inserted a ram's-horn nozzle into an
opening in one of the furnaces. The muscles of his bare
back bunched and gathered as he pumped the leather
bellows to fertilize the melting ore inside the furnace
with forced air. Not for the first time the furnace reminded Saul of a female, shaped in stone to the roundness of the stomach of a woman about to give birth. The
orifice of the birth canal was low, a slit between open
thighs made of heat-hardened clay. The vaginalike entrance was plugged with clay. The nozzle of the bellows
was the male organ. The workmen who pumped the
bellows were the midwives in attendance.

Saul felt uneasy. There was something pagan about
the ritual performed by the workmen in this, the last
stage before birth, something vaguely orgiastic in the
obvious comparison to pudenda, phallus, birth.

Eri donned a thick leather apron that reached below his knees. He bent before the furnace as if in worship, and once more Saul felt vaguely unclean, as he'd felt when he had pretended to be a worshiper of Dagon in the Philistine cities. As if to heighten Saul's uneasiness, Eri was chanting in an unfamiliar language.

Eri was singing the song of the armorer—a song he'd learned at his father's side, that Urnan's father had learned from his father. Centuries before, Belsunu of Babylon had once sung the same words as he worked the metals to blend into bronze in his furnace and his forge. It was a song of the Children of the Lion, as old as the world. The words would have been known to those who built the walls and the great ziggurat at old Ur.

Now Eri pulled the last clay plug. Men stood in silence, some with mouths open. Breathing was difficult while standing in the furnace-hot air. With an audible sizzle the birth began. White-hot, in a molten stream of fire, the metal ran into sand molds and began almost immediately to blacken.

The men felt the heat of the liquid metal on their skin, felt the pride of accomplishment. Now the new metal had to be purged and alloyed with bronze to make it less brittle but still as hard as the iron that was its heart.

In the days that followed Saul became inured to the oppressive heat, for hammers rang through the wadi as Eri's apprentices began to work the new metal. Eri's consummate skill became evident as he lifted his hammer and made the ironstone anvil ring, as a blade took shape under his pounding. At his side a helper sweated profusely as he pumped the bellows that produced white heat in the firebox to bring the metal to a workable texture.

The newly shaped blade sizzled and made steam as Eri plunged it into water. He personally did the filing and polishing with his apprentices gathered round, listening with rapt attention to his explanations of every movement.

Saul held the finished sword in his hand. He, too, had stripped to his loincloth. He pointed the gleaming, sharp point of the weapon toward the sky and said in a low voice, "Lord God, we thank you for giving the armorer's skill to this, our brother, and we ask you to bless his efforts. God of Abraham, give strength to our arms when we wield this weapon against our enemies who defy the will of Yahweh, who deny that this land was given to us by the one God."

Saul stayed in the wilderness until, under Eri's direction, the smiths had turned out swords numbering three score. With the weapons packed securely on donkeys, he told Eri good-bye and was gone. The armory workers had cheered Saul as he departed, for they knew that the keen edges of the weapons they had fashioned would soon taste the blood of the enemy who had destroyed holy Shiloh, the enemy who held captive most of the land that God had given to His people.

Now, for Eri, came a lonely time of many months. He had trained his helpers well so that he no longer had to don the leather apron to tend the furnaces. The streams of fiery metal issued from the birth canals with regularity. From dawn to dark the hammers rang at the anvils. Eri spent his time fashioning swords. Others made iron tips for arrows and long, graceful points for spears. Often he wondered where Saul was and why his friend no longer visited the armory. Eri's feelings were hurt that he was accomplishing such important work and yet was forgotten by his closest friend.

But the nights were even more tormenting than the days. In the darkness, when the land gave up its heat and mantles were needed to guard against the coolness, Eri thought of a smiling young girl with full, red lips and mischievous brown eyes. Thinking of Sarah, dreaming of her, wondering—no, agonizing—if some suitor had been accepted by Raphu to take the girl to his hearth, Eri decided that the work at the armory could continue without his presence. He had more pressing, more personal concerns on his mind, all of which centered around the smiling girl whose eyes had no hesitancy in meeting his.

He had marked his seventeenth birthday on a day

that he finished a sword that he had designed especially for a man of great strength and size, a weapon for his friend Saul. Its blade was of such perfect balance and heft, it could come to life only in the hands of the greatest of warriors. He polished and honed it to perfection, oiled it well, then slid it into a hand-sewn, decorated sheath. He did not pack it with the other weapons being readied for shipment to the north. When the weapons pack train left the secret wadi of the armory, the sword was at Eri's waist, along with his own shorter weapon.

The journey to Saul's village seemed longer in the return. The laden donkeys moved too slowly for Eri's restlessness. He rode ahead, reached the village just as twilight was falling. To his surprise there were no sentries. He rode into the streets of the town before he saw anyone, and then it was an old man who looked at him fearfully and was poised to flee before Eri identified himself.

"It is you, the friend of Saul," the old man said as he edged closer.

"Where is the Lion of the Mountains?" Eri asked.

The old man lifted his hands at his side. "Where there are Philistines, there is Saul."

"And where are the guards to warn of an attack on the village?" Eri wanted to know.

"Our young warriors are keeping the Philistine occupied," the old man said. "There is no longer any need to stand guard."

Eri was doubtful, but he said nothing. He led his ass to Saul's house. A boy came to tend the animal. Eri carried the large new sword inside, placed it on Saul's bed. It had been a long day. He had not eaten since having a meal at midday, but he was more tired than hungry. He cleaned his face and hands, using the water in a clay pan, and was lying on his bed with his eyes closed when he heard his name. He sat up because he had never heard the name sound so beautiful.

She stood in the doorway. She wore a rich, blue linen tunic topped with a colorfully embroidered mantle. Her hair was gathered into a greatness atop her head and on her nape, exposing the long and graceful lines of her neck.

"I have brought food for you, traveler," she said shyly.

"How kind of you, lady."

Flushed with pleasure, she moved to kneel before him, presenting a tray on which were a pitcher of milk, a bowl of a spicy stew, ripe figs, a large hunk of bread.

"Saul has told us of your work," she whispered. "We can do nothing less than honor one who serves our people so well."

"That's a very nice speech," Eri said.

She flushed again and then giggled. "To tell the truth, I spent a long time forming it in my mind before I came here."

"Nicer still, then, to know that you gave it so much thought." He drank from the pitcher. The goat's milk was rich and warm. He put the tray on the couch beside him and she stood, bowing as she backed away.

"Don't bow your head to me," he said.

"I am honored to do so."

"Never to me," he said with feeling.

She looked at him, her eyes going wide.

"In the wilderness, as I worked, I thought many times of this moment," he said. He laughed. "Unlike you, who formed a nice speech, I could think of nothing that I dared say to you."

She lowered her eyes.

"Your beauty would inspire pretty words in one of wit," he said. "I can only think—"

"What little you have said," she whispered, "pleases me more than if oceans of words had come from one much more glib."

"What?" he asked, pleased by her compliment.

"You said that you consider me beautiful," she said.

"In the name of God, I do. I surely do. You are—"

She waited expectantly.

"—beautiful," he finished lamely.

"I am fulfilled," she said, and turned toward the door.

"Please don't go."

"I must."

"I want to see you, to talk with you."

"Yes," she said.

"Tomorrow?"

"At midmorning. East of the town, on the ridge, there is a cave. The entrance to it is hidden by a cedar. You'll recognize the spot by a tall pillar of rock that is shaped somewhat like a woman."

Eri finished off the stew and figs for breakfast and was out and about shortly after sunrise. It was evident that all of the able-bodied men were with Saul. The old ones were tending the fields and the orchards. Young boys played at war, whooping with great enthusiasm.

Long before the appointed time Eri walked down the trail to the olive orchards. The trees were heavy with immature fruit. The orchard was deserted. He sat with his back against a gnarled trunk and listened to the sounds from the village above, all the while dreaming dreams. There had been young Canaanite girls in Ekron who were eager to experiment with the mysteries of life, but never had he seen anything nearing the perfection that was represented by Sarah.

He looked up at the sun. It was only an hour above the eastern horizon, but he could wait no longer. He left the orchard and climbed the hill to the east of the village. He began to feel uneasy when he could not locate the spot that had been described to him, but at last he saw the tall column of stone. True to Sarah's description, the rock took on the shape of a mature woman, and a stir of youthful passion warmed him. He found the cedar hiding the entrance to the cave, and because there was still time, he explored.

The cave had been fitted out as a retreat, a hiding place. There were sealed amphorae that, he guessed, contained water and, perhaps, preserved foods. On a ledge were stacks of bed coverings. It was not unusual, especially in times of trouble, for a family to have such a hideaway.

Sarah came early. She didn't see Eri at first. He sat

in the shade of the cedar tree and was silent. His heart and eyes filled with her. She wore the same linen tunic and embroidered mantle. Her shapely ankles were revealed. Her feet were slender and elegant in her decorated sandals. When she saw him she stopped. He rose and went to her, took both her hands in his. A thrill went through his body. She shivered. Her reaction told him that she, too, had been jolted by their first touch.

Her brown eyes held his. Her lips were parted in surprise. He kissed them. She gasped and tried to pull away, but her confusion lasted only for a moment. She stepped forward, and he felt her firm thighs against his, felt her breasts being compacted as his arms went around her and pulled her to his chest. There was no sense of time left to them. Neither of them would ever be able to guess how long they remained thus, mouth to mouth, body to body, heart to heart. It was only a long moment, but it was eternity, and when he lifted his mouth from hers—having difficulty breathing—his words were spontaneous.

"I have never loved till now," he said. "I have dreamed, and I have speculated. But I could not imagine the glory of you in my arms."

"Nor could I know the fullness of it," she whispered, giving him her lips in quick, soft, pecking kisses.

"You are mine," he said.

"I am yours."

"And I yours," he said. "Forever."

He held her at arm's length. "Is falling in love really this simple?"

She laughed. The sound was sweeter than the tinkle of silver bells. "Well, you will have to speak to my family."

He winced. "What am I to say?"

"You will simply ask Raphu for my hand in marriage."

"And what will he say?"

Her smile faded for a moment, then returned. "I will not allow him to say anything other than yes."

"We will take time to think about what I must say

to him," he said, thinking of Saul's assessment of the man.

She kissed him fiercely. "Are you sure you want to wait?"

He took her hand and lifted it close to his face so that he could examine it, memorizing each bend of knuckle, each line of crease in her soft palm. She stood there, smiling at him, her even, white teeth gleaming with the moisture of her mouth. He touched her arm, bare under the short sleeve of her tunic. It was warm. Tiny hairs of butterfly softness were almost invisible.

"It's all right," she said when his hand stopped as it closed over her upper arm to feel heat and a hint of muscle hardness. "It's all right."

He was shivering as if from a chill. She took his hand and placed it on her breast, and through the linen of her garment he felt the bulge of a nipple, the firm curve of citrus-sized roundness.

"Do you like touching me?" she whispered.

He could only nod as he cupped her other breast with his left hand. She moved closer and pressed against him and lifted her head, giving him her full, deliciously wet mouth. His arms were around her, and after a long, long time, a time during which she began to tremble as he was trembling, he let his hands fall to her buttocks to feel the luscious curves there.

She pulled away, leaving him wanting to cry out, "No, no."

"I must go."

He moaned in frustration. His need for her was the greatest and most wonderful emotion he had ever known. But the thought of standing before her family was daunting.

"Will you wait while others state their suit?" Sarah asked.

Eri's hand went to his sword. The thought of another man desiring his Sarah, touching her, speaking for her hand, was maddening.

"When?" he asked.

"Now," she whispered, giving him another series of swift, incredibly soft, small kisses.

* * *

Sapha's welfare, and that of her only daughter, had become the responsibility of her brother-in-law, one of the richest men in the land of Benjamin. Raphu's home and gardens were surrounded by an extensive wall, a statement in stone of the man's worth, for lesser men's gardens were protected only by thorn hedges. Watchtowers marked the corners of Raphu's property, manned by guards to drive away animals or people who would trespass or take fruit without permission. Inside the wall, Raphu's exalted financial status was in evidence by plantings of purely decorative flowers and aromatic shrubs, in addition to the utile olive, walnut, and fig trees. Near the rear of the large house was a vegetable garden with prolific cucumber vines and beds of onions and garlic, and beyond that the vineyard with vines heavy with immature grapes.

Raphu was a man in his middle years. His bushy black beard was silvering. He wore the rich man's fabric, linen, and the sleeves of his outer garment sported embroideries of gold. He was heavy of body and stern of eye. Sarah's mother, Sapha, told Eri by her appearance what his own love would look like as a mature woman, and he was not displeased, for Sapha had a full-bodied beauty.

He would never be able to remember what he said, for his tongue was dry, his brain fevered, and the words came out in a rush. He would always remember what Raphu said.

"Young man," the rich man intoned in a voice made heavy by many jugs of wine over the years, "while we are, of course, grateful to you for your contribution toward the armed strength of our people, what you ask is impossible. The daughter of Raphu cannot marry a mere craftsman."

The words came so swiftly, so harshly, that neither Eri nor Sarah credited their ears at first. It was Sarah who recovered most quickly.

"I am not your daughter," she said. "Mother, hear me."

"You are the daughter of Raphu by law," Sapha

said. "To dispute his wisdom would be to show ingratitude for all he has done for us."

"I will marry Eri," Sarah said.

"Go to your room," Raphu said harshly.

The hair stood up on the back of Eri's neck to hear the older man speak so to Sarah, and his hand went to the hilt of his sword.

"Would you violate hospitality and draw arms in my house?" Raphu demanded.

"No, that I would not do," Eri said, and his hand fell to his side.

"Leave us," Raphu said to Sarah.

"Eri—" She held out her arms to him, and it was all he could do not to go to her.

"Please, Sarah," Sapha said firmly.

"Yes," Sarah said, "I will obey you now. This does not change my determination."

"I'm sorry," Sapha said to Eri.

"I love your daughter very much," Eri said, surprising himself by being able to speak so calmly.

"Love," Raphu said, "is not something that springs forth like water from a rock struck by the staff of Moses, or like wildfire. Love is the product of wise planning and reason. First one considers the propriety of the match, and then love grows."

"Is money the only measurement of worth?" Eri asked.

Raphu drew himself up. "The sons of the leading citizens of the land of Benjamin pay suit to my daughter."

"And what, sir, do the leading citizens of Benjamin do to remove the Philistine yoke from your people?" Eri demanded.

"Since you mention it, young man," Raphu said, "aside from your status, there is another reason why a match between my daughter and you would be impossible. The Philistines have shown themselves to be reasonable people, interested not solely in conquest but in trade. Wise people have accepted this. It is men like you and your friend, young Saul, who are perpetuating the bloodshed and forcing the Philistines to be restrictive in their rule. I warn you, you are headed for a fall, all of you. You cannot hope to stand against the might of the Philistine army, and even if you were acceptable otherwise, I would not want my daughter to be made a widow at a young age."

Eri held his anger and his disappointment until he was out of Raphu's house. He kicked a tree so hard that it hurt his foot, and he was hopping around, moaning, when he heard something fall to the gravel walkway near him. It was a golden ring. He looked up. Sarah was at her window.

"Wear that in remembrance of me," she said. "And come for me by night."

He put the ring on his small finger, but it went only as far as his second knuckle. He held it in his hand and waved to her.

"Give them some time to forget," she called, "and then come for me."

Eri nodded, waved once more. What she asked was difficult. To steal away a daughter without parental permission was a serious offense in Israel. Moreover, he had to admit that Raphu was right in saying that he was in poor financial condition. He had no home of his own, no place to take a bride.

His evening meal was provided by a woman whose husband was with Saul's army. He expressed his appreciation for her hospitality.

"Because of you my Amos is armed now with a blade that is the equal of any Philistine iron," the woman said. "You have no need to thank me."

He went to his bed in Saul's hut early. It was a long time before he could sleep. Respite from his misery came only when he, after much agonizing, told himself that he could not bring disgrace down on Sarah by stealing her. He was determined to have her, but he would have her with honor and in the tradition of the Hebrews. In the meantime, he would go back to the wilderness and provide more weapons to throw off the yoke of the Philistines.

He thought of Raphu's portrayal of them as attractive trading partners, and visions of his mother's death and father's enslavement flashed across the dark room. *Reasonable people,* he thought, his anger growing. It was not a mystery why a man like Raphu would consider them as such. He rolled over, pulled the blanket over his head, and calmed down enough finally to fall asleep.

CHAPTER TWENTY

Eri awoke with the haunting feeling that someone was in the hut with him. He sat up so quickly that he felt momentarily dizzy. The room was empty. Morning sunlight streamed in through the open window. Dust motes danced in the brilliance. He was not yet fully alert, but he had an awareness that something had changed. He looked around the room twice before he realized that Saul's bed had been slept in and that the sword he had fashioned especially for his friend was gone.

At that moment he heard a joyful shout from outside the hut. He quickly pulled on his clothing and opened the door to a day that God had made—a clean and wonderful morning of fresh, nose-filling aromas and a kind sun.

Outside, Saul was standing facing away from the hut, holding the sword pointing toward the heavens. His head was thrown back, and his black beard glistened with blue highlights in the sunshine. Eri paused in the doorway while his friend let out a whoop and killed the air with a mighty swing of the blade. His momentum turned him toward the hut. With the tip of the long sword pointed at Eri, he poised on the balls of his feet.

"*Here* is a blade!" he shouted. "Here is a weapon fit for a *king*! Am I to think that it is *mine*?"

"How is the balance?" Eri asked, battling to keep the pride and happiness from his voice.

Saul made the blade sing in the air with a series of slashes and thrusts. "Balance?" he asked, incredulous. "Never has a weapon been better crafted, my friend. Never."

Eri grinned, then made a rueful scowl. "Well, I had hoped that you might *like* it."

Saul strode to put his left arm around Eri's shoulder. "Actually," he said, "I might be able to use it. A little weight taken off the tip—"

"Take file to that blade and I'll use it on you, you big—"

Saul laughed and clapped Eri on the back with enough force to clear his lungs of the residual of sleep. "So, what inspired you to crawl out of that hellish hole of unholy heat?" He looked at Eri knowingly. "Could it have been a certain young woman of the village?"

Eri shifted uneasily and said nothing.

It was evident to Saul that something was wrong. "Do I detect signs of rejected love?"

Eri frowned. "The lady's protector thinks that she is above marrying a common craftsman."

Saul's face darkened, and his voice was low thunder. "Why, that hypocritical old scoundrel. After all you've done for our people? Well, I'm not surprised. I'll have a talk with Raphu."

"No," Eri said quickly. "No, it's better this way."

Saul eyed his friend closely, then shrugged. "I'm sure you're right, old friend. We have things to do, you and I."

Eri nodded. He was ready—ready for something, anything, to get him out of the village and away from his disappointment and anger.

"Things are going smoothly at the armory?" Saul asked.

"Production will not slow in my absence. The men I have trained are good craftsmen and hard workers."

"Good, good. It's time you and I had a bit of fun together, just like the old days, eh? You'll need a water flask and a warm blanket for sleeping in the open. We'll leave as soon as you and the others are ready."

By nightfall they were looking down on the Philistine plain. Saul's force consisted of just over twoscore men. They had no horses, but each man was armed with sword and spear, a bow and a supply of arrows. A quick inspection had pleased Eri. All the weapons were of iron and from his forges. It was good, solid work. The quality was uniform even in the small, barbed arrowheads.

"Tonight the lion feeds among the farms of the Philistines," Saul predicted, and he smiled like a predator.

The sun was setting. From far away, down on the plain, came the sound of a dog barking. Across a green width of cultivation sat a Philistine blockhouse with strong wooden palisades.

Saul snorted. "They think they're safe behind those walls."

"That's a strong position," Eri said. "Just how are we going to penetrate it?"

"Have faith," Saul said. "Did not God bring down the walls of Jericho for Joshua with nothing more than a blast of trumpets?"

"I'm glad to know that God is yours to command," Eri said.

"Hush," Saul warned. "It does not become you to flirt with blasphemy." He gestured to his men to get ready.

The raiders descended to the plain with first darkness and moved like the shadows of death across the fields, past the huts of Canaanite farmers and the more substantial establishments of the Philistine masters.

"They will have finished their evening meal," Saul said, explaining his intentions to Eri. "Now they'll be dulling their senses with beer. We'll give them just a while yet."

Half of the Hebrew force, in position in front of the gate, was concealed at the edge of a field of grain. The others were waiting in an irrigation canal, standing knee-deep in water. Saul himself gave the prearranged signal, a soft hoot on a ram's horn, and the house nearest the Philistine blockhouse blossomed into flames fed by oil.

Women screamed. A sentinel atop the palisade shouted an alert. Sounds of confusion erupted from inside the enclosure before the gate was thrown wide and a disorganized group of Philistine soldiers rushed out to run toward the blazing house.

The archers waited until all of the Philistines were in the open before sending their buzzing, stinging missiles of death to strike with deadly accuracy. Even as men fell, some crying out in surprise and agony, Saul bellowed his orders, and with Eri at his side, the half of his force that had been concealed in the irrigation ditch rushed the gate.

Saul was ever at the forefront, leading, inspiring, guiding his men forward. The Hebrews swarmed into the compound and met half-dressed Philistines rushing out of their barracks. The tall figure of Saul was everywhere, the oversized sword thrusting, slicing, hacking.

The fight was over so quickly that Eri was stunned. His own sword was red, having tasted blood. He leaned against the outer wall and watched as Saul's men put the torch to the structures within the compound. Saul found him there. The young commander sank to the ground, his back against the wall. His men continued to work silently. The only sounds were the leap and crackle of the growing flames.

"How many?" Eri asked.

Saul's voice sounded weary. "Fifty, a hundred. Who can tell?"

In the red glow of the fires Eri could see that Saul's tunic was wet with blood. Concerned, he knelt beside his friend and gingerly felt Saul's chest and shoulder. "Are you wounded?"

"The blood is not mine," Saul said.

A man trotted across the open compound and gave Saul a salute. "It is done. No man lives."

Saul got to his feet with an effort. "They won't see these fires in Ashdod, Gath, or Gaza, but word of them will be heard there." He wiped his new sword on his bloody tunic, then sheathed it. "Thank you, Eri. It's a fine weapon. Come then, my lion cubs. Our work has begun, but there is much more to be done."

All the people of the plain were enemies of Israel. Saul's men took as much pleasure in the destruction of Canaanite homes as in the burning of the estates of the Philistines. Before the sun tinted the eastern sky, a huge semicircle of fire ran from the destroyed Philistine guardpost through the lushest part of the plain. Now was the time to retreat to a safe place and rest.

By forced march, the Hebrews put space and mountainous terrain between them and any possible Philistine pursuit. It was late in the afternoon before they reached a prearranged spot to meet allies. It was a remote glen with a hidden entrance, which opened onto a small pool of water on rock. A spring trickled from the stone face of a cliff.

"Drink," Saul ordered his men. "Fill your flasks."

Young boys were waiting there with sheep to be slaughtered. Soon cooking fires were sending up their tantalizing smells, but instead of eating, the exhausted fighters slept. They lay motionless, in the dreamless sleep of the bone weary, where they had fallen. . . .

Eri woke with the scent of cooking meat making his mouth water. Beside him Saul snored mightily. A few men were already eating. The young lads who had prepared the meal sliced off a large portion of meat for Eri. It was so hot that he had to toss it back and forth between his hands as he carried it back to the spot where Saul was still sleeping.

He drew his sword and impaled the meat, giving ease to his pained fingers. Saul stirred with a groan as Eri sat beside him.

"I've more than enough for two," Eri said, his back against the solid rock of the cliff.

Saul sat up, rubbing his eyes, then sliced off a strip of steaming meat with his dagger. "If you want your share, eat fast," he warned, stuffing it into his mouth.

Eri went back to the fires for a whole leg of lamb. For a while there was no talking. After the long, bloody night and the forced march without food to the glen, eating was a very serious matter. When there was nothing left of the leg but bone, Saul cracked it with a rock and picked out the marrow with his dagger. Only then did he lean back and sigh in contentment.

"So, my friend," Saul asked, "how does it suit you being a fighter for the freedom of Israel?"

"I am reminded that I am first of all a craftsman," he said wryly.

"An armorer who knows how to use the weapons he makes," Saul said. "I watched you last night. I saw not a maker of swords but a wielder of the blade."

For a moment Eri relived the brief minutes inside the Philistine stockade. One face in particular came back to haunt him—a boy, no older than he . . . a white-faced, frightened boy running out of the barracks, weapon in hand, to impale himself by his own force on Eri's sword. Even as Eri withdrew the blade, he saw the light go out in the boy's eyes.

"Once, when there were two of them against you, I thought I was going to have to come to your rescue," Saul admitted. "You learned more than the fashioning of arms in Ekron, my friend."

Eri felt that he owed Saul an explanation. "My father, who bore the paw mark of the lion, delighted in designing pretty things of gold and silver. He considered making weapons his secondary occupation. He carried a sword, but he never practiced the art of its use." Eri was surprised by the bitterness that suddenly filled his voice. "When he charged half a dozen Philistine soldiers to protect my mother, he was helpless against them. I vowed then that given the chance, I would learn the use of the weapons of war and death."

"What were you doing while your father was losing the fight?" Saul asked gently.

"Hanging like an ornament on the door of his forge." Eri snorted, and his face flamed red. "I was no help. I swore I would never be put into a position of being inferior in knowledge and skill to an enemy."

Saul was silent for a time. "You have reason to hate them," he said. "What happened to your mother?"

"She died. My father was led away into slavery. I do not let a night go by without praying to God that one day I will see them again, those who killed my mother, that I will have the chance to face them, one by one, with nothing but cold iron between us."

"You would remember their faces?"

"I will never forget," Eri said. "And the names of the officers. The man in command was Galar of Ashdod."

"In God's name," Saul said, "you never told me that."

"And the man who delivered the killing sword thrust to my mother was Jobal, one of Galar's lieutenants."

"Perhaps God will be kind and deliver them to you," Saul said. "In the meantime, we march with the sun."

"I won't be going with you," Eri said.

Saul looked at him questioningly.

"I came to Gibeah for one reason," Eri said. "I had convinced myself that my feelings for Sarah were more important than my work. They aren't; I will return to the furnaces."

Saul nodded. "I repeat my offer to speak with Raphu on your behalf. . . ."

Eri shook his head sadly. "Thank you, but what's done is done. What kind of life could I offer her at the forges, anyway? I had no right to speak for her hand."

Saul said nothing.

"And you?" Eri asked.

"We strike where the Philistine least expects it," Saul said. "He knows by the blood and the ashes that we have been near Gezer. Tomorrow we march north, and when we strike next, it will be on the Plain of Sharon, perhaps near Azor. We have heard that a new garrison is being constructed in the land of Dan. Perhaps we can discourage the workmen before the job is finished."

"May God go with you."

"And with you," Saul said fervently. He arranged his blanket, then put his head down.

Eri lay on his back. He had hollowed out a place in the sandy soil for his hips. Overhead the sky was ablaze. There was no moon. A flash of light burned its way in an arc and died. A sign, a dying star.

"Did you see that?" Saul asked in a quiet voice.

"Yes."

"What does it mean?"

"I am no soothsayer," Eri said, "but I would guess that it means greatness has returned to Israel in the form of a man who is known to the Philistine as the Lion of the Mountains."

"Ha!" Saul snorted, but he was pleased. He was silent for a time, then said, "Eri, take the girl."

"Huh?" Eri grunted in surprise.

"Do you think she loves you?"

"I know she does."

"Then take her. These are not ordinary times. That old pretender Raphu has no right to deny you the woman you love. You are of more worth to Israel than ten Raphus. Go through Gibeah on your way back to the wilderness. Take Sarah with you. Make her your wife so that you do not sin in the eyes of God, and don't concern yourself with Raphu and the girl's mother."

"Don't think that I have not dreamed of doing just that," Eri confessed. "But do you think she'd be happy in the wadi?"

"I think she'd be happy with you, wherever you live. I want to tell you something in confidence." Saul edged closer. "There is talk among the people of wanting a king. Samuel does not approve; he says that God is our king. But if the tribes' wishes are fulfilled and my military successes against the Philistine continue, I will become—" He paused, as if not daring to say the words.

"The king of Israel?" Eri asked, amazed.

"Yes. As far as taking Sarah, you have both my blessings, which may mean nothing right now, and the backing of my sword, which is of *some* worth."

They parted with the morning, and Eri, with a golden bangle in his pouch, traveled toward Gibeah. Saul had given him the piece of jewelry as a wedding gift for Sarah. "Don't tell her, lest she be squeamish about it, that I took it from a dead Philistine," Saul had said.

Because Eri traveled alone, he had a lot of time to think. His thoughts alternated between flying ahead to the honey-smooth face of Sarah and staying in the mountains behind him with Saul. Eri was tempted to believe that the God of Israel was with the big warrior, for Saul had invented a new type of warfare to harass the Philistines. Poor and subjugated Israel was not strong enough to meet the Philistine in pitched battle, as it had at Ebenezer with such disastrous and long-lasting results. Saul traveled light, with a force small in numbers but great in determination and battle skills. He hit the enemy hard and then fled, melting into the mountains. He had made the interior of the country his own, and he knew every hill, every wadi, every glade in the tribal areas of Dan, Ephraim, and Benjamin.

There was no doubt that Saul was a great commander. But king? There was no way to know. Eri felt a tinge of guilt as he thought of his coming happiness with Sarah, for Saul was older than he, past the age at which young men usually took a wife. By all rights he should have begun his family. In an orderly world, Saul would be preparing to celebrate the Feast of the Tabernacles, the Vintage Festival. He should be at his family home near the village, tending his olive trees. The olive was, to the Hebrew, the symbol of life; its fruit was food, its oil fuel for lamps and an ointment for healing, washing, and anointing. In a world at peace Saul would be preparing to give a fat ox to the priests for sacrifice and feasting. He would be warmed with wine, his appetite sated, happy in the midst of his family. Instead he was looking forward to the possibility of having even more responsibility than he had now.

It was not, however, an orderly world. It was a hard, fierce world overlooked—in Saul's viewpoint—by a vengeful God. That God was—in Eri's opinion—more interested in punishing his people for their transgressions against Him than in protecting them from the evil that men do to one another.

In a moment of contrition, Eri almost prayed to God for forgiveness but instead turned his prayer to the memory of his mother, asking her forgiveness for being so doubtful about God.

He reached the rugged, protective hills surrounding Gibeah too late in the day to finish the journey. He was awakened by the sounds of a Philistine column on the march. He heard the creak of the wheels of supply carts, the jingle of harness, a low, moaning call from an ox.

Eri scurried to a point of vantage. Three hundred armed men, fifty of them mounted, were moving toward Gibeah. His heart leaped when he saw a man in armor bearing the insignia of a Philistine general. He recognized the riding stance of an old enemy. "Galar . . ." he hissed.

He tried to pick out Jobal but failed.

He swallowed panic but allowed urgency to give wings to his feet. He took advantage of his knowledge of the countryside and arrived near the village, approaching it from the fields of Raphu, just as the mounted Philistines thundered into the streets. He heard the screams, the shouts, the whinnying of agitated horses. He ran with all his strength, for the horsemen were making quick work of the old men, children, and women of the village.

The leading element of the cavalry was pounding toward the front gate of Raphu's establishment when he saw a familiar form in the fields behind the house. For a moment he was ready to admit that there was one God, and that God was good. Panting, struggling to pump air into his burning lungs, he ran toward the girl he loved.

The sounds of the running horses as they squeezed by twos and threes through the open gate into the well-tended gardens were loud behind him. A mortal scream erupted from the front of the house. Eri watched as the girl put a hand to her mouth and started to run toward the back gate. Eri intercepted her and seized her around the waist. Her struggles caused them both to fall and roll in the sweet, green shoots of grain. She screamed and fought to dislodge him.

"Sarah, Sarah!" He gasped. "Don't! It's me, Eri."

She recognized him. Her eyes were wide. Her mouth was open.

A shout of surprise came from the house. It was followed by a female scream.

"We must go to them," she said.

"No! It's too late."

He lifted her to her feet, then dragged her toward the hillside leading to the cave that was the family retreat.

"Let me go!" she screamed at him.

She was surprisingly strong. She broke away from him, and with the last of his strength he had to pull her to the ground again to stop her.

"Listen to me," he said forcefully.

"Let me go," she wailed. "Let me go."

He slapped her.

Her eyes went wide. "Eri?" she whispered.

"You can't help them," he said. "Come with me."

He led her at a run to the hillside, then up toward the cave. The sounds of death and destruction came to them from the village and from Raphu's compound. After Eri reached the shadows of the cedar tree concealing the entrance to the cave, he allowed himself a respite and tried to catch his breath. He realized too late that Sarah was witnessing horror. She had turned her head to see Philistine soldiers dragging servants out of the house. Three soldiers were raping a young servingmaid. And as Sarah watched, Raphu and Sapha were shoved from the house into the square at the edge of the garden. A sword flashed, and Raphu's head fell to the ground. His body teetered for long moments before it folded and slumped. The man's voice rang in Eri's memory: *Reasonable people . . . reasonable people . . .*

Sarah heard her mother's scream as a soldier thrust his sword into her stomach. The girl started to run down the hill, and Eri had to move swiftly to stop her.

"Mother . . ." Sarah moaned. "Oh, Mother."

"We can't help them," Eri said.

"Mother!" Sarah repeated wildly, struggling in his arms. With the strength of hysteria she threatened to break away from him.

In his exhausted state, he was desperate. He was determined not to let her run down the hill to share the fate that had been his mother's. He drew back his strong, right arm, clenched his fist, and tapped her— lightly, he thought—on the side of her chin. She collapsed unconscious in his arms, and he carried her into the cave.

He made a bed for her, using the stored woolens, and knelt beside her. Eri knew that he had hit her too hard. After a while the screams from the village and Raphu's house were no longer heard, but still the girl did not awaken.

Eri went to the entrance of the cave and peered carefully around the cedar tree. Here and there in the town the soldiers were still taking their pleasure with women. Galar of Ashdod sat his horse in the garden of Raphu, watching as his men finished off the household servants and started fires. Eri was tempted to go down there and murder the Philistine if he could, but he was afraid to leave Sarah. *Another time,* he vowed.

It was late in the afternoon before horns blew and the Philistine soldiers left off their plundering. They put torches to every house in the village before forming to march back toward the west. This, then, Eri thought, was repayment for the burned Canaanite villages and Philistine garrisons.

Sarah awoke in the middle of the night. He was sitting by her side, holding her hands in his. She screamed and tried to sit up.

"Go back to sleep, my love," he whispered, hating

the thought of the grief his beloved would suffer upon seeing the devastation below them. Again he considered going into the village, this time to bury her parents, to spare her that, at least. But in the end he was still afraid to leave her alone, afraid that she might stumble into a Philistine patrol, and he would lose her, too, forever. . . .

When he awoke it was light in the cave. He was sitting on the ground next to Sarah's bed, his head bent to lie beside her breast. Her eyes were open. She stared at him unblinkingly.

"They're all dead, aren't they?" she asked.

"Yes," he said.

"All dead." She rubbed her chin. There was some swelling and a purple bruise. She flinched in pain.

He felt a surge of guilt. "Does it hurt?"

"It's very sore."

"Do you want some water?" he asked.

"Yes, please."

He handed her a flask.

She drank thirstily before looking up. "I must go to them. They will need tending."

He nodded.

She arranged her tunic, sat up, then stood.

"It may not be safe yet," Eri said.

"The dead cannot be neglected. It is the work of a woman to prepare the dead for their return to the dust."

Eri caught her by the arm. "It is not a good idea to go down there, Sarah."

"But I must," she said with a calmness that surprised him. "To leave them lying there in the dirt would be a sin before God." She took his hand. "Help me, please, Eri."

He knew from past experience that Hebrew women were made of stern stuff. He was proud of the way she was accepting disaster. "First we must eat something."

"Yes," she agreed.

She ate dutifully. There was a moment of awkwardness before Eri realized that she needed to answer the call of nature. He went outside into brilliant sunshine and stood guard while she relieved herself. When she joined him, they went hand in hand down the hill.

As they approached the smoldering ruins of the house, he realized his mistake. The scavengers, winged and otherwise, had already been at the bodies of Raphu, Sapha, and the household servants. Sarah came to an abrupt halt. She made a sound as if she'd been struck in the stomach, and then her face went blank.

"Wait for me in the garden," Eri said. "I will see to them."

Her eyes were fixed, staring at nothing. Her lips were slackly open.

"Sarah, wait for me in the garden," he repeated.

She was stiff to his touch. He turned her, led her back toward the garden. Her lax face did not change expression and she made no protest when he seated her on a bench.

He buried only Raphu and Sapha. There were too many of the others to take the time necessary. And only a stone's throw away scores of dead lay in the village streets. When he went back to the garden, Sarah had not moved, nor had her expression changed.

"It's time to go," he whispered.

He massaged her wrists, patted her on the cheek. She continued to stare into the distance, blinking only occasionally. She was pliant and obedient when he took her arm and lifted her to her feet. He guided her to the street. She didn't seem to notice the bodies of the servants or hear the raucous cries of the carrion birds.

His plan was to travel toward Ramah, the home of Samuel, in the hope that that remote place had been spared the attentions of the Philistines. But first he would need money to provide a place of residence for Sarah and for food. In Saul's ruined hut was a small cache of hidden coins. He dug through ashes to retrieve them.

Leading the silent, staring Sarah, he moved cautiously through a devastated countryside. Galar had spared not even the most remote farm. The silvery shimmer of olive orchards was no more. No building stood. No crop was intact. The stench of death was everywhere in the form not only of people but of dead sheep, goats, and oxen.

He almost walked into a Philistine camp but heard the sounds of male laughter at the last moment and circled around toward Samuel's stronghold. The way was blocked by pillaging bands of Philistines. He put his face to the south. North of Jerusalem he hoped to find bands of Hebrews. Even in this he was disappointed.

The days passed. Sometimes there was food in the form of fruit salvaged from ruined orchards. Once, there was a stray lamb that ran to meet him so gladly that he had to steel himself and as he drew his sword remind himself that it was vital to get some solid food into the silent, withdrawn Sarah.

It was necessary to skirt Jerusalem, for that city was occupied by Philistines. He was traveling through unfamiliar country. Others fleeing the Philistine outrages told him that he might find peace in Bethlehem. He continued toward the south with the silent, dazed Sarah clinging to his hand. The countryside was pleasant and unspoiled. Farmers and shepherds, taking pity on the young man with the damaged woman, fed them.

The days were filled with sunshine and soft breezes. The nights were chill. Eri made camp beside water, warmed himself and Sarah with a fire, and then took her into his own bed to warm her with his body. She was pliant. She snuggled to him against the cold and seemed totally unaware of Eri's roiling passions as he held her slim, soft body in his arms.

On a night when it required all of his honor and all of his respect for Sarah to keep his hands off her rounded breasts and away from her soft, moist, secret womanhood, he looked up at the starred sky and appealed to God, speaking not for her but for himself.

"Yahweh," he whispered, "it is said that you made the earth, that you made man himself. In this, the woman that I love, your work was good and yet—" He paused to swallow his indignation. "Be kind to her, for she is your daughter, and she has seen terrible things. Give her back her senses, God of Abraham. Please, give her back to me."

She was awake when he opened his eyes next morning, and a surge of hope shot through him. She was sitting on the woolens beside him, her hands in her lap. But on her face was the same vacant look. In her eyes was the same blankness.

CHAPTER
TWENTY-ONE

In the Philistine city of Ashdod, a new craftsman had made his name in the street of the metalsmiths. A well-formed and well-spoken man who had arrived in Philistia by sea, he had purchased an established shop from the widow and sons of a man who had been taken by death while at his forge. Because the former owner of the forge had fallen facedown into his firebox to send the smell of burning hair and flesh wafting out into the street, superstitious folk predicted that the newcomer would have nothing but bad luck.

For some months he kept to his work. The wives of small merchants and soldiers discovered that his prices were very reasonable. His fame grew. Rich and powerful women came to his shop to purchase his creations in gold and silver to adorn their ears, arms, ankles, bosoms.

The new smith spoke a variety of languages and

had a smooth way with the wives of the rich who came in their slave-borne chairs to shop for trinkets. The stranger was friendly enough, and quite pleasant, but when questioned, he was stingy with personal information. It was obvious from his limited conversation that he had traveled widely. Certainly he had learned the secrets of the Egyptian goldworkers, and he was more than familiar with the gray metal of the Hittites. He turned out jewelry in the Egyptian manner.

In spite of some subtle and other, more overt invitations, he chose not to avail himself of the company of women. He was cordial with men but did not join them in the inns to consume frothy beer and tell ribald stories in a loud voice.

The more perceptive among those who came into contact with the new smith, who called himself Urnan, saw—or fancied they saw—a restlessness in him. A deep-seated dissatisfaction in his eyes seemed to speak of a troubled and secret past.

Urnan's success made him an immediate object of envy among the other metalworkers. In time it was noted by his peers that he was turning out things other than baubles for ladies. On display on one wall of his shop was a selection of weapons that brought the other smiths, one by one and in twos and threes, to examine and admit either vocally or by bitter silence that Urnan's edges were keener and harder, his arrows and spearheads better balanced, his swords capable of song in the hand of a skilled warrior.

Nor were the other metalworkers the only men to notice Urnan's display of the tools of war. Perhaps one of the women who bought his jewelry mentioned to her husband or to a lover that the smith named Urnan made excellent weapons. Perhaps the word was spread unintentionally by one of Urnan's competitors.

At first the soldiers who came were not men of exalted rank. To their surprise they found that weapons fit for a general or a king were affordable. Junior officers equipped themselves with a blade that they believed was as fine as those carried by the lords of the city.

When Guzbaal, son of the lord of Ashdod, entered the shop to be greeted with perfect protocol by a bronzed, powerful man bare from the waist up, his torso glittering with perspiration, Guzbaal found that this smith, Urnan, had a sword made especially for a man of Guzbaal's status. The hilt was jeweled and decorated with gold inlay. The blade was businesslike, deadly, and keen.

"You waste your talents making baubles for women," Guzbaal said gruffly.

"Lord, one has to live," Urnan said with just the right tone of subservience.

Guzbaal laughed. "One who makes weapons like this does not have to worry about earning a living. If you had a contract with our army in the field, you could name your own price, within reason."

"It would be my pleasure to serve," Urnan said. "But I am just a poor craftsman, lord, and know not the ways of the high and mighty. I would hesitate to offer my simple craftsmanship to the great army of Philistia."

"Your simple craftsmanship would please General Galar himself," Guzbaal said. In a gesture of disdain, he tossed gold coins in Urnan's general direction.

Urnan caught the coins skillfully, then bowed his thanks. But the name *Galar* was ringing in his mind. There had been a time in his life when he would have died gladly if he had been able to take Galar with him. Over the years the fiery hatred had been coated over, as an arrowhead driven into a living tree is encased by new growth; but hearing the name awakened emotions that he had thought to be forgotten.

"I will furnish you with a letter to General Galar," Guzbaal said, lifting his chin pridefully. He hefted his sword. "Do this caliber of work for Galar, and your fortune is made. Moreover, you will be serving your people."

Urnan nodded. He was smiling because of the irony in Guzbaal's words. His intention was indeed to serve his people. In that he and the lord were in total agreement, and Urnan would not disabuse the Philistine of the notion that Urnan was a man of Philistia. The

people Urnan intended to aid with his skills were not his
in blood, but he had lived among them for many years
and had taken his first wife from among them. His son,
if he still lived, had the blood of the race of Abraham
from his mother. Urnan still dreamed of finding Eri
someday, then of their going home to the hills of Israel.

"You make me proud and humble, lord," Urnan
said.

All things, it seemed to Urnan, took time. The days
and the months had merged into an endless series of
dawns, days, evenings, nights. Eri would be a man by
now, perhaps with children of his own. He hoped that
Eri had also come to his own peace in life and had, like
his father, found his freedom and fortune.

Urnan came to the conclusion very quickly after
arriving in Ashdod that it would be useless to conduct a
personal search for his son without knowing where to
start. He had last seen Eri near the city, so it was logical
to think that Eri might still be there. When women of all
classes began to frequent his shop, as he had hoped they
would do, he first catered to their vanity with shameless
flattery and embellished whatever beauty or lack of it
they had with golden and silver trinkets. In the process,
he managed to inform each of the ladies that he was a
man in search of a lost son. Not all of them were sympa-
thetic enough to listen, but a few heard his description
of Eri as a boy and Urnan's guess about how Eri would
look as a young man. More than once Urnan was told
that there was a slave in a certain household who answered the description. More than once Urnan used the
excuse of coming to the wrong house to deliver an order
to get acquainted with the servants and ask about a certain young man of Eri's description, only to see a face
that could not be his son's.

There was, he believed, only one way to discover
where Eri had been taken after they were parted. Information would have to come from a member of the party
of soldiers who had razed Urnan's home, who had
raped and slaughtered his wife, who had sold him and
his son into slavery. He knew the names of only two
men who had been involved, Galar of Ashdod and his

lieutenant on the raid, the man who had thrust his sword into Shelah's stomach, the officer Jobal.

With the help of Lord Guzbaal, he was at last to have access to Galar. It was, of course, a risky situation. There was the possibility that when he came face to face with Galar or Jobal he would be recognized, but he would count on the arrogance and pride of the Philistines. To men like Galar and Jobal, all slaves looked alike. Moreover, the years had changed Urnan. His body was fuller, his hair just a bit thinner, and his face lined, not unattractively, by the elements during his stay on the Island of Copper and by the scorching sun of the Nile valley. The healers at the court in Waset had applied solutions to scorch, then fade the slave's brand on his neck.

He converted his Ashdod assets to gold. He was reminded, as he set out on a donkey for the hills past the Philistine plain, of another time when he rode with the profits of his trade and a well-fashioned sword hidden among his poor effects. There was but one difference: He was more than the craftsman he had once been. His strong right arm knew not only the skills of his work but the art of war. Under the tutelage of Kemose's blade masters, he had gained techniques and skills with the sword that made him a match for most—certainly for Galar and Jobal. Once they were dead, he would resume the search for his son.

It was reassuring to Eri to be traveling through a landscape untouched by the ravages of war. The Philistines had not thrown the battering-ram strength of their main armies into the areas south of Jerusalem, in the lands of the tribe of Judah. Border skirmishes had resulted in stalemate, but no great, bloody incursions such as those made into the areas of the north. Flocks grazed peacefully among the rolling hills, and the outlying homesteads around the city of Bethlehem were well tended and prosperous.

Judahites, Eri found, were like their northern brothers in their hunger for news. In exchange for hospitality, Eri described the conditions in the north. It became evident to him that the descendants of Judah had not forgotten their fratricidal war against the tribe of Benjamin. When Eri told of Philistine conquests in the north, his hosts shook their heads and made sounds of regret. But there was an undercurrent of insincerity, as if the Judahites were saying privately and among themselves, "Well, the Benjamites started it all and fought against their cousins to the north as well as against Judah. Whatever befalls them at the hands of the Philistines is God's punishment."

Eri's plans had, from the beginning of the trek, been dependent on Sarah's recovery from her affliction. His first choice, to take her to the stronghold where the seer Samuel held sway, had been stymied by roving units of Philistines. Now his choices were down to two, and neither seemed attractive. One option was to find a place for Sarah and himself in one of the towns of Judah, where he could practice his craft; but this alternative cut him off from the land that had been his home and from his true friend, Saul. The only other choice was to take Sarah to the wadi in the wilderness where the broiling sun, the heat of the furnaces, and the forges combined to make life trying for all but the smiths who loved their work.

He decided at last upon the latter—at least temporarily. He would build a shelter for Sarah at the armory, high on a slope where breezes would moderate the desert heat. He would care for her there until the situation was more favorable in the north. Then he would take her home to Gibeah and live happily and in peace.

Eri had no doubt that the Philistines would be driven out of the homeland. Saul was bigger than life, large in spirit and in the ability to inspire men. He was a natural leader. Eri could accept the possibility that Saul was sent by Yahweh to save Israel. But whether Saul's inspiration and strength came from God or somewhere within him, Eri was certain that one day, because of the efforts of the young commander, he would return with Sarah to the hills where they were born. He was as confident of that as he was in his belief that Sarah would regain her reason and become his wife and mother of his children.

He put Bethlehem behind them, traveling slowly on a day of lowering clouds and sighing wind. To the east was the Salt Sea and the hidden chasm from which issued the smokes of his forges, but he was in no hurry. It hurt him for others to see the girl he loved in her state of detachment, with her staring, unfocused eyes, her blankness of expression, her silence. Her beauty was undiminished. Indeed, as her golden skin was exposed to sun and wind, it took on a deep vibrancy of color that became her.

At night, when he found a campsite near some secluded spring or tiny rill, he tended her as if she were a small child, for she was indifferent to the soil and perspiration that accumulated during the day's journey. He preserved her modesty as best he could, but it was necessary to clean her private parts, for she was sometimes careless. While he washed her clothing, Sarah sat wrapped in a woolen blanket; but more than once she let the covering fall so she might sit in the cool evening air with her young, proud breasts exposed. The delicate in-curve of her waist was exquisite loveliness, the length of her rounded thighs a wonder of pulchritude. Never had he seen anything to match the beauty of her body. Never had he suffered so much from wanting. Never did he act on his desires and take advantage of her.

The next day, the clouds hung low again, touching the tops of the higher hills. But it was the wrong season for rain. Eri led Sarah along the crest of a shallow ridge, through sere, browned grass. Below, sheep grazed in a delightful little valley. Eri looked for the shepherd and saw him sitting apart from his flock, with his back against a boulder. The peaceful scene saddened the young armorer, for it should have been so in Benjamin, where the flocks had been scattered or slaughtered and the homes of the shepherds demolished.

He was leading Sarah on, climbing a slope toward a depression between two hills, when he heard a sound that chilled his blood. No matter how many times he was exposed to the roar of a male lion, the coughing, soughing rattle and bellow of the sound penetrated to some ancient and visceral fear. He pulled Sarah to a halt and turned to see the tawny animal edging forward, tail twitching, stalking the flock in the valley below. Eri cupped his hands to his mouth, preparing to shout warning to the shepherd, but the boy had already seen the lion and was running toward the flock.

The beast attacked in a blur of yellow-brown motion. With one blow of his forepaw he brought down a lamb. The little animal rolled on the ground, then lay still. The lion seized it in his jaws and was turning to slink away when the shepherd neared, shouting, brandishing his staff. The animal turned, dropped his prey, and, before Eri could shout down to the boy to be careful, filled the air with a terrible roar and charged.

Eri held his breath. He admired the lad for having the courage to protect his flock, but it was stupid to commit suicide by facing the charge of a lion with only a staff.

"Stay here," Eri told Sarah, pushing her down to sit on the grass.

He drew his sword and raced down the hill to help the boy. He knew that he would be too late, for the lion was moving with great speed. But if the lad survived the first lunge of the lion, Eri might arrive in time to drive the animal away before it could inflict fatal wounds. As Eri watched in horror, the lion leaped with forelegs extended and with mighty jaws agape. The boy twisted aside and swung his staff with all of his strength. The heavy rod made a sound audible to Eri as it struck the lion between his yellow, fearful eyes. The beast landed awkwardly, stunned by the blow, but was quickly on his feet to press the attack.

Once again the boy skipped aside and smashed his staff down across the lion's nose. The animal's front legs gave way. Eri was still too far away to join the fight when the boy jumped forward, grabbed the struggling lion by its beard, and delivered a slashing, killing blow to the animal's throat with a long, gleaming knife.

Eri, breathing hard, skidded to a stop a few paces

away. The boy was standing at a safe distance, watching the lion's expiring jerks and twitches.

"Well done," Eri commended.

The boy whirled and went into a fighting crouch.

Eri quickly sheathed his sword. "I was coming to help." He laughed in appreciation. "But you obviously did not need me. I will have a tale to tell my grandchildren one day—how I saw a boy with nothing more than a staff and a knife kill a lion."

The lad shrugged. "God was with me. It is my duty to protect my father's flock."

Eri came down the slope and stood on a level with the shepherd. He was not as tall as Eri, but his arms and shoulders were well developed. He had strong, long-muscled legs, and his chest was powerful. He had thick, black hair and a face that was good to look upon.

"I thank you for your concern," the boy said. "I am David, son of Jesse. Our home is there." He pointed his staff to the north.

"And I am Eri. With my companion I travel toward the Salt Sea."

"The Eri who makes fine weaponry for Saul of Benjamin?" David asked.

Eri gave a small bow.

"The men of Judah should be fighting at Saul's side," David said. "You are most welcome—you and your companion. If it pleases you, come with me and take food at my father's table."

"With pleasure and honor," Eri said.

Sarah seemed bemused by the sheep as she and Eri followed David and his charges over a small hill and into another pleasant valley. There they were greeted politely by Jesse, a white-bearded patriarch surrounded by strong sons and many women. The establishment was prosperous but not rich. The food was strictly in accordance with the dietary laws, for Jesse was a man of God. During the meal he stated, with justifiable pride, that he was the great-grandson of Ruth and Boaz.

In his turn, Eri described David's encounter with the lion, using his hands expressively to describe the boy's quickness and the sureness of his blows. David's older brothers laughed with delight. One of them, as he slapped his thigh in proud glee, said, "Little brother, if you continue this, you will deplete the countryside of animal life."

"Not long ago a great, brown bear threatened my flock," Jesse explained, "and my youngest son treated him with the same disdain that he displayed for today's lion."

The women of the house of Jesse had been quick to note that Sarah was afflicted. She was taken away into the women's quarters, and when she was brought back to sit by Eri's side at the meal, her hair was freshly washed, and she was dressed in a clean tunic.

At times Sarah would eat by herself, but on that day she chose to sit with her hands folded in her lap. From his position on the couch beside her, Eri put the food in her mouth with his own fingers.

"How long has the woman been ill?" Jesse asked sympathetically.

"If you don't mind, I'd rather not talk about it during such a splendid repast," Eri said.

The old man nodded, and the conversation moved to other, lighter topics. But Jesse brought up the subject again after the remains of the meal had been cleared away by the women. Sarah was again in their care. Only the male members of Jesse's family remained behind.

Jesse listened attentively to Eri's explanation of Sarah's condition. After the young man had finished, Jesse stroked his white beard broodingly, then asked, "You have cared for this young woman, washing her, cleaning her, changing her clothing?"

"Sir, I have," Eri said.

"Just by being alone with her in the hills you sin in the eyes of God," Jesse said. "I understand your concern for her, and you are to be commended for your loyalty; but what you do is wrong, and you risk God's judgment not only on yourself but on Sarah."

Eri's face flushed with indignation. To think that the stern God of Israel would bring more suffering to Sarah was more than he was willing to accept. And why should he be judged harshly? He had done nothing wrong! He remained silent, however, for he was a guest in this house.

Jesse's face softened. "Forgive an old man for his bluntness, but think about what I have said. Consider, too, the future of this unfortunate woman. What are your plans for her?"

"Eventually, when peace comes, to take her back to her own country."

"But you have said that all of her kinspeople are dead."

"Yes."

Jesse was silent for long moments. "My house is not as rich as some, but there is space in it for one so burdened. Leave her with us, and we will care for her."

Eri softened, realizing that the settlement's patriarch had Sarah's best interests at heart. "You are very kind, but I must refuse your generous offer."

Jesse raised his white eyebrows. "What will you do with her, then?"

"I will take her to my place of work."

"And continue to live in sin?" Jesse asked, not unkindly.

"I don't know what else to do," Eri admitted.

"I take it that you love the girl."

"I do."

"Then marry her."

"I had planned to wait until she regained her senses, until she could participate in the ceremony," Eri said. "But I never intended to subject her to condemnation. I will not permit her to be censured for being alone with me without benefit of marriage."

"Allow me to summon a priest, and you may take Sarah in marriage in this house. My women can be counted on to provide a most festive observance of the occasion."

Eri was struck dumb by the generous offer and by the swift movement of events.

"There is one other thing." Jesse sighed.

Eri's heart lurched. "Yes?"

"One of the more immediate results of marriage is

a child." He smiled and waved his hand to indicate his sons. "If you doubt that, here is proof in the shape of several hulking young men who eat their weight daily."

"My father exaggerates just a bit," David said with a wink.

"Now," Jesse said, "it is obvious that your Sarah cannot care for herself, much less for a child."

Frustration and sadness came over Eri, for during the talk of marriage he had felt resurgence of his desire, that great force that had been building in him from the time he first kissed Sarah. For brief, fevered moments he had been thinking of marriage as consummation of that desire; but now, with great wisdom, the old man was telling him that he could not, even after he was married to her, know Sarah as his wife. To bring a child into the world without a mother to care for her, to add the care of an infant to his burden of tending Sarah, would be out of the question.

"You speak wisely," he said, nodding his respect to Jesse. "I shall govern myself accordingly."

The sons and daughters of the house of Jesse made the occasion a holiday. It was as if one of their own was being married. A priest was summoned from Bethlehem. There was much feasting, joyful singing, and beautiful music from a harp in the hands of David. But as wonderful as the day was, no glimmer of light shone in Sarah's eyes.

At last the festivities were over. In the room prepared for them, Eri removed Sarah's borrowed finery and put her to bed. She curled into a ball and went to sleep immediately.

Eri, still clothed, sat by her side and looked at her. As she slept, her long, black lashes lying on the sooty, soft skin under her eyes, her beauty tore at his heart. But he vowed he would not come into her as a man until she was capable of participating in the union, with her arms reaching out to him for mutual fulfillment.

He heaved a sigh of exhaustion, then lay down beside his wife. It had been a long day, but with the dawn it would begin an even longer one, as he and Sarah would begin the final leg of their journey to the Hebrew armorers' secret wadi.

He built a house for Sarah and obtained a servant, an Ammonite girl who had been brought as a slave from the east. Baalan was slow to accomplish her work but eventually got everything done. The girl was grateful for the considerate treatment she received as a member of Eri's household, and more importantly, the tenderness she developed for Sarah assured Eri that his wife would be well treated while he was at his work.

"She was not always like this, my lord?" Baalan asked early on.

"No, she saw her life and all those she loved destroyed before her eyes," Eri said. "To escape that which she could not accept, she retreated to some far place."

The slave looked deeply into Sarah's eyes. "She's hiding in there somewhere?"

Eri did not know, nor could he guess, where the woman he loved was hiding. A few months after their wedding, he had given Sarah her own room for sleep, for in the night when he held her in his arms, he could not help but pretend that she longed for his love as much as he yearned for hers. He no longer allowed himself to touch her, for to know the sweetness of her flesh under his lips without taking her as his wife was a torture too stern to bear.

And in this miserable way passed the years of greatest trial in Eri's life.

CHAPTER
TWENTY-TWO

When Saul returned to the orchards, hills, and fields of his childhood after yet another excursion against the Philistines to find Gibeah in ashes, his anger was a fire that threatened to consume him. Well after the remains of the dead had been given respectful burial, the stench of death hung heavy in the air. Desolation was all around. Everything that would burn had been torched by the enemy. Stone walls had been tumbled to the earth. On the outskirts of the village the fine mansion of Raphu had fared no better.

With fear in his heart, Saul hurried to the home of his father, in a glen some distance from the main village. As he came near he saw evidence that the enemy had passed, and he steeled himself to find new graves. Instead he came into a bustle of activity. His father and his brothers, with all of the male servants, were salvaging cut stones from the ruins in preparation for rebuilding the main house. Women gleaned the fields and orchards, saving what foodstuffs they could.

Kish had been warned of the coming of the enemy, for he was wise in the ways of war and kept lookouts on duty both day and night. The entire household had retreated to a hideaway in the hills to wait until the Philistines had done their looting and their razing.

"You have arrived just in time for the most interesting part of the rebuilding, Brother," said one of Saul's siblings.

"Praise God that you are safe," Kish said, hurrying forward to embrace his son.

"It looks as if there is work to be done, Father," Saul said. "I am yours to command."

"You serve us better by killing Philistines," Kish said.

Saul nodded.

"Are you hungry? There are food and drink in the cave on the hillside," Kish said.

"I have eaten," Saul said. He cleared his throat and made his question, although he dreaded the answer. "My friend Eri? . . . He had returned to the village to visit the daughter of Sapha."

"His body was not among those we buried," Kish said. "Nor did we find Sapha's daughter."

Saul allowed himself to hope not for Sarah but for Eri. If Sarah was not dead, she was as good as dead. A girl as shapely as she would bring a good price on the slave market in one of the Philistine cities, and by the time she reached the block she would have been well used by her captors. There was, of course, the possibility that Eri, too, had been taken into slavery, but Saul doubted it. Having once known the shame of being owned by another man, Eri would have died before allowing himself to be taken alive.

Now, more men came down from the hills. They were carrying freshly cut building timbers on their shoulders. "Such heavy loads would best be carried by beasts of burden," Saul said.

"When the Philistines came, I turned my animals free to run to the hills so that they would not be wantonly slaughtered," Kish said. "The sheep did not go far. The donkeys? Well, you know the independence of the ass. I've been intending to send someone to look for them. They bear my mark and should be easily found unless they were caught by the enemy."

"This is a chore that I can perform," Saul said. "It will serve two purposes: While I look for the animals I can check on the whereabouts of the raiders."

"As you say," Kish agreed with a nod.

For two days Saul searched without success. He saw more evidence of the rapacity of the enemy in the form of dead animals and destroyed homesteads, but as he neared the land of Zuph, he entered country that was serene and undisturbed. It made him feel slightly uncomfortable to be greeted with great respect and no little awe when he encountered the inhabitants of that land. His stature marked him, made him easily identifiable. He had not realized how widely he was known in the land of Israel, but he didn't fight for glory or for recognition from his fellows. He fought for God and for the land that God had given to his people. He knew the movement to make him a king was ever-growing, but he did nothing to pursue that honor.

Exhausted from his days of searching, he sought out an inn, enjoyed a fine meal, then took to the streets to walk off the feeling of having eaten too much. Word of his presence had spread. A young man approached him respectfully and offered to join his forces in battle against the Philistines.

"Have you a sword?" Saul asked.

"My father has his father's father's sword, said to have been used at the battle of Jericho."

"Iron is needed against the Philistine," Saul told him, eyeing the lad. He was a brawny one, and willing, and Saul was reluctant to discourage such a one as he. "Come to me with the new moon at Gibeah."

"Saul," asked a nervous old woman who had shuffled up beside him, "will the Philistines come here, to Zuph?"

"They go where the winds blow them," Saul said,

"and they will make this land theirs unless all men of fighting age join together to oppose them."

"But we have the protection of the seer Samuel," the old one said.

"Of what metal is the seer's weapon?" Saul retorted.

"If you have come to recruit for your army," the old woman said, "you are too late. Our young men died at Ebenezer. As for Samuel, he fights no more."

"I have come, old mother, in search of my father's donkeys."

"The seer can help you," she said.

"Can he, now," Saul said. He shrugged, thinking that he'd tried everything else, he might as well give the seer a chance. He handed the old woman a silver coin. "Take this to the holy man, old mother, and tell him that I will follow it closely."

"He will help," the old woman said, "for he has the gift of God."

A small crowd had gathered around the tall warrior and the old woman. From the way others listened to her words, Saul assumed that she was respected in the town.

"His mother, Hannah, wife of Elkanah of Ramathaim on Mount Ephraim, was barren," the old woman said in a voice that quavered with age. "When Hannah conceived, it was a miracle from God, and in exchange she promised that her child would be given to God for all the days of his life, and that no razor would ever touch his hair."

Saul chuckled. "I have not seen Samuel for a long time," he said. "I have only to look for the shaggiest man in Zuph to find him."

"Jest not," the old woman warned, "for Samuel speaks to God and God to him. It is from God that he takes his wisdom and his strength."

"His wisdom and his strength did not prevent the destruction of Shiloh," Saul said.

Even as he spoke, his face flushed guiltily. He told himself that jealousy was a childish emotion, beneath his dignity. Although he believed that Samuel had been given credit for more fight than he had actually displayed, the holy man's direction and leadership had kept a semblance of unity in the conquered land. After the fall of Shiloh Samuel had led tribal units to remote areas outside the sphere of enemy control. From his redoubt at Mizpah, on the borders of Benjamin north of Jerusalem, he had encouraged resistance to Philistine occupation.

After returning the Ark to Israel, Saul had gone to join Samuel's rebels. They were warriors armed with pitchforks and other farm tools, and Saul admired the men for their courage—ineffectual though they were against the Philistine. But secretly, Saul was in awe of Samuel. Why, he wondered, would God speak to the old man but not to him?

Saul was glad that twilight had deepened as the old woman talked, so that the townspeople could not see his expression. No, Saul told himself, he had no reason to be jealous of the seer, for Samuel's belligerence had been short-lived. For a time he had been a fierce warrior, but he had retreated to his birthplace on Mount Ephraim to play the soothsayer, the prophet, the giver of God-inspired oracles.

He, like Samson, was a Nazirite, a member of a strict sect consecrated to God by a vow never to drink wine, never to have his hair cut, and never to be in the presence of a corpse willingly. Nazirites were known for their fanaticism, and for that, if nothing else, Saul was cautious when he and Samuel met again for the first time in years.

Samuel was a head shorter than Saul. His beard was an impressive bush that hung to his chest and straggled down from there in isolated tendrils. His hair bushed out to hang below his waist.

"I have been expecting you," he said.

"Then you are not surprised," Saul said. The seer's first words had damaged him in Saul's eyes, for they were, Saul felt, nothing more than a cheap soothsayer's trick. He resisted an impulse to tell the bearded, hairy man that anyone can claim foreknowledge of an event once that event has happened. The same could be said, he felt, of Samuel's next statement.

"You will find your father's donkeys grazing near Rachel's sepulchre on the border of Benjamin at Zelzah," Samuel said, "for that is where they wandered when they were freed."

Saul nodded. "Then my search will be directed there with the morning." He had made no secret of the fact that he was searching for his father's animals. The old woman or any number of men could have told Samuel his purpose. It was yet to be proven that the seer was correct in his oracle; but even if the animals were in the spot singled out by Samuel, that was no absolute guarantee that the prophet had divine inspiration. Someone could also have told him the whereabouts of Kish's donkeys.

"Tonight," Samuel said, his voice as vibrant as a handbell, as penetrating as the shrill notes of a flute, "you will take food with me." He pointed to a hill overlooking the town. A fire burned there at the site of an altar, beside a stone building. "There, on the high place."

"As you will," Saul said.

He followed Samuel to the high place and nodded a bow as Samuel prostrated himself before the holy altar. Two young priests came running from the stone building.

"Serve us meat and the sweet, natural wine of God's earth," Samuel ordered.

Saul did not question the Nazirite's request for wine. He had learned during the time that he was playing tricks on the priests of Dagon in the Philistine cities that it was best to let a self-appointed holy man do most of the talking. It was good that he had not made any remark, for the "natural wine of God's earth" was cool, clear water.

Samuel ate in silence. The two young priests stood near at hand, willing and ready to serve. A night bird swooped past the fire, visible for one tiny moment.

Samuel was the first to finish his meal. He dipped his fingers in a bowl presented to him by one of the priests and waited patiently for Saul to finish and cleanse his fingers with water.

Samuel beckoned to Saul. "We will go down together."

They started down the hill. The two priests trailed along. Samuel stopped suddenly and threw his leonine head back to gaze up into the starry sky. For a long time he was silent; then he turned to the priests and said, "Pass on before us."

Saul waited, wondering what trick the seer would use, for it was obvious that Samuel was setting the scene for something.

"But stand thou still a while," Samuel said to Saul, "that I may show thee the word of God."

Saul was astonished by his reaction—or, more accurately, at his lack of reaction—to what came next. Samuel took a vial of oil from his mantle and reached up to pour from it onto Saul's dark, thick hair.

"The Lord hath anointed thee to be captain over his inheritance," Samuel intoned.

Saul could not find it within himself to make light of the old man's seriousness, and when the seer kissed him solemnly, he neither spoke nor averted his face.

"After you have found the asses near Rachel's sepulchre," Samuel said, "go to the plain of Tabor. There you will meet three men on their way to Bethel. One will be carrying three young goats; another, three loaves of bread; the last, a bottle of wine. They will salute you and give you bread. You will then meet a company of prophets coming down from a high place with a ten-stringed psaltery, a pipe, a harp, and a drum. The spirit of the Lord will come upon you, and you will prophesy with them."

Saul hid his doubt behind a smile. He was reminded of the false trances he had performed during the time that Eri and he were trying to convince the Dagon priests that the Ark should be returned to Israel. It was highly unlikely, he felt, that he would go into a genuine religious ecstasy.

"Go then to Gilgal," Samuel instructed. "Tarry

there seven days, and I will come to you to give burnt offerings and to offer sacrifices of peace."

Kish's donkeys were exactly where the seer had said they would be. Never had Saul felt so befuddled. He considered himself to be a man of God, devout, tainted only by minor sins of omission. He could offer the prescribed respect to the priests of Yahweh, for they were anointed of God. Without being wickedly prideful, he accepted the obvious fact that he stood head and shoulders taller than most men and, figuratively, that he towered over most in deeds. He feared no one. It was not in his nature to think that he was lesser in any way than a self-styled prophet, a radical, fanatical, hair-covered man who had not earned his leadership by the might of his arm. And yet now he wondered. . . . He was not the first, nor would he be the last, to ask, "Just what gave you the right to state that you and you alone have been appointed by God to speak for him?"

So Saul felt resentful of Samuel, but it was mixed with awe and wonder. His thoughts were confused as he drove his father's animals toward his home and on the plain of Tabor.

He began to have the disquieting fear that he was lesser in God's eyes than Samuel when he met three men carrying three kids, three loaves of bread, and a bottle of wine. Without a word, he was given two loaves of bread.

As the men continued on whatever journey had brought them to this particular place at this moment in time, Saul prayed earnestly. He asked that God give *him* revelation, that God speak to *him* to confirm that Samuel was, indeed, the spokesman for the All High.

He was crestfallen when he received no answer . . . and he was not surprised when he met a small group of men coming down from a high place and making music with pipe, harp, drum, and a ten-stringed psaltery. But never was a man more flabbergasted by his own behavior than Saul when he began to sing the praises of God with the company of musicians. The spirit came into him, and he shouted out the praises of

God in a tongue unknown to any mortal man. Just as Samuel had predicted, Saul prophesied with the men of God and became not Saul but another man for a time . . . which, he realized later, could have been as brief as moments or as long as the ages.

The peace of acceptance came to him. He convinced himself that he believed what Samuel said, just as all those not directly under the control of the Philistines also believed him. Perhaps he himself was, as some said, the right hand of God when it came to the destruction of the enemy; but Samuel was God's spokesman on earth. Saul told himself that he was not bowing, figuratively, to another man but to a prophet of God. He said, "Yes, God speaks through Samuel."

When Samuel called, the people gathered, for he had given them hope in dire times, when Israel was shattered by the disaster at Ebenezer. They gathered at a place known as Gilgal, and there many repeated the demand that was growing throughout Israel. They wanted a leader, a man whom they could see with their eyes and hear with their ears. They wanted more than Samuel's prayers and God's invisible blessings that were, it seemed, always postponed for the morrow.

Samuel, stern, gray, his long hair and beard blowing in the hot wind, stood before them with sorrow in his eyes. "You say that I must set a king over you. You ask not for the grace of God but for a man to rule over you. So be it. See, then, whom the Lord has chosen."

He paused, and the silence was heavy, like a fog. Slowly he turned his head. "Where is Saul, son of Kish? A man from the smallest of all tribes is chosen by the Lord. There is none like him among all of the people."

"God save the king!" the crowd roared.

But Saul was not to be seen anywhere.

Men found Saul fussing with his armor, checking the edge on his sword. They led him to stand before Samuel.

The great shout came again. "God save the king!"

Saul said nothing, but again there was doubt in his

heart. In spite of the fact that the prophecies had come to pass exactly as the old seer had described them, Saul experienced a feeling of unreality—almost as if he were living out a nightmare. But the voices of the people were loud, and Samuel solemnized the event by writing it in a book.

Now, he realized, he was linked to Samuel forever. The man who had made him a king could just as easily undo the deed. Samuel answered to God, true; but Saul, even though he was king, answered to Samuel.

In the north the fight to free the land from the Philistine oppressors continued. When next Eri saw Saul, even though years had passed, the men enjoyed a glad and affectionate reunion at the armory. The commander of Israel had come to check on the progress of his army's weapons and to see his old and dear friend. The big, bearded warrior had taken a wife and had already thanked his God for the birth of a son, called Jonathan.

"I am happy for you!" Eri said, and he meant it. But there was a bittersweet quality to his voice, for his Sarah still lived very much in her own world.

"God is good," Saul said. He put his hand on Eri's shoulder. "Be patient, my friend. Have faith."

"I try," Eri said. He and his friend sat on a rock and looked down upon the hidden valley where hammers clanged and forges smoked.

"It is a strange and unpredictable world," Saul said. "But in the end there is God's mercy." He laughed, hoping to lighten his friend's gloom. "Even for an oversized lunk like me. You have heard, I assume, that I am a king."

"And if you are king," chided Eri as he peered around, "just where is your retinue?"

Saul laughed and spread his hands wide to encompass the empty wilderness. "My band of men come to me whenever it is time to fight. *There* you see Israel."

"I see dry sand and rocky cliffs," Eri grumbled.

"Sometimes I ask myself, how can I save this land? How can I, in spite of my great size, lead an army against the enemy? We have never stood in a great battle—our efforts are always hit and run. We have done nothing more than rain arrows down on small groups of Philistines from the protection of the rocks."

"Don't be foolish," Eri said. He had seen regal qualities in his friend long before. "You will build upon your success. Wait awhile. You'll see. Your confidence will catch up with your abilities."

CHAPTER TWENTY-THREE

Eri's life had finally fallen into a pattern that was not without satisfaction. Although there were occasional shortages of the ore from which the fecund furnaces bled molten iron, the equipping of Saul's army proceeded at a steady pace. The men who worked in the hidden wadi, all of them descendants of Abraham, claimed that God was with those who drove the weapons-laden donkeys northward, for not one shipment had been lost to the enemy. In fact, the widespread opinion was that when the strength of Israel had been restored and Saul's army faced the Philistines in pitched battle, the enemy would have an unpleasant surprise: that Israel had weapons of iron of a quality equal to the Philistines' own.

The heat and the work had honed Eri's body to fighting trim. He started each morning with a glorious feeling of fitness and anticipation. It was only in the

225

evenings, when he returned to the home he had placed
high on a slope, that he knew discontentment. Each
time he came into his home he had the hope—after a
while he ceased to admit it, but it was there—that *she*
would greet him with a smile, a word, an embrace. *She,*
Sarah, banished from his thoughts during the day by the
necessity of concentrating on his work, was heavy in his
heart in the lonely night.

She was a complaisant child in the body of a volup-
tuous woman. She could amuse herself for hours merely
by watching a butterfly stitching arcs in the air in the
garden that Baalan, the Ammonite slave, had planted.
Sarah did exactly as she was told, but directions had to
be constant. During the day she walked with Baalan,
and the slave used gentle persuasion to cause Sarah to
exercise her shapely limbs and body, to keep them
youthful and supple. Baalan saw to Sarah's food and
hygiene and kept up a stream of chatter that was disregarded by her beloved mistress.

Sarah's serene expression did not change when Eri
came to hold her hands and look into the lifeless eyes
that once had sparkled with vitality.

In the manner of his adopted people, he took
Baalan to wife and into his bed, where she was a willing
partner. She had never known the womanly joy of being
loved, although in her young life she had been used. Eri
told Baalan of his fondness for her, and she glowed with
pleasure.

In due time, Baalan presented Eri with a sturdy son
whose heft weighed pleasingly in his hands. Eri's first
act was to turn the boy to see whether or not the paw
print of the lion was on his back. There it was, just
above the swell of his tiny left buttock. The boy was
marked, but it was not the mark of a slave—the child
would be an armorer.

When the baby was first shown to Sarah, her reaction caused a wild surge of hope in Eri. She leaned
forward, and her dulled eyes gleamed with interest for a
moment—but for only a moment. After that she would
watch the boy with the same glazed idleness that she
displayed when observing a butterfly.

News from the northern areas came with the ore trains and those returning from delivering the products of Eri's forges. There came with one shipment a letter from Saul, written in a fine hand on coarse parchment but made authentic by a roughly scrawled greeting from Saul himself. It was a request that Eri come to Gibeah with his family because "you are needed here, my friend. You have done your work well in the south. Because of your organization of the work, it will continue without you."

Eri left the desert with several donkeys laden with household goods and clothing. Although Baalan never forgot her place as former slave and secondary wife, she convinced him with a few feminine tears that nothing should be left behind. Eri argued that everything could be replaced after the family arrived in the north, with much less expense and effort than was required to move it. Nonetheless, the young Ammonite had her way.

At times Eri carried his son, whom he had named Sunu. At other times the infant was in his mother's arms. Sarah was able to ride unaided. Progress was slow. They rested in Bethlehem after a long and tiring journey, then set out northward once again.

They skirted to the east of Jerusalem and were, at last, in territory made relatively secure by Saul and his small bands of patriots. The area was abuzz with news. Samuel had called together representatives of the tribes and asked for a formal vote to ratify Saul's kingship. According to local speculation, Samuel was hoping that the men would overturn Saul's appointment. The prophet had never wanted a king for Israel, and certainly not one who might, in time, rival the old man's own power and influence. The tribesmen had voted in Saul's favor, however, and now the young king's name was on everyone's lips. His deeds were told and retold as Eri and his family traveled toward the little village that had suddenly become the capital of Israel.

Gibeah had been rebuilt on its own ruins, but there was none of the splendor that might have been expected in the political center of the Hebrews' nation. Nor was

Saul's residence regal. He lived with his family in a modest stone house in the center of the village. He himself answered Eri's hail at the gate and roared out his pleasure. He came striding out dressed in coarse, common cloth, the long sword that Eri had made for him hanging from his girdle.

"To see you again is reward enough for one day!" Saul bellowed as he smothered Eri in his arms and lifted him off the ground.

"And who's this?" Saul asked in his big, gruff voice when he espied Sunu in Baalan's arms.

Eri lifted the boy's swaddling clothes to expose the mark of the lion.

Saul laughed. "Good, good. We must pass on our skills to a new generation sooner or later, Eri." He looked closely at the expressionless but beautiful face of Sarah. "The same?" he asked quietly.

"I had hoped that bringing her here might . . ." Eri could not finish, for his disappointment was a pain in his chest.

"Let us not dwell on the sadness of life," Saul said. "The village has changed beyond all recognition. But the vines are producing again in Israel, and the new wine is sweet. There are things we must discuss, you and I." He lifted one hand and a servingwoman hurried forward. "Take these ladies to the guesthouse. Meet any requirement they might have."

Baalan was ill at ease in the strange place in the midst of so many people; but when Eri nodded to her, she smiled wanly and obeyed. Saul led Eri into his house, seated him on a comfortable couch, then called out for a servant, who within moments had placed a goblet of wine in his hand.

"Because of you," Saul said, "we can look forward to matching weapons with the Philistines."

Eri nodded acceptance of the praise.

Saul's face darkened. "But it is not the Philistines who will feel the sharp edges of your blades," he said.

Eri looked up, surprised.

"Nahash, the Ammonite, has besieged Jabesh-Gilead, over Jordan," Saul said.

"Surely the Ammonites can't be our most dangerous enemy!" Eri said, upset to think that the still-unproven might of the growing army of Israel might be squandered without striking a blow at the real foe, Philistia.

"It is true that Jabesh-Gilead expects no help from us," Saul said. "In fact, they offered to surrender to Ammon. Nahash accepted the offer—on condition that all residents of the city consent to having their right eyes taken from them."

Eri uttered a startled curse in the language of his ancestors.

"The messengers came today with these tidings," Saul said grimly. "I have sent out a call for the army to assemble."

"Yes," Eri agreed. "You can do no less."

Saul stood and looked out the window. His back was to his friend. "There is one other thing," he admitted. "Samuel. He's taken too many liberties with my kingship. I need to stabilize my power so he can't interfere again."

"But the tribes' representatives just ratified your position! You have nothing to fear from Samuel. Besides, you can't send men into battle and risk their lives simply to silence an old man."

Saul whirled around to face Eri. "But it's so much more than that, don't you see? Israel needs to be united. The tribes must act as one, under one man. So long as Samuel lives, so long as he is believed to speak for God, Israel will remain divided under two leaders with conflicting loyalties and priorities."

Eri sat silently, looking closely at his friend, taking his measure.

"Come, Eri, drink up. We'll test your weapons against the Ammonites, we'll save the people of Jabesh-Gilead, and then we'll go after the Philistines. I promise." He grinned and lifted his goblet. "To the deliverance of Jabesh-Gilead?"

Eri drank.

"And to old friends marching together?" Saul
asked, lifting his glass again.

"Indeed," Eri said angrily. "Long live the king."

The army gathered at Bezek, in the hills of Manas-
seh, directly west of the besieged city on the other side
of the Jordan. The force was mainly comprised of men
of Israel, but others came north from Judah as well, for
the word had spread that Saul was leading the attack
and that all men who joined him would be armed with
iron blades.

The army of Saul came thundering down in a three-
pronged attack upon the unwary Ammonites. Saul,
standing head and shoulders above the masses, led the
way at the center. Eri was at his side, and their swords
tasted much blood that day. Men who had never fought
with iron weapons were flabbergasted at what they were
able to accomplish. The unblooded army was an unstop-
pable surge of destruction against the Ammonites.

As the Hebrews fought the invaders in hand-to-
hand combat in the streets, the oppressed residents of
the town hung out their windows and cheered. Whenever they could, they also took part in driving the for-
eigners from their midst. Jabesh-Gilead was saved, and
the city was now a firm ally of Saul.

The news spread rapidly. The homeward march
was triumphal, and an air of high excitement prevailed.
Saul was in high good humor, feeling he had accomplished his purposes. Eri's mood lightened, too, for to
see his weapons used to such great effectiveness was
gratifying. Soldiers slapped him on the back and
thanked him profusely for his efforts. Perhaps, he
thought, Saul had been right to go after Nahash. . . .

On a chill evening when the heat of the campfire
was pleasant on his face and hands, Eri sat on a stone
and watched his friend make the rounds of the camp of
the army. His progress was marked by the flow of
soldiers into clumps around him, and by their loud good
wishes. A movement at his side turned Eri's head.
Young Jonathan, Saul's son, nodded greetings and sat
down to warm his hands at the fire. The boy was likable

and open-hearted, and he was handsome like his father but not yet as tall. He had not been allowed to fight in the forefront at Jabesh-Gilead, and that had caused him to fret.

"There will be battles enough for you when you're older, Jonathan," Eri consoled. "The Philistines won't be driven from our land all that quickly."

"I know, Uncle. It's just that I feel ready now." A sudden outburst of cheering attracted his attention. Jonathan nodded toward it. "The men would march through fire for him, and so would I."

"It is because he tells them what he believes they are capable of doing," Eri said, hoping the boy would realize that the same truth applied to him. "His determination and faith make it so. He not only says, he does. He has credibility in the form of past deeds. One has only to look at him to know that there is a king in Israel."

CHAPTER
TWENTY-FOUR

The old, buried memories and hurts seemed to grow more vivid as Urnan passed beyond the cultivated fields into dry, sparsely wooded hills on his way to the Philistine garrison. The letter of introduction to General Galar was in his pack. A melancholy came over him, and he despaired of ever being reunited with those he loved. The proud and beautiful woman who had become his wife in Egypt—and their child, if she had not terminated the pregnancy—was as good as dead to him, cut off from him by distance and by the hostility of those who controlled the Nile Delta. To return there would mean being taken captive by the Libyan-controlled faction, if, indeed, the Libyans had not seized the entire nation. Just as the young girl who had given him his only son was hopelessly beyond his reach through death, Tania was gone from his life forever.

And Eri? There were times when he felt that it

might be best if he let the dead past lie. Eri had been a handsome lad, smooth-limbed and comely. He would have become the plaything of some Philistine, and only God knew what a life of inflicted perversion would have done to the lad.

So it was with a heavy burden of gloom that Urnan followed the tracks of Philistine carts and the wide swath of desolation left by the army to a mountain village called Michmash.

The sentry to whom he presented his letter from Guzbaal could not read, so Urnan was taken to an officer who straightened his shoulders and became very polite after scanning the missive.

Galar of Ashdod had matured. In his prime he was even more physically impressive than he had been when he watched his men savage and kill Shelah. His winter-sky-blue eyes were made keener by sun lines and by a touch of gray in his eyebrows and his hair. His nose was more hawkishly prominent. His chin jutted belligerently, as if it had been carved from stone. He took the letter from Urnan's hand and read it at a glance. His piercing eyes examined the smith.

Urnan kept his hand near the hilt of his sword. He was prepared, should Galar recognize him, to die even as his own blade pierced the Philistine's stomach.

"We are grateful to Lord Guzbaal for his consideration," Galar said. He held out his hand. "Your sword, smith."

Urnan tensed. His hand went to the sword. For a moment there was a question in his mind whether his blade would be drawn with intent to die fighting, but there was no light of recognition in Galar's cold blue eyes. Urnan drew the sword, flipped it, caught it by its tip, and handed it hilt-first to Galar. There were no jewels on the haft. That would not have been commensurate with Urnan's status. It was a utilitarian blade; but the balance was perfect and the edge sturdy but keen.

The general examined the weapon. He made the blade swish as he slashed the air, then handed the sword back to Urnan. "Yes, we need weapons of this caliber. But you will be of more value to us at your own forge in

Ashdod. We move often in the field, and you would not always have proper working facilities."

"Forgive me, Lord General," Urnan said with a little nod of his head, "but is there no need for the mending and repair of weapons after a clash with the enemy? I could be of great use to you in that."

Galar nodded.

Urnan's immediate goal was to find some way to stay with Galar's army, to get on speaking terms if not with the general himself, then with Jobal or one of the other soldiers who had been at Shiloh.

"I ask, General, that you allow me to serve by setting up a portable shop for repair work. I would be most grateful, and I would feel honored to be allowed to serve my country under the command of our greatest general."

Galar nodded, lifted his chin in a small gesture of preening. "Your request is granted. For the time being, consider this garrison your post. Build your shop with an eye toward mobility, for soon we will be moving south."

As it happened there was a shop available, for one of the army's smiths had died of fever only days before Urnan's arrival at Michmash. Soon Urnan was at work, and there was plenty of it. He became known among the garrison as a talkative, friendly man who was willing to do a soldier a favor, who put little extra touches of craftsmanship into the repair of a breastplate, who could hone a sword to razor sharpness and still maintain the integrity of the blade.

Urnan's disarming chatter and his flow of questions to those who came to him for repairs turned up the information that a captain named Jobal was currently in the field with a foraging party.

In the weeks that followed, Urnan saw Galar only twice, once at a distance and once when the general came into the shop. When he entered, Urnan's back was to him.

"You wasted no time in getting to work," Galar said.

Urnan turned quickly, saluted. "There was need, General."

Galar was staring at Urnan. The smith had removed his tunic in the heat and was wearing only a loincloth.

"Turn around," Galar ordered.

"Sir?"

"Turn your back to me."

Urnan obeyed. He heard the creak of leather as the general stepped closer. Galar traced old scars on Urnan's sweat-moistened shoulders with the tip of his crop. "Why would a smith have the mark of the lash on his back?"

Urnan turned to face the general. "When I was a young apprentice, sir, my master felt that I had a rebellious streak."

"Ummm," Galar said, his eyes squinted as they studied Urnan's face. "I cannot banish the feeling, smith, that I have seen you before."

"I would remember had I ever been in the presence of Philistia's greatest warrior," Urnan said, bowing his head.

The general stared at him for long, uneasy seconds, then drew a sword from the sheath at his waist. "This blade has not been sharpened in some time."

Urnan recognized the weapon immediately. It was the bronze blade he had fashioned for himself in happier times, the weapon that had been taken from him after his attack on the soldier who had been violating Shelah so long before.

"An interesting piece of work, sir," he said.

Galar was watching him closely. "I pride myself on my modest but interesting collection of swords. What would you say of this one?"

Urnan hefted the blade. "The work of a fair craftsman. Well balanced. The alloy tells me that it was probably fashioned in the hills to the west of the Salt Sea, for there is a certain redness in the blend of copper and tin. As a bronze blade goes, it is a good piece of work, but hardly the match, of course, for good Philistine iron."

Galar took a deep breath, and Urnan held his, ready to attack with the blade of his own making.

"Polish it," Galar said. "Hone it."

"I will, lord," Urnan said, bowing.

After the general left, Urnan wiped nervous perspiration from his forehead. It was evident that Galar was probing his memory as one does for the temporarily lost name of an old acquaintance. Should Galar associate Urnan's face with that scene near Shiloh, it would mean death or a return to slavery.

Every instinct of survival told Urnan to flee the Philistine garrison; but Jobal had not returned from the field, and that man represented the only hope for getting a clue to Eri's possible whereabouts. Certainly Urnan could not dare question the general about a slave boy. Such a mention would, no doubt, be the key to Galar's lost memories.

When Jobal entered the garrison he came with prancing horses and the sound of trumpets. One of Jobal's soldiers carried a severed head on the tip of a spear—a Hebrew head, Urnan guessed, by the dark hair and black beard. On the very day of the patrol's return one of its members came to Urnan's shop for repair of his breastplate, which had been dented by a blow from a sword.

"By Dagon," the soldier bragged, "he didn't live to strike again. That was his head we carried home."

"I'm sure that he was not the only Hebrew to feel the bite of our iron, since you were under the command of such a brave officer as Captain Jobal."

The soldier shifted uneasily. "Actually," he said, "the Hebrew cowards will not come out and fight unless they outnumber us at least twenty to one."

"But one man fought?" Urnan asked.

"He was trying to hide behind the robes of a shepherd," the soldier said weakly.

Urnan felt that it was best to drop the subject. He began work on the breastplate. "Have you served with Jobal long?"

"Since I was a lad."

"Then you fought at Ebenezer?"

"Just a boy I was then," the soldier said, "and between you and me, smith, shaking like a leaf when the Hebrews, yelling like demons, came charging at me." He pulled himself up, thrust out his chest, and said, "But I soon learned that there was nothing to fear."

"Wasn't Jobal a junior officer then, under the command of Galar, himself just a captain?"

"That's right," the soldier said.

"I had a kinsman who fought at Ebenezer with Galar. He said that after the battle Galar led a force into the hills to destroy small pockets of resistance."

"That he did," the soldier said. He sighed in fond remembrance. "Those were good days. The general—captain then—believed in letting a man enjoy the fruits of victory." He made an obscene gesture. "And some of them were sweet indeed."

Urnan held back a desire to use his hammer on the soldier's smirking face instead of on the metal of the breastplate. "My cousin said that he participated in the sacking of the Hebrews' most holy place, at Shiloh."

The soldier looked at Urnan with new interest. "What was your cousin's name? I was at Shiloh."

Urnan picked the first Philistine name that entered his mind. "He was Hagab, of Ashdod."

The soldier scratched his head. "Can't place him."

"Yes, well, he was a very ordinary-looking fellow." Urnan concentrated on his work. He was finishing the job with a careful polishing of the metal when Jobal himself entered the shop.

The soldier leaped to his feet. "Sir!"

"Be at rest," Jobal said.

Urnan gave the captain a salute, lifting his hammer and bowing his head.

"I am in need of a new sword, smith," Jobal said. "The general said that you do good work."

"I thank the general for his praise," Urnan said. "I think, sir, that I have just the thing for you."

"Good, good," Jobal said. "But finish with the breastplate. This is a good man here. Be sure that his armor is strong."

"Thank you, sir," the soldier said. "By the way, Captain, the smith had a kinsman with us at Ebenezer and afterward."

Jobal looked at Urnan and raised an eyebrow in interest.

"Fellow named Hagab," the soldier said. "Can't place him myself."

"Nor I," Jobal said. "Where was he from?"

"From a small village outside Ashdod," Urnan said.

"Hagab . . ." Jobal said. "No, I don't remember any Hagab."

"He told the smith all about how we destroyed Shiloh," the soldier said.

Jobal's eyes narrowed.

Urnan had finished polishing the breastplate. He handed it to the soldier, turned away, picked up his own sword, and faced Jobal.

"Shiloh," Jobal said, his hand on the hilt of his short sword. "Yes." His eyes flared. The sword leaped into view. His smile was the grin of a reptile before its strike. "You were a piss-poor swordsman then, smith. Have you improved?"

Urnan's answer was a swift slash that opened the throat of the soldier who was coming to his feet, puzzlement on his face. It was necessary to reduce the odds and to give him a chance to force Jobal to talk about Eri.

Blood pumped from severed arteries, splashing Jobal's feet and legs as the soldier collapsed. He jumped back just in time to prevent Urnan's sword from wounding his shoulder.

"I'll try not to kill you, smith," Jobal said, "because I think it will be amusing to learn how you managed to escape from the mines."

The Philistine came in a rush, his blade flashing. Urnan stepped back, parrying the slashing blows, and Jobal increased his attack. Urnan had proved, in that brief exchange, that he had learned something since Shiloh about swordplay.

Urnan felt the hot touch of Jobal's sword on his left arm. Blood ran down, feeling like crawling insects.

Jobal, emboldened, thrust forward, only to have Urnan's blade bury itself in his stomach. The Philistine's strength faded. He lifted his blade but did not strike. His fingers went limp, and the sword fell to the packed earth floor of the forge. Urnan pulled his blade out with a jerk, and blood gushed as Jobal sank slowly to his knees. He clasped his gut.

Urnan lifted the wounded man by his shoulders and placed his back against the base of the iron anvil. He knelt in front of Jobal. Jobal's eyes held his.

"You thrust your sword into my wife's stomach," Urnan said.

"So it *is* you."

"There was a boy—my son. He was still with you when I was taken north from a point near Ashdod. What happened to him?"

To Urnan's puzzlement, Jobal laughed. The sound became a wet cough as blood filled his throat. "You came . . . to find—"

"My son," Urnan said. "What did you do with him?"

"Fool," Jobal said. "Dead."

Urnan put his hands on the Philistine's shoulders and squeezed. "He was killed?"

"Sold. Dead . . . now though."

"But you don't know for sure?"

"Hurt," Jobal said. "I—hurt."

"Where was my son sold?"

"Ashdod. Slave . . . market."

"To whom was he sold?"

"Don't know," Jobal said. He coughed, and Urnan had to jerk his face back to keep from being splattered with blood.

"Pretty boy," Jobal said. "Pretty boys don't live—"

Urnan shook the Philistine's shoulders, but there was no response.

It was time to leave. Quickly he cleaned the blade of his sword, donned his tunic and girdle, and thrust the sword into its sheath. It was growing dark. A glow of red came from the firebox. He stepped out from under the shed that shaded the forge and right into the arms of two burly soldiers.

"Here, what's the hurry, smith?" one of them asked. "What's all the disturbance?"

Urnan was pushed back into the shop. A soldier exclaimed in surprise when he saw the two dead men on the floor.

"It's Captain Jobal!"

Jobal was not dead. As one soldier moved quickly to bend over him, he opened his eyes and rasped, "Tell Galar—smith . . . of Shiloh."

Urnan bunched his muscles, then used all of his strength to break the loose hold that the other soldier had on him. His left arm flamed with pain, but he was free and running. He tripped and fell, and the weight of two soldiers was quickly on his back.

He stood before the general in torchlight.

"He killed Jobal?" Galar asked in amazement.

"And Bulbul," said a soldier. "Bulbul, too."

Galar stepped forward and looked into Urnan's face. "Why, smith?"

Urnan was silent.

"The captain said something just before he died, General," a soldier said.

"What?" Galar demanded.

"I didn't really understand it, sir. But he wanted me to tell you something. Called your name, sir, and said something that sounded like Shiloh."

"Shiloh?"

"Yes, sir."

Galar shook his head in sudden comprehension. "By the gods," he said, "I *thought* I knew you. You told me, near Shiloh, that you were an armorer." He turned to the soldiers. "How did he kill Jobal?" He thrust his face into Urnan's. "You sneaked up behind him, didn't you, you Hebrew pig, just as the coward Saul ambushes our patrols."

"We heard a fight, General," one of the soldiers said. "Went on not too long, but we heard blades clashing."

"But he couldn't kill Jobal in a fair fight—not a smith, not a Hebrew."

"Give me my sword and face me yourself," Urnan challenged. But it was a foolhardy notion. He was feeling light-headed from loss of blood.

"Don't tempt me," Galar said, eyeing the smith's wound. The torches flickered. Shadows played on the general's face, throwing the sharp planes into deep relief. "Have his wound treated," he ordered. "Stop the bleeding. I will deal with him tomorrow."

CHAPTER TWENTY-FIVE

Once again the smell of superheated charcoal wafted about on the breezes of the hills of Israel. The ring of iron on iron reverberated among the rocky crags, and the hiss of hot metal being tempered in water confirmed that there was a smith in the land of Benjamin. Long years had passed without one—ever since the Philistines had outlawed smiths among the oppressed.

Eri was placing himself, his family, and the entire settlement of Gibeah at great risk by openly operating a forge. If he were caught by the Philistines, he would suffer the most terrible tortures they could devise. It was at Saul's request that Eri had established his family in a pleasant house among the olive orchards on the outskirts of the town that the king had made his capital. Life was settling into a comfortable routine for the armorer. Baalan managed his household skillfully, and the man and his second wife had developed a genuine fondness for each other, although he did not feel the passion for Baalan that he always harbored for Sarah. To make the Ammonite woman's life easier, Eri had taken two young domestic servants, one male and the other female. Because of the long and persistent conflict with the Philistines, there was no shortage of orphans looking for shelter in exchange for hard work. Baalan was able to devote the majority of her time to caring for her child, Sunu, and the childlike Sarah; but never did she fail to have a meal hot and ready when Eri came from his work.

As for Sarah, her condition was unchanged. Being back in the village where she was born, where she had grown to be the young woman who witnessed the slaughter of her family, had no effect on her condition. When Eri took her to the cave that had once been her family's emergency retreat, she wandered around idly, picking up a rock with a touch of color or plucking a wildflower, but showed no sign of being jarred into awareness at the scene of her trauma.

Gibeah had been rebuilt. The village, being in the center of the territory where Saul conducted his hit-and-run war against the Philistine occupation, had more protection than many areas. Nonetheless, the residents lived on a keen edge of suspense because of Saul's presence and Eri's. Although work continued on the wall that surrounded the heart of the settlement, the townspeople knew that no wall, however strong, would stop a concerted attack by the bulk of the enemy forces.

Gibeah's primary defense was the army of Saul. Even though the fighting force had grown with each military success, it was still very small when compared to the size of the power and weaponry of its foe. There were those who feared that Saul's continued harassment of Philistine forces was sure to bring down retribution. When Jonathan, Saul's oldest son, brought word of his father's latest triumph, the town was abuzz with excitement and worry.

Eri was at his forge, as usual, when Jonathan came into the village at the head of a small force of men. Eri heard the shouts of greeting and wanted to know how the Hebrews had fared. He struck the spearhead he was forming a few precision blows, then put it back into the fire and nodded to his helper to work the bellows. While the iron was heating, he stepped out into the sun. Jonathan raised one powerful fist and shook it high in the air in victory.

"Hail, Jonathan!" Eri smiled fondly. He had watched Jonathan develop from a boy into a magnificent young man. The son was an image of the father, tall, regal of bearing, fair of face. He was now recognized by his father as a brave warrior capable of leading other men, and his skill as an archer was without peer.

"Uncle," Jonathan said, taking Eri's arm in a firm clasp. "Have you heard?"

"Rumors," Eri said. "Come into the shade."

"It is a day to be in the light of God's sun," Jonathan said. "Our people have destroyed the Philistine garrison at Geba."

"Saul is well?" Eri asked.

"The king is indestructible."

"Bless God and forgive Jonathan's arrogance," Eri said, rolling his eyes heavenward.

Since childhood, Eri had been impressed by the devotion and piety of those who claimed to be Yahweh's Chosen People more than by any evidence of divine guidance or protection given to the Hebrews. In fact, if one formed his opinion strictly on the present condition of the Chosen People, one had to wonder just what kind of God they worshiped, for they lived in a precarious condition. God had given the land of Israel to those who followed Moses and Joshua, but now the people were in danger of losing all that had been gained by the men of old.

And yet, when Eri and Baalan took Sarah and Sunu to hear the priests of Yahweh and the sounds of prayer were in the air, a feeling of rightness and peace came over him. There had been no doubt in his mind, even as a youth, that the stone image of Dagon had been a manmade thing of no spiritual value. The God of Israel was entirely a different matter.

When Eri prayed, which admittedly was not often,

he prayed to the one God. And when he heard Jonathan's words and saw the light of triumph in the young man's eyes, he formed a silent prayer for his friend Saul, for the men who fought with him, and for their people.

"You're right, Uncle," Jonathan said, "I must not risk the sin of pride." He clenched a fist. "But, by the name of God, my father did crush them!"

Saul returned to Gibeah a few days later. The years had changed him little. His great mane of hair was still stygian black, his beard stiff and fierce, his arms more mighty than ever. His friendship with Eri remained unaltered as well. He and Jonathan, whose closeness with Eri was a joy to all three men, took meat in the house of the armorer and laughed at the antics of young Sunu.

When the meal was finished, and Baalan had taken the silent Sarah and the boy to the women's quarters, Eri poured wine. Saul reclined on a couch, his leonine head resting on an ornately decorated pillow. "The great blow that was predicted to fall on us in revenge for Geba has not come," he said.

Both Eri and Jonathan were silent, waiting for the king to continue.

"But the enemy has gathered his forces," Saul said.

Jonathan spoke softly. "My scouts say that there are many chariots and horsemen and a forest of footmen with spears."

"Scouts always overestimate the strength of the enemy," Saul said with a disdainful wave of his hand. "Moses sent twelve spies, one from each of the tribes, to search out the land of Canaan. They found a land of milk and honey; but they said, 'Oh, Moses, the people of that land are strong, and the cities have great walls.' They said, 'Oh, Moses, the fierce Amalekites are in the south, and then there are the terrible Hittites, and the Jebusites, and the Amorites, and the Canaanites by the sea.' "

Saul sat up, grinning. He minced his words, holding up his hands as if to ward off a blow. "And, 'Oh, Moses, there are the giants, the sons of Anak. Oh, Moses, in their sight we are as insignificant as grasshoppers.' " He put on a fierce look. "And when the people heard all of these dire tidings they wept and soiled their clothing in fear and wished that they had died in the wilderness so that they would not have to face the ferocious people in Canaan."

He pointed a finger at Eri to emphasize his next words. "Only one man stood unafraid—Caleb, of the tribe of Judah. He told the calamity howlers to be still, and he said, 'We can overcome. We can do it. Let us go at once and take for our own this land that God had promised to us.'"

Saul looked first at Eri, then at his son. "Where is my Caleb?" he asked.

"Here," Jonathan said quickly.

"And here," Eri said.

Saul laughed. "Good, good, for I would miss both of you sorely if I had to punish you, as Moses banished all those who doubted from entering the Promised Land." He rose, and his head almost touched the ceiling. "The numbers of the enemy do *not* match the sands of the seashore. They are *not* invincible. They *can* be beaten."

"I hear, and I believe," Jonathan said.

Saul reached out and mussed his son's hair with a great paw of a hand. "I must go to Gilgal." He made a sour face. "I have been summoned by Samuel. He heard that I'm ready to take on the Philistines, and he wants to bless me and burn a sacrifice beforehand."

Eri's eyebrows shot up. "Are things smoother between you two?"

"An uneasy truce," Saul replied.

The armorer nodded knowingly. He had recently heard a rumor regarding the prophet and the king: Someone had dared to challenge Samuel by reminding him that he had anointed Saul with oil at God's direction to be prince of his inheritance. In response the old man blustered that he had succumbed to pressure applied by the people and that Israel needed no king but Yahweh.

"I will go with you to Gilgal," Jonathan said.

"No, no. Stay. Stay with your men, for if the enemy

decides to venture from his position at Michmash, there will be only you to stand in his way."

"I obey, of course," Jonathan said.

Wherever Saul went, people gathered to see the king and, now, to be blessed by the prophet. It was supposed to be a great occasion. Although the Hebrews saw the king, there was no priest to make sacrifice and call down God's kindness. Seven days after the time of the prearranged meeting, Samuel had not arrived in Gilgal.

Saul grew increasingly impatient. First, he interpreted Samuel's absence as yet another sign of disrespect. Second, he did not want his forces to interpret the prophet's nonappearance as an omen against their success. That in itself could cause defeat. Third, the gathering of Hebrew civilians presented a tempting, defenseless target for a Philistine raid and would be easy prey for even a small enemy force venturing forth from Michmash.

Saul, eager to have the crowds dispersed before the Philistine decided to move against them, usurped the duties of the priest. He himself presented the burnt offering to God and the peace offering.

Many bizarre and twisted reports of the occurrences at Gilgal reached Eri and Jonathan. After hearing of the king's actions, they wished they had been at his elbow to advise him to be patient. Perhaps only one report, brought to them by a young officer of Saul's army, was not exaggerated. Samuel, the young man said, had been enraged when he heard that the king had acted without him. Then the prophet had accused the king of acting foolishly.

"Ooo-hoo! Even having God's protection, that priest is a brave man," Eri said, for he knew his friend.

The young officer continued. "Samuel said that the king had gone against God's commandments—"

"More so Samuel's commandments," Jonathan interrupted angrily.

"—and that Saul's kingdom would not continue."

Jonathan's face went white, and a visible shudder

passed through him. "When the spoilers come from the Philistine garrison, I would like to see Samuel fight them off with nothing more than the word of God," he said bitterly.

Eri, frightened by the blasphemy, raised his hand to silence the young man.

But his blood was up. "When the cavalry charges and the spearmen follow up, let Samuel throw his holy scrolls at them!" Jonathan erupted.

Now it was Eri's time to shudder. He went back to his work with a sense of foreboding making the bright, sunlit day seem less radiant.

CHAPTER
TWENTY-SIX

Samuel was growing old, and it was not often that he chose to leave his home. When he traveled he never burdened an animal with his weight and let it be known that those accompanying him should be on foot as well. He was still a powerful man, and his stride was vigorous. His tresses and his beard, neither of which had ever felt the blade of a razor, were silvered, long, and so formidable that he looked as if he wore a tunic of hair over his other garments.

The prophet came to Gibeah on a day of summer heat. He walked through orchards of olives and fruit, then past fields where men, women, and children worked side by side under the blazing sun. The heat was not unusual, just a typical summer's day in the hills west of the great Salt Sea.

Just after midday he rested in the shade of a rocky outcrop outside the village while several members of his entourage went ahead to announce his arrival. Others watched idly as a group of women and children gleaned a field of once-harvested grain.

Samuel was musing in prayer when a commotion broke out among the women in the field. A feminine wail of anguish came to his ears. Then he saw a girl run at top speed toward the nearest group of buildings, one of which, judging from the smoke and sounds that issued from it, was a forge. As the wailing from the field intensified, a man ran from the forge into the field. Samuel guessed this was the smith, because he was naked from the waist up and his arms were strongly developed.

Samuel got to his feet, straightened his back slowly, then moved into the grain field. He watched as the smith threw himself to his knees beside a small boy who had fallen to the ground.

Stalks of grain slashed at Eri's arms and legs as he came racing into the field. He found his wife Baalan weeping piteously as she knelt beside her son in the heat. She looked up tearfully when Eri fell to his knees and lifted Sunu into his arms. The child was so still, so pale, so seemingly weightless and fragile. His chest did not rise and fall with breath.

Eri recognized the symptoms immediately. The boy had fallen victim to the sun. He had seen grown men stricken in the same manner. "We must get him into the shade," he said, rising with his son in his arms.

"Hold!" a deep voice commanded.

Eri turned his head and was amazed to see the prophet Samuel. For a moment he wondered if he were hallucinating. He had not seen Samuel in a matter of years and was shocked to see that age was overtaking the prophet.

"Put him down," Samuel ordered.

"It is the sun," Eri said. "We must get him into the shade."

"He breathes not," Samuel said. "There is little time. Do as I say."

"My child . . . my child . . ." Baalan wailed, plucking at Sunu's hair.

There was an almost eerie quality of command in the voice of the long-haired one. Baalan wailed anew as Eri knelt and placed Sunu on the stubble-covered ground.

Samuel grunted as he lowered himself to his knees. He lifted his hands to the Lord and prayed in a voice that rang out over the field and reverberated back from the rocky crags that ringed the little valley.

Eri knew true panic, for Samuel had said that time was short. Although he accepted the God of Israel, he did not believe that the power of prayer would bring his son back from the dead. And he had heard too much of the conflict between Samuel and Saul from the king's point of view; he was predisposed against the prophet's abilities.

The last words of Samuel's prayer rang out. Eri placed his hand on Sunu's forehead. It was damp and hot. The boy's face was pale, but now his lips were turning blue. His chest was still. Baalan was nearly convulsed with her sobs.

Samuel bent over the small body. Eri formed words of protest, but something stopped him. He watched as Samuel opened the boy's mouth with his fingers, then covered the orifice with his lips. The sound of Samuel's exhalation was audible as he forced his own breath into Sunu's mouth. A gasp went up from the women.

The sun burned down. Baalan wept softly now, sounding as if all hope was gone. Eri was whispering, "Help him, please help him."

For an endless time the old man bent over the boy, huffing his breath into Sunu's mouth. His silvering hair cascaded down to hide the small head and bony shoulders from sight, so if Sunu's chest moved, only Samuel knew. He intensified his efforts, and the boy gasped and began to breathe. The old man straightened and lifted his hands in thanks to the Lord.

"Now take him indoors," Samuel said. "Cool him with damp cloths and give him water to drink."

Eri held his son in his arms and looked into the

eyes of the prophet, one of which was beginning to
cloud whitely with the blinding disease of age. "Thank
you," he said fervently.

"Give your thanks to God," Samuel said. "And
when the boy is older, tell him that the God of Abraham
saw fit to give him life for the second time."

"I will, Samuel," Eri promised.

Samuel looked upward, toward the hills. His forehead was wrinkled in thought or in puzzlement. He
lifted his hand in blessing and turned away, only to
pause indecisively. "You are the smith Eri?"

Eri was not impressed that Samuel knew his name.
Israel was a small nation, and there was but one smith in
the unconquered territory. "Who is greatly in your
debt," he acknowledged.

The old man's face became serene, as if he had just
made a satisfactory decision about a troublesome matter. "Gird yourself and be ready," he said, "for soon you
will hear a call. It will come from someone of your
blood."

"But I have no surviving kin," Eri said. He had
given up his father for dead many years before. The best
guess of those who knew the ways of the Philistines was
that Urnan had been sent to the mines of Kittem, where
the life expectancy of a slave was measured in months.

Samuel raised his bushy eyebrows. "Nevertheless, a
call will come."

"Samuel, I know that you probably came here to
meet with Saul. But later, when you and the king are
finished with your business, please come to my home.
You will be most welcome. My women will prepare food
and drink for you and your company."

Samuel shook his head. "No, my work here is
done," he said. "I have nothing to transact with the
king."

True to his word, as Eri and the women carried
Sunu toward the house, the prophet turned, and with
his protesting and puzzled entourage, strode away in the
direction from which he had come.

* * *

Sunu was weak for several days. Baalan kept him quiet, and Sarah took enough interest to help bathe his forehead with cool cloths. Saul, miffed that Samuel had come to the outskirts of Gibeah without even paying his respects to the king, came to find out how the child was faring. Baalan had accepted Samuel's miracle without question, but Eri remained troubled. He had much to do, for the Philistines were active, sending out companies of soldiers from their garrison at Michmash to ravage the countryside.

Saul and the main army went into the hills. Jonathan and his small company ventured forth from Gibeah on scouting trips, mainly to be sure that the enemy did not turn his attentions toward Saul's once-ruined capital. The young man fretted, for he had orders from his father to avoid the enemy if possible, not to venture too far afield to find the Philistine, and, in short, to act as a garrison for the village.

There came a day, however, when it was impossible to avoid contact with the enemy. A patrol of Jonathan's men came face-to-face with a small group of Philistines in a narrow wadi, and in the brief and deadly fight all of the Philistines except one were killed. The survivor was brought in chains into Gibeah and presented to Jonathan.

"Mercy, Great One," the Philistine begged.

Jonathan had seen the ravaged villages left behind by the Philistine. He knew better than most that Israel was fighting not only for the land that had been given to the Chosen People by God but for their very survival as a people. In the bitter war between Hebrew and Philistine, only God could afford to show mercy, and Yahweh was known as a stern God. Both Jonathan and the captured soldier knew that the Philistine would die. It had become a question of how quickly or how painfully death would come.

"How many men, horsemen, footmen, and chariots are at Michmash?" Jonathan asked.

"I am but a poor soldier," the Philistine said. "I cannot number them. They are there in the ten thousands, surely."

Eri, who had noted the return of the patrol, came into the small square in front of Jonathan's headquarters in time to hear the exchange. Jonathan looked up, nodded, and said, "Here is a fellow who can't count."

"My lord," the captive said, "I speak the truth. I know not how many there are exactly. I know only that when the chariots move, their dust blocks out the sun."

"And footmen?" Jonathan asked.

"As many as grains of sand on the seashore," the soldier said.

Jonathan snorted in derision. "I believe our guest will estimate more accurately after he hangs by the wall for a day or so." He lifted his hand, and two of his men sprang forward. "Fasten him to a wall. Damage him as little as possible so that he can contemplate his inability to count."

"No, lord," the Philistine begged. "At Michmash the chariots number fewer than a hundred, for there is not much room to maneuver them in these hills."

"Good, good," Jonathan said. "And footmen?"

"Truly, I know not. I can only say—"

"That they do not match in number the grains of sand at the seashore," Jonathan said grimly.

"No, lord. Three thousand, perhaps four. There are three companies of at least a thousand foot each."

"Tell me where Galar pitches," Jonathan said.

"The main force is pitched around Gibeah."

Eri blanched when he heard that news. He and Jonathan exchanged quick looks. Neither knew when Saul and his men were expected back, and the village was defenseless without them.

"Be more specific," Jonathan ordered the captive.

"In front of the village is a deep valley. The only approach from the escarpment is guarded by a squad of men who are rotated four times between dawn and dawn."

"A squad consists of how many men?" Jonathan asked.

"Ten, lord."

"Who are Galar's captains?"

"I knew only my own, lord. His name was Jobal."

Eri, who had been listening with intense interest, lifted his head. His eyes narrowed. Even after all the years that had passed, the name *Jobal* was a sourness in his mouth.

" 'Was'?" Eri asked.

"He is dead, lord, killed by an armorer."

"Tell me of this," Eri said, moving forward.

"The smith came to us from Ashdod," the Philistine babbled, "and he was a good armorer. Once he straightened one of my leg guards when everyone said that it was ruined beyond repair."

"Why and how did he kill this Jobal?" Eri asked.

"Not only the captain," the soldier said. "First he cut the throat of a friend of mine, and then he ran his blade into the captain's belly. He almost got away, too. He fell, and we caught him, and after the general, uh, talked with him we put him to the tree."

When it was desirable to shame a dead enemy, his body was suspended from a tree or fastened to a wall. On occasion such an action was taken while the enemy was still alive. If a relatively quick death was wanted, the man was fastened to a wall with metal spikes through his palms and feet. Death came from suffocation, for if the victim let his weight hang by his arms, the position inhibited breathing; and if he put his weight on the spikes through his feet to lift himself in order to draw breath, the pain was excruciating.

The soldier, trying to be helpful in the hopes of earning a quick death, continued talking. "Funny thing —the general knew this smith from sometime long past. He called him the smith of Shiloh."

Shock numbed Eri. "A name. Did the smith have a name?"

"Urnan," the Philistine said. "His name was Urnan."

The injustice of it made Eri want to protest to the God who had become intensely real to him after Samuel's miraculous revival of Sunu. It was possible, of course, that there was another Urnan from Shiloh who was a smith, but in his heart Eri knew that that was highly unlikely.

"What was done with his body?" he asked, thinking there might be some way he could sneak into the Philistine camp and give his father an honorable burial.

"It was still alive and kicking when we left camp this morning," the Philistine said. "General Galar wanted the smith to last a long time. No spikes. No rope around the neck."

"He's still alive?" Eri demanded.

"They last for days like that," the Philistine said. "It's the thirst that kills them eventually." He turned his eyes to Jonathan. "By the gods this is a dry and terrible land, and I hate being thirsty. That's why, lord, I beg you to give me my end with a sword."

"Where in the camp is the tree on which the smith hangs?" Eri asked.

"At the passage," the soldier said, "where everyone can see. Where the men who guard the high place overlooking the valley are always alert."

Eri turned to the men who had brought the Philistine before Jonathan. "You have this man's sword?"

The sword was presented to Eri. "Loose his hands," he ordered.

The soldiers looked to Jonathan for confirmation. The leader nodded. Eri handed the Philistine his sword.

"Maybe we'll met in hell, Hebrews," the Philistine said, as he positioned his short sword point-first at the v of his ribs. He cried out before the blade penetrated, not afterward, as he used the strength of his arms to drive his sword into his diaphragm and his heart. He slumped to the floor in death.

"Remove him," Jonathan ordered, and the men did his bidding. Alone with Eri he said, "You believe that the man hanging on the tree in the Philistine camp might be your father?"

"It is my father," Eri said, for he had just remembered the words of Samuel. *Gird yourself and be ready, for soon you will hear a call. It will be from someone of your blood.* "I will enter the garrison as a Canaanite tradesman."

"Galar will never accept the presence of a tradesman in a war zone," Jonathan told him.

"I have lived among them," Eri said. "I speak their language."

"Eri," Jonathan said, shaking his head slowly, "I don't know why God has willed that I come to love you so much. But you are my dear friend, and I will not allow you to sacrifice your life uselessly."

"I must go," Eri said.

"Certainly. There is no question of that." Jonathan held up one hand to silence Eri's questions. "I know that place. I know the very tree that holds the man you think might be your father. With a small force of men—"

"You have your orders," Eri said. "I will not be responsible for influencing you to go against the king's commands."

"His orders were for me to prevent my men from engaging the enemy," Jonathan said. "My company will not be involved. We will be two."

"Impossible!" Eri said. "Better that I go into the garrison as a Canaanite."

"Uncle," Jonathan said patiently, "in my father's absence I command Gibeah and all those who reside here. While I respect your age, which is greater than mine, and your wisdom, which is considerable, I insist that we go about this thing in my way. Otherwise I will have to chain you to your anvil so that you will not disobey *my* orders. I tell you I know this place. Listen to me—" He bent to the ground and drew in the dust, explaining his plan.

"The tree stands here," Jonathan said, "within a half acre of land, which a yoke of oxen might plow. We will cross over there."

Eri had no choice but to agree.

They crossed the valley in the night. They waited until the singing of a small group of Philistine soldiers faded into silence, until there were no more shouts of disappointment or triumph from those who gamed for stakes. They reached the base of the steep cliff in the silence of midnight.

Jonathan had briefed Eri well. Israel was a small

territory, actually, and the Hebrews had lived in it for
generations. Each physical feature had a name. On each
side of the cliff was a crag: On one side was the sharp
rock called Bozez, on the other side Seneh. All around
was darkness, and above them, an unknown number of
Philistines. Eri could only hope that the captured enemy
soldier had been truthful in saying that no more than
ten men guarded the small, open area on the brink of
the cliff in front of the village.

On the other side of the valley awaited a chosen
force from Jonathan's small army. They had orders to
stand, not to advance regardless of what happened atop
the cliffs.

Climbing to the top of the cliff would have been a
challenge for Eri and Jonathan even in daylight. Ex-
tremes of heat and cold had shattered rock over the
centuries, making the handholds uncertain. Each upward movement had to be tested so the men could be
sure that the rock would not crumble under a foot or in
the grip of the hand.

Jonathan went first. The drop below them deepened with their upward progress. There was no going
back, for climbing down in the darkness would have
been more difficult than scaling upward. A small moon
rose as they reached within a few cubits of the crest.

Suddenly they heard movement from above, and a
voice called out softly in the language of the Philistines,
"Who goes?"

Eri hugged himself as close to the cliff as he could.
Jonathan, above him, was also motionless.

"What is it?" another voice asked.

"Someone climbs the rock," the first voice said.

"Who goes?" came the demand.

Eri called out in the enemy's language. "Two
soldiers of Saul."

Jonathan hissed in anger.

"We are discovered," Eri explained. "We can't go
down."

There was a laugh from above. "The mountain pigs
come from their holes," said a Philistine.

"Stay there until we come to you," Eri called up.

Again there was laughter. "We don't plan to move, Hebrew. Come up, and we'll show you a thing or two."

"They will fall on us and push us back as we reach for the top," Jonathan said.

"I think not," Eri whispered. He knew the enemy, knew their pride.

"Well, we are in the Lord's hands," Jonathan said as he began to climb.

Jonathan was the first to reach the top of the cliff. When Eri heaved himself up and clambered quickly to his feet, his sword in his hand, he could see the weak moonlight gleaming on the armor of four Philistine soldiers.

"Which one shall I skewer on my blade?" asked a burly soldier. "The smaller one or the larger one?"

"Try me!" Jonathan said, and leaped forward.

His blade flashed. There was a heavy clash of metal, followed by a cry of agony and surprise.

Eri had no time to see what had happened, for two of the enemy rushed at him. He went in low, on his knees, and his blade plunged into the soft underbelly of a Philistine, below the man's breastplate. Then Eri was fighting for his life, catching and parrying a blade by the flashes it made in the light of the moon. Suddenly a great shout of alarm went up, and he heard the pounding of feet.

Eri and Jonathan ran forward to position themselves in a very narrow passage they knew of atop the cliffs. They stood side by side, and there was just enough room to wield their swords as men rushed toward the clash of battle. Eri stepped on the leg of a dead man but regained his balance in time to meet the wild rush of another Philistine.

Iron on iron . . . grunts of effort . . . hard breathing . . . sprays of perspiration and blood . . . the thud of a blade as it struck bone and the clash as it rang off armor. Eri's arm lifted and thrust and slashed. Once, he felt the sting of a cut as a blade narrowly missed decapitating him. Blood ran down to his chin as he stepped over still another man who had fallen either to his own blade or Jonathan's, to feel the impact as

iron slipped between the hinges of Philistine armor and
penetrated flesh.

Sounds of confusion went up from the main Philistine camp. Torches flared, and horns blared. The shouting of the officers came to Eri's ears even as he fought
for his life against yet another surge of men—many,
many more than ten. The captive had lied. Eri knew
that Jonathan had, by himself, killed more than ten, and
still they came. The footing in the narrow passage was
slippery with blood, and still they came. Eri's arm was
getting heavy. He knew it was only a matter of time
before he would be too exhausted to fight anymore.
Then they would kill him. The frustration of it nearly
drove him mad, to be so near to his dying father and yet
to be dying himself.

Across the valley Jonathan's men heard the clash of
blades, heard the alarms, saw the glow of torches, and
listened to the shouting. The Hebrews tried to understand the orders that were being given, but distance distorted the words. There was, however, no mistaking the
frenzied movement in the main camp. The captains
were forming their men. Horses squealed in fright as
drivers hurried to hitch them to chariots. The wheeled
vehicles of war would be useless against Jonathan and
Eri, of course, for there was no access for them to the
small, enclosed area.

"They will surely die," said the man whom Jonathan had left in charge.

"No, look!" said another, pointing.

"It is God's will," someone whispered, for instead
of advancing toward the two men in the embattled pass,
the Philistine army was beginning to retreat. It was evident that the Philistines, who for weeks had been expecting an attack from Saul, thought that the entire
army of Israel was about to surround them.

"Let's go!" the leader said, and took his men on
the run toward the road approach to Michmash.

As the small force of Hebrews advanced on the
much-larger enemy group, they made a great noise of

shouts and cries, thinking to add to the Philistines' confusion.

A hush fell atop the cliffs. Befuddled, Eri, in a fighting crouch, turned this way and that, looking for an opponent. Jonathan was still at his side. Behind them, in front of them, and under their feet were the bodies of the enemy.

"In God's name," Jonathan said, his chest heaving, "I have stood with a man."

"And I," Eri said.

Eri's entire body ached with exhaustion, but he forced himself forward. Ahead, in the open portion of the field, was a gnarled olive tree. Among the shadows Eri could see a dark mass. He reached up and touched a bare foot. The flesh was warm. A moan escaped Eri's lips, and a shudder passed through him.

"Climb up and cut him loose," Jonathan said. "I'll catch him."

Eri's foot slipped on the bark, and he scraped his knee against the roughness of the tree. He could not see the man's face. He put his hand out and felt movement as the chest rose and fell. "Urnan?" he whispered.

There was no answer.

"Jonathan, climb up here, too. I need help bracing him."

The young man joined Eri on a branch and leaned forward, both hands flat against the chest of the Philistine captive. That held the man securely while Eri severed the ropes around the man's wrists with a blade that had been dulled during the battle. Next, after Jonathan dropped down from the tree, Eri cut the ropes that supported the body at the belly and chest. He held the man's weight as best he could; but he lost his grip, and the inert body tumbled down at Jonathan. Both men crashed to the ground.

"He's breathing," Jonathan said as Eri jumped down from the tree.

The man's face was still in shadows. Eri moved the body, let moonlight fall on a countenance that was so much like his own that he caught his breath.

"Is it—?"

"It is he," the armorer whispered.

"He has felt the lash," Jonathan said, for his hands were reddened by blood from Urnan's back.

"How can we get him down the cliff?" Eri asked.

"That, thank God, won't be necessary," Jonathan said. "We are greater warriors than we thought, Uncle."

Eri was examining his father's face in the dim light.

"I believe we've frightened the entire Philistine army into running," Jonathan said. "We can take the easy way down into the valley."

Eri looked up through his tears. It was as Jonathan had said. The Philistine camp was empty. The rumble of the heavy supply carts was receding in the distance.

Jonathan, who had more experience in such matters, made a litter from Philistine garments. He used double thicknesses of sturdy spears for the carrying handles. He told Eri that it would be wise to be gone from Michmash by the time the morning light revealed the true size of the attacking Hebrew force.

By dawn they had taken the long road into the valley and were listening to the excited praise of the men.

Urnan's eyes opened as he was being carried back toward Gibeah. At first his lids seemed heavy. He blinked and exerted a great effort to see where he was, but his gaze was blurred. A man walking beside the litter told his companions to stop. They lowered the stretcher to the ground, and the first man knelt beside it. Urnan's unfocused eyes played over his face.

"Father," the man said. "Father, can you speak?"

Father? Ah, yes, a courtesy. "Yes," Urnan said, making an effort to focus his vision.

"You are safe. You're with friends."

"Yes."

Urnan squinted with great effort, and his mouth opened in a failed effort to speak. He was given a flask of water and assisted in the drinking. His head sank back, and his vision cleared. He looked again at the man helping him and was struck momentarily dumb by gazing into what seemed to be a more youthful image of his own face. Could it be? he wondered, disoriented. He reached out his hand to seize the man's arm.

"Eri?" The word was weak, strained.

"Yes, Father. It is I."

Silence. Then, "Eri." The name was thick with tears.

"Yes," Eri said. "Rest now. We're going home."

The Hebrew army's watchmen sent runners to the king's tent when the Philistine host began to withdraw in total confusion. Before dawn Saul sent cavalry to harass the disorganized rear guard, and many carts and oxen were captured. Even as Saul watched from a high crag, some incident panicked a portion of the enemy, and fighting broke out between two groups of Philistines.

"We have them," Saul whispered, more to himself than to his officers.

"We are but few," said a captain who had come north from Judah. "With the light the Philistines will reorganize."

"If they flee from shadows," Saul said, "they will crush one another underfoot when Hebrew iron is applied to their rear."

"I fear, Lord King," said Saul's mightiest captain, "that you risk losing the entire army if you choose to engage the enemy in his superior numbers."

Saul roared in sudden rage. "Cursed be the man who lags behind!" he thundered. "Let all men smite the enemy. Let battle be the order of the day until not one Philistine lives. To hasten this end, here is my command: Let no man pause to rest, or to drink, or to eat. Cursed will be the man who touches food before the fall of evening or until our revenge on the enemy is complete. He who pauses to eat, be he of my own blood, will die!"

It was a long, long day. The running battle raged from near Michmash to Aijalon, and when it was over, Saul rejoiced and shouted his thanks to God for having given him the victory.

In the first hush of darkness Saul returned to

Gibeah. His clothing was wet with the sweat of his exertions, but the blood that soiled his armor, his weapons, and his sandals was not his own. He had given orders for the correct ritual slaying of herds of captured sheep and cattle, so that the fighting men, famished after their long, hard day of battle, would not sin by eating the meat with blood.

There he was told, for there was that quality in some men that engendered jealousy of the great, that his own son Jonathan had disobeyed the stern and dire injunction not to touch food during the day.

Jonathan was called before the king. The young man was greatly beloved by most, so the officers and elders and priests stood and watched grimly as Saul, deathly pale, questioned him.

"Tell me what you have done," he said.

"Father," Jonathan replied, "I heard not your order. As we came through a wood I saw bees making honey in a tree. I thrust the butt of my spear into the hive and ate the honey that adhered to it."

A hush fell. Saul's face was anguished.

"Lord King," a harsh voice called out, "do what you think is right."

"I gave an order," Saul said, and his voice was heavy. "If I do not enforce that order with my own son as I would with others, then it will be myself and Jonathan on one hand, and all of Israel against us."

"I am to die because I tasted honey?" Jonathan asked quietly.

"Surely you must die," Saul said, his voice breaking.

Eri stepped forward. "Then I with him, Lord King," he said. "We did not hear your orders, for we were involved in killing the enemy before Michmash and in bringing my father home to Gibeah."

"And I," shouted a soldier. And then, by twos and by threes the company gathered around Jonathan.

Saul tried to hide his relief. "Is it the will of the people that Jonathan be spared?" he bellowed in question. "He has smitten the enemy. Does that make him worthy of forgiveness?"

The roar from the soldiers was in the affirmative.

"Then so be it!" the king proclaimed, to the loud approval of all but a small few who had gathered. Then Saul beckoned to Eri. Eri stood beside the king, who bent to whisper, "Urnan? Urnan is here?"

"Truly," Eri said, his face split in a grin. "He has been wounded and lashed, but he will live. My women are giving him tender care."

"By the thunder," Saul growled. "Urnan, who found me at Ebenezer and cared for me in my illness and brought me home." He clapped Eri on the back, causing him to take an involuntary step forward. "Let me know when he has recovered enough to talk."

"That I will," Eri said joyously.

Saul grinned, his lips red through his black beard. "My friend, do you suppose there just might be a God, after all?"

CHAPTER TWENTY-SEVEN

Urnan's wounds were healing nicely. Watching his grandson at play had put a smile on the man's face and helped him endure the days when he had strength only to lie in the shade and suffer the ache in his healing arm, the itch as the lash marks scabbed over on his back. Father and son spent the days and evenings together, engaged in the bittersweet diversion of describing the separate lives they had lived since that moment so long before, when they last caught sight of each other outside Ashdod.

Urnan roared with laughter when Eri told of the methods Saul and he had used to convince the Dagon priests to return the Ark of the Covenant to Israel. He could identify with Eri's sorrow when his son recounted the events leading up to the onset of Sarah's madness.

For his part, Eri was fascinated by Urnan's description of the wonders of Egypt, of many-gated cities, and the splendor and grandeur of the pharaohs' tombs. He noticed that his father could not speak of Tania, the beautiful Egyptian princess, without his voice becoming husky.

"Will you go back to Egypt?" Eri asked.

Urnan was silent for a long time. He was by no means an old man, although there were times when his body reminded him with aches and pains that he was no longer a youth. His child was now a man in the prime of life.

"The thought of it makes my heart leap in expectation, just before it sinks down in consternation when I think of the barriers that lie between her and me." He shook his head. "If I were ten years younger . . ."

Soon he was walking slowly to Eri's forge, to sniff at the familiar odors and to give unsolicited advice to the smiths and the helpers. He was pleased by Eri's skills. As soon as there was strength in his own arm he began to teach his son the secrets of the Egyptian armorers, then goldsmiths. He presented the first product of a collaboration with Eri, a whimsical scarab with eyes of lapis, to the mother of his grandson, and the gift in glowing gold caused Baalan to weep with happiness.

It was a quiet and pleasant time in the land of Israel. As a result of Saul's efforts, the Philistines had retreated all the way back to the plains and coastal cities. The yoke of Philistine occupation had been lifted. Once again the shepherds could graze their flocks anywhere in Israel without fear. Burnt offerings sent their smokes heavenward to Yahweh in thanksgiving.

Eri saw little of his friend Saul in those days, but through Jonathan he was kept apprised of the enmity that continued to fester between the king and the man who had crowned him. In spite of the repeated successes Saul enjoyed in the military arena, the old man was still unwilling to remove his hands completely from the reins of state.

When Jonathan came to the smith's house, he was wearing armor. He was a splendid sight, tall and elegant. His hair and his beard were neatly trimmed. His strong nose and his bold eyes, sun-crinkled at the corners, were truly those of a prince.

"Well, Eri," Jonathan said, "if you can tear yourself away from home and family and abandon the hammer for the sword, your services will be much in demand again."

"Why?" he asked quickly. "Are the Philistines on the march again?"

"No, no," Jonathan answered. "We march south, directed by God." He paused and, with a smirk of distaste, added, "Or by Samuel."

"But why into Judah?" Eri asked in puzzlement.

"Our spiritual leader has decided that it is time to redress old wrongs," Jonathan said. "We march against the Amalekites."

"They offer no threat to us," Eri said. He wanted to say, "No, no, let war be damned." Life was sweet. He had his son and his father. Sarah was physically well taken care of, and his relationship with Baalan was warm and satisfying.

"Ah, Uncle," Jonathan teased, "every true Hebrew remembers that the Amalekite was the first enemy to be faced when we came up out of Egypt. They attacked Moses and Joshua in the Sinai. And when the people first attempted to enter the land that God had promised, it was the Amalekites who stood in the way."

"But that is so long past," Eri protested.

"God—and Samuel—have long memories," Jonathan said. He shrugged and spread his hands. "I hesitate to ask you to leave home just when you're getting reacquainted with your father. . . ."

"If the army moves, I will move with it," Eri said.

Urnan, who had been listening silently, said, "And I."

Eri smiled indulgently. "I think that you had best stand aside for this clash."

"But—"

"I agree with Eri," Jonathan interrupted. "No, Urnan. Our carrying you half-dead on a litter from the camp of the Philistines is too recent and your wounds too severe for you to think of joining us."

"Baalan and Sarah and the boy will be glad of your company and your protection," Eri said.

"You both appeal to my less noble instincts," Urnan said with a grin. "With your silvery speech you have convinced me."

Eri stood at Jonathan's side to hear the singing and chanting of the old prophet. The smoke of sacrifice was still in the armorer's nostrils when Samuel stood on the steps of the altar on a high place. Saul, head and shoulders above those gathered around him, resplendent in his armor, bowed his head only slightly in deference to the last judge of Israel.

"Saul!" the old man bellowed. "Hear now the words of the Lord. The Lord of Hosts says, 'I remember what the Amalekites did to Israel when Israel came up from Egypt, how they lay in ambush and how they smote Israel sorely.' Now the Lord says to you, 'Saul, go and smite the city of Amalek. Go and destroy it utterly. Spare them not. Slay every man, every woman, every infant and suckling. Kill every ox and ass and sheep and camel. Leave not one stone standing.' "

Eri sneaked a glance at Jonathan, who was looking at his father. Then Eri shifted his eyes to Saul's face. The king's expression was blank, but his eyes were burning with a fury unlike anything that Eri had ever seen. Eri knew his friend well enough to know what he was thinking: The king was exhausted after the long years of battle and strife, and he had accomplished what he had set out to do. All he wanted to do was go home and live simply and in peace. Now, to be sent by Samuel on this faraway, onerous, and, as he saw it, unnecessary excursion, was ridiculous. But to kill everything in their path was heinous. For a moment Eri thought Saul was going to fly at Samuel and strangle him. But the king kept a tight hold on his temper instead.

After the blessing was made, the army started out in the midst of great celebration. After a short while the experience felt good to Eri—the long march, the companionship, the feeling of being a small part of a whole. The army trekked through desolate splendor in the

Negeb, where water was of more value than gold. The nomadic Amalekites, having been warned by their scouts of the strength of Saul's army, moved their flocks and herds deeper into the wilderness of Paran, toward Sinai, where the first clash between the two groups of wanderers had occurred so long before.

Two Israelite units trapped a small band of Amalekites in a wadi, where they had gathered for water. As it happened, Eri and Jonathan, at the head of Jonathan's company, came upon the scene late. The Hebrews had obeyed Samuel's instructions. Nothing lived. The water that trickled from a rocky escarpment mixed with the blood of men, women, and children, along with their animals.

Eri turned away in disgust. Jonathan gave orders to his second-in-command to take the men down to the waterhole, clear it, and refill their waterskins.

"We'll give them time to clean things up," Jonathan said to Eri. "Then we'll go down. It is said that this spring is one of those that Moses brought forth by striking the stones with his staff."

"I have enough water to last," Eri said, although the water in his skin had been taken from a muddy sink and was rank and stale.

Jonathan put his hand on Eri's shoulder. "Senseless slaughter is distasteful to me as well, Uncle, but the men were obeying the word of God."

"The word of Samuel," Eri said heatedly.

Jonathan made a mock gesture of sheltering his head from heavenly bolts. "You risk the wrath of Yahweh so lightly?"

"Never," Eri said. "But neither can I make sense of what he asks of us or how he influences our lives. When we heard that there was a smith hanging on a tree at Michmash, I prayed that it was my father and that he would be alive. It was, and he was. And yet for years I have prayed every night and a dozen times during the day that my wife be brought back to me, and there she is, as beautiful as she was as a girl. But her wits are—" He spread his hands. "—where?"

"The ways of God are not always clear to a mere man," Jonathan said.

"Can it be God's will to kill women and children? And the animals?"

"Who is to say, other than Samuel?" Jonathan asked. "It makes a form of brutal sense to slay the Amalekite children and infants, for they would grow up to be the enemies of Israel. But it seems to me that it would be much wiser to eat the sheep than provide a banquet for the carrion birds and the jackals."

When the army was at Shur, which was near Egypt, word came to the main encampment of Saul that the Amalekites, having no place to run, were gathering at a site called Havilah. With great shouts the men of Israel came down on the massed nomads, and the iron weapons smashed the Amalekites' bronze blades. But Eri took no pride in his craftsmanship on this day.

Jonathan's company was a mounted force. The striking point was made up of a dozen captured Philistine chariots. Eri watched from a dry, sunbaked prominence as the chariots lifted dust in plumes behind them. The slashing blades that whirled from the hubs of the great wheels caused havoc in the Amalekite ranks. He watched as the horsemen split the enemy into two groups to be swarmed over by masses of footmen.

The battle was over before the sun was high. Eri turned away and rode into the desert to escape the screams of women, the terrified bleating of sheep and groaning of dying oxen. He returned with the sunset. As he topped the last rocky ridge to look down upon the scene of the battle, he heard, to his shock, the sound of sheep and the lowing of cattle.

CHAPTER
TWENTY-EIGHT

Sarah liked watching the boy Sunu. She was intrigued by all of his activities—playing, eating, bathing, even sleeping. As the summer's heat was moderated by the changing season, the woman spent long hours each day sitting in the shade of the apple trees that Eri had planted in the gardens. Sunu was in a youthful stage of hero worship. His father and Prince Jonathan were, to him, the mightiest of men. In his imagination they matched fabled Samson and even that greatest of all warriors, Joshua.

Eri was still in the south with the army, and no word had come from him to his family. To help allay Sunu's missing his father, Urnan crafted for the boy a very light breastplate of calf's hide and whittled him a sword of olive wood. The slaying of imaginary Philistine and Amalekite enemies in the garden was pitiless and prodigious, and thus, by causing enemy ranks to dwindle, Sunu was helping his father to come home soon.

Filled with fatherly concern, Urnan had become interested in studying Sarah. He was absolutely stymied by her condition. She had the face of a praying angel—beautiful, peaceful. He wondered what torment still lay within and how to unlock that door. Thus it was that he noticed her dark eyes following the mock battles of the young warrior. As the days passed he realized that only Sunu seemed to elicit a show of interest in Sarah.

Urnan moved his stool so that he could sit beside her. He talked to her in a low, quiet, soothing voice. He spoke of how handsome the young boy was growing to be. He made laughing comments about Sunu's play. He asked such questions as, "Would you like to have a child of your own, Sarah? Would you like to have a son of Eri's to hold in your arms?"

The weeks passed in this manner, with no response from the woman. Baalan seated Sarah in the garden in the morning after the day's first meal. Urnan joined her there after he had made the rounds of the shop to see that the workmen were doing their jobs of turning out armaments for Saul's army.

On a whim, Urnan guided Sunu, tired from an epic battle, to stand by Sarah's side. "Be nice to Mother Sarah," Urnan told the boy. "Give her a kiss."

It took some persuading, for Sunu was at a stage where females of any age were anathema. At last the boy kissed her on the cheek. He blushed. "She smells good," he admitted.

At first Sarah did not cooperate, but Sunu did. At Urnan's request, he repeated the gesture every day, and it was a matter of only a week before one of Sarah's arms closed about the boy as he gave her a kiss—and a few more days before, when he was fresh from his bath, she would comb his hair back from his brow in long, slow, rhythmic strokes.

Urnan explained to Baalan what he was trying to do. He was encouraged to continue his efforts to break through the shell of indifference. "Sarah," he would whisper over and over, "you can have a boy of your own, but you must try. Come back to us, Sarah. Come back, and soon there will be a child at your breast. *Your* child, Sarah. Eri's child."

The nights were becoming chill. In the evenings Urnan joined Baalan and Sarah in the central room of the house, where a fire burned on the grate to make things cozy. He told Baalan and Sunu, who listened to his grandfather's stories with avid interest and with wide eyes, about his friend the Egyptian prince, who could impose his will upon others through the force of his eyes.

"Would that he were here," Baalan said, "to awaken Sarah from her long sleep."

"Tell her to play with me," Sunu said. "Put your eyes in hers like Remose did."

"His name was Kemose," Urnan said. "And I do not have his gift."

"Perhaps you learned something from him," Baalan suggested.

Sarah was staring into the fire. Urnan knelt before her. "Look at me, Sarah," he said.

But she continued to gaze at the fire. He turned her head and looked into her eyes. She cocked her head slightly. "Sarah," he whispered. "Hear me, Sarah. The choice is yours. You retreated from life, Sarah, but you can come back. You can come back and be one of us. You can know love, and you can have the child that you want so much."

She tried to move her head, to look away. He held her with his hands on either side of her face. "Sarah, you are not the only one to have known sadness. Once, I watched helplessly while the woman I loved, the mother of my son, was brutalized and killed. I saw my son led away into slavery. You are not the only one. What did you see?"

She struggled, but he held her head by force. "Did you see the Philistines kill your mother? Is that why you hide behind madness? Did you see her blood gush like water from a spring created by Moses? Did you—"

She screamed once, piercingly, and fainted.

With the morning she was the same, a body that moved, ate, slept, and walked when led by someone—

but a shell that remained empty. But that night, in front of the fire, after Sunu had gone to sleep, Urnan talked to her, deliberately describing images of merciless slaughter. The horror, he hoped, would be so vivid that Sarah's mind would be jolted. Suddenly she began to weep, and as he spoke, her sobs caused her entire body to spasm with their force.

"Sarah," Urnan said, his eyes boring into hers. "Now you will speak to me. I am Urnan, father of Eri. Speak to me."

Her weeping abated. She settled back onto her couch and, with tears running down her cheeks, watched the leaping, fluttering flames. Again it appeared that her mind had withdrawn unto itself.

"Put her to bed," Urnan said sadly.

"Come with me, Sarah," Baalan said, taking Sarah's arm.

Sarah looked up. "Yes," she said.

"Oh, yes, my dear," Baalan whispered, looking at Urnan with a triumphant smile. "Come, and I will help you prepare for bed."

"Yes," Sarah said again.

Agag, onetime king of the vanquished Amalekites, trudged tiredly along behind the horse of a Hebrew officer. His hands were tied together, and a line led from them to the pommel of the officer's saddle. Saul was at the forefront of the army as it marched northward through Judah. Jonathan and Eri rode side by side as Jonathan surveyed the ranks of his soldiers and the animals that were being herded along with the army. Not all of the Amalekites' animals had been spared; but when the soldiers begged to be allowed to save the best of the sheep and oxen to be taken back with them into the hills of Israel, the king did not forbid it.

The greatest puzzle, however, was why the Amalekite, Agag, still lived. The survival of both the animals and the man who had once ruled the nomadic bands was in direct opposition to God's command as interpreted by Samuel.

"For myself," Jonathan said, "I would rather be

dead and food for the scavengers than led into captivity in chains."

"You haven't experienced slavery," Eri said, "and still you abhor the thought of it. Is it not time, Jonathan, to outlaw the practice from Israel?"

Jonathan gave the question no thought at all, for he was pondering Agag's presence. "Could it be that my father is finding that it is lonely in high places?"

"He has become a different person," Eri acknowledged.

"Does he see a symbol of his own kingship in this wretched little man? Does he feel akin to Agag?"

"It is curious that he would let Agag live, while slaughtering all of his people," Eri said.

"The sheep and the cattle can be well utilized as sacrifices to Yahweh," Jonathan pointed out.

"Or to augment the herds of the people who have lost animals to the raids of the Philistines," Eri added.

"But *this* man, this so-called king," Jonathan said. "Uncle, I see nothing but trouble when I look at him. Wouldn't it be best if I take my sword to him and prevent his entering the land of my fathers?"

"Once, we survived disobeying the king's orders," Eri said. "I don't care to take that risk again."

A part of the army camped at Carmel, all of them extremely pleased to be back in their native hills. Saul and the balance of the men marched on to Gilgal. There, on a chill morning, Samuel arrived, walking, leaning on his staff. His hair almost touched the ground, and it was the white of summer clouds. Eri quickly found Jonathan, and the two men hurried to Saul's tent, where the prophet angrily faced the king.

"At Carmel and now in this place I hear the bleating of sheep and the lowing of cattle," Samuel said.

Saul's stance was proud. His chin was high. "For the people I have spared the best of the animals."

Samuel's face darkened. He pointed one gnarled finger at Saul. His thunderous voice had lost none of its power with age. "Shall I tell you what the Lord said to me last night?"

"Say on," Saul said with a curt nod.

"When I anointed you king over Israel, there were those who expressed surprise. Many said that you were too young, that you were a member of the poorest and smallest tribe of Israel."

"I remember," Saul said.

"Now you think you have grown greater than God himself," Samuel thundered. "The Lord sent you to consume the Amalekites!"

"And in that I have obeyed," Saul said.

"Yet you bring the animals alive, and you bring the king of the Amalekites."

"The sheep and the cattle will be sacrifices to the Lord," Saul said, but his face did not show a desire to appease the stern prophet.

"The Lord delights more in obedience than in burnt sacrifices," Samuel said. He drew himself up. "Saul, you have rejected him."

"Not so!" Saul protested.

"And since you have rejected God," Samuel said, "He has stripped you of the kingship."

Saul's eyes narrowed. His hand went to the hilt of his sword. His knuckles showed white as he grasped it. But then his hand came away. He bowed his head and said, "If I have sinned, it was because I was concerned for the welfare of my people. If I have transgressed the commandment of the Lord, I pray that my sin will be forgiven."

"You cannot be forgiven! No longer are you king!"

Samuel turned away, and Saul went after him. As Eri watched in horror, his friend took hold of Samuel's robes to stop the man. Saul's face was nearly purple. "I've had all I can take of your—" Accidentally he tore the fragile gauze of the mantle. The sound ripped outward in waves.

Samuel whirled on him, and his eyes were like burning coals.

"I-I'm sorry," Saul said. "I didn't mean to—"

"As this mantle is rent," Samuel said, and his voice was hollow with the sound of threat, "so has the Lord rent the kingdom of Israel away from you this day. The kingdom is no longer yours but belongs to another who will obey the word of the Lord."

"I know not the man who can take the kingdom from me," Saul warned darkly. "But I ask you, Samuel, not to turn your back on me. Perhaps I have sinned, but I have also served the Lord and my people with my heart and my right arm. Am I now so devoid of honor? Do I not worship God?"

Samuel studied Saul. "Bring the king of the Amalekites to me."

"Let it be done," Saul said immediately, and two lieutenants who had watched the face-off leaped to do his bidding.

Eri and Jonathan had to step back as the Amalekite came shuffling in. Heavy chains shortened his steps and dangled from his wrists. The links were not, as were most metal products in that area, a product of Eri's shops. He had never forged a chain—not in all the years of his work.

Agag stood with his head high. Samuel held out his hand for the sword of one lieutenant, then strode toward the Amalekite. The prophet raised the weapon. The Amalekite king lifted his chin still higher and made no sound as Samuel began to smash at him with the sharp blade. The Amalekite went down, his blood drenching the earth. But the prophet was not satisfied. As the Hebrews watched in fascinated revulsion, Samuel hacked and hacked at the body until it had been hewn to pieces, the bones separated at the joint of shoulder, thigh, and knee.

Saul stood motionless. His face was white with anger. His eyes were terrible.

But Samuel met his gaze. There was a heaviness in the air, as if from an impending storm, and yet the sky was cloudless. "Come no more to me until the day of your death," the prophet said. Then he turned and stalked away.

CHAPTER TWENTY-NINE

Eri came home, to be clasped to his father's breast. Sunu whooped with joy and launched himself, to be caught in midair by the smith. Baalan smiled with joy and waited her turn, which came with Eri holding both of her hands and returning her smile before he kissed her.

"You look well, Husband," she said.

"I am well," Eri said. "You have made me proud, as always, Baalan, by the way you have managed the household in my absence."

"She had some help," Urnan said.

"Yes, we helped," Sunu said, nodding his head vigorously. "And Grandfather says that when we begin to harvest the olives, I can climb the trees to shake down the fruit," Sunu reported.

Eri raised his eyebrows, for that was the task saved for the older boys in the village. "We'll see," he said, and looked at his growing son with new eyes.

"Are you hungry?" Baalan asked.

"Not so much so that I can't keep our customary mealtime schedule," Eri said.

"Some figs and a glass of milk cold from the spring?" Baalan asked.

"No, I'll wait," Eri told her, patting her fondly on her shapely rump. She jerked away, pretending embarrassment. Eri looked around. "And Sarah?"

Baalan's face sobered. Her smile was gone. "In the garden."

"I'll speak to her," Eri said.

"Yes, of course," Baalan said with a nod.

"Father, Sarah can—" Sunu's excited revelation was cut short by his grandfather's hand over his mouth.

Eri smiled at his son and mussed his hair. "We'll talk later, you and I. And we'll see how well you have learned your swordplay lessons from your grandfather."

Eri was determined that his son be able to protect himself as well as to fashion the arms that afforded a measure of freedom from the many threats that beset a man of Israel. No longer was it enough to be a master craftsman, an armorer. Once, a smith with the mark of the lion on his body would have been welcomed in any nation and valued for his skills. In the land of the Philistines, in the world as it was, the old values were lost.

He found Sarah sitting on her couch, half reclined, as he'd seen her sit so often. The white linen of her mantle draped her shapely breasts. The skirt was hiked to reveal her lower legs, and they were honey-skinned, smooth, shapely. As usual, Baalan had done a masterful job of arranging Sarah's hair to complement her lovely round face. Eri made no effort to be quiet. She heard his steps and looked up.

"I've come home, Sarah," he said.

To his surprise, her face flushed, and she lifted one hand to place her fingertips on her cheek. There was something different in her eyes.

He knelt before her and took her other hand in his. "Have you been a good girl?" In spite of her lack of response, it was his custom to talk to her, and because of her condition, the talk was often that of a man speaking to a child who understood little and answered nothing. "Yes, I know you were. For you're always a good girl, aren't you?"

"Yes," Sarah said.

He was shocked into silence.

"Yes," she said. "I know you."

"Sarah?" his voice cracked.

"You must be my Eri's older brother, for you look much like him," Sarah said with a shy smile that tore at Eri's heart, for it was the same smile he'd fallen in love with when she was not yet sixteen.

"Not his brother," he said. "I am he, Sarah. I am Eri."

"No," she said, "for my Eri is very young and more beautiful than you." She realized what she had said and blushed more fiercely. "Forgive me—"

"Only you are still as beautiful as you were when we were so young," he said.

"But where is Eri? They told me he'd be coming soon."

Eri heard a sound, looked up. Urnan, Baalan, and Sunu had entered the garden.

"When? How?" Eri asked.

"Was it a pleasant surprise?" Urnan asked, grinning hugely.

"God has seen fit to bless me," Eri whispered.

"This man won't tell me where Eri is," Sarah said.

Baalan stepped to the side of the couch and took Sarah's hand. "You have not listened to me, Sarah. I told you that Eri would be different."

"No," Sarah pouted.

"I have told you," Baalan said patiently, "that you've been ill, that years have passed. Did you not understand?"

Sarah looked up, and the concentration on her face was touching. "I tried to understand, Baalan. I did try."

"Then look at your husband," Baalan said. "Look at this face and see Eri, for it is he. Just older." She smiled. "And, I'm sure, far more handsome than he was as a callow boy."

Tears ran down Sarah's face. "That is not Eri," she

said. "Please, please, don't be cruel, Baalan. That man is too old. I could never love him."

Baalan slapped Sarah quickly. The sound rang out in the garden. Sarah gasped and put a hand to her cheek. "Little fool," Baalan said harshly. "You had his love, and you abandoned him. You had what I have prayed for, and it was not enough to keep you from seeking to escape, not enough to enable you to endure sorrow. Are you going to throw away his love again?"

Sarah put her hands to her face and wept. "May I go to my room, Baalan?" she asked in a child's voice.

"Let her go," Eri said, heartbroken.

Sarah ran through the garden, to disappear into the house.

"That's what I was trying to tell you, Father," Sunu said. "Mother Sarah can talk."

"Give it time, Eri," Urnan urged. "Recovering one's wits is, I would guess, as great a shock as losing them."

"She's been getting better and better," Baalan said.

"How did it come about?" Eri asked.

"She loves the boy," Urnan said. "I kept telling her that she could have a child of her own."

"He used the magic of the Egyptian Kemose," Baalan said.

Urnan shrugged. "I think it was words more than magic."

"I'm cold," Sunu said.

"Take him inside," Eri told Baalan.

"Come with us," she said. "It's almost time for the meal."

"I want to walk alone for a while," Eri said.

"Then I'll go along with Baalan and Sunu," Urnan said, and before he left he enclosed his son in a comforting embrace.

Eri nodded. He watched them leave.

The sun was low, and there was a chill that foretold winter was in the air. His mood was as bleak as the weather. Eri pulled his mantle around him and walked to the farthest extent of his gardens. Once, he had been very much impressed by the gardens of the house of

Raphu, the man who had taken in Sarah and her mother, and his own gardens were patterned after those. They usually gave him much pleasure, but on that evening as twilight came and the evening star became visible, a heaviness hung in his heart, for he had lost Sarah once more. To lose her and to go through the years wanting to take her into his arms had been, he realized, more painful than he'd ever admitted. But now, to hear her voice, to see life in her eyes once more, to have her returned to him . . . only to have her reject him because of her private vision of a younger Eri—it was too cruel to accept.

It was the nature of the followers of Yahweh to be frank in their discussions with God. Asking questions, wailing out with one's soul, "Why? Why? Why?" was not blasphemy, not rebellion against God. There, in the growing darkness as star after star found the strength to gleam in the blackness of the heavens, he asked more than why. He demanded to know the reason for such harshness not only against him but against Sarah.

"Perhaps it was merciful of you to give her forgetfulness after the slaughter of her mother and Raphu, and if that was your original purpose—to spare her pain —then I can understand," he pointed out, talking to the Most High, sending his voice upward and outward into the silent heavens. "But this? Why this? Why would you return her wits to her, along with the memories, memories as painfully vivid as if it had all happened yesterday? Why would you do that and then deny me my love by having her think of me as a boy? Yes, I wish you'd take the time to explain that to me, because I do not understand it."

There was more, much more, but the cold air penetrated his garments, and he sought the comfort of the house. He had only questions, not answers.

Sarah did not participate in the meal. Eri ate little, although Baalan had ordered the servants to prepare all of his favorite foods. Afterwards, he was restless. He told Baalan, Urnan, and Sunu a few tales about the campaign in the south but did not mention the terrible massacres to which he had been witness. They could tell that his heart was not in his story-telling.

"Go to her," Baalan urged.

He shook his head. "She knows me not."

"You are her husband, her lord," Baalan said.

"She loves another," Eri said.

"She's just confused," Urnan said.

"No, she remembers Eri as a youth."

"Go to her," Baalan insisted. "Talk to her."

He took a deep breath and blew it out. "Perhaps you are right," he said, pushing back from the table.

Only Urnan noted the look of pain that filled Baalan's eyes as Eri left the room.

Sarah was seated on her bed in her nightclothes, a tunic of woven wool. A lamp was burning, and the glow of it accented the golden hue of her neck, her cheeks, her hands.

"You're not sleepy?" Eri asked.

"No," she said. She looked at him, bending close to examine his face in the dim light. "I'm very troubled."

"Don't be troubled. Lie down. Go to sleep."

"Baalan tells me things, and I can almost believe them. But then—"

"There is time," he soothed. "Everything will come to you in time."

"Tell me how it was before—before my mother and the others were killed," she whispered.

"You were slightly more than a girl," he said, smiling at the memory. "You were considerably thinner than you are now and—"

"Baalan says that I am older, too, but I have nothing—nothing. . . ." She shook her head.

"You were as slim as a boy, and your hair was thick and beautiful. It shone blue-black in the sunshine. And your eyes! They sparkled like spring water at midday. And your breasts were no bigger than an orange."

She laughed and looked down at the bulging front of her nightdress.

He laughed. "Yes, in that you can tell that you've grown older."

"Was I very foolish?" she asked.

"Only if you consider it foolish to have fallen in love with me," he said.

"Oh, no," she whispered. Tears wet her cheeks. "Will you help me, E-E-Eri?" It took three tries for her to get out his name. "Will you help me to remember how to grow older?"

"As God loves us all, yes."

She closed her eyes. "Do you remember how you kissed me there in the gardens?"

"I do."

"Would you kiss me again?" she asked. "If you think it will help me to remember," she added shyly, then closed her eyes and offered up her lips.

He was trembling. Her mouth was a ripeness, a fruit warmed by the sun, and all of the need that he had suppressed for so many years shook him as if he were a boy in the first throes of passion. He made himself tear his lips away from hers. He looked at her.

Her eyes were still closed. "It is you," she whispered. "Oh, Eri, it *is* you."

"Yes, yes," he said. "Yes, my love, my wife."

She gave one small cry, and for a moment there were tears of pain. She kept her eyes closed, but she clung to him, by words and actions let him know that she wanted more. And in the end, reaching up to him, she cried out again, in surprised completion.

He left her sleeping. He covered her carefully, pulled on his clothing, crept quietly out to the open courtyard. The moon had risen, and the night was cold. Sarah's awakening had happened just as he had prayed it would. So why was there an emptiness in him? he wondered. Why a feeling of wrongness and dissatisfaction?

He stood looking up at the sky while he voiced his sincere thanks to God. It was some time before he became aware of a soft sound emanating from a shadowy alcove. He could make out the familiar shape of Baalan. She was huddled on a bench, her legs and feet drawn up under her, a cloak around her draping down to touch the paving tiles of the courtyard.

"Baalan?"

She started, snuffled, and tried to stanch her tears. He sat beside her and took her hand. "You'll get cold out here," he said.

"Yes. No," she said. "I-I didn't mean to disturb you."

"Nor did you." He kissed her on the cheek and tasted salt tears. "Why are you crying?"

She turned away and said nothing.

He put his hand on her chin and turned her to face him. "Wife," he said, "in the excitement of my return, and in the pleasure of discovering that a miracle had happened in regard to our Sarah—"

She hiccupped and sniffed, for she was touched by the choice and the truth of his words *our Sarah*. In the years that she had tended Sarah's needs, she had come to be quite fond of the woman.

"—I have not expressed to you my joy at seeing you again," he finished.

She began to weep anew.

He laughed softly. "I missed you sorely, my little Ammonite. The nights were long without you, and my bed seemed very cold."

"Eri, don't—" she began.

He understood. "Don't what?" he teased.

"Nothing," she whispered, crestfallen.

"Don't say that I love you unless it is true?"

She wiped tears with the back of her hand and nodded.

"Nor will I," he said.

"Sarah—"

"She, also, is my wife," Eri said, "and was in name before you, but in name only."

"And now?"

"You are the mother of my firstborn," he said. "And even if you're not getting cold, I am."

She rose and took his hand.

In bed she clung to him. He took pleasure in the warmth of her, and the softness, and the good, familiar way she fit against his body . . . and that was all, for a time. She did nothing to arouse him other than lifting her face to his for a kiss.

In those days Eri, the smith, armorer to the army of Saul, king of Israel, was a happy and contented man.

CHAPTER THIRTY

Kaptar, prince of Waset, managed to evade his mother and the hordes of women who tried to manage his life by making it thoroughly unexciting and unfulfilling.

Kaptar was a sturdy lad, tall for his years, which would be measured in single digits for less than one more year. His eyes were large, and in accordance with court custom, the women had lined them with kohl to emphasize their handsomeness. He cleared the last barrier between himself and temporary freedom by first distracting the eunuchs guarding the outside entrance to the women's quarters and then darting past their fat, grasping arms. Whooping with joy, he ran with speed and grace across a courtyard, past the stables of the king, and into that portion of the royal enclosure where interesting things happened.

The prince was a frequent visitor to the shops of

the royal smiths and metalworkers, and because of his status he was treated with reverence and politeness. Actually, he was not the pest that he had once been. He was a strong lad, genuinely intrigued by the techniques of bleeding metals from the bones of the earth and fashioning them, each to its own use, as arrowhead or necklace, sword or a ring for the finger of his royal mother, the princess Tania, or for his uncle, the high prince Kemose.

"So, Prince Kaptar," said the boy's favorite smith, "what will it be today?"

"Show me how to polish a finished blade," Kaptar requested, stripping off his fine royal linen tunic.

The old smith obeyed, and soon Kaptar was seated on a floor made hard by the bare feet of generations of smiths. He bent over a roughly finished sword balanced across his legs and worked diligently on it. Rust and dirt soiled his loincloth and his bronze skin. Sweat poured down his sides.

When a regal lady in white linen made her way daintily into the shop, holding her skirts high to avoid the dust, he looked up proudly. "This I have done myself, Mother," he announced, brandishing the sword, which, in one spot at least, was taking on a finished polish.

"You are filthy, young man," said Tania. She turned to the old smith. "I hope he's not being a nuisance."

"Lady," said the old smith, "the boy is most welcome here, as you know."

"Too welcome," Tania, princess of Waset, said with a smile. "What am I going to do with you, Kaptar?"

"Soon, when I have learned to pour molten gold, I will make you a bracelet of such surpassing beauty—"

Tania laughed. The paw print of a lion, the same birthmark that had been on the lower back of the boy's father, was clearly visible as Kaptar sat on the floor in the position of a scribe. The boy's mark was high on his left side, at his waist. The sight of it brought memories to the beautiful woman, and although her bed was not always empty, there arose a longing in her that made her feel weak for Urnan. She saw her beloved's face daily in the face of their son. She averted her gaze.

"When he has succeeded in soiling himself from head to foot, smith, send him back to me," Tania said.

With vivid memories of her happy times with Urnan causing her both joy and pain, she walked back toward her quarters.

Ahead, she saw the giant form of Prince Kemose standing in the path and waiting for her. She smiled and took his arm.

"And what is the boy creating today?" her kinsman asked fondly as they strolled together.

"Some grand and dangerous weapon."

Kemose chuckled indulgently. "Even without the strong physical resemblance, there is no doubt that Kaptar is Urnan's son."

"He is with the smiths at every opportunity."

"By the gods, I miss that man!" the prince told her. "He was a great friend to me and this nation." He shook his head in remembrance. "I never approved of my brother's exiling him. With your safety at risk, Urnan had no choice but to kill Musen's men. He had no way of knowing that Paynozem feared a Libyan uprising."

Tania pulled Kemose to an abrupt halt. "What are you saying? That the Libyans did *not* kidnap my husband? That Paynozem had Urnan taken away?"

"It was a punishment neither you nor Urnan deserved," Kemose told her.

"Then—then he might still be alive somewhere," she said faintly. "Why have I never heard from him? Why has he never come back?"

"These are questions I cannot answer, Princess. Who knows what awaited him in his homeland?" Kemose took her hand and kissed it. "I must go. Tell Kaptar I must postpone our swordplay from tomorrow morning to the afternoon."

She nodded, then watched her kinsman walk away. "So, Urnan," she whispered, for there was no one in the huge courtyard to hear, "where are you?"

Epilogue

∞∞∞∞∞∞∞∞∞∞∞∞∞∞∞∞∞∞∞∞∞∞∞∞∞∞∞∞∞∞∞∞∞

A debilitated sun, yellowed and wearied by its battle with the dark and roiling clouds that had besparkled the city with a thin dusting of snow, gave an illusion of warmth to a small group of listeners surrounding the scholar. The old man sat halfway up the stairs of the great, angular temple that was Solomon's greatest glory. A wind sighed from the north.

"You have heard it said that we are a stiff-necked people," the scholar said in his soaring voice. *"We will debate with God himself, and woe to a brother should he contend with us. There was a king in Israel. He was a mighty king of valor, victorious in war and loved by his people, and yet there were those who turned against him and worked to see him fall."*

"Because he defied God," said a young woman with a water vessel balanced on her shoulder. *She stood as if unable to decide whether to go on about her errand or stay to hear the scholar's words.*

"Did God really speak through Samuel?" the scholar asked in a soft voice.

"Samuel was a prophet of God," said three or four of the listeners at once.

"Samuel was but a man," said a young man with a quiet voice.

"And so was Saul only a man," the scholar reminded. *He sighed and pulled his mantle closer about his shoulders, for the late sun gave no warmth. "It is written that Saul was without the enlightenment given by God to other*

291

leaders of the Chosen People; yet it was Saul who drove the Philistine out of Israel and back to the cities along the coast. It was Saul who allied the Children who lived east of the Jordan with Israel and who renewed cooperation with Judah to the south. There was indeed a king in Israel."

"Tell us of David. Tell us of the courageous Jonathan and his friends who were Children of the Lion."

"And what of Egypt?" asked the young woman, setting down her vessel and taking a seat.

The scholar looked up at the sky, which was darkening. "Another time," he said, rising stiffly. "Another time, when there is a friendlier sun, we will talk of all that. We will consider how the strife of civil war continued to consume the greatness of Egypt and how the chariots of the Philistine once more ground Israel under their iron-shod wheels. And we will sit upon the ground and speak of the death of kings."

The Children of the Lion—Volume XVII
A SONG OF ZION
by Peter Danielson

The dark passion of jealousy rages in King Saul, causing terrifying outbursts of violence against his beloved family and friends. In spite of the king's continuing victories against the Philistines, archenemy General Galar closes in, and a new star is rising—the lad David, blessed by Samuel and favored even by Saul's son Jonathan and closest friend Eri.

When David slays the nine-foot-tall Philistine Goliath and wins Saul's most beautiful daughter in marriage, civil war erupts not only in the king's family but across the land of Israel.

Who is Saul's betrayer? Can it be the lovely Sarah, wife of Eri, with her child's brain trapped within her lush, womanly body?

Read A SONG OF ZION, Volume Seventeen of THE CHILDREN OF THE LION series, on sale in 1994 wherever Bantam Books are sold.